ABOUT THE AUTHOR

Fiona O'Brien left an award-winning career in advertising to write fiction. She lives in Sandymount, Dublin.

ALSO BY FIONA O'BRIEN
and published by Hachette Books Ireland

None of My Affair

No Reservations

Fiona O'Brien

HACHETTE
BOOKS
IRELAND

First published in Ireland in 2009 by Hachette Books Ireland
An Hachette UK company

First published in paperback in 2010

1

A CIP catalogue record for this title is available from the British Library

ISBN 978 0 340 96283 1

Typeset in Plantin Light by Palimpsest Book Production Limited,
Grangemouth, Stirlingshire

Printed and bound by Clays Ltd, St Ives plc

Hachette Books Ireland
8 Castlecourt
Castleknock
Dublin 15

Hachette UK Ltd
338 Euston Road
London NW1 3BH

www.hachette.ie

For Kate Thompson,
who convinced me there was life beyond slogans and jingles,
and who, over a memorable lunch, persuaded me to write that
first full page A4.

Prologue

'Problem at table twenty-two,' the young French waiter murmured discreetly in Dom's ear.

'So deal with it.' The handsome proprietor smiled in greeting as a well-known actress and her new husband swept past him en route to their table.

'They're asking for you.' The waiter kept a smile fixed on his face.

'On a scale of one to ten?' Dom continued to glance through the reservations list.

'Twelve.'

'We've never had a twelve.' Dom raised an eyebrow.

'We do now.'

'What is it?'

'WUT.' This was restaurant shorthand for Woman Under Table. Dom had learned the lingo during the many years he'd spent working in the restaurant business, honing his skills until he'd finally realised his dream of setting up on his own.

'At table twenty-two?' Dom did some quick mental arithmetic. The table in question comprised an elderly heiress, Mrs Randolph Fitzgerald, and her son and daughter, both in their sixties – they were regulars. No love was lost between them and they had been drinking steadily since they arrived. The heiress, celebrating her eighty-ninth birthday, had been putting away an impressive number of double gin and tonics.

'How bad is it?' Dom glanced towards the table, where, sure enough, only the man and woman were visible. They looked remarkably unperturbed and were continuing with their meal, the place between them vacant. The immaculately starched white linen tablecloth that reached to the floor clearly concealed their absent mother. Dom was glad he'd decided on long tablecloths. They were not only elegant, but also convenient, it turned out.

'Never settle for anything but the best,' his mentor, Marco, had told him in L'Aurelius on the Place des Vosges, Paris. L'Aurelius was one of France's great restaurants, with three Michelin stars, where Dom had earned his restaurant stripes.

'How bad is it?' Dom asked now.

'Pretty bad.' The waiter fingered his collar and coughed. 'She was complaining of chest pains.'

'Oh, shit.'

'Precisely.'

'Is there a doctor in the house?' Dom's eagle eye swept the room. Everything was just as it should be. It was Friday and they had a full house, as usual. The perfectly choreographed staff were weaving their way between tables, discreetly serving and taking away the dishes that were effusively referred to as the best food in Dublin in the hottest new restaurant. So far, nothing appeared to be amiss, and that was the way Dom intended to keep it.

'Yes, P.J. O'Sullivan, table three. I've mentioned we might need his help.' The waiter indicated the doctor, who made eye contact with Dom. He was ready to act.

'Thank Christ for that!' Dom took a deep breath. At least that was something. 'You've called an ambulance?'

'It's on its way, five minutes, no sirens.'

'Good. No disturbances, you know the drill. Code Red. Alert all staff.'

'This is a first.' Small beads of sweat broke out on the waiter's forehead.

'That's what this business is all about,' Dom smiled grimly. 'Just follow the drill. Have Tanya take over on the desk.'

As he moved smoothly towards table twenty-two, nodding

and smiling at well-known diners, no one in the restaurant could have guessed that beneath his cool exterior, the much-admired proprietor had a cold trickle of sweat running down his back.

Dom Coleman-Cappabianca was charm personified. He was kind to girls, decent to men, gave money to beggars and couldn't pass a charity ticket seller without buying two. Dogs crossed the street to be petted by him. He was, as his mother never ceased telling him, a big softie. He was also utterly professional. This particular Friday evening, he was going to have to employ both qualities to the very best of his ability.

I

'Watch it, lady!' yelled Carla Berlusconi, skipping nimbly aside and narrowly avoiding being drenched by a passing SUV. The driver, blonde, imperious and unconcerned, mouthed into her mobile phone, cruising through the vast pothole, spraying water and pedestrians alike in her wake. 'Bitch,' Carla muttered, pressing on quickly, the cold November rain making her feel more irritable than usual.

Dublin, she had decided, was not a good city for pedestrians. Oh, sure, you could walk most places, but there were way too many cars. In her native New York, people used the subway, although granted, there was no decent public transport here. It was cool, though. She liked to walk. It reminded her of Rome, her spiritual home. Carla could never understand why her parents had moved to New York, both of them, before they had even got married; it was where they had met each other. If you could live in Italy, where else was there? In Rome, young people walked everywhere or raced around on scooters, but here, it was four wheels or nothing.

It was just as well she lived centrally and liked to walk, and it did keep her toned. Carla would never be one of those skinny girls. She was all Italian curves. She had inherited her mama's hourglass figure and that was just fine with her. Too bad Gino, her erstwhile boyfriend, had mentioned he preferred thinner girls. Was he history or what! Carla loved her food and wasn't going to play the skinny game for anyone. Anyway, she was through with men, which was one of the reasons she'd come to Dublin. Her father was the other. She'd had to get out of New York if she was ever going to strike out on her own, and Dublin had seemed as good a place as any to get some space.

Carla liked Dublin and the people, who were friendly, but also curiously shy. She also liked the fact that people didn't pigeonhole you according to what you did for a living or where you came from. Just as well in her case, Carla smiled. If they'd known about her background, she would never have got away with her present job, waiting tables in the hottest restaurant in town.

That wasn't the only hot thing about it – the proprietor, Dom, the guy who'd interviewed her and given her the job, was drop-dead gorgeous. She smiled, remembering the interview just over six weeks ago, when forcing herself to be positive despite the gloomy economic forecast, she had walked in off the street determined to get a job. Answering his questions, it had been all she could do to stop herself from staring at him he was so beautiful. He made her think of the Italian statues she'd seen when she'd visited her grandparents in Italy. He had dark brown eyes, with a slightly hooked nose and dark hair that fell over his forehead. He was half Italian too, on his mother's side, which would account for the olive skin. But looking at Dom was as much as she was going to do. She'd had it with men and careers. Neither had worked for her so far. Apart from Mr You Could Lose a Couple of Pounds, the few serious relationships she'd had thus far had all bitten the dust because of her dedication to work and the unsocial hours it had demanded of her. Getting to the top of the heap career-wise had left her lonely and frustrated and had culminated in the spectacular family row that had seen her leave New York.

Carla sighed. She'd had enough. No men and a complete career break were what she had decided. She had told Dom that she had worked in restaurants pretty much all her life, and that, at least, was true.

'When can you start?' he'd asked her.

'Right now, if you like.' She couldn't help smiling at the way his face broke into a wide grin.

'That's the spirit I like in my staff.' He had shown her around the restaurant and introduced her to the others. She had allowed herself to wonder if that was all he might like about her, but only for an instant. This was work, she reminded herself.

Dominic's had been the right choice. It was fun and her co-workers were great – everyone, that is, apart from Tanya Sherry, Dom's girlfriend. It hadn't taken Carla more than one minute in Tanya's presence to work out that the manageress was a tough cookie and was one of those women who viewed all other women as competition. Carla hated that type of thing. Tanya reminded Carla of those icy New York women with perfect manicures on the lookout for a man to bankroll them. But that aside, something told her Tanya wasn't quite what she seemed, that beneath her perfectly groomed exterior, she wasn't as assured as she appeared. Nobody that uptight could be.

Tanya was a public relations executive who had somehow assumed the front of house position. This seemed to mostly involve entertaining her friends and contacts on a regular basis and reminding Dom just how indispensable she was to him. The staff loathed her almost as much as they loved Dom. Privately Carla had come to the conclusion that far too much of Dom's profits were being eaten up by Tanya comping her friends for lunch and dinner. But who was she to comment?

All the same, yesterday Tanya had noticed Carla looking speculatively at a table of her friends as yet another bottle of good wine was sent over – none of it paid for. Tanya had quickly sent Carla to the storeroom on an errand, dismissing her with a steely smile. Mind you, Tanya's ice-cold demeanour had come in useful last week when that old lady had died. The poor woman had had a heart attack right at the table – or was it after she had slipped under it? Apparently she had been so comatose with alcohol she wouldn't have felt a thing, the doctor had said. He'd been really nice, the doctor, kind and concerned, preserving the old lady's dignity right up to the end. Her family, on the other hand, had been horrible about her. They hadn't even seemed upset. That was the trouble with family feuds, she thought sadly – you could take them too far. Nothing was worth that.

She thought affectionately about her own family: her old-fashioned, fiercely protective father and her three hand-some, hot-headed brothers. She was still furious at their outdated and downright stupid machismo attitude towards her proposition. Well, that was their problem. They would find out just how much she had done for them in their own good time – without her. She was going to stick to her guns come what may, but all the same, she hadn't bargained on missing them quite as much as she did.

Reaching the restaurant, she ran down the side alley and keyed in the security code that let her in through the staff entrance. At ten o'clock in the morning, Dominic's was already a hive of activity. Carla avoided the kitchen and its cacophony of shouts and crashing pots and pans and made for the staff room. She was deliberately early for her shift and enjoyed the twenty minutes or so of calm before the inevitable storm began.

'Howya, gorgeous?' Paddy, the elderly kitchen porter looked up from his paper, grinning at her as she stowed her coat and pulled off her boots, replacing them with her work shoes.

'Wet,' Carla said, pouring herself a cup of steaming coffee and hungrily eyeing the plate of pastries that Astrid, the Austrian pastry chef, put down on the table.

'Have one.' Astrid pushed the plate towards her. 'I've tweaked my recipe.'

Carla sat down, bit into a feather-light puff and shook her head. 'Oh my God,' she sighed. 'This is divine. What did you put in it?'

Astrid smiled. 'I could tell you, but then I'd have to kill you.'

'You're killing my waistline for sure. I've put on at least ten pounds in the last month.'

'Nothing wrong with a few curves on a woman,' Paddy interjected. 'In my opinion, women only slim for other women. Men like something to hold on to.'

'Yeah, well, I'd quite like to hold on to my figure, or what remains of it.'

'At least your skin doesn't suffer,' Astrid said moodily. 'Mine has gone berserk since I started working here. Dry one day, greasy the next, and look at this!' She pointed to an offending spot on her forehead.

Privately, Carla had to agree Astrid wasn't looking her best. She had lost weight, her fair colouring had become sallow and deep purple shadows nestled underneath her beautiful eyes.

Despite Astrid's protestations, Carla knew full well it had little or nothing to do with work, and everything to do with her on-again, off-again relationship with the larger-than-life Rollo, Dominic's temperamental and egotistical head chef.

'Full house again?' Carla asked.

'Yes, both sittings,' Astrid said. 'Thankfully I get to escape this afternoon, my weekend off. I don't think I could stand another moment of Tanya sticking her nose in and getting under everybody's feet. I have no idea what purpose she serves here.'

'Search me,' said Carla, agreeing with Astrid's bewilderment, 'but Dom seems to think she's vital.'

'Pah,' Astrid scowled. 'He's a man, what would he know? In any of the restaurants where I trained, someone like Tanya would have been thrown out faster than yesterday's leftovers.'

As if on cue, they heard the *click clack* of stiletto heels that heralded Tanya's arrival. She popped her freshly blow-dried head around the door and despite her bright smile managed to look disapproving. 'Ah, there you all are. I was wondering where you were hiding. Paddy, somebody's parking in one of our spaces, be a dear and shoo them off, would you? And Carla, *Socialite's* booking has increased by three, see that the place settings are organised, will you? They're at the corner table, as usual.'

'It's already full. We'll have to move them.'

'Nonsense, I've promised them the corner. There's plenty of room for three more, just whoosh them all up a bit. They won't mind being cosy.' She pointedly checked her watch. 'Whenever you're ready, of course,' she added briskly before disappearing.

'That's crazy,' Carla muttered. 'They're going to be packed in there.'

'They won't care,' Astrid said witheringly. 'All that crowd wants to do is drink for the afternoon. Food is wasted on them. It's the same every Friday. Anyway,' she said, getting up, 'I'm out of here. See you Monday.'

When Paddy and Astrid had gone, Carla cleared away the pastries and changed quickly, putting on her working outfit of freshly pressed black shirt and tailored trousers covered by an immaculate white apron. She pinned her hair up, cursing at the fact that it was frizzing nicely thanks to the earlier shower she had got caught in. Then she went to work setting and checking her tables.

The restaurant interior, she had to admit, was spectacular. In its previous incarnation, Dominic's had been an old furniture shop and storeroom. It was impossible to believe now, after being lavishly refurbished by the celebrity Italian architect, Lorenzo Benadutti. The ambience was understated and modern. Gleaming terrazzo floors and cool white walls formed a uniform palette for the array of simple but beautifully designed walnut tables. Cleverly disguised and adjustable lighting ensured just the right ambience at midday or in the evening. The walls were hung with modern Irish art belonging to some serious collectors, on loan from their owners for public exhibition who thereby enjoyed the generous tax break it allowed them. Cleverly positioned mirrors ensured diners could discreetly see and be seen.

At the back of the room and to the left was the *pièce de résistance*, the state-of-the-art bar where every type of alcohol known to man was arranged in tiers against a mirrored wall. The designer bottles stood row upon row in a pyramid effect, backlit by a host of changing coloured lights, giving rise to its name, Chameleon. The bar, in contrast to the stark styling of the main restaurant floor, was intimate, with an array of comfortable tub chairs and sumptuous sofas, covered in opulent silks and velvets, the low tables in between lit by pretty candle lights.

Satisfied that her tables were in order, Carla risked poking her head into the kitchen.

'Hey,' she said, ducking out of the way as Pino, a Latvian sous chef, rushed past, a tray of garnishes held above his head as he made for his station.

'Not a good time,' he muttered as Carla followed him. 'He's depressed today. Says it's the fucking rain, but he and Astrid are fighting again.' He glanced meaningfully in Rollo's direction, who was shouting at a new assistant, the poor boy cowering in fright.

'What's new?' Carla said. 'That looks good.' She sniffed at a whole salmon gently poaching in a fragrant court bouillon. 'I didn't think salmon was on the menu today.'

'It's not. It's for that stupid party we're catering tomorrow,' Pino said as he chopped a row of spring onions with vehemence. 'I come to learn from an acclaimed chef and end up doing party food a monkey could prepare.'

'Shit. I forgot,' Carla said, her visions of her Saturday night off at the movies shattered.

'Yup. You and me, babe, and the assistants we'll have to babysit. The latest three don't even speak English.'

'Last I heard, speaking wasn't a requirement. What was it Dom said? Perfect food and drink, perfectly timed, perfectly served, and we are to glide seamlessly through the rooms, catering to every whim of our host and hostess.'

Carla had been surprised when Dom agreed to cater this particular party, given by one of Dublin's elite business tycoons to celebrate his fiftieth birthday. Dominic's didn't usually cater, unless it was for a valued customer or a close friend of Dom's, but on this occasion, according to Astrid, who had overheard the conversation, Tanya had been adamant.

'It's such a high-profile gig, Dom. Money's no object and half of Dublin's invited, or so I hear,' Tanya had said. 'Television coverage too, lots of media types. It'll be a good PR exercise. I'll be there, of course, to make sure everything's up to scratch.'

'All right,' Dom had acquiesced, 'just as long as it doesn't interfere with the rest of the kitchen – and no matter what, I will *not*, under any circumstances, have to attend said party.'

Tanya had pouted. 'Oh, Dom. Just for a half an hour or so – it would be such fun.'

'Not a chance. I can't stand the man, he's an ostentatious git. In fact,' he'd scowled, 'I'm not sure we should be having anything to do with it. It's not exactly the type of image I want Dominic's to be associated with.'

'We need the money, Dom,' Tanya had said, playing her trump card.

'Fine, whatever,' he'd sighed. 'You organise it.'

'She totally manipulates him,' Astrid sighed when she relayed the conversation to Carla. 'He's too nice a guy for her.'

The discussion about the fiftieth birthday party had been weeks ago and Carla had clean forgotten that she and Pino had signed on to head up the team of staff that would cater the function. If nothing else, the extra money would be useful.

'What time's kick-off?' Carla asked.

'We have to be at the house at ten tomorrow morning. I'll pick you up. Make sure you don't forget your costume.'

'Costume? What are you talking about?'

'For the party – it's themed, you know, fancy dress.' Pino grinned as he whisked a béchamel sauce. 'Luckily for me, I'm a chef and already wear a uniform – I refused on health and safety grounds to wear anything else. You, on the other hand, are a mere . . . what was it?' Pino frowned in mock concentration. 'Ah yes, a serving wench – that was what Tanya said. I believe she is collecting your costume as we speak.'

'Don't bullshit me, Pino!' Carla laughed, well used to his wind-ups.

'No bullshit, Carla,' Pino grinned evilly. 'The theme of the party is the Tudors. That means you and the rest of the staff will be dressed as medieval serving wenches. I look forward to seeing you in your outfit. I'm sure you'll look adorable.'

Carla was about to protest when she was silenced by a roar and the sight of Rollo bearing down on them, meat cleaver in hand. At six feet two inches of well-built muscle, he was an intimidating prospect.

'Nobody speaks in my kitchen without permission!' he roared at Carla. 'Get out! I won't have my chefs disturbed.'

'Oh keep your hair on, Rollo,' Carla replied, slipping into fluent Italian, his native language. 'I was only checking the menu, and then I got distracted by those fabulous Capelletti,' Carla said, referring to the cones of pasta stuffed with chicken, cheese and eggs she had spied at the other end of the kitchen. 'How can a girl stay out of the kitchen when there's such temptation inside?'

Rollo's face creased into an enormous smile. 'My little Carlita with the J-Lo body! Always you can make Rollo smile, eh?' He put an arm around her shoulders and bent down to whisper conspiratorially in her ear. 'But Astrid, she no make me happy.' He shook his head emphatically. 'Astrid makes me sad, and that is very bad for Rollo. Sad chef, he make sad food.'

'You could never make sad food, Rollo, even if you tried,' Carla said. 'And Astrid is just a bit depressed because of the weather. I think she's a little homesick too.'

'Why she not say that to me?' Rollo demanded. 'To me, she say that I no love her.'

'She doesn't want to worry you. You know Astrid would never do anything that might stress you, she knows how important your role is, how crucial the kitchen is to you. How we *all* depend on you.'

Pino and the other sous chefs within earshot hid their smiles as Carla expertly stroked Rollo's enormous, but eggshell-fragile, ego.

Rollo nodded earnestly. 'Yes, yes, you are right as usual, my Carlita. I will talk to Astrid this evening, maybe take her for a weekend home.' His face lit up at the idea. 'Then she will be happy, yes?'

'That's a great idea. Just make sure you give Tanya plenty of notice. Losing her chef and pastry chef for a whole weekend could be traumatic for her.'

'I don't speak with Tanya!' Rollo banged his fist on the counter. 'I answer only to Dom. He will understand that my Astrid needs holiday.'

'Sure he will. Just don't tell him it was my idea.'

'My lips are sealed, Carlita,' Rollo grinned. 'Now, tell whoever is out there that no one comes into the kitchen before lunch until I say so.' He swatted her on the behind with a tea towel.

'Whatever you say, Chef!'

Just then, Tanya came through the swing door. 'Carla,' she began crossly. 'I've been looking—'

'I said no one!' Rollo roared, advancing ominously in her direction. 'Out! Everybody, *out!*'

Tanya rapidly obliged, followed by a grinning Carla.

* * *

Upstairs, in his apartment above the restaurant, Dom put down the phone to his mother and shook his head despairingly. He didn't know what had got into her, and her move from the family home into the mews at the bottom of the garden was bewildering, to put it mildly, not to mention upsetting. Although he loved her dearly, she seemed to be going through what he could only describe as some sort of midlife crisis. Probably better if he stayed out of it, as his father had advised him to. In Dom's experience, marriages were best left to their own devices, even if the one in question was his parents'.

Dom Coleman-Cappabianca adored women – simply because he had no justifiable reason not to. And the feeling, by all accounts, was mutual.

It was hardly surprising. His mother, Cici, a noted beauty with sloe eyes and the seductive gaze of Goya's naked Maja, doted on him, and his younger sisters, Sophia and Mimi, practically hero-worshipped him. Dom had inherited his mother's dark Italian looks and his father's height and broad-shouldered, lean build. His looks, together with his affable, laid-back personality and his genuine delight in female company, ensured that women everywhere loved him right back – some to distraction.

It had always been that way. Even in his exclusive all-male boarding school run by an order of Benedictine monks in the heart of the Irish countryside, Dom had attracted affectionate looks and lingering, indulgent glances from teachers, matrons and cleaning ladies alike, not to mention the local village girls. On Valentine's Day and his birthday, Dom's post had grown to such unseemly proportions as to warrant the abbot bringing the matter to the attention of Dom's parents, explaining that the 'fan mail', for want of a better description, had become a rather inappropriate and indeed unfair distraction to the other boys.

His mates, on the other hand, thought it was hilarious. Dom was completely unaffected and great fun, and

although highly intelligent, his dyslexia meant academics were
an obvious struggle. He wasn't annoyingly obsessive about
sport either (apart from his beloved polo, which he played
in the holidays), and, most important of all, he was more
than generous when it came to setting the guys up with his
numerous female contacts. As a result, his popularity only
increased.

School holidays were spent travelling abroad with his family
when he was younger – both Cici and James were adamant
about encouraging their children to learn about different
cultures and languages. Later, when Dom's interest in food
and wine became evident, summers were spent working in
private vineyards in France and Italy, the US and Argentina,
where he was able to improve his already competent polo
playing. It was on one of these happy, sun-filled working
holidays that Dom was initiated into what was to become the
other great passion of his life.

Eagerly encouraged by girls his own age and several considerably older and more experienced ones, Dom became a
willing and naturally talented student eager to be shown and
instructed in the age-old skills of how to please a woman,
happily discovering in the process that he had a God-given
talent he effortlessly excelled in. It was a talent that would
bring him equal measures of delight and bewilderment and
not a little bother over the years.

On his eighteenth birthday, working at a chateau in the
Loire and at the height of a passionate six-week affair with
his employer's wife, the very beautiful and experienced
comtesse, their liaison was discovered and Dom was unceremoniously discharged and packed off home after a flurry
of disgruntled emails from the cuckolded *comte*, leaving a tearful,
but not at all remorseful, *comtesse* mourning his departure.

James, Dom's father, was furious with him on hearing the
news. Cici, his mother, had been philosophical and not a little
amused. 'What do you expect, James? He is a beautiful and

eager young man, and half Italian, fied husband. 'Just be thankful it's Do... daughters.' She had laughed at the horri... face at the prospect.

Unwilling at the time to face his father's inevi... and warnings, Dom had hopped on a train to Pa... what he had left of his hard-earned wages renting ...ny studio apartment off the Rue Saint-Denis and got a job as a *plongeur* working under a female chef who liked the look of him. It was there, in the sweltering, electrically charged, stressed atmosphere of the kitchen, that Dom discovered his real calling. He vowed then that he would open a restaurant of his own and set himself a goal of ten years from that day to do it.

Now, strolling through that very restaurant to take his mind off things, Dom smiled with pleasure. They had just completed their first year in business and already Dominic's was a thundering success with diners and critics alike. It hadn't been easy – he and the rest of the staff had worked relentlessly – but it was finally paying off. He looked around methodically, checking every detail as if for the first time. There was no letting up in this business, where the tiniest slip could cost a restaurant dearly, and even though his staff were the best, the buck stopped with him. Today, in preparation for Friday lunch, one of their busiest sittings, everything seemed to be in order. The tablecloths were pristine and starched, the cutlery and glasses gleaming. Over in the corner, he watched as the new girl he had hired, Carla, worked quietly and efficiently.

She had been a real find, though initially he hadn't been sure about her. At the interview she had seemed almost too polished, too competent to be applying for the job of waitress, but then, he reflected, those were exactly the qualities he was looking for in his staff. She was cheerful, too, and had proved a real hit with her co-workers and diners alike.

bore an amazing resemblance to Jennifer Lopez, which was going down well with the male diners. Dom grinned. Having a pretty girl around never hurt, and Carla certainly was very pretty. Gorgeous, even. She looked up suddenly, caught him gazing at her, and flashed him one of her ear-to-ear smiles. Dom beamed back at her.

Even her working outfit of black shirt and trousers, covered by the traditional white apron, failed to hide her curvaceous body, and Dom found himself wondering just what those delicious curves would look like without it – then pulled himself up abruptly. That was the kind of thinking that got a man into trouble, and Dom didn't have time for that kind of trouble any more. Besides, he was her employer. It was completely unacceptable for him to flirt with her. Those days, he sternly reminded himself, were well and truly over.

Dom had had many romances, but sooner or later every girl had begun to put pressure on him, with one or two taking it to quite frightening levels. He remembered one girl in particular who had rung him and told him she'd taken an overdose after he had gently ended their relationship. Although it had only been a few of her mother's Valiums and it hadn't been serious, Dom had rushed over and called an ambulance. He still shuddered to think of the awful day. No matter how nice or gentle he was about it to women, they just couldn't seem to cope when he felt it was time to move on and reacted with varying degrees of petulance or hysteria. So Dom had decided women were off the menu – at least for a while – until he'd met Tanya.

Tanya was different from his other girlfriends. She was attractive, naturally, but was also cool, calm and very collected. She never shouted at him or threw hissy fits if he was late or was unavoidably detained by work. She made things easy for him too, organising the decoration of his flat, which he had never got around to, and making sure he didn't forget his mother's or sisters' birthdays. She was also doing an

amazing job with the PR for the restaurant – the reviews they
were getting were consistently fabulous. Although Dom knew
they were deserved, he also knew a lot of it was due to Tanya's
relentless work on his behalf. And so far, she seemed perfectly
content to take their relationship one day at a time, which
was only about as far as Dom could think lately. Their relationship was very civilised, he reflected. No demands, no
screaming at him, no tempestuous outbursts. It was a nice
change.

The restaurant began to fill promptly at quarter to one, with
a seemingly automated file of glamorous patrons processing
through the doors. There were a few early birds, not regulars,
who had taken their places at half past twelve to get ahead
of the rush so they would be seated comfortably to watch
the parade of beautiful, high-profile diners guaranteed to
make an appearance every Friday.

Dom was there to greet them all.

There was the usual crowd, of course – Tanya's weekly
group of PR people and journalists, jovial, enthusiastic, back-
slapping guys and thin, hungry-looking, accessory-laden
women. They would eat little, consuming only who was in
attendance, who they were dining with and whether or not
they were worth writing up. Food would be toyed with, many
bottles of champagne and wine ordered, and at some stage
of the afternoon, they would stagger on to either the
Shelbourne Hotel or Doheny & Nesbitt's pub, possibly
followed by the Four Seasons Hotel to bolster their stamina
for the long Friday night ahead.

The real diehards would continue clubbing. Reynard's for
the older set, and Krystal for the young celebrity wannabe's:
models, actresses, sports personalities, all who would be
photographed outside looking nonchalant and spend what
remained of the wee hours eagerly awaiting the Sunday papers
and glossies that would hopefully feature them. To his left

Dom noticed a famous Irish rock star, clearly on a visit home as he lived in London. He was accompanied by a very attractive blonde, not his wife, who was stealing surreptitious glances in the mirror to make sure people had noticed them.

Dom was annoyed. Tanya should have tipped him off, and she hadn't. Rick Waters expected special treatment, and that included an obsequious welcome on arrival. He always reserved a table under his code name, and it would have been in the book. Dom made a mental note to check the database – these kinds of slip-ups could cost a restaurant dearly.

'Mr Waters!' Dom greeted him respectfully, although of course they were on first-name terms. 'To what do we owe this honour? Haven't seen you in a while, can I get you a drink?'

'Howya, Dom.' Rick smiled up at him and winked. 'Champagne's already on the way, thanks. This is Melanie.' He waved towards his companion by way of introduction. 'She's my new sound engineer, aren't you, love?'

Melanie smiled obligingly. 'I've been dying to come to Dominic's,' she said, clearly overawed. 'I couldn't believe it when Rick said he was bringing me here. It's not even a special occasion or anything.'

'I can think of two good reasons, eh, Dom?' Rick stared pointedly at her generously displayed cleavage nestling in a black, fluffy, low-cut jumper and laughed loudly at his own humour.

Dom's smile didn't quite reach his eyes. He hated men who treated women like accessories to be flaunted, even if the woman in question, as was clearly the case here, was more than happy to oblige.

Luckily the champagne arrived just then, followed closely by Tanya. 'On the house of course, Mr Waters,' she murmured as the waiter poured a tasting glass.

'Good girl,' Rick said, delighted to see that Melanie, his date, was clearly impressed.

Dom made his escape. 'Enjoy your lunch. If you need anything . . .'

'Don't worry, mate, I'll holler.'

I don't doubt for a minute you will, thought Dom, smiling as he moved away.

He made his way through the room greeting customers, appearing for all the world like the delightfully charming host he was. But behind the welcoming words and gracious manner, he was alert, constantly monitoring the apparently effortlessly choreographed show that unfolded before him with military-like precision.

Dominic's had attracted the fun crowd for sure, but the food was taken seriously.

Food was Dom's passion. Ever since he could remember, Dom had been in love with good food. He understood it, so much so that he realised early on in his training that although he could cook well himself, he lacked the extra five per cent that would have made him a great chef, and Dom wouldn't settle for anything less. In the kitchen, he firmly believed, as he had been taught, that 'good is the enemy of great', and Dom wasn't afraid to admit he didn't have what it took. He didn't have the fierce determination, the drive, the particular kind of genius that makes a revered chef. Dom's strengths lay in motivating the team that made up his kitchen, seeking out unusual ingredients, fusing together ideas, techniques and styles and, of course, dealing with the public, who adored him. In short, Dominic Coleman-Cappabianca was too nice to be a great chef, but he made a fantastic restaurateur. Which was just as well, because he certainly wasn't cut out for the family business.

James Coleman, Dom's father, had made a fortune in computers in the early 1980s. One of the few successful entrepreneurs who held on to his business and didn't sell out to the big guys, he had become one of the big guys himself through diversifying into software and other techie stocks.

Not unnaturally, it was his father's dream, or rather assumption, that Dom would follow him into the rapidly expanding business that was Coleman Technologies Ltd. But it wasn't to be. Apart from being dyslexic, Dom loathed studying, although he had loved school, and had graduated with little in the way of scholastic results, but with a great deal of laid-back charm. This, coupled with his stunning, dark good looks, made him a happy target for every young woman in Dublin upon his graduation. And Dom was willingly seduced by what was to become the *other* great passion in his life.

Now, focused as he was on the job in hand, Dom, as usual, was unaware of the female diners whose glances trailed him as he wove through the tables. Today, wearing an immaculate charcoal grey Jermyn Street suit and a crisp, pale pink open-necked shirt that set off his dark colouring beautifully, he looked more handsome than ever. His hair, freshly washed and damp around the edges, was just beginning to wave, the unruly forelock falling into his eyes at regular intervals. It made more than one woman present want to reach up and tenderly brush it back.

He was chatting briefly with an up-and-coming politician and the journalist who was buying him lunch in the hope of garnering an interesting political titbit when the occupant of a table to the side caught his attention.

There was no mistaking P.J. O'Sullivan, the infamous doctor. He was well built, with shoulders like a prop forward, a handsome, craggy face and shaggy, greying hair. It seemed that half the restaurant knew him and were waving hello. Rick Waters, the rock star, had even left his table to go over and greet him.

P.J. was a friend of Dom's father, and although he had only met him once or twice socially, he had done Dom a great favour in helping him out so discreetly last week when the unthinkable occurred and Mrs Fitzgerald had departed this world, slipping elegantly underneath her table right there in the restaurant. Dom would never forget it. He made a mental note to make sure P.J. got a very good bottle of whatever he was drinking on the house. By any standards he was a good-looking man, if dishevelled. He was a little heavier, maybe, a little worn looking, but nothing a bit of TLC wouldn't take care of. Then Dom remembered hearing that he had lost his wife to cancer about five years back. That would account for it. They had adored each other. He seemed slightly uncomfortable too, which wasn't like him, as if he felt too big for the table he sat at, hiding behind his menu and taking a quick swig of the glass of red in front of him. In fact, if Dom hadn't known better, he'd have said he was nervous, but that was ridiculous. Or was it? As the doctor's lunch companion strolled into the restaurant and joined him, Dom realised that it was Alex O'Sullivan. They were father and son, although he would never have put the smooth, suave financial adviser and P.J. O'Sullivan together. It just went to show.

Dom glanced over at the other corner table, today set for eight. It was already full except for one vacant seat, and its occupants were chattering ten to the dozen. Today, they were a gay milliner, whose outrageously chic hats were the crowning glory to every outfit; a property developer; not one, but *two* members of Viper, the biggest band on the planet; a well-known social diarist; a sports commentator; and a model turned vocalist who was enjoying a number one hit single in the UK. The champagne had arrived and there was an air of eager anticipation around the table. Dom checked his watch. Of course she'd be the last to arrive. It was all part of the theatre.

As if on cue, a slight hush descended as the whole restaurant looked up for a split second to acknowledge her arrival.

The Sophia Loren lookalike stood at the top of the steps and paused for just enough time to show off her outfit, which was, Dom had to admit, magnificent. A figure-hugging midnight blue silk suit clung to every curve, the scooped out neckline of the jacket showing off her décolletage to perfection. The skirt was to the knee and tight. The collar and cuffs were trimmed in matching navy fur, and a pair of navy suede high-heeled boots encased the famous legs. On her head sat one of the aforementioned milliner's creations: a midnight blue, wide-brimmed hat that curved dramatically around her face, emphasising the already spectacular bone structure. No one else could have carried it off.

'Cici!' the milliner cried, leaping up from the table and rushing to greet her. 'You look fabulous.' He air kissed her on both cheeks.

She sauntered down the steps, nodding and smiling to staff and friends alike until she reached Dom, when she paused again, making a great show of removing her navy silk gloves and proffering her cheek to him, which he duly kissed.

'Hello, darling,' she beamed at him. 'Don't *you* look nice today. That shade of pink is divine on you.' She patted his cheek fondly.

Embarrassment crawled all over him. 'Hello, Mum.'

'Well, aren't you going to escort me to my table, darling?'

'Sure,' he said glumly.

Now the real work would begin. If Cici had arrived, then Friday lunch at Dominic's had officially begun.

'Damn,' James Coleman cursed under his breath as he sliced his third drive of the day.

'You'd want to get that shoulder of yours seen to,' his partner, Mike, said, shaking his head. 'Your game's shot to pieces, and in case it's slipped your memory, the club championship's less than three weeks away.'

'You're right, and I haven't forgotten. I'm going to pull out.'

'Don't be ridiculous.' Mike's swing stopped in mid-air. 'We've won it for the past four years. One more and we get to keep the trophy. Just get your bloody shoulder sorted.'

If only it were that simple, thought James.

'Let's call it a day,' Mike said, not pushing it. 'I'll see you back at the clubhouse?'

'Sorry,' James turned away and slotted his driver into the bag. 'I've got a meeting. Have to dash. I'll call you tomorrow.'

'You work too hard, you know that?' Mike looked at him quizzically. 'Should take things a bit easier, James. You're not yourself these days. Surely the company can survive without you for a while? You should take a holiday, take that gorgeous wife of yours away somewhere exotic and chill out – after the championship, of course.' He chuckled. 'How is Cici, by the way?'

'She's great.'

'Tell her I said hello. We should have dinner soon, just the four of us. It's been too long. I'll tell Janet to organise it.'

'Sure, great, whatever.'

'Well don't sound so enthusiastic.' Mike sounded hurt.

'Really, Mike, I've got to go.' James was already making long strides towards the clubhouse, golf bag slung over his shoulder. He turned briefly. 'Dinner would be great.'

Mike shook his head as he watched his friend walk away. Something was up. James Coleman was most certainly *not* his calm, courteous, collected self these days. He wondered what it could be. Not business problems anyway; James's company was *huge* and doing better than ever. He was worth millions. Normally the man was utterly unflappable, but lately his behaviour seemed distracted at best, strained at worst. In fact, Mike reflected, it was downright worrying. He thought about calling him now on his mobile and pinning him down, asking what the hell was going on with him. Instead he shrugged. Who was he to be nosy?

James turned his sleek black Mercedes 600 coupé into Wellington Square and pulled up outside number 15. The car had been chosen only after careful consideration, the same consideration that he applied to everything in his life. James Coleman was not a man who rushed into things. On the contrary, whether in his personal life or his business dealings, James moved with the utmost deliberation only after analysing every minute detail and nuance of the matter in question. It made for a straightforward life. Consequences to potential actions had to be anticipated or mayhem ensued. The Rules applied at all times, and if you followed them, desired results were achieved – or at least they had been up till now.

He walked up the steps to his home and reached for his key, taking a barely perceptible breath before inserting it in the lock and turning it.

Inside, the long hallway greeted him as always. The warm timber floors, polished to perfection, were covered by an intricately patterned Persian runner leading to the base of the stairway. The narrow Edwardian hall table held a large silver salver containing the day's post, and a vase of elegantly arranged flowers stood in pride of place. The large mirror that ran the length of the table had been found at an auction at Adam's and hung now above it, dutifully enhancing the width of the rather narrow space. James caught sight of himself in it now and frowned. His face seemed shrunken to him, pale and rather pinched against the bold dark red backdrop of the walls. He took off his long navy cashmere overcoat and threw it on a hall chair, not bothering to hang it, and watched it slither to the ground. He walked into the drawing room, straight to the drinks cabinet, and poured himself a large gin. He sat there, sipping it mechanically, for fifteen or twenty minutes before realising the room was in complete darkness. He turned on a table lamp and tried, for the umpteenth time, to make sense of the mess that had become his life.

If there had been warning signs, he certainly hadn't seen them. Looking back, he still saw nothing that would have alerted him that all was not as it should be. In fact, as far as he could tell, things had been good, better than good even.

'Darling,' Cici had said to him one evening after dinner.'I think the mews could do with a makeover. It's looking a bit tired these days. I was thinking of redecorating it. What do you think?'

'I think that's a great idea.' He had looked up from his laptop and smiled at the enthusiasm in her voice. 'Go right ahead, I'm sure you'll do a wonderful job. Just don't expect me to get involved, you know how I hate all that stuff.' He went back to his share portfolio. 'Only please, no builders around the house, I beg you.'

'Of course not, sweetie. It will be my little project. You won't even know it's being done. I'll surprise you with the finished result.'

'Cici, you never cease to surprise me, as you well know. And you're right, redecorating the mews will be a good investment. Maybe we can rent it out. It's silly to have it lying there empty, unless one of the children wants it for a while, of course.'

'Unlikely, darling. Dommy has to be near the restaurant, and the girls, well, they're gone for this year at any rate. It's just you and me now,' she had said.

He remembered, with a rueful smile, the first time he had set eyes on her. He had wandered into the Shelbourne Hotel after a boring business pitch over dinner at his club nearby and made straight for the famous Horseshoe Bar, where a friend of his had arranged to meet him. There was no sign of the friend, but sitting at the bar was a stunning young woman gulping champagne as she endeavoured, in heavily accented English, to tearfully relate to the barman, who was listening, enthralled, the story of her first miserable day in Ireland.

Perhaps it was the fact that she was in evening dress that

intrigued him, or that the white chiffon confection plunged
in a Grecian neckline to enhance the most incredible breasts
James Coleman had ever seen that made him approach her
and ask if he might join her and buy her a drink.

She had turned towards him then and the slanting, chocolate brown eyes had surveyed him, looking up at him from
under thick, curling lashes. Suddenly she smiled and crossed
her legs, allowing the dress, which was full length, to shift,
revealing a thigh-high split that displayed long, shapely, olive-
skinned limbs.

'I'd be delighted,' she said.

After that, everything had happened very quickly.

They'd had a few more drinks, champagne for Cici, but
when James had been about to order a martini, Cici had
interjected.

'Please, let me choose for you.' She had let those eyes rove
over him again and a playful smiled curved suggestively. 'A
Carpano, for my new friend,' she instructed the amused
barman. 'An Italian drink for an Irish gentleman, yes? A martini
is too . . . James Bond. Too predictable. And you, James, I think
are not so predictable as you would like me to think, no?'

James, captivated and wildly flattered, had no intention of
disillusioning her. And he hadn't been predictable, not that
night.

'Has anyone ever told you that you look remarkably like
Sophia Loren? A very young Sophia Loren,' he added hastily.

'All the time.' It was true; there was no mistaking the resemblance. 'But you,' she said, 'you are too aristocratic looking
to be a movie star.'

'Well I can assure you I am not an aristocrat, and much
as I wish I had a magnificent castle in the depths of the
country to lure you away to, I'm afraid I do not,' James said
equally playfully. 'How long are you here for?'

'I had planned to stay for a week, but now I must go back
to Italy tomorrow. I would go sooner if I could,' she scowled.

'What on earth for?'

'My boyfriend, he is . . . how you say . . . a Don Juan, a cheat, a liar.'

'Then why go back to him?'

'He is here. I came over to be with him. That is the problem.'

James listened as she related her romance with the handsome army officer who was now a famous member of the Italian show-jumping team. James wasn't well up on things equestrian, but even the dogs on the street knew it was Horse Show week in Dublin. The yearly event brought traffic to a standstill and was the highlight of the social season every first week of August, when, after the day's competitions, a series of glamorous balls were held in various hotels in Ballsbridge, close to the Royal Dublin Society, where the Horse Show was held.

'But . . .' he racked his brain to remember, 'today was the Aga Khan trophy, the Nation's Cup. The Italians won, didn't they?'

'Yes, they did, and as we speak he and the rest of the team are celebrating at the ball that I left.'

'But why did you leave?'

'He didn't know I was coming. It was to be a surprise. I arrived at the hotel and went to the bar, where they were drinking before the ball. I could tell by the faces of his teammates that it was a mistake. And then I saw him with the girl who was supposed to be his ex-girlfriend. He had invited her to the ball.'

'What did you do?'

'I picked up a drink and I threw it in his face. Then I left. But now,' she grinned defiantly, 'now I am glad that it happened. Otherwise I would not be sitting here with a very handsome Irishman.'

'I'm very glad it happened too. He may be an accomplished horseman, this boyfriend—'

'Ex-boyfriend,' she corrected him.

'But he's clearly a complete fool in every other sense.' James checked his watch. It was half past ten, almost closing time. 'Have you eaten?' He was suddenly ravenously hungry.

'No. But perhaps I should, so much champagne . . .'

As it was Horse Show week, James knew they would have no chance of getting into a restaurant at that late stage.

'I live quite close by,' he risked. 'If you want, we could have something to eat at my place. I can't say I'm a good cook, but I'll fix us something.'

'But I am.' Her eyes lit up. 'I am a very good cook. We go to your place and I cook for you, yes?'

So they had. James had automatically gone to look for a taxi, but when Cici learned that his flat was in nearby Baggot Street, she insisted on walking.

'But you can't,' James protested, 'not like that, in your beautiful dress and those sandals.'

'Of course I can. Come, let's go.'

So he had taken off his jacket, placed it around her shoulders and they had strolled the ten-minute walk to the Georgian house where he had his flat. And she had cooked for him – she made the best spaghetti puttanesca he had ever tasted in his life.

He had somehow persuaded her to stay on for the week in his flat. There was nothing inappropriate; James was far too much of a gentleman to suggest anything untoward. Cici stayed in the second bedroom and they spent a wonderful week together as James showed her around Dublin and proudly introduced her to his clearly astounded and envious friends. Before she left, he proposed to her and she accepted. She went back to Rome to make the appropriate arrangements. Her parents, she informed him, had been killed in a car crash and she lived with an elderly aunt who would not be sorry to see her go, and the feeling, she assured him, would be mutual.

They were married three months later, in a quiet ceremony

in the Irish College in Rome and returned to Dublin, where James set about building his fledgling computer business and Cici, in true Italian fashion, settled down to babies and cooking, embracing domesticity as passionately as she did everything else in her life.

They had three children: Dominic, Sophia and Mimi. All of them had inherited their parents' dark good looks, but it was Dominic who was most like his mother in temperament. The girls, on the other hand, took after their father. They had done well at school and were presently abroad, Sophia studying art history in Florence and Mimi travelling the world on a year out from her political science degree at the Sorbonne in Paris.

Dominic, of course, had his restaurant, where by all accounts Cici was spending far too much time in the company of the kind of people James would rather not think about. It wasn't that he was jealous as such – he was too hurt, too miserable, too genuinely bewildered at the extraordinary turn events had taken. Why had his beautiful, devoted and adored wife, at forty-nine years of age, suddenly announced she wanted a trial separation? And had plotted to conduct that same separation in their newly revamped mews house under his very nose? It was . . . James searched for the appropriate word and failed. Bizarre was the closest he could manage.

What was he supposed to do? What would he say to people? *My wife has left me and she's living at the bottom of the garden.* If it weren't so bloody tragic, it would be funny.

He drained the remains of his drink and wandered down to the kitchen. He wasn't hungry, but he knew he should force himself to eat something, and the fridge, as always, would be well stocked by their Filipina housekeeper, who was carrying out her duties as usual. If she knew of her mistress's whereabouts, she made no mention of the matter. James was thankful for that at least. It was bad enough to come home to and wake up to the relentless loneliness of a house he had once regarded as a happy, love-filled home without fielding embarrassing questions.

Despite himself, he felt the familiar siren call of the kitchen window, which looked out onto the back garden and from where he could see the downstairs windows of the mews. He knew he shouldn't, but he couldn't help himself. He peered out and saw the mews lit up, looking warm and inviting, the outlines of several people moving about, glasses in hand. Cici was in residence, and obviously entertaining. James wanted to feel angry, enraged even, but all he could feel was the knife twist of loneliness that cut him to the quick. Then the curtains were pulled.

Just at that moment, his mobile rang.

'Dad?' he heard Dominic's voice. 'If you, er, don't have any plans, Tanya and I were wondering if you'd like to join us for a bite to eat this evening?'

Trying to inject a semblance of levity into his voice, James assured his son that he would be delighted to.

Never, for as long as he could remember, had an invitation been so welcomed.

2

P J. O'Sullivan was not a man made for sleeping alone.
Yet this was exactly what he had been doing for the
past five years.

Today, another bleak late-November morning, was, as he
knew it would be, the worst – the one he steadfastly resisted
waking up to.

Every year it was the same. No matter how much he drank,
how late he stayed up or what kind of pill he took, he tossed
and turned, dreaming fitfully. Sometime towards dawn, the
gnawing emptiness would invade his artificially induced sleep
and consciousness would return. Then he would feel keenly,
as always, the sense of loss afresh.

Today would be her fifth anniversary.

Five long years without Jilly. A sixth about to begin.

He shoved the palms of his hands into his eyes and
groaned. A headache was hovering if he thought about it
and he had a crick in his neck. Hardly surprising when he
realised the awkward angle he'd been sleeping at – on his
stomach, one arm caught under his rib cage, the other
stretching out across the empty bed as if reaching for her
would bring her back.

Not to think, that was the trick. Definitely not to think.

He would focus on the throbbing in his temples, taste the
bitter dryness of his mouth, dismiss the erection that deserted
him as quickly as his dreams of her.

He would not think about the amazing life they had had
together. The chaotic, colourful life that had been his – his

and Jilly's. Nothing else had mattered. Together they had been an island of their own.

Wonderful, warm, spontaneous, exuberant Jilly. Wife, lover, soul mate. A woman who made everybody happy, and without whom life was unbearably lonely. No, he would definitely not think about that.

The alarm clock beside his bed told him it was 6:30 a.m. It was earlier than he usually woke, but this wasn't a bad thing. The sooner he got on with it, the sooner this day would be over, and he truly hated this day.

Downstairs, he opened the door to the kitchen and was greeted by Bones, his golden Labrador, who at ten years of age was, like himself, overweight and out of condition. Neither of them cared. P.J. let him out and made the first of the many cups of coffee he would drink that day.

Back inside, after his morning amble, Bones sat beside him, alert now, looking wistfully at the toast P.J. spread thickly with butter, which Jilly would have reproved him for.

'Don't listen to what they say, Bones,' he said, throwing his dog a piece he caught deftly and wolfed down, 'cholesterol is great.' Bones thumped his tail in agreement.

Mind you, P.J. thought, it had got the better of that poor old dear who had pegged it in Dominic's last night. He shook his head at the memory of the bizarre turn events had taken the previous evening in his favourite restaurant. He had to hand it to Dom – he and his staff had handled the whole thing superbly. Without a hint of the drama unfolding, they had managed to resurrect the old lady from under the table and prop her up, and while staff had gathered discreetly to conceal the activity, P.J. and Dom had managed to hold her up between them and get her out to the ante room, where the paramedics took over. She had been pronounced dead from a massive heart attack. P.J. had been rather impressed. As a way to go, eating and drinking with gusto in a first-class restaurant before slipping quietly under the table showed a certain amount of brio. Very convivial, really – by all accounts, it was the way she had conducted most of her life.

P.J. and his dog sat there for a while companionably, long-time breakfast partners taking comfort from the ritual that began their day.

The kitchen had been Jilly's favourite room, 'the heart of the house', she said, where they had retreated to cook, eat, drink, laugh and entertain and, when they couldn't make it upstairs, have wonderful sex.

The spacious old room had captivated her and responded eagerly to the hours of painstaking restoration she had undertaken with the help of various workmen, students and friends. Lino had been pulled up to reveal impressive flagstones, walls stripped and replastered and painted warm colours. Original brickwork was exposed and cleaned and, best of all, a hidden stone fireplace unveiled.

The ramshackle larders had been stripped out and a large, American-style stainless-steel fridge-freezer installed along with a huge, comfortable sofa. The old cream Aga had also been overhauled and proclaimed functional. It sat now, as it always had, radiating heat between the two large picture windows that looked out onto the square.

'Won't it be awfully posh?' A note of worry had crept into Jilly's voice despite her excitement at the thought of moving into the wonderful old house.

'Not once *we're* installed,' P.J. had retorted, grinning.

It had come as a complete surprise that his dotty old maiden aunt, Barbara, rumoured to have been a hell-raiser in her day and who studiously avoided all her relatives bar P.J.'s late father, her brother, had left him her splendidly decaying old house in Wellington Square upon her death. And so, ten years ago, with their two children, Alex, twenty, and Bella, just ten, they had become the latest residents of the elegant and much-sought-after location that was Wellington Square.

Even then, riding on the back of the soaring Celtic Tiger,

the prices the houses fetched were thought ludicrous at five, even six million. Now you wouldn't get one for ten. Some of them had a mews at the back, which made them even more valuable. Theirs also had a granny flat to the side.

Along with the house, his aunt had left P.J. a decent sum of cash, which meant that with a loan on top they could actually manage to undertake most of the work needed on the old place. Of course, it wasn't nearly as grand as some of the houses on the square, all recently renovated as they changed hands or long-time residents took advantage of increasing their ever-escalating property interests, but he and Jilly had achieved the home they had dreamed of, even though it had meant living in what felt and looked like a building site for a long time, managing with a kettle and a microwave in an upstairs bedroom.

It had been fun. But then, everything had been fun with Jilly.

From the moment he had set eyes on her, he knew she was the one.

Knebworth House, 1979, Led Zeppelin belting out across the grounds, but P.J. was hearing a different kind of music. Catching sight of her, dressed in wellies and a charmingly inappropriate vintage summer dress, she was a vision of loveliness amongst the crowd of heavy metal rockers and early punks. Taking in her masses of long copper and blonde-streaked curls, her golden skin, the wide sensual mouth, head thrown back as she laughed uproariously at something her mates were saying, P.J.'s breath caught. The girl was sex on long, lissom legs. She had turned suddenly then, caught him gazing at her, and smiled at him. He left his friends and walked over to her. She seemed a little out of it, and so was he. He took her hand. It felt like the most natural thing in the world.

She was a psychology student, had just taken her final exams and was waiting for results. When he told her he was a med student, she had laughed and said he looked far too sexy.

'That makes two of us,' he replied.

'I like you,' she said, her eyes crinkling at the corners when she smiled.

They split from the others, walked, talked, got high, talked some more, got hungry and grabbed a burger and chips from a catering van. They spent the night in his tent, and the next, and though the rock concert had come to an end, P.J. knew something much, much better had begun.

He didn't want to leave her, but he had to get back. One of his mates had a car and they were heading back to Holyhead to catch the ferry.

'Can I have your number?' he'd asked her.

'Sure.' She pulled a piece of paper from the back pocket of her jeans and wrote it down.

'Don't you want mine?' he heard himself bleat.

'If you want to give it to me,' she grinned.

'Come to Dublin,' he said.

'Maybe I will.'

'I'll call you.'

'Of course you will.' She had kissed him then, lightly, and turned, swinging her backpack over her shoulder.

P.J. felt as if someone had kicked him in the guts.

Back home, he told himself he would forget about her, that in time she would fade into one of the many hazy, happy, soft-focus memories that formed his summer breaks.

She didn't.

His mates gave him a hard time. Rugby-playing students like himself, they took full advantage of this rare opportunity to wind him up mercilessly. He thought he was hiding it well. They told him he was pathetic.

He tried, he really did. There were other girls, other nights. University resumed and he made the Rugby Firsts, but he never stopped thinking about her.

'She's really got to you, hasn't she?' his best mate, Joey, said, looking at him quizzically. 'Pity she's English. I mean, if she was *here*, there'd be some hope,' he went on as P.J. scowled at him, 'but what's the point? You'll probably never see her again. Best forget her, mate.'

She called him that night.

'I'm in Dublin,' she said. 'I think we'd better meet. I'm pregnant.'

He met her in town. She was standing, as they had arranged, outside the Bailey, a pub off Grafton Street that was considered way too posh and expensive for any of his student mates to frequent. He saw her first, as he turned the corner.

She didn't look pregnant. She looked beautiful, her slim, long legs encased in flared jeans, a multicoloured woolly hat pulled over her blonde curls and a matching long, skinny scarf wound around her neck. When she saw him, her face lit up and suddenly nothing mattered, nothing at all.

'I wasn't sure you'd come,' she said, pulling back finally from the lingering kiss their initial tentative peck had become.

'Try and stop me,' he grinned. 'C'mon, let's go inside, we can talk.'

At three in the afternoon, the pub was fairly empty.

'I'm sorry about this,' she began.

'Don't be,' he said. 'It's not your fault.'

'I was on the Pill, but I'd had food poisoning. I suppose that did it. It must be an awful shock for you.' A line of worry creased between her eyes.

'For you too.' He wanted to reach out and stroke the line away. 'How, um, how far along are you?' *Stupid question!* his brain screamed. *Do the maths! You're studying to be a doctor, for Christ's sake.* 'Sorry, sorry, stupid question – I didn't mean—'

'No, it's okay. Two months, a couple of weeks ago.'

'Two months eleven days then?' he grinned.

'You've been counting too?'

'I couldn't get you out of my head. I can't stop thinking about you.'

'Me neither.'

'Have you told your parents?'

'Yes. They're okay, they're cool.'

Cool parents? It was an oxymoron, a thought he couldn't quite get his head around. Not when your twenty-one-year-old daughter suddenly announced she was pregnant.

'Have you?' she asked. 'I mean, will you?'

'Not yet. I thought we should meet first.' He didn't want to contemplate that prospective discussion – not yet.

'That's what my parents said. That I should tell you and we should talk it over, see, um, what we want to do. They'll support me whatever we decide.' Her eyes were clear and certain.

'That's, er, very decent of them.' It was – decent, sensible, considerate. P.J. tried to imagine these liberal, calm-sounding people and couldn't.

'Will your parents . . . be upset?' she ventured.

He tried to search for the appropriate word and couldn't. 'It'll be a surprise,' he said brightly. 'They'll get used to it.' It was time for the million-dollar question. 'What *do* you want to do?'

'I don't want to get rid of it – you know, have an abortion.'

'No, no, of course not.'

'I don't want to get married either. That would be silly. I don't mean, you know . . .'

'No, I know what you mean.' He didn't know anything, really, but he hastened to assure her, this beautiful creature with her wide, innocent gaze and clear thinking, who was – the thought both terrified and beguiled him – carrying his child.

'What about you?' she asked. 'This can't have been on your list of things to do before you're thirty.' She smiled, but she was searching his face. 'What do *you* want to do? I mean it's crazy, you don't even know me.'

'But I want to.' He didn't have to think about it – he just had to say it. 'I want to get to know you.'

The concern left her face and was replaced by something light and hopeful. 'That's good, because I want to get to know you too.'

He reached across the table to take her hand, and they sat there, grinning foolishly, like the young, idealistic people they were, with their whole lives stretching before them.

His parents were not cool about it. Astounded, dumbfounded, disbelieving, certainly. Not cool.

'She's trapped you, you stupid boy,' his mother cried. 'This – this girl, whoever she is. She's ruined your life.'

'You bloody fool!' His father shouted. 'You're a medical student for God's sake! What were you thinking?' He was pacing up and down the drawing room.

'For Christ sake stop crying Maureen!' He snapped at his wife, who was perched on the edge of a Chippendale chair, wringing her hands.

His father's voice was cold. He was an intimidating man at the best of times but now, angry and taken aback, P.J. sensed for the first time that he was not someone to be crossed.

'Do something!' His mother was hysterical now. 'You're a doctor aren't you – a surgeon. You have contacts – can't she . . . you know . . .'

'No!' P.J.'s voice surprised him, sounding as firm and decisive as it did. 'That's out of the question. Jilly is – we . . . we're having this baby.'

'And how, precisely, are you proposing to support a wife, and a child, as a fourth year medical student?'

'That's another thing, we're not getting married either. It would be stupid.'

'Oh, sweet Jesus,' his mother moaned. 'The girls, your sisters, what an example to them – they'll be ruined. Tell him, Charlie, *tell* him. You'll *have* to get married if you're having this child, it's the only thing you can do.'

'We don't and we won't.' P.J. was feeling weary now. He was all out of fight.

'You've got it all worked out, haven't you?' His father leaned against the mantelpiece. 'Well I wish you luck young man, I really do. You're going to need it.'

'We'll manage.'

He left home the next day.

There wasn't much to pack. His books were the biggest problem. Otherwise, he just needed some clothes and his guitar. Joey had borrowed a small van and was waiting outside as arranged, looking sheepish.

'That's it.' P.J. said, hoisting the last of the boxes in. 'Hang on for a mo' will you, I've just got to go back inside to . . . you know.'

P.J. went upstairs and knocked on his parent's bedroom door. His mother had taken to bed and had not been seen or heard all day.

'Mum,' he called, softly. 'Can I come in?'

There was no reply. He sighed. 'I'm off now, Mum, I'll be in touch, okay?' He thought he heard a sniff, but he wasn't sure. He went back downstairs. His twin sisters were standing in the hall still in their school uniforms, silent, for once, looking worried and much younger than their seventeen years.

Shit, this was going to be worse than he had expected.

Lydia, the younger of the pair, by five minutes, opened her mouth to say something and then, to his horror, began to cry.

'You'll come back, won't you?' blurted Jane, the elder. 'I mean, it's not like you're gone for ever or anything?'

'No, no, 'course not. Don't be mad! C'mere.' He hugged them awkwardly.

Just then the door to his father's study opened and his

father emerged looking grim and, P.J. noted with a pang of guilt, as if he had aged overnight.

For a moment they regarded one another.

'You're off then?' his father said.

'Yes, Dad, I am.' He met his father's eyes and saw something flicker briefly, something he didn't recognize.

'Right. Well, then.'

His father reached into his jacket pocket and withdrew an envelope. 'Take this P.J.' He held it out.

'No, Dad. Thanks, it's good of you, but I . . . I can't.'

'Of course you can, man.' His father was brusque but P.J. could see the emotion in his eyes. 'Dammit, this is no time for pride. You have a child to support now, and the rest of it. It's just to get you on your way. I still think you're a fool, but you might as well learn the hard way, if that's what you want. Don't give up on your studies, son.' His voice almost caught. 'You're a born doctor.'

'Thanks, Dad.' P.J. croaked.

'And P.J.?'

'Yes?'

'This has all come as a terrible shock to your mother but if you get into difficulties . . .' He paused. 'You know we're always here for you. You can always come home – the three of you.'

For a horrible moment P.J. thought he was going to cry, as the full implications of what he was doing hit him. And then, thankfully, his father retreated back inside his study and closed the door.

Outside, P.J. climbed into the van.

'Are you right?' asked Joey.

'Yeah, let's hit the road.'

'Was it heavy?'

'Yeah.'

'Jaysus, I don't envy you, P.J. I mean, sorry – that's not what I mean, y'know . . . Did the folks throw the head?'

'Yup. Big time.'

Joey shook his head in awe, 'Respect, man. I mean, it's tough stuff, y'know, we're all behind you mate.' He shook his head again. 'Jaysus, I hate to think what my folks would do to me. Ma, well, she says she thinks you're mental but you know what mothers are like.'

'Yeah,' said P.J., darkly. 'I do.'

Things happened very quickly. They found somewhere to live through a friend of a friend's mother. The parent network had gone into action, it seemed, fuelled either by genuine sympathy or the huge collective relief that it wasn't one of *their* children having to negotiate this unfortunate turn of events. Sympathetic enquiries were made about the young couple, genuine advice offered and many knowing looks exchanged across dinner tables. To their credit, not one parent ever came out and said 'I told you so' or 'now you see why we're always telling you to be careful. They didn't have to – they could see the sobering effect this sudden visitation of adulthood and its attendant responsibilities produced on their own offspring. Besides which, everyone was inordinately fond of P.J. He was bright, funny, respectful and totally unaware of his good looks.

In fact, the only real tragedy, it was agreed among the womenfolk, was that P.J. was a terrific catch and more than a few mothers had harboured hopeful ambitions to acquire him as a son-in-law, an ambition their daughters had happily concurred with. Now, the disappointment was palpable.

'It's such a *waste*,' said Clodagh McLaughlin, Joey's mother, as she doled out a chicken casserole with more force than usual. 'He would have made some girl a wonderful husband, and from such a good family too. His parents must be devastated, poor things, I must ring Maureen this week, see how she is.'

'He *is* making someone a wonderful husband, isn't he?' Her husband interjected.

'Oh they're not getting married, dear, just living together, you know, shacking up, isn't that what you young people call it?'

'Same thing,' Vicky, Joey's sister, threw her mother a resentful look. 'She's got him hasn't she? So much for your warnings about playing fast and loose Mum, hasn't done this Jilly any harm.'

'It won't last kissing time.' Clodagh McLaughlin sniffed. 'Mark my words, they'll be history before the baby's a year old. And he can say goodbye to his career. She's ruined him, that's what she's done, that English tart.'

'Why don't you just shut up! All of you!' Joey stood up angrily from the table. 'Jilly's a lovely girl, and stunning looking, P.J. couldn't be happier. I for one would consider myself more than lucky if I could meet a girl half as fabulous as Jilly.' And he stormed from the room.

'Well!' exclaimed his mother, 'I knew it, I just *knew* that all this would be a bad example for the rest of them.'

Vicky opened her mouth to protest but her mother glared at her.

'I think the less mentioned about young P.J. and his circumstances the better, for the time being at any rate,' said her husband, his mouth settling in a thin line of disapproval.

It shouldn't have worked, but it did.

Once he had organised a flat, P.J. borrowed a van and got the ferry to Holyhead and drove down to Oxford to pick Jilly up.

He had found his way easily to the picturesque, orderly village on the outskirts of Oxford. Their house was just as she had described it: a pretty, regency home overlooking a weir where swans glided by serenely.

Jilly opened the door to him, grinning, and brought him

inside. In the sitting room, her parents rose to greet him, if not effusively then with considered interest. There was no chilliness, no undercurrent of resentment.

Jilly's mother was Swedish, a teacher, and had passed on to her daughter her Scandinavian good looks. Her father was good-looking too, in that aristocratic, even-featured English way, and was a professor of classics. By the time lunch was served, everyone had relaxed a little.

'I can see what Jilly sees in you,' her mother said to him matter-of-factly in her lilting accent as she regarded him. 'You have a lot of sex appeal.'

P.J. nearly choked on his roast beef, although there had been no trace of suggestiveness in the remark.

'Er, thank you, I think,' he said colouring and feeling hugely embarrassed.

Her husband allowed himself a smile. 'Really Freda! Steady on old girl! Young P.J. won't be as used to your direct manner as we are.'

'But I am right, no?' she laughed at them as she and Jilly got up to clear the table.

Then it was time to set off. Jilly's belongings were loaded into the van and goodbyes were said. As Jilly hugged her parents warmly and kissed them both, P.J. was again astonished at how unlike his own family they were. How unaffected, demonstrative and loving they were, and so generous to him, a stranger, taking away their only daughter.

'Good luck,' said Jilly's father to them. 'Be kind to each other.'

And then they were waving to them, to the receding village, to the landscape they were leaving behind as they set out for Dublin, and their first home together.

Their flat was in the basement of a rundown house in Leeson Street, owned by an elderly and very deaf widower. What it lacked in mod cons, it made up for in spaciousness, consisting of a reasonable bedroom, a small bathroom, a tiny galley kitchen and a sitting room. There was no furniture, precious little light and far too much noise, particularly late at night, when the basement nightclubs on either side of them pulsed music through the walls.

To Jilly and P.J., it was complete heaven.

The arrangement suited everybody. The widower, Billy, was happier with a young couple below him in the house, particularly a medical student. In exchange for keeping an eye out for him and Jilly doing his shopping now and then and listening for the doorbell he couldn't hear, the rent was minimal.

They were the envy of all their friends, who, still stuck at home and mostly studying, thought the dark, dimly lit flat terribly exotic. Their bed was a large mattress on the floor, orange crates made perfectly acceptable bedside tables and, thanks to a tip-off from a hospital porter, P.J. was able to salvage a table, some chairs and a few stools destined for the dump. Three evenings a week, he worked in a bar and Jilly got a job as a temporary secretary, and between them they made ends meet. Weekends were spent painting and decorating, their friends lending a hand. Exhausted, they would open some cans, send someone out for pizzas or burgers, then sit around the rescued hospital table, laughing and talking and playing music long into the night.

The baby arrived bang on time. On 1 June 1978, Alexander Charles Patrick O'Sullivan made his entrance to the world. Everything had gone perfectly according to plan. P.J. had been rather disappointed about that – he'd envisaged a dramatic dash to hospital, breaking traffic lights and possibly a police escort. Instead, Jilly woke up at six o'clock with mild contractions. By lunchtime, they took her packed case and got a taxi to the hospital.

Despite her calmness throughout the pregnancy, Jilly was suddenly uncharacteristically nervous.

'It's okay, I'm here. Everything's going to be fine,' P.J. reassured her, looking into her eyes, wide with worry. She had refused to attend the hospital on a private basis, although she could have, and now greatly missed the presence of a familiar and trusted gynaecologist.

By four o'clock, she was exhausted. Then, alarmingly, the baby's heartbeat faltered. The monitor set off a flurry of action.

'Baby in distress.' The stern voice of the midwife cut through the delivery room.

P.J., having watched hundreds of deliveries and assisted with several himself, now felt as terrified and helpless as Jilly looked.

'Oh, please,' she whimpered. 'Don't let anything happen to my baby, please.'

Suddenly the swing doors burst open and a tall, gowned figure strode towards Jilly's bed. 'Thank you, Nurse, I'll take over now.'

P.J., relief coursing through him, recognised the clipped, confident tones of his father's golf partner, one of the most respected gynaecologists in the country. P.J. had never been so glad to see anyone in his life.

'Mr O'Gallagher!' The midwife looked surprised and not altogether pleased. 'You're not listed as being on call this evening.'

'A happy coincidence, Nurse. Just happened to be passing by. Now, let's see what the problem is here.'

Jilly began to cry as Tony O'Gallagher examined her and assessed the situation quickly. When he spoke, it was with kindness but there was urgency in his voice.

'Forceps,' he commanded. 'And suction. You're doing splendidly well, Mum, just another minute or two, good girl . . . here we go, stand back please, people, let's give Dad a ringside seat . . . ready P.J.?'

And suddenly everyone was cheering and slapping him on the back, and Jilly was holding their perfect new baby in her arms.

Not far away, in his consulting rooms in Fitzwilliam Square, P.J.'s father smiled into the phone. 'Thank you, Tony, I appreciate that. It was good of you to make yourself available to keep an eye on things.'

'Nonsense,' replied his old friend, 'Worth it all to see you the first granddad on the block! Hope it improves your game. Congratulations old chap, give my best to Maureen.'

'Will do.'

Then Charles Richard Ignatius O'Sullivan poured himself a large tumbler of Jameson's finest, leaned back in his chair, and, with an impressive surge of emotion, drank a toast to his first grandson.

It is a well-known fact of life that babies are great peace-makers and Alexander Charles Patrick O'Sullivan was no exception. A model child from the outset, Alex embraced routine the way other children resist it. He fed when he was supposed to feed and slept when he was supposed to sleep, so soundly and so still that sometimes Jilly woke him up to make sure he was still breathing.

He looked remarkably unlike either of his parents. This further endeared him to his four doting grandparents, who spent many an hour speculating upon, and claiming, every emerging feature as one of their own.

And all the while, P.J. and Jilly grew closer and fell more deeply in love.

What had started off as a haphazard, blinding haze of attraction developed into a mutual appreciation and dependency that grew stronger every day. It wasn't all plain sailing, of course. They had their ups and downs like every young couple, the most memorable of which was when P.J. disappeared for three days to play with his mates in their band. He had negotiated a free pass for one night, but it inexplicably turned into three.

At first vexed, then genuinely worried, Jilly had tracked him down to an inner city 'studio', where Viper, his mates' burgeoning band, was writing and recording.

Joey let her in. Through the haze of smoke and alcohol fumes, Jilly spied P.J. lying against a wall, his arm protectively resting on his beloved guitar and a silly smile on his face.

'You fucking selfish bastard!' she screamed in fury. 'I thought something had happened to you!'

The silly smile got bigger. 'Hey, babe,' he said sleepily. 'It's beautiful of you to find me. Really beautiful.'

'That's it!' Joey shouted, joint dangling from his lips as he scampered to the keyboard. 'That's the lyric! Fucking brilliant, guys!'

As he played a haunting riff, Jilly sat down beside P.J. and, taking a swig from the vodka bottle, gave up the fight and began to hum along with the tune.

It was Viper's breakthrough single, and 'Beautiful to Find Me' went on to be a hit.

A few years passed, and suddenly it seemed like all their mates were getting married and settling down and having babies too. The earlier drama they had caused felt like another lifetime. Now everyone was in the same boat. The guys moaned to P.J. about sleepless nights and the girls were glad to have Jilly to confide in and seek advice from as someone who had been through it all before.

They were happy days.

P.J. eventually qualified and won a place at M.D. Anderson, the renowned medical establishment in Texas, to pursue his chosen specialty of oncology. It was there that Bella arrived unexpectedly. The spitting image of her mother, the longed-for second child had surprised and overjoyed them. In an ironic twist of fate, despite Alex's instant arrival, they had been unable to conceive thereafter. 'Unexplained infertility' was the diagnosis, though neither Jilly nor P.J. had been unduly upset. They had Alex and, of course, each other. Jilly had resumed her psychological studies and qualified as a counsellor. By the time she discovered she was pregnant with Bella, Alex was almost ten.

An orderly and precise child, Alex was as unlike his parents as it was possible to be.

'Do you think they gave us the wrong baby leaving the hospital? P.J. asked Jilly more than once, shaking his head as he watched Alex methodically tick off a to-do list.

Jilly grinned. 'It won't hurt to have one organised member in the family.'

'Guess what?' Jilly had said to Alex one warm May Texas evening, ruffling his hair as he came in from tennis practice.

'Mom, don't do that,' he'd moaned, ducking his head, although he grinned as she hugged him in a vicelike grip. 'I don't like guessing. What's cooking?'

'Big, juicy steaks,' P.J. said.

'Great.' Alex looked approving. 'Can Freddie come over?'

'Sure, there's plenty,' said Jilly. 'Alex?' Jilly called as he made to run to the phone.

'Uh huh?'

'We're having a baby, honey. You're going to have a little brother or sister. How about that?'

'How about that indeed!' added P.J., looking pleased as punch.

'When?'

'December. It'll be our big Christmas surprise. Isn't that fantastic?'

'I don't like surprises, and I've already made up my mind what I want for Christmas.'

Alex turned away quickly, but not before P.J. had caught the mutinous expression that crossed his face.

Three years later, they returned home to a very different Dublin. The city was alive, vibrant and confidently about to clamber aboard the back of the Celtic Tiger. P.J., whose medical credentials were spectacular, had been offered, amongst other positions, a consultant post in St Edmund's, one of the three big teaching hospitals in the city.

He and Jilly bought a nice house on the south side, near the hospital, and Alex attended his father's old school, Blackrock College, where he studiously avoided rugby and attained top grades in everything, especially mathematics, which he excelled in, finding satisfaction in intricate and foreign calculations that P.J. couldn't come close to understanding.

He'd hoped that moving back home might bring Alex out of himself a bit more, help them bond. It was silly, he knew – as if Alex going to his old school would bring them closer, help Alex understand him better because they'd walked the same corridors, run around the same muddy playing fields in the same jerseys. But it hadn't happened. Whatever way he looked at it, he and Alex were just too different, and finding common ground was becoming more and more difficult.

Bella, on the other hand, was a three-year-old bundle of energy who looked just like her mother and was showing signs of having her father's personality. She adored P.J. and worshipped her big brother, following him around at every opportunity, a pastime Alex found, and failed to hide, profoundly irritating.

There was only one problem. P.J. wasn't happy. It wasn't his domestic life; that couldn't have been better. It was work. Not medicine per se, but rather hospital politics. He loathed the game-playing, the wasted hours arguing with the Board, and he hated the Health Service most of all, the lumbering, blood-sucking, inefficient body that was the common symptom in every illness.

'You're not happy, are you?' Jilly asked him one night, stroking his hand as they sat quietly in the kitchen, sharing a joint.

'That obvious?'

'How bad is it?'

'The pits,' P.J. smiled ruefully. 'I thought I could cope with it, you know, enjoy the bits I liked and ignore the rest, but it gets to me so much. I don't want to be a property developer masquerading as a physician, I want to be a bloody doctor – someone who can help make sick people better, and when that's not an option, make them as comfortable as they can be, by whatever means are at my disposal.' He let out a long, angry sigh.

'Then why don't you do that?'

'What? You mean give it – all this – up?'

'Why not, if it's making you miserable.'

'Wouldn't you be disappointed? I mean, all those years of training, Texas, the exams, having no money. Jesus, it must have been so hard for you, and now, just when I could reap all the rewards, to chuck it all in?'

'You wouldn't be chucking anything in. Your training will always stand to you, and to your patients, probably more so if you can use it the way you want to. Set up your own practice, hon, a general practice. Go back to what you enjoy – being a doctor. On your own terms.'

So he did, and never regretted it for a moment. It had been the right move to make.

From then on, things got better and better.

They converted the garage of their semi-d. P.J. had his surgery downstairs and Jilly had a room upstairs, where she saw her clients.

Word spread quickly about the practice, about the wonderful young doctor with the kind and sympathetic manner who was more like someone you'd want to have a pint with than a remote, judgemental member of the medical profession. The word on the street was that he was open-minded too, and creative in his prescriptions. Best of all, it was said, Dr P.J. O'Sullivan could work out what the hell was wrong with you when no one else could. His diagnostic skills were legendary. The more superstitious among them said he had the 'gift'. More than one consultant had been pulled up in his tracks when P.J. had spotted a rogue symptom they had overlooked or dismissed. It made him inordinately popular with patients, but not with the medical establishment. Dr. P.J. O'Sullivan was a maverick. In other words, he was trouble.

Patients came to him from all over the country, and he never turned anyone away. If you could afford it, he charged top dollar. If you couldn't, you didn't pay or you made a donation at your discretion to the Cancer Fund.

Rock stars, actors and stressed-out whizz-kids attended him. He didn't lecture anyone about their lifestyles or tell them to shape up or he wouldn't treat them. 'Look, I smoke and drink myself. What would I be doing giving you a hard time about it? They'll kill you more likely than not, but we all have to die of something, don't we?' he'd chuckle.

He could as easily be found playing doctor on stage behind the scenes at one of the many rock concerts he was invited to (his old band, Viper, was now a famous rock group) as making a house call to a frightened, vulnerable pensioner.

No one ever came empty-handed to the surgery. Whether it was a bone for the dog, a bunch of flowers for Jilly or a leg of lamb for the freezer, even the most hard-up patients brought something for their dearly loved doctor and his gorgeous wife. P.J. and Jilly never wanted for anything.

Then his aunt died, and they inherited the wonderful house on Wellington Square. P.J.'s surgery was moved to the mews, and Jilly counselled her clients from a cosy room at the back of the house.

They never changed. P.J. still looked like a reject from the 1970s, according to Alex, and Jilly was as unaffected and natural as ever.

They had five years in Wellington Square, five blissful years, before the cancer struck, and when it did, it was quick.

Metastatic lung cancer. No warnings, just a niggling pain in her back and a devastating diagnosis. Six weeks later, Jilly was dead.

They had considered everything. No treatment plan had been unexplored, no centre of excellence ruled out. But P.J. knew, the way he always did, instinctively, that this was a losing battle. The specialists were kind, but adamant – there was nothing to be done, nothing that would save her or extend her life. Examining the evidence for himself, P.J. had to agree with them.

Gavin, one of their oldest friends, now an eminent Cedars-Sinai-trained oncologist, had sat with P.J., head in his hands, and watched helplessly as his dearest friend picked up a glass from a sideboard and flung it against the wall, where it shattered. Then he sobbed inconsolably.

For the short time that remained to her, she was kept out of pain.

Her last words were 'Love you, baby,' whispered, barely caught. She died in his arms seconds later, at home, Bella beside her on the bed crying softly, and Alex, stern and white-faced, who waited till the end, then turned and left the room quietly.

People had been kind, unbelievably kind, but for P.J., nothing would be, could ever be, the same again.

He continued with his practice, of course, drank a little more, smoked a little more than was good for him, but he kept it together. He had to, for the children. Bella was devastated, and fourteen was too young for a daughter to lose her mother, especially one as wonderful as Jilly. He worried about that – about her first date, about buying the right clothes, her wedding even, all without Jilly.

Alex was a worry too, in a different way. He seemed to be coping, but he never referred to his mother and seemed exasperated if P.J. tried to. He continued to be as remote, as controlled and as much a mystery to his father as he had ever been.

But they had managed.

Five long years without Jilly. P.J. shook his head. It didn't get any easier.

He left the kitchen, went upstairs, showered and dressed, then grimaced at the reflection that peered back at him. Alex was right; he did look like a relic from the 1970s. But was that such a bad thing? Mick Jagger, Ronnie Wood, plenty of guys way older than him wore their hair long – he felt lucky to still have any. It was greying now, but still there. Anyway, Jilly had liked it long. His face still looked pretty much the same – a few more creases, the hooded eyes maybe a bit heavier and, he had to admit, blearier. Sure, he could do with getting a bit more exercise, losing a bit of weight, but why? And he was comfortable with his gear, even if Alex wasn't. Jeans were acceptable at any age. Maybe the sweatshirt was pushing it a bit for work, but God, it was comfortable. And ankle boots had come back into fashion again – he had read that somewhere – even if he had never realised they had been out of it. That was one of the best things about working for yourself – you could wear what you liked.

Downstairs, he collected Bones and they set off for the morning surgery. All the way down the garden to the mews. 'Ready old chap?' he said to his adoring dog. 'Let's see who's on the list today.'

He tried to motivate himself, he really did. He tried to remember the gratitude of so many of his patients, the challenge of decoding a trail of tricky symptoms, the genuine pleasure of helping and seeing someone get well.

But underneath it all was the nagging reality. *What the hell use was it being a doctor, a good one, when you weren't able to help the one person in the world who meant everything to you?*

3

Candice Keating regarded herself in the full-length mirror of her designer bedroom and smiled approvingly. The tight, elaborately worked corset pushed up her boobs to make them look twice their normal size and had sucked in her waist by at least three inches. The heavy, full skirt of the dress was a bit cumbersome to walk around in, but who cared? The effect was fabulous.

'You look amazing, Candy, really amazing,' her friend Katy breathed admiringly, trying to get a glimpse of herself unsuccessfully in the mirror Candy was monopolising.

'I do, don't I?' Candy turned sideways, appraising her reflection from this new and engaging angle.

'Is my hair all right?' Emma fidgeted with a blonde tendril.

'Leave it, Em, it's fine.' Candy turned to her friends, both dressed as ladies-in-waiting. 'You'll ruin it if you start pulling at it. Dylan's the best hairdresser in the city. He didn't spend all afternoon here for nothing. Don't undo all his good work.'

'It feels weird, up like this,' grumbled Emma.

'You both look fine. Now remember what I said – no messing and no getting pissed, at least not until we're on our own later. There's going to be loads of press people and I know at least one TV station is covering it. And if *she* comes over to us, you're to ignore her, got it? Unless Dad's with her, in which case you can nod, but no smiling or simpering and playing up to her.'

'I can't wait to see her, though – up close, I mean,' Katy said, a note of awe creeping into her voice.

Candy scowled. This was exactly the kind of attitude she was at pains to discourage. 'She looks exactly like she does in her photos. Like a slut.'

Her friends' eyes widened and they giggled. Candy Keating might be a bossy, stuck-up, spoiled, opinionated pain in the ass, but she more than made up for it by her advantageous associations. Her father was one of the wealthiest men in the country and by all accounts was happy to spend that money in as obvious and extravagant a manner as possible, which included, among other things, catering to Candy's every whim. Since Katy and Emma, as her two best, and possibly only, friends were regularly included in many of these dubious demands, they felt that such glamorous outings and events more than made up for their friend's other shortcomings – which were multiple.

Tonight would be the best of all, when they would be going to the party of all parties: the fiftieth birthday party thrown by Candy's multimillionaire father, Ossie Keating, and his model girlfriend, Shalom deLacey, bane of Candy's life, would be there. Anyone who was anyone was going, including loads of celebrities. It didn't get any better.

'D'you think they'll get married?' Emma mused, adding a final coat of pearlescent midnight blue to her nails.

'Not if I have anything to do with it.'

'Why do you hate her so much?' Katy was curious.

'I don't hate her. She just makes me sick, that's all.'

Emma and Katy exchanged looks.

Before the subject could be debated further, the bedroom door opened and Candy's grandmother poked her head in. 'Are you decent, girls?'

'Come on in, Gran.'

'Well, don't you all look splendid. You could have walked straight from a film set.'

'Hi, Mrs Searson,' the girls chorused.

'How many times do I have to tell you to call me Jennifer?'

she said fondly to Emma and Katy before turning to her granddaughter.

'What a perfect young queen you make, Candice.'

'Thanks, Gran.'

Emma and Katy made wild eyes at each other and tried not to laugh. They loved Candy's gran. She was terribly posh and a bit scary, but she said the most outrageous things and didn't give a hoot about what the recipient of her acerbic remarks might think. A glamorous seventy-six years of age, she had trouble with her hip and since her hip operation had taken to walking with a silver-topped cane, which she didn't hesitate to bang on the floor or indeed prod people with if the situation warranted. Now, dressed in a fuchsia pink quilted satin dressing gown and full make-up, she lowered herself regally onto Candy's bed, crossed her legs and took a sip from the gin and tonic she clutched in her hand.

'My feet are killing me.' She rotated her ankle and stretched out one of the offending feet, encased in her favourite gold ballet slippers, before returning her appraising gaze to Candy. 'I must say, it was well worth getting those costumes over from Paris. At the time I thought that stylist creature was off her rocker, but that rig-out does wonders for you, Candice. Although I do wish you wouldn't cover up your lovely freckles with that mask of make-up,' she frowned. 'Still, you look wonderful, dear, and your lovely red hair makes you a perfect young Elizabeth.'

'It's strawberry blonde.' Candy looked at her coldly as her friends tried not to snigger.

'Yes dear, whatever. Your father will be so proud of you. He won't have eyes for anyone else.'

Candy was slightly mollified. 'I do wish you were coming, Gran. Won't you change your mind, for me? There's still time.'

'Yes, Mrs – I mean, Jennifer,' Katy encouraged. 'Do come.'

'I'd rather have bamboo shoots inserted under my nails than accept such a vulgar invitation.'

Candy glared at her while Katy and Emma collapsed into giggles.

'It's not vulgar, Gran. It's going to be brilliant, and loads of celebrities will be there.'

'Exactly,' Jennifer said. 'And your mother shouldn't be going either. I told her, but of course she wouldn't listen to me.'

'What did you tell me, Mother?' Charlotte Keating appeared at the door, smiling, but her tone was deceptively light.

'Good God!' Jennifer's mouth dropped open. 'Tell me, I *beg* of you, you are not going in that – that regalia.'

'Why not? It's entirely appropriate, I think, and even you, Mother, approve of me in black.'

The girls were riveted.

Jennifer looked outraged and the temporary plate the dentist had given her until her implants were ready, began to slip as she searched for words. 'But you're going as . . . as . . .'

'Catherine of Aragon. Yes, Mother, I am. I'm chronologically spot on – after all, I *am* the first wife.' She tilted her head to one side. 'What's wrong with that? It's a fancy dress party – it's all in good fun.'

'Are you out of your mind?' spluttered Jennifer. 'You'll be a laughing stock.'

'No I won't. If anyone's laughing, it will be me.' She looked at the girls approvingly. 'You look terrific, girls. If you're ready, we should get going, the car's outside.'

'I think you look brilliant, Mrs Keating.'

'Thank you, Katy.'

'Fantastic,' added Emma.

'Now come along. Mother, will you be all right?'

Jennifer harrumphed loudly. 'Of course I'll be all right. It's you who needs your head checked.'

Downstairs, standing in the hallway, the girls watched as Charlotte descended the stairs, followed by Candy, who was looking mutinous.

'She looks amazing, doesn't she? Who'd have thought it?' whispered Emma.

It was true. Charlotte Keating was a very good-looking woman. She had inherited her mother's pale skin and black hair, which tonight was caught up gracefully in a Spanish headdress from which a black lace mantilla flowed. Her dress, which was in period, was fitted with a billowing skirt and made her already slim figure look even more dramatic. The black corset top accented the pearly white skin of her décolletage and arms, which were tantalisingly covered by a sheer veil of black chiffon. The whole effect was both dramatic and startlingly elegant.

'She looks better than any of us,' Katy agreed wonderingly.

As Charlotte picked up her black pearl-encrusted evening bag from a chair, she checked for her keys and then hurried the girls out and into the waiting chauffeur-driven car.

'Hurry up, Candy,' she said to her daughter, who was taking a last, lingering look in the hall mirror.

'All right, all right, I'm coming.' She brushed past her mother angrily. 'Gran was right,' she hissed at her. 'You look like a crow. Why do you always have to get it so wrong?'

Charlotte took a deep breath and slid into the front seat of the car. She had been looking forward to the party, but now she wasn't so sure. Perhaps her mother was right after all. Maybe it was a mistake to go. But why? She and Ossie had a perfectly civilised post-marital relationship – everybody knew that. She was genuinely happy for him, for his new relationship. She only wished her daughter, and indeed her mother, could be too.

'What do you mean, he's in property?' her mother had asked archly after Charlotte had introduced Ossie to her parents all those years ago. 'He doesn't even have a house, he only rents that place he's in.'

'He's investing in property, speculating. He'll have a house of his own soon, it's just that now he has to spread the risk on other stuff, offices and things.'

'He's not right for you, Charlotte. Mark my words, he'll lead you a merry dance, a chap like that. I know the type well. Social climbers, want to marry the perfect girl so they can run a perfect house and provide a perfect family for them to cover up their own inadequacies. Then the minute they make the big time, they're off without so much as a backward look. You won't listen to me, I know, you've got that stubborn look on your face, but if you marry that chap you'll be throwing yourself away. Remember, Charlotte – origins will out.'

'Your mother's right – for once.' Her father had looked up from *The Irish Field* he was studying intently. 'He's not our type – not yours either.'

And that was all that had been said on the matter.

But it was too late. Charlotte was already in love with the funny, witty, larger-than-life character who was, as her parents pointed out, so unlike anyone she had ever met before.

Up until then, her life had been an orderly, diligent affair that ran mostly as it was meant to. She had grown up, along with her two older brothers, on the stud farm in Kildare, an hour or so from Dublin. Secondary school was spent boarding at an exclusive convent where she had excelled at sports and made many good friends. This was followed, despite protest-ations (her parents had insisted) by a stint in finishing school at St Mary's Ascot.

After school, she had applied successfully for a post as a trainee estate agent in Dublin, and it was there, showing one of her first properties, that she had encountered Ossie Keating.

'Just what do you think you're doing?' she had whispered angrily, anxious not to attract attention from other viewers inspecting the three-storey-over-basement house.

The tall young man with brown wavy hair a shade too long, wearing a camel-hair coat over jeans and shiny, pointy-toed boots, took not a jot of notice of her. He continued to pull at and eventually removed a large chunk of damp wallpaper and held it up for inspection. 'See?' he grinned infuriatingly. 'Rot – and lots of it,' he added loudly. 'You'd need plenty of dosh and a builder who owes you more than one favour to get this place anywhere close to liveable. It's way overpriced.' Then, with a nod and a further dismissive glance around the property, he had disappeared, and most of the other viewers had promptly followed.

Charlotte had been livid. The ignorant, arrogant oaf! She checked her clipboard for his name. Ossie Keating. Sure, the house was a bit run down – a lot run down, actually; it hadn't been lived in for over twenty years – but the proportions were wonderful and its location in the old world, elegant Wellington Square, so close to town, was second to none. At £120,000, it was a seriously good buy. The auction was the following week.

Despite the recession, there was a fair amount of interest in the property, and bidding began briskly with three eager parties. Charlotte, sitting beside the auctioneer, looking neat and composed in her pleated skirt and Laura Ashley blouse, was keeping written track of bids. It went quickly to reserve price and then on to £140,000, where two parties dropped out and the remaining bidder waited expectantly for the auctioneer to close the deal. Then another bidder entered the fray. As the price reached £150,000, the property was proclaimed sold. Charlotte looked up from her notes to inspect the buyer. He was standing at the back of the room leaning against the wall, wearing his camel-hair coat and a cheeky grin. He waved up at her. It was none other than Ossie Keating.

'Have a drink with me,' he said to her after everybody had shaken hands and Ossie had signed the various deeds of sale. 'I think this calls for a celebration, and I don't have anyone else to celebrate with right now.' He'd looked at her expectantly.

'I have to get back to the office to finish the rest of the paperwork,' Charlotte had said.

'No need, Lottie,' her boss said, happy at the unexpectedly high price they had achieved. 'Go right ahead. See you tomorrow.'

'Allow me to introduce myself,' he had said with mock gallantry. 'Oswald Keating. Delighted to make your acquaintance. And you are . . .?' He held out his hand.

'Charlotte Searson.' She took his hand and he shook hers firmly.

'Well, Charlotte Searson, you shouldn't allow your boss to call you Lottie.'

'Why not?' she had asked.

'Because you're definitely a Charlotte.'

They had gone for a drink in the nearby Shelbourne Hotel, and before she left to go home, Charlotte had agreed to have dinner with him the following Friday.

He took her to a good restaurant in an upmarket hotel. Charlotte was nervous and shy, but Ossie was engaging company and she soon found her natural reserve disappearing as she laughed at his stories and escapades. He was generous too, and always paid in cash and tipped heavily. He was well known in these restaurants and the waiters and maître d's were always happy to see him and greeted him warmly, sometimes, Charlotte felt, with overfamiliarity. After dinner, they would sometimes go to a nightclub, where more people would greet him, and there would be shouts of laughter and winks from his mates.

Her parents kept a house in town, on nearby Merrion Square, and Charlotte had a flat in the basement. Ossie had been impressed. She had always taken her upbringing for granted, but with Ossie, she began to see it through new eyes. After two months of dating, she had introduced him to her parents, who had been polite – overly polite. Charlotte knew immediately what that meant – they didn't approve.

Thankfully, Ossie seemed unaware of the undercurrent and was his usual laid-back self. He had dressed up for the occasion without any prompting on her part and wore a pair of dark green corduroys with suede laced-up shoes. His shirt was brushed cotton and checked and his jacket was a bright green and brown tweed. A red tie covered in horseshoes completed the outfit. He'd even had a haircut. Looking at him, he could have been auditioning for a part in *The Irish R.M.*, and Charlotte's heart went out to him. She'd have preferred if he'd worn his jeans and cowboy boots, but clearly he had gone to great trouble on her behalf and she told him he looked terrific.

'Only the best for my girl,' he'd winked at her. 'Told you I cleaned up nice, didn't I?'

He was chatty and respectful to her parents and complimented her mother heartily on the pheasant served at lunch.

'Nice place you have here.' He waved his knife to illustrate his enthusiasm, and Charlotte cringed inwardly as she saw her mother all but flinch. 'Charlotte tells me you're big into horses, Mr Searson,' he went on, chewing rather excessively, Charlotte noticed for the first time. 'I'm a fan myself. Got an eye for a good filly.' He winked at Charlotte.

'I've bred some of the best bloodstock in Europe, yes,' her father said pleasantly.

After coffee, Charlotte said they had to go, otherwise they would hit all the Sunday evening traffic.

The next morning, Charlotte rang her mother to thank her for lunch. No mention was made of Ossie. Hating herself for it, Charlotte couldn't help asking.

'Well, what did you think of him, Mummy?'

There was the briefest of pauses. 'Revolting. And your father agrees with me. He said there'd be no use telling you, but you know me, Charlotte, I'm your mother and I'm not one to mince words. You're obviously in the grip of some sort of sexual excitement or something, but I would strongly advise you to look elsewhere. Good God, Charlotte, his table manners alone are appalling and he was dressed like a bookie, for heaven's sakes.'

For the first time in her life, but not the last, Charlotte had hung up the phone on her. Her hands were trembling.

Her mother had hit on at least one home truth. Charlotte was having ecstatically satisfying sex, and was enjoying every delicious minute of it.

Ossie noticed how subdued she was in the following days. 'They don't like me, do they, your folks?'

When she had protested, he silenced her with a kiss and seemed not at all put out about the situation. 'Don't worry about it, babe. When they see us surrounded by half a dozen kids and all the millions I'm going to make, they'll know you made the right choice.'

'What?' Charlotte almost dropped the cup of coffee she had just poured.

'You heard me.' He stood in front of her, smiling, confident. 'You *are* going to marry me, aren't you?'

'Ossie . . . I . . .'

He took the cup from her hand and placed it on the counter behind her. 'Because if you don't . . .'

Charlotte gasped as his hands found their way under her skirt and reached up until they had found her panties, which were then unceremoniously pulled off. 'Because if you don't,' he was lifting her onto the countertop and pushing himself between her legs, 'I'm going to have to tell your parents what a naughty little convent girl you really are.' He was holding her hair back and kissing her neck, undoing his jeans with his free hand.

'Won't I, Miss Searson?' He opened her blouse, unhooked her bra, and flicked his tongue lightly across her nipple. 'Well?'

'Oh yes!' Charlotte murmured, winding her arms around him. 'Yes, Ossie, yes, yes, yes.'

★   ★   ★

The wedding was an elegant affair, held, of course, at home, on the stud farm. They were married in the little village church, where Charlotte and her father arrived in a horse-drawn carriage.

Afterwards, three hundred and fifty guests partied long into the night in a vast, chiffon-lined marquee and the newly-weds made their getaway to Dublin, from where they flew to London and then on to an island-hopping tour of the Caribbean.

They arrived back three weeks later, sunburned and sated, to Charlotte's flat, where she set about making them a late-night snack before going to bed. But Ossie had a surprise in store for her.

'Don't unpack just yet, Mrs Keating,' he said. 'There's something I want to show you.' He collected his car and she slipped into the front seat as he drove off.

'What on earth is all this about?'

'Wait and see.' He turned into Wellington Square, in darkness apart from the street lights and a few night lights that shone from elegant sash windows.

'Remember I told you yesterday I got the go-ahead to develop the Cabinteely site?'

'Yes.'

'Well, it means I won't have to turn this place into flats like I was going to.' He pulled up outside number 42. 'It's all yours, Mrs Keating. It may be a wreck, but if you'd care to take on the task of turning it into the elegant family home for us that I know you would, money will not be an object.'

'Oh, Ossie, really? Really and truly?'

'It's all yours, Charlotte. That's the first bit of good news you can give those disapproving parents of yours!'

So she did. It took two long years while number 42 was gutted and painstakingly rebuilt, and once the builders had finished, Charlotte went to work. Six months later, a home that spoke of generations of good taste welcomed its new owners. For once, her mother had nothing negative to say – after all, she had been consulted and much involved in the decorating project.

Nine months after they had moved in, almost to the day, their daughter was born.

'What about Candice?' Charlotte asked, cradling her newborn while Ossie cracked open the champagne.

'Call her whatever you like, darling,' he beamed, looking proudly down at the small pink face that hiccupped loudly at him. 'She'll always be Princess to me.'

Those were the happiest times, Charlotte always thought later. She had relished homemaking and looking after Ossie and their little daughter and ran a fabulous house. Nothing fazed her. No last-minute surprise sprung by Ossie that he had to entertain a dozen people at short notice or throw a party for such-and-such was a bother. Charlotte came from a long line of capable, confident women and had the upbringing to match. Their parties, when they threw them, were the talk of the country – for all the right reasons.

All the while, Ossie's property interests flourished and he made more and more money. He even won her parents over, bit by bit, particularly when he bought his first racehorse. Trips to Cheltenham, Royal Ascot and local courses were a regular part of their calendar, and now they were doing it in the best corporate style.

The fact was, it was impossible to insult Ossie. He took everything in great good humour whether or not it was intended as such. He was clever too, and slowly but surely, the flash clothes were replaced by more subdued, stylish ones and his table manners and sometimes raucous behaviour were modulated. When he appeared one day, ready to take them to the Grand National, sporting a Barbour jacket, trilby and racing glasses, Jennifer murmured to her daughter, 'I've seen it all now. Who'd have thought it?'

Charlotte hunted every season, as she always had, until

one cold, unforgiving November day, when she had the fall that preceded her first miscarriage, and the four that were to follow.

Ossie was marvellous. No one could have been better to her, more concerned, more understanding, but the loss, the desperate, fluttering hopes that were dashed time and time again, left Charlotte bereft in a way she could never have anticipated.

She blamed herself constantly and never got on a horse again. Instead, she threw herself even more into her role as the perfect wife, doing course after course, fund-raising for endless charities and entertaining royally for the husband she felt, but couldn't bear to acknowledge, slipping slowly but surely away from her.

She didn't blame him. Ossie had always wanted a big family and had never made any secret of it – nor had she. He was larger than life himself and never happier than when he was organising and amusing great crowds of people. Ossie was a provider, a fixer, a builder of empires. It did more to him than he knew that he couldn't help, fix or provide the one thing they both longed for.

Eventually, she was advised to stop trying for the sake of her health, both physical and psychological, and she reluctantly agreed to have her tubes tied. By that stage it didn't matter. Something inside her, something nurturing, life-giving and hopeful, had already withered away.

It was in May 2004, shortly before their twentieth wedding anniversary, that Ossie told her that he was leaving her, that he had met someone else and was in love. Charlotte sat down and listened as a great vacuum inside threatened to consume her. She took deep breaths and resolved not to make a scene. She sat up straight in her chair and folded her hands on her lap, remembering from somewhere in the dim and distant past a voice telling her that deportment was everything, even in the most unlikely of situations.

'I see,' she said quietly. 'When will you be leaving?'

Ossie looked uncomfortable. 'Well, over the next couple of days. I thought . . . that is, we have to talk to Candice, explain it to her.'

'Yes, yes we do. They say it's better for both parents to sit down and talk about . . . it. Although I think I'll leave most of the talking to you, if that's all right. I – I wouldn't really know what to say.'

'Charlotte, please.' Ossie looked wretched. 'I never meant for this to happen. I never meant to hurt you. You've always been a wonderful wife and mother. We've just grown apart. Things move on – life, people move on.' He looked at her hopefully.

'It certainly would appear so.'

'Look, I know you must be angry with me, hurt. You have every right to scream at me. Please, say something.'

'I think you know by now that's not my style,' Charlotte said quietly. 'But I will say this – if you're going, I'd like you to leave now, tonight.' She had to stop herself from offering, out of habit and despite the roaring in her ears, *Would you like me to pack for you?*

'But—'

'Tonight, Ossie. That's all I'm asking.'

He sighed deeply. 'Whatever you say.' He got up from his chair. 'Don't you even want to know who she is?' He seemed puzzled, unsure now.

'I imagine I'll find out in good time.' Charlotte gave a little smile. 'What's important now is that we tell Candice. I'll go into the kitchen and make some coffee. You'd better call her down.'

In the kitchen, she went mechanically about her task, grinding fresh beans, putting them into the coffee-maker and watching the dark liquid filter through as if she was seeing it for the first time, a thing of wonder. She poured three mugs, adding vanilla essence to Ossie's, just the way he liked it.

Then she sat down and sipped her coffee and watched as
Ossie appeared at the door, followed by Candice, looking put
out to have been dragged away from her bedroom, her iPod
and her endless emails. And then the surreal scene began to
unfold as Ossie haltingly began telling Candice how much
they both loved her.

'Princess, you know how I – how much we both – love
you, don't you?' he looked at her beseechingly.

He didn't get any further. The expression on Candice's
sixteen-year-old face said it all – a flicker of bewilderment,
followed closely by horror, then disgust. 'You're getting a
divorce, aren't you?'

'Princess, please, let me explain.'

'Darling.' Charlotte reached out for her hand across the table,
which was instantly snatched back. 'Let Daddy talk for a minute.'

'There's someone else, isn't there?' Her eyes were blazing.
'You've met someone else and now you're leaving us.'

'Please, Princess, just let me—'

'Shut up!' she shouted, jumping up from the table. 'Shut
up! I don't want to hear this.'

'Please, Candy.' Charlotte was appalled. 'Please sit down
and listen.'

'To what, exactly? How much you love me, blah, blah,
yeah, right. How people grow apart? Give me a fucking break.
I've heard it all before. I watch television. I know how the
script goes.' She was shivering now.

'Please, Princess.'

'Stop calling me Princess – I hate it. I hate you both!'

Charlotte and Ossie watched immobilised, frozen as their
daughter fell apart.

'And you,' she spat at Ossie. 'Don't think I don't know
about these things. You've been seeing someone, haven't you?
Sleeping with some . . . some *slut* and you haven't even got
the guts to come out and say it!'

'Candy, that's enough!' Charlotte's voice was sharper than

she intended, but she could hardly take in the scene of horror that was unfolding.

'Who is she? Who is she?' Candy screamed.

Ossie sat speechless, stricken. His mouth opened but no words came out.

'I knew it. I just knew it. You've been different. You've been dressing funny and using stupid trendy words. You think you're so cool, don't you? Well, you're pathetic. Just a pathetic old man having filthy sex with some tart. Well go on, go! I never want to see you again! And don't think you're any better!' She regarded Charlotte with utter contempt. 'This is all your fault! I bet you never even noticed anything. You're always so busy playing Mrs Perfect. Doing your stupid charity stuff and courses and telling me how I should behave. Well it hasn't got you very far, has it?'

Ossie tried one more time, getting up awkwardly to reach for her.

She backed away from him as if he were about to strike her. 'Don't come near me! Don't touch me! Don't you even dare try.' Tears were pouring down her face. 'You disgust me!'

And with that she ran from the kitchen, up the stairs and into her room, where they heard the door slam and the thumping sound of music begin. Charlotte looked at her husband as he sat with his head in his hands and took a shuddering breath.

'It was never going to be easy,' she said quietly. 'She adores you, she always has. It's hard for her. You're her knight in shining armour. And you indulged her dreadfully. We both did.'

He looked at her, still shocked and numb. 'I thought I was just loving her. She was all I . . . all we had.' His voice caught.

'Don't, Ossie.' Charlotte felt the twist of pain begin. 'Not now.'

'What will we do?' He seemed helpless.

Charlotte sighed. 'I think it's best if you go now. Take an overnight bag; you can get the rest of your things later. I'll talk to her when she's calmed down. It'll take a while, but she'll come around.'

'She hates me.'

'No, she doesn't. She adores you. That's the problem.'

Charlotte sat and listened as her husband went upstairs, packed a case and came back down to her.

'Charlotte?'

'Yes?'

'You know the house is yours, don't you? I would never . . .'

'Thank you, Ossie, I appreciate that. I suppose the lawyers will sort out everything else.'

'You won't want for anything – ever. You have my word on that.' And then he turned and walked down the hall and out of her life.

Outside, she heard the gravel crunch as he drove away. She poured herself another cup of coffee and sat down again, moulding her hands against the cup for warmth, hardly noticing the trembling in her fingers.

Had she somehow always known this day would come? Was that why she was so calm, so controlled? Or was she in shock? Why, at this moment, when this bombshell had been dropped in their lives, why was it her daughter and not her who was behaving like the wronged wife?

Later, as Charlotte wearily made for bed, she stood outside her daughter's bedroom, which was now silent, and knocked gently. 'Candy? Can I come in?'

There was a shuffle, and then the door opened. Candy stood there in her pink pyjamas, clutching her favourite teddy. Against her white, blotchy, woebegone face, her freckles stood out more than ever, and her eyes, red from crying, regarded Charlotte with accusation. She looked about twelve years old. Seeing her, Charlotte's heart constricted.

'I know this seems awful now, but I promise you, we'll be

all right, really we will. Daddy adores you. You'll always come first in his life, whatever happens. You're the most important person in both our lives. Nothing will ever change that.'

Candy looked at her mutely.

'Try and get some sleep, darling. We'll talk about it in the morning.'

'There's nothing to talk about, is there?' Her tone was flat, matter-of-fact, but Charlotte could see the pain in her eyes. 'He's gone. And,' she added, with a sudden look of loathing, 'I bet you never even tried to stop him.' With that, the door closed.

In her room, Charlotte undressed, put away her clothes and cleaned her face. Looking at that face in the mirror, she marvelled that it could seem so normal, so unchanged, when inside she felt as if an earthquake had struck, destroying the familiar landscape she held so dear and rearranging it with jagged, harsh cracks and ridges she could no longer recognise or negotiate.

She climbed into bed, turned off the light and lay very still, knowing with sudden clarity that this must be her destiny – to be alone and to try with every fibre of her being to make that aloneness bearable, endurable. Most of all, to convince her stricken, terrified daughter that life as she knew it would go on, would continue to be full of new and exciting adventures, and that her father, wherever he might go and whoever he might be with, would always provide a life that would include her, first and foremost.

It was then that she allowed herself to cry, great, heaving sobs that wracked her body. She cried for herself, for Ossie and for Candy. For her broken dreams and for her lost babies, and most of all she cried because yet again, her mother had been proved right.

Sometime towards early morning, she fell into an exhausted sleep. When she awoke at half past eight, she was resolved. Whatever it took, however monumentally difficult it might be, she was going to make sure this divorce would be amicable and civilised. She would be the perfect ex-wife. There would be no drama, no self-pity, no recriminations. Satisfied that she had another sensible task to devote herself to, Charlotte showered, put on her minimal make-up and dressed briskly. She listened briefly at Candy's door, from which there was no sound, and decided to let her sleep or keep to herself for as long as it took for her to appear. Then she went down to the kitchen and made herself some strong coffee and toast. She would need fortification, she reflected, to get through today, and a good breakfast had always stood her in good stead. Then, taking a deep breath, she prepared for the first, most daunting of the tasks that lay ahead. Picking up the phone, she dialled and waited for an answer.

'Mummy, she said, 'there's something I have to tell you.'

In the event, Jennifer's reaction had been restrained and as sympathetic as she could manage. Her concern, along with Charlotte's father, had been the effect this would have on Candice.

Eventually, of course, things did settle down. The separation and divorce moved smoothly enough and everyone breathed a sigh of relief when the last Is were dotted and the Ts crossed. Her parents took her and Candy to lunch in Guilbaud's when it was all final.

'At least you've got the house,' Jennifer said.

'That was never in question.'

'You never know. Make sure you hold on to it. These days they can go back at any time and try to change arrangements, you know.'

'Thank you, Mummy, but let's discuss something else for a change, hmm?' Charlotte said lightly.

In the following months, Ossie became Enemy Number One in Jennifer's books. It was more than just motherly support for her newly single daughter, Charlotte suddenly realised. Over the years, Jennifer had become fond of Ossie. She had let her guard down with him. She had also come to enjoy the privileges associated with having a multimillionaire son-in-law, not least of which was talking about him to her friends. In a flash of insight, Charlotte understood that her mother, of all people, was feeling deserted and abandoned too, and unlike her daughter or granddaughter, she made no bones about the fact that Ossie Keating had made a big mistake in taking this course of action – one that, she, Jennifer, of course, had predicted many years ago.

Two years after the divorce, Charlotte's father had died of a heart attack. Jennifer had found him, thinking him to be dozing in his chair, his half-moon reading glasses perched on the end of his nose, a copy of *The Irish Field* on his lap and an unfinished tumbler of whiskey on the table beside him. It was only when she tried to rouse him and his two beloved Jack Russells, Bonnie and Clyde, sitting at his feet in front of the fire had begun to howl that she realised he was gone.

Ossie had been wonderful. He had been there at the funeral, alone, standing discreetly in the pew behind Candy and Charlotte. Afterwards, he had offered to and gladly taken on the monumental task of selling the stud farm and disposing of the bloodstock, making sure every mare and foal fetched their rightful market price. This was almost too much for Jennifer to bear, but Charlotte was intensely grateful to him. By the time the estate was finalised, Jennifer was left a very wealthy widow. She came to stay with Charlotte, along with the dogs, for six weeks, and despite her protestations, Charlotte knew she was glad of the invitation.

'I refuse to be a burden to anyone. I'm quite capable of managing on my own, you know.'

'Of course we know that, Mummy. It's just until you get used to things. Then we can find you somewhere nice of your own.'

It turned out to be a happy arrangement, more so than anyone could have imagined. When Charlotte discussed the possibility of turning the basement into a separate apartment for Jennifer with Ossie, he declared it to be a marvellous idea and once again the builders were brought in to number 42.

Jennifer pretended to be furious when the idea was put to her.

'Don't be ridiculous, Charlotte! All mothers and daughters irritate the pants off each other. I'd drive you mad, and you me.'

It was only when Candy appealed to her that she made a great show of relenting.

'Please, Gran, for me? I'd love to have you here in the basement, and you'll hardly know Mum is in the house. We can all meet up for Sunday lunch or by appointment.'

Charlotte hid a smile as she saw her mother wrestle with the invitation she was dying to accept.

'Candy's right, Mummy. It would be good for her, and for me.'

'What about the dogs?' Jennifer was suspicious.

'Naturally you can have the dogs. Candy and I love dogs, you know that. The only reason I never had one in the house was because Ossie wasn't keen on them.'

'Well, as long as we all live independently and I have my own separate entrance to come and go through, and my own house rules . . .'

'Absolutely.'

'I suppose we could give it a try. But I won't be beholden to anyone, Charlotte. I'll pay my own way. I'm a very independent woman.'

'Of course, Mummy. Let's just see how it goes.'

And it went very well. The basement was converted into two bedrooms, a sitting room with a small dining area and a small, cosy kitchen with its own bright red Aga. This was extended to include a small conservatory leading onto a private patio where Jennifer could continue to enjoy her gardening. And every Sunday, as arranged, they met for lunch either upstairs, when it was Charlotte's turn, or downstairs when Jennifer cooked, and, as it turned out, on many other days of the week as well.

Charlotte realised with a start that they were almost there. The car had sped along the motorway as she was lost in thought, and the girls had been chattering away in the back – now, they couldn't be more than five minutes away. Suddenly, for no reason at all, she felt a fluttering begin in her stomach.

'Will we be on TV?' Katy was asking. 'And how will we know? My mum is dying to see anything and she warned me to text her.'

'If you are,' Charlotte said, 'it will probably be tomorrow. I imagine they'll do a slot on one of the entertainment programmes, you know the ones?'

'Maybe I'll finally be discovered,' Emma said. 'My sister's dead jealous.'

Moments later, they turned off the motorway and onto a slip road that climbed steadily, then another left turn, where up ahead, an impressive pair of wrought iron gates came into view.

'Look!' cried Katy. 'TV cameras at the gate, and loads of paparazzi.'

She was right. As they turned through the gates of Windsor Hall and past the pretty gate lodge, a flurry of flashes went off – but that was just for starters.

Charlotte knew Ossie never did things by half, but this was extraordinary.

Along the half mile leading up to the old manor house, the drive was lined on either side with blazing effigies of martyrs, interspersed with the odd faux head on a pike, producing squeals of horror from the girls.

They drew to a halt a little way before the house as a dark figure emerged in medieval dress. 'No cars beyond this point, order of the King.' Another three figures appeared and opened the car doors. 'From here, my ladies, you will journey by sedan chair.'

Charlotte and the girls emerged and were guided to separate sedan chairs, which were duly lifted and transported the remaining distance, where they were set down.

'Ready girls?' Charlotte smiled at their barely contained excitement. Even Candy, who was trying to be nonchalant, was goggle-eyed. As they were ushered into the house, still more people were arriving on horseback.

They were escorted through the main hall on through to the back of the house, where steps led down to french doors thrown open into the biggest marquee Charlotte had ever seen. It must have been the size of a football pitch, and brilliantly disguised as a great medieval hall. It was simply spectacular – there was no other word for it. Stepping into it, one was transported into another world. Everywhere, from elaborate table arrangements to garlands hung from the walls and ceilings, were the fabled white Tudor roses. Lute players strolled among guests, acrobats formed human pyramids, tumblers frolicked and jesters in lurid colours played to their delighted court. Tables groaned with every kind of food, dwarfed by whole boars and even swans.

'Some refreshment, my lady?' a rather embarrassed waiter in hose smiled at her, proffering a selection of drinks from his tray. Charlotte avoided the mead and asked instead for champagne, although there were no glasses of it to be seen. When the waiter indicated a pewter tumbler, she laughed. Only Ossie would provide pints of champagne. She looked around. The girls had already deserted her, and there was no sign of their host. Tumbler in hand, she made to enter the fray. She was stopped by the royal proclaimer, who shouted loudly, 'My lords and ladies, Her Majesty, the dowager queen,

Catherine of Aragon!' Before she could move any further, at least three photographers were clamouring for a shot. She posed and smiled obligingly and then excused herself as she saw the TV cameras and crew about to bear down.

'Charlotte!' A male voice greeted her and laughed loudly. 'What a fabulous outfit. Wonderful choice, my darling. You look amazing!'

Charlotte recognised a familiar voice, although it took her a second or two to work out who was disguised as the elegant figure of Sir Francis Drake. She recognised a good friend of Ossie's, Philip Carter, who she was very fond of. 'I can return the compliment, Phil. I must say, you're looking very dashing yourself. Back from your travels?'

'Sent to singe the King of Spain's beard and all that!' he chuckled. 'Actually I'm just back from a spot of golf in Portugal, but close enough. Quite a production, this, isn't it?'

'I'll say. Speaking of which, where is Ossie? Have you seen him?'

'Oh, the King is not here to greet the guests, Charlotte. We're here to greet *him*. In fact, according to my source, they should be appearing any moment now. Come with me.'

Charlotte followed him towards the back of the marquee, where everyone was heading. Outside was just as spectacular. Bonfires and braziers blazed, roasting ox, pigs and sheep.

'Better behave yourself,' said Phil, pointing at an executioner at his station looking menacingly out at the crowd.

'If I haven't lost my head by now,' Charlotte grinned, 'I think I'm probably safe. I'm much more likely to end up over there.' She pointed to a set of stocks, where an old hag was being pelted by her husband.

'In the stocks? Why?'

'According to my mother, my choice of outfit will make me a laughing stock. Let's just say she didn't approve.'

'I think it's a marvellous choice – very droll – and Ossie will think it's hilarious.'

'I hope so.' Charlotte felt suddenly nervous.

'Speaking of losing heads,' Phil scowled, looking serious, 'we all think he's off his rocker, you know. It was mad enough to leave you, but this . . . this girl, well . . .'

'That's kind of you to say so Phil, but it's all water under the bridge now, really, and I'm glad Ossie's happy.'

'What about you, Charlotte?' He looked at her keenly. 'Anyone special in your life?'

'Not at present, no,' she said lightly.

'There should be. If it wasn't for Jackie,' he said, referring to his long-time wife, 'I'd be in there like a shot!'

'No you wouldn't,' Charlotte laughed. 'You're incorrigible, but thank you.'

Suddenly a loud gong boomed and a voice called for silence. 'My lords and ladies, prepare for the imminent arrival of His Majesty, the King!'

As a fanfare of trumpets went up, Charlotte gazed, along with everyone else, as her ex-husband, dressed as Henry VIII, held out his hand to escort his rather younger queen.

As they processed regally towards the marquee, the TV crews and cameras fought for coverage. Taking their place at the head of the top table, Ossie welcomed his guests and ordered the dining to commence: 'Eat, drink and be merry, my friends!'

Wandering to her table, Charlotte was glad to see she was seated with Phil and Jackie. As far as she could see, the top table where Ossie and Shalom, his partner, sat was mostly made up of celebrities. She recognised one newsreader, several actors, a few members of Viper and what she supposed to be many models. Ossie's new friends seemed to be made up entirely of Shalom's set. Charlotte certainly didn't spot any familiar faces among them. As she chatted to Jackie on her left, who was eager to catch up with her, Phil, on her other side, nudged her. 'Interesting choice of costume for Ossie's queen, don't you think?' he murmured. 'She's dressed as Jane

Seymour, beloved wife number *three*, when technically speaking, she should have come as Anne Boleyn.'

'Perhaps,' Charlotte grinned, 'she was being sensitive to the implications.'

'What?' Jackie asked. 'Losing her head? Oh, I don't think so. Far too late for that,' she giggled.

'Hey, wench! Over here!'

Carla scowled as Pino thrust a platter of poached salmon at her. 'How's it going?'

'Hideously well, as far as one can tell. At least there haven't been any catastrophes yet. Although there's way too much food. I've never seen anything like it.'

'At least we didn't have to worry about the big stuff. Can you imagine?'

'No, I can't. I thought hiring a "historical culinary expert" sounded off the wall, but looking at those medieval barbeques, I'm very glad they did. There are whole animals being roasted out there!'

'A truly medieval barnyard, I believe,' Pino agreed. 'Terrible waste, though. There's no way this crowd will get through it.'

'No, but I know of at least three homeless shelters who'll be only too thrilled to take the leftovers, and as it's part of our contract to clear away *everything*, I've organised for the catering trucks to drop them off tonight.'

'Clever girl.' Pino looked at her admiringly. 'Now get going with that salmon, or the only hot thing will be you in that *very* delectable costume.'

Carla struggled up the stairs from the main kitchen, cursing her outfit, which was becoming unbearably sticky. Although it was November, the heating inside and outside had been a priority and she was beginning to perspire profusely. In the marquee, she deposited the salmon on the main banqueting table and made her way outside for a breath of fresh air.

Fishing in her voluminous skirts for the pocket she had been relieved to find, she extracted her cigarettes and lit up. From here, she was able to watch what was going on inside relatively unobserved. The main course was now pretty much winding up and the staff were busy taking away plates from diners who were obviously working on getting plastered. Gallons of the finest wines and champagnes had been freely flowing all night, and there was no sign of things letting up. There was only the desserts to go, followed by coffee and liqueurs, and then the dancing would begin. By that stage, the clearing up would be in full swing and the worst would be over. Carla smiled wryly. It sure was one hell of a party. She couldn't even begin to think how much it had cost this Ossie guy. He'd seemed nice enough when she'd been briefly introduced to him earlier, if a bit over the top. But then, anyone who wanted to dress up as an overweight medieval king had to have issues. Clearly spending the annual income of a small country on a fiftieth birthday party and inviting the national press and television stations to cover it said something – though quite what, Carla wasn't sure. She wasn't keen on his partner though. Sure, she was pretty in that fake, plastic kind of way. Earlier in the day, in her clingy velour tracksuit, airbrushed, perfect make-up and lacquered ringlets, she hadn't looked bad, but tonight, in that Tudor outfit, her breasts looked as if she'd stuffed a baby's bottom down her corset. And the name! Who in their right mind called themselves *Shalom*? Of course, Carla knew it meant 'peace', but that was pushing it. She was some 'piece' all right – piece of work, more like. Carla watched her now from her vantage point. She hadn't taken her eyes off Ossie all night, simpering and cooing at him, and like all men he was lapping it up. Typical, thought Carla. As long as their enormous egos were being stroked, men like Ossie were happy to bypass the other, considerably smaller parts of their anatomy, such as their brains.

'Carla!' The sharp voice made her jump. She wheeled around, fag in hand, to see Tanya regarding her coldly. Although she was in evening dress, Tanya was not, interestingly enough, dressed in party mode for the Tudors theme. Instead, she wore a strapless column of black silk jersey, which was strikingly simple and looked as if it cost a fortune.

'You are not being paid to stand around outside smoking. What are you thinking? Get back inside immediately. Dessert is about to be served and you should be in there supervising. I might remind you that you are representing Dominic's tonight, and that kind of behaviour is not what we expect from our staff, particularly when they're meant to be on duty at one of the most prestigious social events of the year.' She was almost quivering with anger.

'I was taking a break and getting some fresh air, that's all.' Carla finished her cigarette and stubbed it out under her foot, counting to ten slowly. 'Everything is perfectly under control.'

'Is that so?' Tanya's voice dripped sarcasm. 'Then perhaps you'd be good enough to ensure it remains that way. And if anything happens to that costume you're wearing, cleaning or repairing it will come out of your salary.' She turned on her heel and walked away.

Carla was furious. Who the hell did Tanya think she was? And why, oh why, had she caught her on the one and only five-minute break she had taken all evening? For some reason she couldn't work out, Tanya definitely seemed to have it in for her, and Carla's patience was running out. She didn't give a damn what Tanya thought of her, but she did enjoy working at Dominic's, and if Tanya had her way, Carla was pretty sure she'd have her fired in the morning. Carla couldn't understand what Dom saw in her. Tanya was overbearing, rude to the staff and clearly knew little or nothing about how to run a restaurant. Yet Dom, who had a first-rate training behind him, seemed to rely on her and trust her advice. It didn't make sense. Tanya was one of those women who bulldozed their way into a man's life and simply took over, and by all accounts that was what she was doing with Dom. They hadn't been together long, according to Astrid, but already Tanya had taken over Dom's apartment, reorganised his social life and had somehow persuaded him that her public-relations duties involved floating around the restaurant and generally getting in everybody's way, not to mention getting their backs up.

'Don't worry,' Astrid had said to Carla, 'it won't last for ever. She's determined to marry him. That's why she won't let him out of her sight. Once she's got the ring on her finger, she'll disappear to play Mrs Society Wife. Then she'll be out of our hair.'

For some reason, that hadn't made Carla feel any better.

Now, she hurried back inside, where, right on cue, Pino was lining up the desserts to coincide with what Carla hoped would be the final spectacle of the evening.

Medieval kings were apparently fond of a surprise pie, so a giant one had been duly constructed on Shalom's instructions. Instead of four and twenty blackbirds being sprung on an unsuspecting audience, a flock of fifty doves were to rise up out of the pie. This was greeted by great shouts and applause from the guests and followed by a well-known boy band weaving in and out of the tables, quite unsteadily at this stage, singing 'You Raise Me Up'.

As he sat watching it all unfold, Ossie was quite clearly delighted. Looking at him as he leaned over and kissed Shalom, Carla couldn't help smiling as she saw a girl at a nearby table, dressed as a young Queen Elizabeth, pretend to put her fingers down her throat in disgust for the benefit of her two friends, who giggled with delight.

Ossie rose to his feet and welcomed his guests as Shalom sat gazing up at him, hanging on his every word. He kept it short, thanking everyone for being with him to share his fiftieth birthday and congratulating Dominic's on providing such wonderful food for the event.

'But tonight isn't just about me,' he continued, looking down at Shalom, an expression of tenderness softening his face. 'I ask you all to raise your glasses to my partner, Shalom, who worked so hard to make tonight special for me,' he paused, 'and to the baby she and I are expecting next June. Who could have thought of a more perfect birthday gift? My darling, you are simply wonderful.'

As people raised their glasses and toasted their hosts, a round of applause broke out among some of the rowdier groups in the room.

At Charlotte's table, Jackie noted the pain that registered on her friend's face before she stapled a smile to it and raised her glass along with everybody else.

'You didn't know about this, did you?' she murmured sympathetically.

'No,' Charlotte replied, 'I didn't.'

'The bastard!' Jackie whispered furiously. 'That selfish, insensitive bastard. He should have told you first. I can't imagine what you must be feeling.' She quickly poured more champagne into Charlotte's glass, but Charlotte wasn't listening. She was watching, with horrified comprehension, as Candy, frozen to her seat for the announcement, now got up from the table and walked around until she stood in front of her father, then picked up the nearest plate of dessert and flung it straight into his face. As Shalom's mouth dropped open and she cringed backwards, Ossie, covered in what appeared to be pavlova, gasped in shock while a flurry of flashes went off to capture what was later widely agreed to have been the highlight of the night.

Jennifer was still watching television in the upstairs sitting room and enjoying a little nightcap when she heard the front door slam and footsteps clumping across the hallway. 'Charlotte?' she called. 'Surely you're not home this early?'

'It's me, Gran,' Candy said, pausing on the stairs.

'Candice? What are you doing back at this hour?' She checked her watch, which pointed to eleven p.m. 'Come in here at once!'

Candy sighed and trudged back downstairs and into the sitting room, where Jennifer was propped up in her favourite winged armchair.

'Is your mother with you? Where are the girls?'

'I left them behind. They're still there, at the party.'

'Did you tell them you were leaving?'

'No. I assume they'll have guessed as much though.' Candy plonked down onto a sofa.

'Well that wasn't very sensible, was it?'

'She's having a baby.' Candy looked mutinous, but Jennifer could tell tears were threatening.

'Well.' Jennifer sat up a little straighter in her chair. 'I can't say that comes as a huge surprise. Here.' She held out her glass to Candy. 'Be a dear and top me up, would you? I think I'm going to need some fortification before your mother gets back.'

'Me too.' Candy got up and filled two glasses, pouring herself a vodka and tonic. 'I only had one glass of champagne at the stupid party anyway.' She handed Jennifer her gin and tonic and sat back down, taking a mouthful of her drink.

'Do you mind, about this baby?' Jennifer regarded her shrewdly.

'Mind? It's disgusting. He's fifty, for heaven's sake.'

'That's not a deterrent, apparently. Anyway, that's his problem, not yours.'

'It'll be twenty, no, twenty-one years younger than me. It's obscene.'

'Precisely. You'll be far too busy having an exciting life of your own to even notice a baby. Just be thankful it isn't living *here* – then you'd know all about it. Take it from me, Candice, babies are extremely overrated. I know, I've had four of them.'

'That's it, though, isn't it?' Candy blurted. 'That's the end. He'll have loads of babies with *her* and he won't have any time for me.'

'Don't be ridiculous, Candice. Really, you're blowing this all out of proportion.

'Am I?'

'Yes. Babies are a novelty. The first one is a lovely fantasy until it arrives, and then it's bloody hard work. I can't imagine your father relishing sleepless nights and changing nappies – he's not that sort of man, not at any age. And this isn't his first baby – *you* were. Give him three months and he'll be tearing his hair out – and extremely grateful to have a daughter he can actually converse with.'

The first glimmer that disaster might yet be averted flickered in Candy's face. 'D'you really think so?'

'I'm sure of it. Now, if you take my advice,' Jennifer took a swig of her drink, 'you'll tell everyone you know that you're thrilled with the news.'

'It's a bit late for that.' Candy looked sheepish. 'I threw a plate of pavlova in his face. Everybody saw me.'

'You what?' Jennifer looked appalled.

'He announced it, when he was making his stupid speech, in front of all those people. I couldn't help it. I wanted to kill him. I wanted to wipe the smug look off her stupid face.'

'Well,' said Jennifer, inhaling deeply, 'I imagine you did that all right.'

'It was such a shock.'

'Yes, yes, I can see that.' Jennifer was thoughtful. 'What about your mother? What did *she* do?'

'I don't know. After I threw the pavlova at him, I ran out. There were loads of cars and drivers outside, I just got in one and came home.'

'I see.'

Candy started as they heard the front door open.

'That'll be your mother. We're in here,' Jennifer called to her.

Charlotte came in, looking pale and drawn minus her head-dress, which she carried under her arm. She flung it on the sofa. 'Candy,' she said, sitting down beside her daughter and putting an arm around her shoulders. 'I wish you hadn't run off like that. You gave me a terrible fright. Are you all right?'

'Of course she's all right, stop mollycoddling her. She's twenty, not ten years of age. Isn't that so, Candice?'

'It must have been an awful shock for you. I don't think Daddy thought it through very well, how to break the news.'

'What's new?' Jennifer was withering.

'Please, Mummy.' Charlotte gave Jennifer a warning look.

'Gran's right, Mum,' Candy sighed. 'I'm sorry I, um, over-reacted like that. It was silly of me. I'll apologise to Dad tomorrow.'

'You'll do no such thing!' Jennifer was adamant. 'Your mother will have a little talk with him, won't you, Charlotte? Just like Candice and I had a little talk before you came in, and we've decided it's very good news about this baby. At least that's the line we'll be taking with anyone who's nasty enough to enquire about it. Don't you agree, Charlotte?'

'Do I have a choice in the matter?'

'Candice, go up to bed and get out of that ridiculous costume. Everything will seem much better after a good night's sleep.' She proffered her cheek for a goodnight kiss. 'I might say the same applies to your mother,' she said, looking meaningfully at Charlotte, 'but first I'd like a word. So good-night, Candice dear, sleep tight.'

'Goodnight, Gran. And thanks.' Candice closed the door softly behind her.

'I need a drink.' Charlotte made for the drinks trolley and poured herself a brandy.

'I'm not surprised.' Jennifer looked at her keenly. 'How do you feel about it?'

'Ghastly, if I'm honest. I suppose I knew it was inevitable, but to announce it like that, it was such a shock, such a . . .'

'Slap in the face?'

Charlotte nodded miserably. 'Ossie always wanted a big family. Frankly, I'm surprised they waited as long as they have. I'd sort of steeled myself to expect it, but still . . . it hurts.'

'Ossie always wanted a big family with *you*, Charlotte,' Jennifer said gently but firmly. 'He may discover that children with this other creature will be *quite* a different kettle of fish. Very few women – none that *I* know, at any rate – have your talent for seemingly effortless yet exquisite homemaking. I'd wager Ossie's missing that more than he lets on.'

Charlotte smiled gratefully. 'Sometimes, Mother – not often, mind – you say just the right thing.'

'I have my moments.' Jennifer hauled herself out of her chair. 'Now, let's get to bed. I suspect we'll need to be on top of our game to deal with that daughter of yours tomorrow.'

Charlotte groaned. 'Oh, God, if you'd seen her . . .'

'I rather wish I had,' Jennifer said, chuckling.

In her bedroom, Charlotte undressed slowly, struggling to unhook herself from the elaborate corset-topped dress. It was funny, she thought, stepping out of it, it was the little things you missed a man for. Right now, she'd give anything to have someone undo her dress and help her out of it, laugh about the bizarre evening and climb into bed and cuddle up with.

Now she hung the dress up carefully on its special hanger and regarded it fondly. It was sentimental to have kept it all these years, but every time she had tried, she just hadn't had the heart to give it away. When the invitation came for the party, with the instructions for guests to come appropriately dressed as Tudors, Charlotte had immediately known what she would wear. While stylists everywhere were bombarded with requests from frantic guests the minute the invitations had landed and were scouring every theatre supply company in the country and beyond, Charlotte had simply unearthed her beautiful wedding dress, feeling a little thrill of satisfaction that she could still fit into it, and had it professionally dyed black. No one, not even Ossie, had recognised it. The dress had served her well on both occasions. Tomorrow, she resolved, she would take it to one of the charity shops. After all, she reasoned, wedding dresses, current *or* vintage, were not part and parcel of a divorced wife's wardrobe.

Collapsing into bed, Charlotte fell asleep almost immediately and dreamed of Catherine of Aragon, locked in the Tower, existing solely on pavlova pies.

After everything had been cleared away, the kitchens tidied up and the catering trucks sent off, stocked with leftover food for the shelters, Carla decided to go for a stroll. Apart from anything else, she needed to find a loo, and the car that would be taking her and Pino back to town wasn't due for another forty-five minutes. Pino was on his phone, presumably relating the events of the night in rapid Latvian to a friend, accompanied, not surprisingly, by bursts of laughter.

Making her way up from the basement, Carla found herself in the main hall of the house and paused, tilting her head to admire the soaring ceilings above her, with their ornate decorations, and the great sweep of curving staircase that rose ahead. Impulsively, she made her way upstairs, past regal portraits of men and women who regarded her haughtily. Presumably the ancestors, she guessed, although they looked far too formidable to belong to the Ossie guy or his consort, but hey, who knew? Popping her head around the doors of a few sumptuously decorated bedrooms that looked as if they had featured in the pages of a glossy interiors magazine, she kept going until she found a separate guest bathroom, hurried inside and locked the door.

What a night! She shook her head, thinking of the spectacular display of daughterly rage they had all been treated to, courtesy of the young Princess Elizabeth, who turned out to be Ossie Keating's only daughter – to date, that is. Clearly, her reaction to the news that she was about to have a baby half-brother or sister in her life didn't exactly thrill her, and considering the way the news had been delivered, Carla couldn't say she blamed her. It was a hell of a stunt to pull though. Ossie's face covered in pavlova had just about made everyone's night. After the gasps of shock, people had found it impossible to keep a straight face. It was just way too funny – although presumably not for the family involved. Still, she thought, straightening her skirt, washing her hands and splashing some cold water on her flushed face, that was life – the old had to make way for the new. Not that you'd know it as regards her *own* family, she scowled, remembering the angry scenes she had left behind her. She missed her brothers, and her father – but she wouldn't think about that now.

Instead, she regarded her reflection in the mirror and almost laughed out loud. With all the fuss and hard work, she had almost forgotten the costume she was wearing. Now, with her cheeks flushed from heat, tendrils of hair escaping to curl around her face and her breasts pushed up in the red silk corset lined at the neck with a white pleated silk ruffle, she could have taken her place beside any of the portraits she had passed adorning the staircase. Pino had been right – she looked just like a lusty medieval serving wench, straight out of central casting. It was a good look, she acknowledged, if you liked that kind of thing, though thoroughly impractical. Even coming up those stairs had left her fighting for breath, and her waist was cinched in so tightly it was all she could do to take in tiny gasps of air.

She had just dried her hands when the handle on the door

turned. 'Just a minute,' she called out, hoping it wasn't Tanya, following her around again. 'I'll be out in a sec.' Making sure she had left the bathroom just as she found it, down to straightening the hand towel with military precision, she made her exit.

For a moment, she thought she was alone, that whoever had turned the handle had gone away, and then she saw him leaning against the wall, glass of champagne in hand.

'Carla,' he said, straightening up and taking a step towards her.

'Dom,' she breathed, suddenly feeling both awkward and guilty. She hadn't known he was coming to the party.

'You look . . . gorgeous.' His eyes roved over her appreciatively, resting for a split second on her décolletage, which, she felt sure, was now suffused with the slow flush of embarrassment that had started in her cheeks. God, he looked sexy. He was in jeans, and the pale blue shirt open at the neck set off his dark skin beautifully. He pushed his hair back from his face and smiled, shaking his head slightly as if to clear it. He was obviously a little worse for wear. She'd never seen him even slightly tipsy in all her time at Dominic's. He was so adamant about professionalism, unlike some restaurateurs she had known in her time.

'I was just . . .' She paused, feeling beyond stupid. What was she doing? She didn't have to justify herself to anyone. She raised her eyes to his and saw only amusement, and something else, something warm that locked with her eyes and then flared between them.

'Just what?' He was grinning now, leaning towards her with a gorgeous, inviting, lopsided grin.

'I was just about to . . .' And then she did it. She couldn't help herself – she reached up and kissed him. She didn't think about it, she just did it, impulsively, and suddenly he was kissing her back, quite fiercely, one hand cradling her head, the other around her waist, pulling her closer. And she kept kissing him, just as he kept kissing her, as he moved backwards, taking her with him, until he had pulled her into one of the bedrooms she had passed, kicking the door shut with his foot. When he came up for air he flicked on the light.

'Christ, you're sexy,' he murmured in Italian, and the sound of it, of her native language, aroused her even more. She didn't care that she was in someone else's house, that she was in this ridiculous costume or even that he had a girl-friend – a girlfriend who was possibly searching for him at that very moment, prowling the house. All that mattered was that she was with him and he was kissing her.

Suddenly she gasped, laughing. 'Wait a minute. I can't breathe, really. This corset is so restricting.'

'Then let's do something about that,' he said, untying the silk bow that laced it together at the back, allowing the tightly boned material to give finally. She took a deep breath and gasped again as Dom's hand found her breast, cupping it, caressing it exquisitely, and he was kissing her again, kissing her neck, his thumb tracing her lips. And then his mouth trailed downwards, his tongue tracing circles on her skin, and then finally his lips closed on her nipple and he was sucking and licking and holding her, moulding her to him and she never wanted him to stop. And then—

'Dom?' The unmistakable voice called from the corridor. 'Dommy? Where are you?'

She froze as Dom wrenched his lips away. 'Shh,' he whispered, holding her still, and then the voice became fainter as its owner moved on down the corridor in her search. For a moment, they looked at one another, desire written all over their faces, and Dom pulled away abruptly. 'I'm sorry,' he said, running his hands through his now-dishevelled hair. 'That was unforgivable of me.'

'No, no,' she heard herself saying as she fumbled to haul her corset back to its original position. 'It was my fault. I shouldn't have. It was . . .' Oh God, this was awful, it was dreadful. It was agonisingly awkward and – worst of all – it was over. The glorious moment had been broken.

'Let me help you with that.' Dom was behind her. She could feel his hands trembling as he pulled the ribbon ties together, drawing them tighter. 'There,' he said, letting out a long breath. 'Not my finest example, but one of the advantages of having sisters is becoming adept at doing up tops.' He was trying to make light of it. That made it even worse, and Carla felt her face flame. He turned her around gently to face him and put his hand under her chin, tilting it until she met his eyes. 'I *am* sorry. You must believe me. And it most certainly was not your fault, it was mine, every bit of it. Will you forgive me?' He searched her face.

Carla pulled herself together. Tanya was his girlfriend, it was *her* he was interested in, and he was clearly embarrassed by what had happened. How could she have encouraged him to kiss her? He was the drunk one; *she* should have behaved better. 'Of course.' She forced herself to smile. 'There's nothing to forgive. These things happen. We're both adults. This has been quite a party and we've all had a lot of wine – don't give it another thought. I won't.' She was giving him her brightest, fakest smile now and willed him to go. She was still finding it hard to breathe and it had nothing to do with her corset.

He seemed reluctant to leave her, then opened the door softly, his eyes still locked on hers. 'Are you okay?' He seemed genuinely concerned.

'Sure. You'd better go.'

'It had nothing to do with the wine,' he said quietly. 'I want you to know that.' And then he closed the door behind him.

'Oh God,' she whispered to herself when he had gone. How could she have been so stupid? How could she even have tried to fool herself? She was crazy about him, and now he'd think she was just a slutty waitress who'd stuck her boobs out at him on purpose. 'Oh no,' she moaned, sitting on the bed, putting her face in her hands as tears ran down it. 'Why did I ruin everything?'

Dom hadn't been planning on attending the party – in fact, he'd been determined to avoid it at all costs, despite Tanya's protestations. But it had been a long week and at the last minute, satisfied that Dominic's final orders had left the kitchen, he had decided to jump in a taxi and have a look in, even if it *was* late. Judging by Tanya's incessant text messages, it was a spectacular event that absolutely *had* to be seen to be believed. At this stage, the formal dinner would be over, so he wouldn't have to sit through that, and it wouldn't hurt to have a few drinks and relax for a change – he'd been working like a dog. And, as Tanya was always reminding him, it was important to be seen at social events to keep up a high profile for the restaurant. It was the one area of contention between them: Dom absolutely refused to be a 'couple about town'. He believed that if the food was good enough and the atmosphere pleasant enough, Dominic's would attract the right clientele. But Tanya didn't give up easily and continued to pester him, and tonight, for a change, he had given in. In more ways than one, it turned out, with possibly disastrous consequences. What on earth had he been thinking? To follow Carla upstairs (well, not really follow, more trail helplessly after her, despite every warning bell that was sounding in his head), waiting until he could strate-gically bump into her, and then – well, he just couldn't take his eyes off her in that sexy outfit, that corset moulded to every delicious curve, her flushed cheeks and shining eyes, locked just as firmly with his. And then she had kissed him and there had been no stopping himself. It had been madness, sheer madness. What if Tanya had walked in on them? She didn't deserve that, and thank God it hadn't come to that. But it had been a close shave.

Tanya could be irritating, but she meant well. She was incredibly organised and made sure all the annoying little things he didn't have the time or inclination to deal with got done. In short, she made his life easy – not interesting, but Dom had had enough of interesting. In his experience, it meant drama – particularly where women were concerned – and he had had quite enough of that. Tanya was a refreshing change, always pleasant and unperturbed, although sometimes Dom almost wished she would lose her rag with him and lose control. But even in bed, Tanya was calmly proficient and capable, always taking care of his needs before her own. Dom shrugged – and he was complaining? There wasn't a guy he knew of who wouldn't be very happy with that arrangement.

But he couldn't get Carla or that kiss out of his head. He would have to pull himself together. His womanising days were over. What he had done had been incredibly irresponsible. Carla was his employee, for heaven's sakes, and now they would have to face each other in the restaurant. He shuddered, but it wasn't only with apprehension, he realised. There was a definite sense of delicious anticipation lurking there as well at the thought of seeing her again.

TAKE THAT! screamed *The Irish Sun*.

CANDY, WARRIOR PRINCESS! proclaimed *The Irish Star*.

TUDOR FEAST ENDS IN FACE-OFF! *The Irish Daily Mail* led with.

GOB SMACKED! quipped *The Echo*.

The shot under every headline was the same: Candy, wearing an expression of rage and triumph, Ossie, face splattered with pavlova, and Shalom, diving for cover, hands protecting her face, mouth open in horror.

The papers lay carefully arranged on the kitchen table and Jennifer was perusing them one at a time while she had her toast and coffee. She didn't usually read the tabloids, but this morning, having reflected on the amount of media presence at Ossie's party, she had correctly guessed that Candice's spontaneity might well have been captured. She had rung the newsagents and had their delivery boy bring them over. She wasn't disappointed. She checked her watch: 8:30 a.m., not too early to ring her daughter.

'Yes, Mother?'

'I know it's a trifle early, Charlotte, but I think you should know this whole episode with Candice and her father has been covered by the tabloids in glorious Technicolor. I have them here.'

'Come on up, I've just put some coffee on.'

'I'm on my way.'

Armed with the evidence, Jennifer lowered herself onto the stair lift that stood at the bottom of the stairs. Normally she avoided using it, but when she had a drink in hand or had to carry her walking cane or, as at present, something awkward, she was glad of it. She settled herself in, pushed the button and sailed upstairs to the door that separated her basement flat from the main house. Safely deposited at the top of the stairs, she got up and went into the kitchen, where Charlotte, already dressed, sat at the table. She poured another coffee for her mother.

'I thought you'd better see for yourself.' Jennifer put the papers down and sat opposite her.

'How bad are they?'

'Not *that* bad. The shot's the same in every one. Actually, there's a very nice one of you and Ossie earlier in the evening in the great hall.'

'Oh dear God,' Charlotte murmured as she leafed through the pages. 'This is frightful.'

'Depends what spin you put on it,' Jennifer pronounced.

'Spin?' Charlotte echoed, looking at her incredulously.

'Yes, spin. That Max Clifford person makes a fortune out

of it. I've seen him lots of times on television. He does an awful lot of charity work too, you know. Apparently it's all about how brazen you can be about things. Luckily for Candice, I would have thought that's rather a forte of hers. She takes after her father in that respect. Speaking of whom,' Jennifer advised, 'you shouldn't speak to him until we've got this sorted out. His behaviour was barbaric.'

'To be fair, he did try and take me aside once or twice in the evening, and he mentioned he had something he wanted to talk to me about, but someone or other always interrupted us.'

'Shalom, no doubt.'

'Well, yes, now that you mention it.'

As if on cue, Charlotte's phone began to ring beside her on the table. Picking it up, she saw Ossie's number on caller display.

'Don't answer it,' Jennifer commanded.

Charlotte held the phone in her hand and chewed her lip.

'Really, Charlotte, I mean it. His behaviour was appalling, both to you *and* Candice. You've got to stop jumping every time he clicks his fingers. It'll be on *her* instructions, you know.'

'What on earth am I going to say?' The phone stopped ringing. 'I'll have to deal with it sometime.'

'Yes, but not just now, dear. We have to think about this, think about what's best for Candice and how to salvage the situation to her advantage.'

'Salvage what situation, exactly?' Candice stood in the doorway in her dressing gown.

'You've made rather a splash in the newspapers this morning. Not entirely unexpected, I suppose,' Jennifer said. 'It really was monstrously ignorant of your father to invite the media. You do know, of course,' she said as she regarded Candice directly, 'that a lady's name should appear in print on only three occasions?'

'What occasions?' Candice had sat down and was already engrossed in the first headline.

'On her birth, her engagement and her death. That is the official line, and the correct one. Anything else is vulgarity personified.'

'Well, it's a bit late for that, isn't it?' Candice grabbed a bit of toast and poured a mug of coffee. 'If you don't mind,' she said, gathering up the papers, 'I'd like to look at the rest of these upstairs. See you later.'

'How extraordinary,' murmured Charlotte, looking bewildered. 'She didn't seem in the slightest bit distressed. I thought there would be a major tantrum at the very least.'

'That,' said Jennifer, pursing her mouth, 'is a bad sign. A very bad sign indeed.'

Upstairs in her bedroom, Candy got back into bed, flicked on the TV for background noise and settled herself down to read every single word.

'Poor Little Rich Girl', the first article was headed, and the others were variations on the same theme. The articles, which were sketchy on hard facts, had at least grasped the general details that her multimillionaire father had left her and her mother for Shalom almost four years ago. Best of all, though, one paper had been more thorough than the rest and had correctly named Shalom as Sharon, which was her real name, or had been until she'd changed it by deed poll. It also gratifyingly painted her mother as a woman of immaculate taste and dignity, implying that Shalom, along with her new name and shop-bought body parts, was anything but.

Candice was described as an aspiring actress, according to 'sources'. 'If her performance last night was anything to go by,' said the *Mail* reporter, 'I don't doubt an Oscar-winning role is imminent!'

Candice grinned. This was even better than she could have hoped for.

Her phone rang, interrupting her reverie. Looking at it, she saw her father's number flash on screen and deftly pressed the 'reject' button. He could piss off! There was no way she was going to talk to him now. Gran was right about that at least.

It rang again almost instantly. Candy cursed under her breath and picked it up crossly, until she saw that it was Emma calling.

'Candy,' she said breathlessly, 'why on earth did you run off like that? We had a brilliant time. Katy got off with Eamonn from Guyz, he's been texting her all night, and I've got an audition to model lingerie on a spot for *TV 2000*!' Emma could hardly contain her excitement.

'Really?' Candy sounded bored. 'Clearly you haven't seen the newspapers then?'

'What do you mean?' Emma was on her guard. 'We didn't say anything except good stuff about you. After you left, they bombarded us.'

'Good,' Candy said. 'That's just as well. And if they ask you anything else, say nothing until you've cleared it with me first.'

'What's going on?'

'You might say I've become an overnight celebrity,' Candy said.

'Ohmigod,' Emma breathed.

'Exactly. We need to discuss strategy. Meet me at three o'clock in Dundrum. Coffee at Harvey Nicks will be on me. Oh, and Emma?'

'Yes?'

'Make sure you and Katy look the biz, okay?'

4

'The doctor will see you now, Mr O'Reilly,' Sheila O'Connor said imperiously, drawing herself up to her full height of five feet ten inches. She peered suspiciously at the prospective patient now crossing the path she guarded so vigilantly between the waiting room and the confessional that was the doctor's office.

A newcomer to the practice, the man looked simultaneously chastened and apprehensive, without quite knowing why.

'Take a seat,' Dr P.J. O'Sullivan stood up from behind his desk and shook his hand, indicating the battered leather tub chair in front of him, which the man sat on gingerly, twisting his cap in his hands, still under the watchful gaze of Sheila.

'Your next two patients are waiting, Doctor.' Her tone was heavy with meaning. 'Mrs Kelly was *particularly* punctual. I've already explained to her that you're running twenty minutes late.' Sheila frowned, clearly disapproving.

'Yes, thank you, Sheila. As I've said many times, a doctor's surgery cannot be run with the precision of a Swiss railway station, much though we would all like it to be. I'm sure Mrs Kelly will understand. I will give her my full and undivided attention when I see her.'

'If you could just shave off five minutes on the next two patients, Doctor, it would greatly—'

'Thank you, Sheila,' P.J. nodded firmly to her. 'That will be all.'

Sheila reluctantly retreated and closed the door behind her.

The patient checked his watch anxiously and was now looking rather alarmed.

'Take no notice of her,' P.J. grinned. 'I don't. She's well used to it.'

'I really don't want to be taking up any more of your time than is absolutely—'

'Nonsense.' P.J. waved a hand. 'I have all the time in the world, and so do you. Sheila – that is, Ms O'Connor – is a first-class secretary in many ways, but she also suffers from OCD, with a touch of bi-polar thrown in.'

'OCD?'

'Obsessive Compulsive Disorder.'

'Oh,' said the patient, sounding not in the least reassured.

'In other words, she means well, but is rather more driven by a longing for orderliness than the rest of us. I have to admit I take an unkind delight in pushing her buttons.' P.J. smiled. 'Now, Mr O'Reilly, if I may take a few details . . .'

The man automatically answered the usual perfunctory medical history queries, and while P.J. took notes, his patient took in his surroundings.

The room was not quite like anything he had ever seen before, certainly nothing that resembled a doctor's office. Patrick O'Reilly had heard a lot about the infamous Dr P.J. O'Sullivan and had imagined his surgery to be a clinical cross between a squash court and a recording studio. Certainly judging from all the famous people who went to see him and spoke so glowingly of him, he never expected anything like this.

The mews P.J. ran his surgery from was a delightfully quaint converted coach house. Inside was a bright, spacious waiting-room area, open plan, with two large picture windows, plenty of single chairs and armchairs and two large sofas that had seen better days. They were all covered in various patterns of faded but immaculately clean chintz. A real fire crackled in the centre of the room, in front of which sat a large wicker dog basket. A vast array of magazines (in fairness, some of them up to date) from *Golfer's Monthly* to the *Sacred Heart Messenger* to *Vogue*, *Harper's* and other high fashion bibles sat in meticulous order on various tables. Fresh flowers and a few interesting plants perched on windowsills, and the resident cat, Psycho, lounged in a corner of the sofa, purring loudly. Presiding over all sat Sheila O'Connor at her pristine receptionist's sentry just inside the door.

Inside, in the surgery, was a whole other story. Paddy O'Reilly had seen untidiness in his time, coming as he did from a small farm shared with a widowed father and four feckless brothers, but this . . . well, this was something else.

Behind the doctor, as he scribbled his notes, was a set of floor-to-ceiling shelves that ran the whole wall, groaning with paperwork. Real paperwork, mind, not neat, typed, orderly stacks of it, but handwritten, unwieldy *masses* of the stuff, like something from a bygone era. His desk, too, obviously antique (if you could manage to see the tiny patch of visible leather-topped mahogany), was covered in more of the stuff. There was paper everywhere – and no rhyme or reason to any of it, apparently. More extraordinarily, the cat that had been sleeping in the waiting room had obviously slipped in through the open door while Sheila had been dispensing instructions. It sat now, a handsome marmalade creature, on the desk, imperiously kneading a pile of handwritten notes for all it was worth. The doctor, Paddy was unnerved to see, paid not a jot of notice.

At the far side of the room was a real log fire, in front of which basked the fattest Labrador Paddy had ever seen. The dog looked at him now, groaned and wagged his tail. He seemed doubly incongruous beside the standing real-life skeleton that inhabited the corner, sporting a trilby, a scarf and a cigarette clenched between his teeth. To cap it all, the strains of some rock band were playing on the sound system.

'You don't mind animals, I hope?' P.J. asked pleasantly. 'I find they have a remarkably therapeutic effect on people. And Psycho here,' he said, indicating the cat, 'provides a first-class filing system. All I have to do is find the paper with the most hairs on it, and I have to hand my most recent notes.' He beamed.

Paddy felt a bit weak but swallowed and nodded, a watery smile on his face.

'They also provide me with the perfect introduction to my cat scan and lab test jokes,' P.J. chuckled. 'Now, what is it I can help you with?'

For an awful moment, Paddy felt the whole room come to a standstill. All movement ceased. Sound faded. The cat had paused in his activity and was regarding him with an accusatory stare and the dog was ogling him, his mouth open and panting. Paddy felt his head begin to swim. He tried to speak, but no words came out. He looked at the cap in his hands, crushed in his clutches.

'Paddy,' P.J. began. 'May I call you Paddy?'

Paddy nodded mutely.

'You must remember that there is nothing – absolutely *nothing* – you could divulge to me that I haven't heard or dealt with before. I realise that doesn't make it any easier for you, especially at a first consultation,' he continued, 'but for what it's worth, I am completely unshockable and resoundingly resilient. And I'm fairly sure that once you share your problem with me – whatever it is – I'll be able to help you, or if not, I'll direct you to someone who can.' P.J. paused to draw breath, hoping against hope that Sheila would not avail of this opportunity to knock discreetly on his door, three times in a row, to remind him he was over time. It was one of many signs that usually indicated she was becoming lax in her medication, and at times such as this, it could have disastrous results. P.J. waited patiently and held his breath.

'It all started about eleven months, two weeks ago, to the day. I'm an accountant, so I remember dates and things like that. I'm very precise.' The cap was fairly spinning in his hands.

P.J. added to his notes and nodded encouragingly.

'Well,' Paddy took a rasping breath, 'there's no other way to say this, Doctor . . .'

'Yes?' P.J. was beginning to feel as agonised as his patient.

Just then, Bones, the Labrador, farted loudly and thumped his tail in approval. The sound made Paddy jump.

'I, er, beg your pardon,' P.J. risked, 'on his behalf.' He grinned. 'As you can see, this is a place of free expression. You were saying?'

'Ican'tgetitupanymore.' The words tumbled out in a rush. Paddy looked first startled, and then as if he might cry.

'A common occurrence, if an inconvenient one,' P.J. nodded knowingly. 'I've suffered from it myself,' he lied. 'Show me the man who hasn't and I'll show you a liar.'

Before his eyes, Paddy expelled a shuddering sigh and regained five, if not ten years. His face, which had been taut, was flooded with relief and he sat up straighter in his chair, an expression of hope and interest replacing despair.

P.J. listened now as the floodgates opened and Paddy related the story of his boardroom barracuda of a wife and her increasingly dissatisfied views of their marriage and indeed their four young children. He wrote him a prescription and took mental notes. It was a textbook case: ambitious, dissatisfied, resentful wife, bewildered, emasculated and increasingly anxious husband.

'We'll have to rule out obvious physical indications, but as you don't smoke or drink, it's unlikely to be a factor.' He handed him the prescription. 'Take these and come back and see me in two weeks. The results of the tests will be back then and we can investigate further if necessary. And remember, Paddy,' he said, tapping his head, 'problems in the bedroom are almost always about what's up here and not about what's down there. That applies to both men and women. If I had a penny for every man who came in here with similar confidences . . .'

Paddy got up and shook his hand heartily. 'Thank you, Doctor, you've been a tonic. I feel better already.' He made for the door.

'Oh, and Paddy?' P.J. regarded him sternly.

'Yes?'

'I think it would be not only appropriate, but thoroughly advisable for you and your wife to abstain in the intervening period until you see me again. Do you think you can manage that? Doctor's orders, if anyone asks.'

The look of relief that crossed his patient's face was positively celestial.

'Whatever you say, Doctor. Whatever you say.'

'Be sure to reassure relevant parties that your emotions are steadfast and that you are merely taking time out to unravel a stressful situation, one which, unresolved, will only contribute to further marital confusion. I have no doubt, no doubt whatsoever, that this situation is entirely resolvable. I wouldn't say that if I didn't believe it. We'll talk further next time.'

'Thank you, Doctor. Again, you have no idea what a load off my mind that is.'

'Take care, Paddy, good to meet you.'

As P.J. went back to his notes and took a gulp of a very cold cup of coffee, another new and hopeful patient took his leave and vowed to tell everyone he knew that it was true, this Dr P.J. O'Sullivan was the real deal, every bit of it. He was halfway down the street in his new BMW, whistling a happy tune, when Paddy realised he had forgotten to offer any kind of payment for the consultation, and, more astonishingly, not one person had prompted him for it – not even the Sheila person, who had very pointedly looked at her watch on his departure. He resolved to write a very generous cheque on his return. It was the least he could do.

For the rest of the day, P.J. continued to see patients, dealing with the usual ailments that presented at this time of year:

flu, a couple of respiratory infections, stress, depression and, interestingly, a rash on an attractive young woman that he strongly suspected might be syphilitic. A few of his regular cancer patients checked in to have him monitor their progress and have their oncologist's ongoing treatment plan explained to them. Nothing too out of the ordinary, and thankfully no bad news to break. He had a cup of coffee and a banana for lunch and by the time he saw his last patient out, he was both tired and ravenous.

'You work too hard, and left to yourself your eating habits are appalling.' Sheila stood at the door, shaking her head.

'Keeps me out of mischief, Sheila, you know that. And don't I know you'll have a lovely dinner waiting for me up at the house.'

Sheila allowed herself a smile. 'It's your favourite, roast chicken with all the trimmings.'

'What would I do without you?'

'Seven o'clock sharp, mind.'

'On the dot, you have my word. Bones and I will go for our evening constitutional and I shall be thinking of chicken every step of the way.'

Sheila checked her watch. 'What time do you have?' She looked at him suspiciously.

'Two minutes past six, exactly.'

She nodded, satisfied. 'We're in sync then.'

'Now don't let me delay you, Sheila. Your duties here finish at five thirty, there's no need to be waiting around here for me.'

'It's no bother.' Sheila was looking longingly at the mound of papers on the desk. 'If you'd just let me tidy that lot up for you . . .'

'Now Sheila, you know the drill.'

'Just the once. I hate to think of—'

'I know my filing system is unorthodox, but it all works perfectly well the way it is.'

'But the Lord only knows what's lurking under that pile. What your patients must think.'

'They think I'll help them to feel better, and that's what I try to do to the best of my ability.'

'And animals in the surgery.' Sheila was edging in now. 'You'll be reported any day now.'

'Sheila.' P.J. was firm. 'If you don't get going, I'll be late on my walk, and then dinner will be delayed, won't it?' He played his trump card.

She looked torn and backed out reluctantly. 'Well, if you're sure.'

'Don't worry, I'll lock up.'

When Sheila had gone, P.J. heaved a sigh of relief. It was always touch and go, finishing up. Sheila kept the house and surgery religiously organised, but P.J.'s office was strictly out of bounds to her. It was the only way the arrangement could survive. The upside was he got to maintain his unbelievingly untidy office just the way he liked it. It had always been the same, ever since he had been a student: P.J. was reasonably tidy with everything else, but his paperwork was sacrosanct. He lived happily with great disjointed mountains of the stuff, covering every possible surface, and was able to find exactly what he wanted at any given moment, even notes dating back years. It gave him an inordinate sense of triumph. He also claimed it was good training for continued mental alertness. He didn't need any of those awful computer games to test his skills, he simply had to think about a particular set of notes and somehow an instinct would arise and he would be drawn unfailingly to the exact piece of paper he wanted. The downside was that he had to do his own dusting and hoovering. It was a small price to pay. The streamlined-looking computer that sat on his desk was used purely for internet research purposes. The only exception he made was to allow Sheila, under his supervision, to clean out and reset the fire. Other than that, unless he was there himself, he kept the office locked.

It drove Sheila mental. Well, it would have driven any woman mental, P.J. supposed, but then, Sheila was not your average woman.

She had come into their lives eight years ago, an anxious, troubled woman of indeterminate age in a well-worn but immaculate overcoat and headscarf. He remembered the day well. She sat down in front of him, plucking at the strap of her handbag, and P.J. had noticed her hands were rubbed raw. It turned out she lived with an elderly and demanding aunt as her carer in return for bed and board. P.J. had correctly diagnosed Obsessive Compulsive Disorder. An intelligent and reasonably well-educated individual, Sheila had begun and been fired from a succession of jobs earlier in life due to her various eccentricities.

Organising her treatment, however, had proved rather more difficult. 'Oh, I don't believe in medication,' she had pronounced. 'It can lead to dependency, and I'm a very independent person.'

'I don't doubt it for a minute, Ms O'Connor.'

'I'd just like to be able to relax a bit more, not get so upset about things and how they should be.' The look of despair that flitted across her face had moved him.

'This medication will help you to do just that. I'd also like you to see my wife, Jilly, for some talking therapy.'

'Talking?' She was wary.

'Yes, counselling. It will help.'

'Isn't that expensive? You see, I don't think my medical card will cover—'

'No need to be concerned about that at present. Look, I'll make a deal with you,' P.J. reasoned with her.

'What's that?' He had her attention.

'If you take these tablets for two weeks and have an appointment with my wife, and if you're still against the idea of medication at your next visit, we'll do it your way.'

'My way?' She looked suspicious.

'You're the boss. That's the way this surgery is run.'

'Well then, I suppose, for two weeks . . .'

And the pills had helped, just as he knew they would. So, of course, had a few sessions with Jilly, who had proclaimed her adorable. 'She *is* funny,' she had said, laughing over dinner that night. 'Sometimes it's all I can do to keep a straight face with some of the things she comes out with.'

Eager to make a bit of extra money, Sheila had put forward the possibility of coming in on a Saturday morning to help with a bit of cleaning and typing, and took to it with relish. The old aunt had eventually died and left her home to her son in America, who promptly sold it. Not a penny went to Sheila. Homeless and jobless, Jilly and P.J. took her on full time, insisting she would be invaluable to them, as long, of course, as she agreed to live in the adjoining granny flat. The arrangement proved to be a successful, if unpredictable, one.

Sheila adored them. This adoration was demonstrated not by any obvious outward affection, but rather a relentless and determined effort to organise and protect Jilly and P.J. from the hazardous possibilities that lurked everywhere. People (the postman was terrified of her), especially patients, were considered a particular threat. She would regard them suspiciously, interrogate them imperiously if unsupervised, and watch with an eagle eye while they sat in the waiting room, silently daring them to touch or move so much as a magazine. It was an uneasy alliance, seeing as they were the sole source of income for her employers, but it made for many hilarious episodes, and as far as his patients were concerned, she only added to the appeal of P.J.'s practice.

Sheila had been a lifesaver, though, since Jilly's death. She kept house and mealtimes as if her life depended on it, which, in a way, P.J. supposed it did. They quite simply would never have managed without her. And now, well, with Bella away studying music in Florence and Alex married, P.J. was glad of Sheila's regular, if eccentric, presence. She was a good cook too, and although P.J. was himself, he knew he would never have bothered about regular meals on his own.

Outside, P.J. and Bones set off for the park a short stroll away. He usually enjoyed this time of day, getting a bit of fresh air and laughing at Bones's enthusiastic efforts at retrieving, which preferably involved hurling himself into the lake, where he would swim powerfully, returning with his trophy. Today, though, P.J. was lost in thought and not as attentive as he might have been.

'Sorry, old chap,' he said to his dog, who was looking perplexed and had dropped his ball at P.J.'s feet for the third time without a response. 'I was miles away. Here you go.' He flung the ball back into the water.

Why was it that Alex always had that effect on him? P.J. frowned. He would have loved to have a good relationship with his only son, to be able to do all the man-to-man stuff, going to rugby matches and having the occasional pint. But Alex wasn't into rugby and favoured smart wine bars over familiar pubs.

It wasn't that they had a bad relationship, as such; he just didn't know how to relate to him. Alex made him feel uncomfortable, and for the life of him P.J. couldn't work out why. Take last week, for instance, when they had met for lunch in that trendy restaurant, Dominic's. It had started off well. P.J. had been deliberately early and had ordered a good bottle of red, a very expensive bottle of red, one that even Alex would approve of. He had made an effort, too, to dress properly and had even had a haircut – well, a trim at any rate. He had stayed away from any incendiary topics and let Alex steer the conversation. Then a couple of people – well, perhaps four or five, maybe – had come over during the course of lunch to say hello to him, including the proprietor, and Alex had positively bristled. To cap it all off, Alex had recounted his latest investment scheme at length, which sounded remarkably risky to P.J., if possibly very profitable. He had listened, nodding encouragingly, and made all the right noises, and then Alex had said, 'Well, that's good. I was hoping you'd be one of the first to come on board.'

P.J. had had to say that he had suggested no such thing, and that he would not be investing in this or indeed any other of Alex's business interests, on family principle. The rest of lunch had passed in relative silence and Alex had made a speedy and resentful exit.

P.J. sighed now, thinking of the day. He had taken the afternoon off especially and had been left with a hefty bill (although he had insisted on paying) and the remains of the bottle of red, which he'd finished.

He wondered if he had been wrong. Should he have invested in the scheme anyway, just as a vote of confidence in his son? Somehow, he didn't think it would have made any real difference. Whatever he did, Alex seemed to think it was always exactly the wrong thing.

'Come on, Bones!' P.J. called his dog. 'Let's go home.'

As Bones galloped towards him, ears flying and soaking wet, P.J. grinned.

'Just as well we have each other, isn't it, old chap?' he said, setting off home. He checked his watch. It was ten minutes to seven. Sheila would not be disappointed.

'Why don't we have your dad to Sunday lunch this week?' Catherine, Alex's wife, suggested. She sat down on the sofa beside her husband and put her feet up, rubbing her growing bump tenderly.

'Not a good idea,' Alex replied sourly.

'Why not?'

'I told you about how he wouldn't even invest in my proposition.' Alex looked irritated.

'Oh, that.'

'What do you mean, o*h, that*? This is what I do,

Catherine, this is how I make my living. He won't even endorse or support me in that. Nothing I do is good enough for that man.'

Catherine sighed. It was a phrase she'd got used to whenever Alex talked about his father. She wished she could get to the bottom of his bitterness with his dad, but no matter how often she tried to talk about it, Alex refused to have any real discussion about it, apart from muttering that they were different.

Only once, on a night when they'd been out with friends, one of whom had been talking fondly about their own father, had Alex said anything.

'He's an old hippie. All free love, act first, think later. I can't stand that type of thing. Besides, he's not—' He'd broken off, as if he'd been about to say something, then thought better of it.

'He's not what?' she'd asked.

'Nothing,' he'd said.

Catherine thought she might never get to the bottom of it. She understood that not everyone adored their parents the way she did; she was lucky. But it pained her that Alex, who she loved so much and who she knew to be kind, could be so cold to his poor father.

'You know that isn't true, Alex,' she said now. 'He really cares about you. I know he does.'

'The only thing he cares about is himself and his bloody practice. He never had any time for me; neither of them did. If they weren't working, they were getting high and mooning at each other across the kitchen table. It was pathetic.'

'Doesn't sound very pathetic to me.' Catherine reached for his hand. 'What's wrong with adoring your wife, might I ask?'

'I do adore you.' Alex softened momentarily. 'You know that. And I know we'll both make wonderful parents.'

'I hope so, but they don't come with a manual, you know. No matter how much you read, no one can teach you how to be a good parent. We'll just have to do the best we can,' she sighed.

'It'll be a cinch,' Alex said. 'I'll just do the exact opposite of everything Dad did.'

Catherine didn't push it. She was tired, and as she was pregnant, she wasn't drinking. The thought of having to listen to Alex begin a well-rehearsed rant about his father without a soothing glass of wine in her hand didn't appeal.

'Honestly,' he began, 'you should have seen him. Before I'd even sat down he'd ordered practically the most expensive red on the list. He didn't even think to enquire as to what I might have fancied. Then all through lunch the most ghastly people kept coming over to interrupt us. Joey and Sharkey from Viper, some awful rock star, Rick something or other—'

'Rick Waters?'

'Yes, that's the one.'

Catherine's eyebrows shot up. 'Rick Waters doesn't talk to anyone. He's notoriously rude.'

'Oh, Dad probably cured him of some horrible dose of the clap or something, no doubt. And then of course that twit that owns Dominic's came over to fawn over him – well of course he would, having just offloaded one of the most expensive bottles in the restaurant,' Alex scowled. 'I've never seen anyone crave attention like my father. It's really quite extraordinary.'

'I'm going to have a bath, hon.' Catherine got up. She hated seeing Alex like this, angry and bitter. 'See you later.'

'What? Oh, fine, darling, I won't be long.'

'No rush. I'm looking forward to a nice long soak.'

Catherine went upstairs and wondered for the umpteenth time what P.J. could have done to make his son resent him so much. She was fond of P.J. and she knew he wanted to have a close relationship with his son, but there wasn't an awful lot he could do. The reason, she reflected, was pure and simple. Her husband was quite clearly consumed with jealousy of his father, and neither father nor son cared to confront or even acknowledge the fact.

'Two hundred and forty-eight, two hundred and forty-nine, two hundred and . . . fifty.' Tanya collapsed back onto the floor and pulled her knees into her chest. It didn't get any easier, but two hundred and fifty stomach crunches was the way she began her morning and so had her mother before her. The reward was a flat-as-a-board tummy and a figure a model could be proud of. What other way was there? Tanya couldn't understand people who didn't look after themselves. That was the way to flabby middle age and other unthinkable possibilities. She didn't bother with a personal trainer either. That was for wimps. If you could push yourself, then what was the point of paying someone else to? Although it would be nice, she mused, to have some tasty piece of eye candy to help relieve the tedium of working out. All in good time, she reminded herself. When she was married to Dom, she could have all the personal trainers and other perks she was looking forward to that rich women took for granted. Right now, it was an inconceivable expense.

Tanya's attitude to spending was strangely skewed. She would be ruthlessly mean with herself in some ways, and then in others, like shopping, particularly for clothes, she would splurge uncontrollably. After all, she reasoned, she took care of herself, kept herself in terrific shape all the time; she deserved to treat herself occasionally. Like that fabulous dress she had bought for Ossie Keating's Tudor party Dominic's had catered. Tanya had no intention whatsoever of dressing up in some ridiculous Elizabethan number that wouldn't show off her slim figure or long, toned legs. Instead, she had bought herself a fabulous strapless designer gown. It had cost a fortune, even with the generous discount the designer had allowed her in return for like favours when she booked at

Dominic's. Quid pro quo. That was the way it worked. Girls in business understood each other.

Mopping her face with a towel, she headed for the treadmill and began to pound her way through three miles. The smart flat tucked away in a discreet development off Stephen's Green complete with treadmill had been a godsend. A rich banker friend of her mother's was newly divorced and decided to relocate to the States for a year. Not wanting or needing to rent out his ultra-modern, no-expenses-spared apartment, he had been looking for someone suitable to 'house sit' and take care of it in his absence. Tanya's mother had pounced on the opportunity for her equally ambitious daughter to avail of, and now she had the home of her dreams, albeit temporarily – and she didn't even have to pay a penny. If Tanya had believed in good fortune, she would have said she was blessed. But she didn't believe in luck. As the heaving shelf of self-help books in the spare bedroom was testimony to, Tanya was firmly convinced that you made your own luck. She had visualised and believed that the perfect flat would find her – and it had. Better still, so had the perfect man.

She had hardly believed her eyes when Dom had strolled into the polo grounds in the Phoenix Park that Saturday afternoon where she had been organising the PR for a charity function a friend of hers had been involved in. Tall, dark and impossibly handsome, he had, unbelievably, been on his own, clearly meeting a couple of male friends who were equally well dressed and hosting a boys-only table at the summer barbeque.

She didn't waste a minute. Waiting until the food had been served and finished, she kept an eagle eye on the table. The moment one of the guys had gone up to the bar, she seized her chance. Slipping into his vacated chair on the pretext of selling raffle tickets she had purloined from one of the young girls employed to do exactly that, she went into action, flirting and flattering them all shamelessly. The boys, who had been hitting the Pimms steadily since arriving, were in great form and gentlemanly enough to insist she join them in a glass or two while they fought over who bought the most tickets. When Dom mentioned he was opening a restaurant the following month, she had immediately advised him on the vital importance of PR for the occasion and had generously offered her services.

'Really,' she had said in the low, sultry voice she had practised so carefully, 'it would be a pleasure. I've just gone out on my own too, and although my company has taken off hugely, I've never done a restaurant launch before. It would be a feather in my cap, and,' she lowered her voice to a whisper, 'I wouldn't dream of charging you anything like full rates until you were up and running and I had proved myself. Why don't we discuss it over lunch?' She handed him her card.

'Well, thanks, er, Tanya,' he had said, genuinely pleased. 'That's awfully decent of you.'

'Not at all. Now, I must get back to work,' she had said, getting up from the table, making sure she left him with an impression of her attention to efficiency and a good view of her long, shapely legs. 'Call me on Monday and we'll set something up.'

They had met for lunch and Tanya had sized Dominic up. Like many handsome, well-bred young men, he was, she correctly guessed, heavy on charm but not terribly astute. His education had been expensive and well rounded, but clearly he was no academic and happily lacked the killer punch and drive that would have made him a ruthless businessman. On the contrary, Dom appeared to be kind, creative and totally absorbed in his passion for food and the restaurant he was about to open. And best of all, he was single and his family was loaded.

Not being terribly organised either, Dom had been happy to let Tanya oversee all the irritating aspects of the opening night – and she had made sure it was a blinder. Calling in all favours and her not inconsiderable contacts, she had made sure that Dominic's got absolutely rave reviews and was regularly referred to in newspapers and magazines as the current and indeed only place to dine, or to see and be seen in. From there, it had been easy. She simply moved from organising the PR to organising his life. The apartment he lived in above the actual restaurant had been converted, but Dom had never got around to properly decorating it or making it into any kind of a home. With the help of an interior decorator friend, Tanya had accomplished in weeks what Dom had happily left unfinished for months. She had arranged a woman to come in twice a week to clean and iron for him and, having been introduced to his friends, began to host a series of casual dinner parties in her flat for him, away from the relentless demands of the restaurant. Soon, Dom began to wonder how he had ever managed without her. She made sure he ate properly, worked out and even stored all his family's birthdays and relevant dates and anniversaries on her computer so she could remind him what was coming up and to purchase the appropriate gift or flowers.

After gentle but insistent nudging on Tanya's part, it wasn't long before he introduced her to his parents. Tanya had been slightly worried about that. Although she was enormously pleased at this crucial move forward in the development of their relationship, she realised how important it was that she pulled it off to her advantage. She had met Dom's parents, Cici and James, briefly at the restaurant, but to be invited to their elegant home in Wellington Square and be presented as his girlfriend – well, that was a whole other ball game. And she had prepared assiduously for it. All the same, Tanya had found the experience intimidating and not a little unnerving. She had dressed carefully for the occasion in an immaculately cut knee-length wool pencil skirt teamed with a white, pintucked designer shirt with double cuffs. At her neck she wore a string of discreet pearls with matching studs in her ears. She had her roots done, her hair trimmed and blow dried. Black Prada medium-heeled pumps and a matching handbag completed the ensemble. The whole effect was polished, yet demure, she decided.

She had been welcomed warmly upon arrival by James and ushered straight down to the enormous kitchen, where Cici and the girls were chattering away ten to the dozen.

Cici, Tanya was rather alarmed to see, was clearly a fabulous cook and one of those women who made throwing together a delicious yet deceptively simple meal seem utterly effortless. Tanya was quiet and carefully polite throughout dinner, answering when she was spoken to and watching her table manners. She was relieved not to be bombarded, as she might have been, with any overly intrusive questions about her life and background, and complimented Cici warmly on her cooking and her beautiful home. The whole thing, she felt, beginning to relax as she took a sip of her Chianti, was going very well. Seated beside James, who was charming, she enquired about his business and appeared fascinated as he recounted the latest wonders of technology with enthusiasm.

As Dom and the girls cleared away plates, Tanya excused herself and escaped to the loo to freshen up. Inside, she smiled at her reflection. She looked every inch the elegant career girl, calm, poised and together. No one could ever guess about the uneasy interior. The Coleman-Cappabiancas were as far removed from her own family as it was possible to imagine – charming, accomplished and with that annoying confidence that only the very rich and educated exuded. Of course, being half Italian helped, she thought grudgingly – it gave Sophia, Mimi and Dom that whole understated glamour thing.

Tanya's own upbringing had been vastly different. Things had not been easy for her, an only child, when her father left her mother when Tanya was only three years old. He had fled to America with his secretary and left a mountain of debts in his wake. The house had to be sold and a much smaller one acquired in a less-than-desirable suburb, and her mother unwillingly went back to work as an air hostess. She had impressed upon Tanya from an early age that men were not to be relied upon unless they had substantial amounts of money to make up for their other, more obvious drawbacks.

There had been no glamorous schools or holidays for Tanya, but she hadn't been afraid of hard work, figuring her cool, blonde good looks and frightening determination would supply what life had taken away from her – the right to claim her place in a world of class and luxury, where she would never have to worry again.

Working as a secretary, she had found her way into PR and had risen rapidly through the ranks, stepping consciously on any offending toes that happened to be in her way. Along with passing her exams and acquiring the industry quali-fications, she had attended every evening course she could find on fine art, antiques and wine-tasting. All that eluded her was the man who would be her ticket into that other, rarefied world, and now he had finally turned up.

On her way back to the kitchen, Tanya paused for a second, listening to the sound of voices engaged in lively discussion. She took a chance and slipped into one of the huge, double reception rooms, flicking on the light and having a quick look around. The room was decorated beautifully and the furni-ture and paintings had to be worth a fortune. Solid silver frames stood on every available surface, encasing photos of happy family gatherings and many of Cici, looking gorgeous, in what Tanya supposed was her native Italy.

'Are you lost?'

Tanya started guiltily as Sophia stood smiling in the doorway.

'I must have taken the wrong turn,' Tanya replied, 'and then I couldn't resist looking at all these lovely photographs. Silly of me – I have no sense of direction.' She moved smoothly past her.

'An easy mistake to make,' Sophia replied genially. 'It could happen to anyone. Let me show you the way back, it's just down these three little steps.' She was still smiling, but her eyes were cold.

Back in the kitchen, coffee was being served and the others didn't seem to notice that her absence had been longer than usual. But as Dom poured a cup for her, she heard Sophia rattle off a rapid fire of Italian to her mother. Did she imagine it, or did Dom's pouring falter ever so fractionally?

So what if his stupid sister had caught her having a little look around? Dom had never mentioned the incident to her, so clearly it hadn't bothered him. That had been over a year ago and she had been in the house many times since, and now, thankfully, Sophia and Mimi were both studying abroad. Mind you, Tanya thought, pounding away on the treadmill, she wasn't at all happy about recent events in the Coleman-Cappabianca household. She frowned, thinking of the unorthodox arrangement that was in place at the moment, with Cici living in the mews at the bottom of the garden and behaving for all the world as if she was single, and James, as the song went, drinking doubles at the thought of it. It wasn't an ideal state of affairs at all as far as Tanya was concerned. Quite apart from anything else, parents on the verge of splitting up were not at all conducive to hastening a son towards a timely and eagerly awaited proposal of marriage. Something would have to be done, but just what Tanya hadn't yet figured out. Still, she reasoned, at least the restaurant was doing well. It kept Dom's mind off other, more disconcerting events. And Tanya loved being involved with it all.

There was only one fly in the ointment. The books, despite chock-a-block bookings, were showing a distinct loss. Eric, the accountant, had been rather concerned about it. Tanya had briskly instructed him not to worry Dom with it at the moment, as he had so many more important things to deal with.

If she was honest, she wasn't altogether surprised. She had been comping her PR friends to beat the band. But it was all for a good cause, she reassured herself. How else had Dominic's got to be so well known and well spoken of, and so quickly? Of course, the food lived up to the reviews, but it was only because of Tanya's relentless pursuit of publicity that they appeared so frequently in all the best columns, and that required a lot of favours in the shape of reduced bills and many free bottles bestowed. Speaking of which, his own mother, Cici, wasn't above showering champagne on her 'friends', and Tanya hadn't once seen her pay for it. Oh well, it wasn't her problem. Not yet anyway. Dominic's was going from strength to strength and the staff were worked off their feet.

Thinking of staff, Tanya scowled. They were all fine, except the chef, Rollo, who was an arrogant and temperamental bastard, but Dom claimed he was the best in the business. Then there was that Carla girl. Tanya didn't like her, not one little bit. She was far too uppity. Sometimes, to watch her, you'd think *she* ran the restaurant. And men adored her. She had that Latin American vibe going on, people were always saying she was the image of J-Lo. And she'd seen the way she looked at Dom when she thought she was unobserved. She fancied him big time and she flirted with him, weaving that sinuous body of hers in and out of tables and wiggling her bottom whenever he was around. She'd seen Dom looking at her too – what man wouldn't with all that sashaying going on under his very nose? It would all but make you dizzy. Still, Tanya reflected, that was the least of her worries. Dom's parents' marital situation was a far more serious impediment to her hopes of procuring an engagement ring any time soon. Carla and her carry-on was just a silly irritation. After all, what would a man like Dom ever see in a ditzy, New York waitress with an ass to match her clearly inflated self-opinion?

5

Cici examined herself in the full-length mirrors of her dressing room. Every morning, after a leisurely bath, she assessed her naked body from every angle. That way, there were no sudden shocks. Approaching fifty, it was holding up pretty well, all things considered. She was, as the French say, comfortable in her own skin. Cici didn't believe in being neurotic about ageing; she fully intended to enjoy every bit of herself that worked and tolerate and encourage the bits that didn't. All the same, she had done well in the gene pool. At five feet eight inches, she was reasonably tall and her long legs were still shapely, especially in high heels, which she favoured, not just for the inches they added but for the way they made a woman walk. How a woman carried herself was so important. It said more about her than words or any amount of money ever could. Her breasts were still impressive, despite fighting an ongoing battle with gravity, but at least lying down, they were splendid, and when she was upright, the situation was helped by fabulous underwear – another vital weapon.

After three children, her waist was no longer what it had been, but her softly rounded tummy simply added to her overall femininity. She wasn't entirely happy with her arms, but so what? Anyway, they were easily covered up. Her face, thanks to fabulous bone structure, was still striking, and her olive skin supple. She maintained it with occasional shots of Botox and fillers but was rigorously vigilant about looking natural, in no way altered. That was the trick. The minute a woman looked in any way 'done' was the minute you saw fear on her face – and nothing, but *nothing* was more unattractive, whether you were seventeen or seventy.

She wondered what to wear. She was lunching, of course, in Dominic's, but today it would be a table just for two. Thinking of her lunch date, she smiled. He really was too adorable: tall, blond, good-looking, terribly intelligent and with that particular brand of earnestness that only the young could carry off without appearing totally idiotic. Not that he was *that* young, she reflected; at thirty, he was two years older than her own son, Dom.

She had met him at a press reception to announce details of a fund-raising event in aid of a local children's hospital, where he had approached her, quite directly, and told her she was the most stylish woman he had ever set eyes upon. He edited a popular women's magazine she knew well, called *Select,* a contemporary mix of style bible and current affairs, and for the rest of the evening had remained glued to her side, much to her delight and to the dismay of many other, much younger, women who threw regretful glances in their direction. After the reception, she had agreed to have dinner with him (why not?), and he had chosen a nearby Italian place that Cici hadn't been in for at least twenty years. It was cheap and cheerful, the food good, if predictable, and the charming waiters greeted her as a long-lost friend.

She told him about coming to Ireland from Italy and how strange and unfamiliar she had found it all at first, especially the men, who, she had been astonished to discover, did not *look* at women – at least not the way Italian men did, lingeringly, assessing almost all of them favourably.

'In Italy, men celebrate women, all women – young, old and in between. It was a severe culture shock for me to arrive here and be deprived of all that attention I took so much for granted,' she laughed. 'Luckily, my husband was very supportive and understanding.'

'What a lucky man, your husband,' he said enviously.

'Oh,' she demurred, suddenly flustered under his intense gaze, 'I'm not so sure he would share those sentiments.'

'You *are* still married?' He looked questioningly at the large solitaire diamond and wedding band she wore.

'Yes, yes, in a manner of speaking . . .'

'Separated?' Hope flickered in his eyes.

'Well, yes, sort of . . . it's complicated.'

'Of course, I'm sorry.' He was genuinely contrite. 'It's absolutely none of my business.'

'No, you have every right to ask. It is I who must apologise for seeming so indecisive, but that's just it, you see. I'm not at all sure whether I *want* to be married or not any more.'

'Ah, I see.' He looked amused. 'Then for tonight at least, let's pretend you're not.'

'I'm afraid I must warn you that I can be very good at pretending,' Cici said flirtatiously, back on safer ground now that she'd been honest.

'Good,' he grinned, 'so am I. I've always thought too much reality can be a little harsh for the soul.'

She had found him endearing, and interesting. He had a double first from Trinity College and a Masters in English from Oxford. During his student years, he had worked, among other things, as a barman, a carpet cleaner and a general dogsbody at a national newspaper: 'That's where I caught the bug, when I realised newspapers, publishing, was for me.'

He had earned his stripes at several London broadsheets, most recently on the *Sunday Times*, and his rise through the English media had been meteoric.

Intrigued, Cici asked, 'Why did you—'

'Throw it all away to edit a women's glossy?' he finished her question. 'There was a girl . . . it went wrong, a misunderstanding that got blown totally out of proportion.' He shrugged self-deprecatingly. 'She was unbalanced, became a bit obsessed, you know the kind of thing. It was easier to move away. Anyway, I was restless, curious to come home again, see if I could hack Dublin. I put out the word and *Select* approached me, made me a very decent offer, actually. That was three years ago. The rest, as they say, is history.'

'You've packed quite a lot into your history.' Cici looked at him admiringly.

'When I want something, I go after it with a vengeance.'

'And when you have it?'

'Then I savour it.'

Something in his tone, or was it his expression, made Cici swallow suddenly. She dabbed the corners of her mouth with her napkin and checked her watch. 'Goodness, it's late,' she said. 'Let's get the bill.'

He had insisted on paying, had walked her to a taxi rank and very much wanted to see her home.

'That's sweet of you, but thank you, no. I've had a most unexpected and enjoyable evening.'

'Then we must do it again.'

'Perhaps,' she said enigmatically, slipping into the taxi.

'Here's my card. Call me next time you're pretending not to be married.' He smiled briefly and walked away.

She hadn't called him, of course, although she had thought about it – and him – quite a lot.

But she did meet him again. He seemed to be at every function she had attended over Christmas. Cici had many young friends of both sexes, and although she flirted outrageously with the young men who admired her, she wasn't really attracted to any of them. They were amusing and fun to have at her Friday lunch table in Dominic's, but that was as far as it went – until Harry.

It didn't matter where she was or how many men of whatever age she was surrounded by, he would wait, patiently, intently, studying her, until one by one they left and only he remained, this strangely beautiful young man who had eyes only for her. And so she had agreed to meet him for a drink once or twice, and then lunch once or twice, maybe three times, and today, Cici smiled, today would be the fourth.

He intrigued her. He never pressed her, had never, since that first dinner, enquired or referred to her marriage, and he was terrific company. There was something about him, something she couldn't define, that made her feel alluring again, in a way she hadn't felt for years.

She decided on black, which was unusual for her, as she generally preferred complementing her looks with brighter colours that local Celtic complexions struggled with, but today she wanted to look dramatic. Black cigarette pants, a clinging, silk jersey T-shirt and a long, knee-length wraparound cardigan. Black high-heeled ankle boots completed the outfit. Her hair had been recently restyled, slightly shorter than usual, with a sexy angled fringe and flicked out at the back, very sixties. She picked up her newest oversized handbag, slung it over her shoulder and took a final approving look in the mirror, checked she had her phone and made for the door. Downstairs, on the hall table (always handy, which meant she never forgot), she picked up the bottle of Chanel No. 5 and dabbed some at her wrists and behind her ears. She was ready.

He was there before her, waiting eagerly, and noticed her the moment she walked through the door, standing up imme- diately from the table to greet her. As it was a Tuesday in January and they were meeting at three o'clock, Dominic's was pleasantly quiet, most people already winding up their lunches and heading back to work or home. Dom was nowhere to be seen, and then Cici remembered he was away on business, sourcing and selecting a variety of new organic cheeses from France. Before Cici reached the table, Tanya appeared at her side as if from nowhere and feigned surprise and delight at seeing her.

'Cici, how lovely to see you. We weren't expecting you.' She sounded puzzled.

'That's because I haven't booked, Tanya,' Cici beamed, 'but I can see my table and indeed my lunch companion is waiting.' She walked smoothly past her to her table, where Harry bent to kiss her cheek.

'Oh,' said Tanya, 'of course, how silly of me. Let me get you a glass of champagne.'

'It's already on the way, thanks,' Harry said, never taking his eyes off Cici as she sat down opposite him.

'I see. Well, if you need anything . . .' She hovered, disapproval seeping from every pore.

'If I need anything,' Cici gazed back at Harry, sounding amused, 'I'm sure it will be taken care of.'

'We'll let you know.' Harry looked up at Tanya, dismissing her with a nod.

Cici giggled as Tanya glided away. 'She makes me feel like a naughty schoolgirl, caught playing truant.'

'Aren't you?' Harry grinned. 'Although you're far more delectable than any schoolgirl I ever came across.'

'You're incorrigible.'

Just then the champagne arrived, poured deftly by Carla, and they ordered quickly, not needing to see the menu.

'Shall I tell you today's specials?' Carla asked.

'No thank you, not for me,' said Cici. 'I'll have the grilled chicken Caesar salad.'

'And for you, sir?'

'Fillet steak, rare, and a salad.'

Over lunch, Harry suddenly became serious. 'I was wondering,' he ventured, 'how you would feel about doing a photo shoot.'

'A photo shoot? What for?'

'A special issue of *Select*. I want to do a feature on Ireland's most stylish women. If I had my way,' he smiled, 'I would devote the whole section to you, but that would be unfair.' He watched as Cici's face softened. 'But I'm hoping that you'll agree to allow us to at least feature you?'

'What would that involve, exactly?'

'Ideally, we would shoot you at home in a selection of different outfits, which you would, of course, have complete control over. The interview – the article, that is – would cover how you live, your innate sense of style, the kind of clothes you like to wear, how you entertain, that sort of thing.'

'Hmm, interesting.' Cici took a sip of champagne. 'Would I have final approval on the shots?'

'That goes without saying, and I myself will be doing the interview and naturally would supervise the whole thing. We'd recommend hair and make-up people that we usually use, but if you prefer your own people, then that can be arranged.'

'It sounds like fun.' Cici sat back in her chair and smiled. 'I don't see why not.'

'I was hoping you'd say that.' He raised his glass to her. 'I can see the spread already. You'll be our most beautiful and intriguing subject.'

'I hope you're not planning on asking me any inappropriate questions.'

'How could anything at all about *you*, Cici, be inappropriate?'

Cici gave a throaty laugh. 'I see what you mean about going after something you want with a vengeance.'

'It's the only way.' His eyes held hers, and she didn't flinch, not even when he took her hand across the table and brought it gently to his lips and his leg brushed hers, for a second longer than could be considered accidental, under the table.

Shalom was doing something very unusual. She was eating. Rather a lot, actually, even more than for two. She hadn't bargained on feeling constantly ravenous, having long ago suppressed her overly eager appetite into complete sub-mission. The fact that it was making itself felt again in such a demanding, insatiable manner had come as a complete surprise. But not as big a surprise as the fact that she was humouring it – indulging it, even – searching for ways to appease it even *before* the hunger pangs struck. This morning, and it was only eleven o'clock, she had already put away five slices of buttery toast, two doughnuts and three squares of Toblerone, and that was *after* her freshly blended morning smoothie, which was all she usually allowed herself.

It was all Candice's fault, of course. Since the fateful night of Ossie's party before Christmas and the horrific pictures and unflattering press coverage Shalom had been subjected to, she had been in a state of shock.

She had been thoroughly disgruntled to discover that once his initial anger had blown over, Ossie had proclaimed the whole incident to be laugh-out-loud funny and had even declared that Candice had displayed great 'spirit' to have acted in the manner she had. That all changed, though, when he discovered that Candice was freezing him out. Over Christmas she had refused to take a single one of his calls and it had drived Ossie to distraction.

'Darling,' Shalom had risked advising him after she had listened to him leave yet another pleading voice message on Candice's phone, 'you mustn't let her upset you like this. It's so bad for you, for your stress levels. Really, it's Candice who should be apologising to *you*.'

'She's only a child, Shalom,' Ossie had retorted, exasperated. 'My only child. This is difficult for her. It was a mistake not to explain things to her gently. I should have told her and her mother beforehand, at an appropriate time, together.'

Shalom had been livid but instead had said reproachfully, 'It's not a "thing", our baby, and there was never going to be an easy way to tell Candice, or Charlotte. You have a new life now Ossie, and you owe it to me and our baby not to let anything else distract you.' Two big tears rolled down her face. 'After all, I'm doing my best, and it's all terribly upsetting for *me*.'

'Sweetheart,' Ossie was immediately contrite, 'I'm so sorry, please don't cry. You know I can't bear to see you upset.'

He had put his arm around her. 'Every time I open my mouth these days, I appear to put my foot in it.'

Shalom sniffed.

'Why don't you go out and buy yourself and the baby something lovely? I have to go to the office, I'm late already, and I hate leaving you like this. Promise me you'll forgive me?'

'Of course I forgive you, darling. I know you didn't mean to upset me. I suppose I'm just sensitive at the moment, you know, a bit emotional.' She had smiled tremulously through her tears.

'Good girl,' he said, sounding relieved as he picked up his briefcase and made for the door. 'I'll see you later.'

Shalom hadn't forgiven him at all, but she was determined not to allow Candice and her carry-on to upset her relationship with Ossie.

Shalom couldn't stand Candice. The girl treated her with thinly veiled contempt at best and at worst was downright rude to her. Charlotte, on the other hand, on the few occasions she had met her, had been friendly and polite, almost disinterested. Shalom didn't really know what to make of Charlotte; she had never met anyone quite like her. She had seen photos of her, of course, in the society pages, organising this or that charity event. Ossie had always said she was a formidable fund-raiser. But in the flesh, Shalom had been taken aback to find that Charlotte was really very beautiful. She was tall and thin – she had a great figure, actually, only she didn't show it off the way she could have in all those boringly elegant clothes she wore. She had beautiful, pale skin, enormous dark eyes, and her hair, still dark and silky, fell in a mass of natural waves to her shoulders. She didn't wear enough make-up, in Shalom's opinion. If she did and got herself some funky, figure-hugging gear, Charlotte could be a real head-turner. Shalom didn't understand why she didn't get herself a stylist and a proper makeover with all that money she had. No wonder she hadn't got a man since Ossie left her.

After meeting Charlotte for the first time, Shalom had been intrigued. She would never in a million years have put Ossie and her together. She couldn't for the life of her think what Ossie would find attractive about her. She had even asked him about it later, when they were in the car.

'Did you ever really fancy Charlotte?'

'What?' Ossie seemed taken aback. 'What sort of a question is that? Of course I fancied her.'

'How?' she probed. 'In what way, exactly?'

'Charlotte's a very beautiful woman, obviously, but it wasn't just her looks. There was something fresh and unspoiled about her. She was terribly prim and proper and had no idea how sexy she was. I never thought she'd look at me, really. I used to love shocking her. She was so easy to wind up.' He laughed. 'I fancied her rotten.' A wistful look had come over his face and Shalom had quickly changed the subject, knowing instinctively that she had been heading for dangerous territory. After that, she stopped asking about Charlotte.

Their daughter, Candice, was another matter altogether. Ossie and Shalom had officially been together for over a year before he agreed to introduce them. Initially Shalom had just assumed he'd been being protective of her, and then she discovered that it was Candice who was refusing to meet *her*. When she had finally agreed to the introduction (and even Shalom didn't know that it had required clearing Candice's considerable credit-card debt and an increased limit on the same card), the encounter had been excruciating.

They had agreed to meet in the lounge of the Four Seasons Hotel for afternoon tea. The plan was that Ossie would pick Candice up from home and they would get there first, then after a respectable fifteen minutes or so Shalom would join them. This way, Ossie and Candice would have time to chat and relax. After all, she reflected, at seventeen and twenty-seven, a ten-year gap was really nothing between girls. Once Candice realised that Shalom wasn't an evil stepmother type but a glamorous, fashion-conscious young woman, she would relax and realise that they probably had a lot in common. She would be able to talk to her about clothes and hair and make-up, advise her on a style to cultivate – something Candice's own mother clearly had no intention of doing by the looks of things.

Shalom almost felt sorry for Candice. She had seen photographs of her and caught a glimpse of her once or twice when she had followed Ossie in the early days (unbeknownst to him) and parked across the road in a borrowed car, wearing a wig and sunglasses, so she could get a look at the women in his life. Candice, she was secretly relieved to discover, had not inherited her mother's dark beauty. In fact, from what Shalom could see, Candice was the living image of her father. It was almost comical. She even walked the same way, with a rather ungainly gait, and stood with her two legs planted firmly apart and her arms folded, particularly when she was making a point. Her colouring was fair, she had nice skin, and her light red hair was silky and poker straight. Shalom had assessed her shrewdly. She was no looker, but it was nothing that couldn't be improved upon. First of all, the girl was overweight by a good stone and a half. Puppy fat, maybe, but Shalom would have got rid of it, sharpish. Her face was quite pretty, really, and on the rare occasions when she smiled (mostly in photos, as far as Shalom could tell), she was like another person, the sulky mouth upturned and sweet, revealing straight, even teeth achieved by the braces that Charlotte insisted she wore in her early teens. Either way, Shalom had reckoned, Candice wouldn't be a problem. She had worried that she might be a younger, frostier version of her mother, with a snooty manner and the kind of bone structure achieved from generations of good breeding that no surgeon, sadly, had yet managed to replicate.

The girl she saw from her car window was really nothing but an awkward teenager. Once they got to know one another,

Candy would be relieved to find she had a sympathetic friend who would be able to help her with things her mother wouldn't or couldn't. With these reassuring thoughts in her mind, Shalom drove off home to her mother (she was still living at home at that stage) to report on the evening's findings. 'The daughter', as Shalom's mother, Bernie, referred to Candice, would not be a problem.

Her pleasing fantasies had come to an abrupt halt upon officially meeting Candice that first time, a year later.

Shalom had thought long and hard about what to wear, and in the end she decided to go for a funky, if more casual than usual outfit. As it was mid-summer, she chose her favourite pair of white Dolce & Gabbana skinny jeans, matching white high wedge sandals and a clingy black strappy T-shirt which revealed her toned stomach and cute little navel ring.

'There, you can't go wrong in black and white.' Bernie surveyed her daughter proudly. 'No point in hiding that figure of yours, pet, it's what he fell for in the first place, don't forget.'

Shalom had shown up late, as arranged, attracting not a little attention as she breezed into the hotel and joined Ossie and Candice in the lounge.

'Ah, here she is.' Ossie stood up to greet her, rather awkwardly, Shalom felt, and said to his daughter, 'Princess, I'd like you to meet my friend Shalom.' He had looked hopefully at Candice.

Shalom had held out her hand politely and said as she had practised in front of the mirror, 'Charmed to meet you. I've heard so much about you.' She kept a smile fixed on her face as Candice looked her up and down disbelievingly and took her hand gingerly, as if it might be infected.

'How do you do,' she said. And that was all she had said – to Shalom at any rate – deliberately excluding her from the conversation as she chatted away to Ossie, telling him about school, horses and how Jennifer, her grandmother, was going to show her and two friends how to pluck and cook a pheasant. 'Gran says it's a crucial part of a young woman's culinary training. "No good having manicured hands if you don't know what to do with them!"' Candice said in a perfect imitation of Jennifer's plummy tones. Ossie had roared with laughter while Shalom sat, still smiling politely but quietly simmering with rage.

Eventually, the strain had become too much even for Ossie, who got up, muttered something about settling the bill and said, 'I'll leave you two girls to have a little chat.'

'Candice,' Shalom leaned forward and began her well-rehearsed worst-case-scenario speech. 'I know this must be difficult for you, but can't we at least try to be friends? You know—'

'Shut up.' Candice's voice was dangerously quiet. 'What makes you think I'd want to be friends with a tart? Just because you're sleeping with my father doesn't mean you've pulled the wool over my eyes. You'll never weasel your way into my family, not if I have anything to do with it. And there's nothing friendly about you either. You've broken up a marriage and broken up my family. As far as I'm concerned you're just a gold-digging slapper. And you look like – like a stupid drag artist.' That last bit she had heard from Emma, who had reported that those were the words *her* mother had described Shalom with after seeing her picture for the first time in *VIP* magazine.

Just then, Ossie came back, smiling broadly. 'Come along, girls. Time I got you back home, Candy.'

And Candy had smiled sweetly and said, 'Thank you for tea, Daddy, it was lovely, and very nice to meet you too, Shalom.'

The drive home had passed in ominous silence, with Candice sitting in the back sending and receiving endless text messages, which appeared to be the cause of much giggling.

'Bye, Daddy,' she chirped, getting out of the car. 'See you soon. Take care, Shalom.' And she ran eagerly up the steps to her home.

'At least one of you seems to be in good spirits,' Ossie said, seemingly oblivious to the undercurrent. 'I must say,' he continued, 'I do think you could have made a bit more effort, Shalom. You didn't say one word to her the whole way back.'

Shalom had turned to him in fury. 'Don't you even dare!' she cried. 'That girl is a monster. I tried my very best. I was charming to her and she said the most horrible, horrible things to me when you left the room.'

'Really, sweetheart,' Ossie sighed. 'I think you're exaggerating. You must be imagining it. I thought she was very civil to you. You mustn't be jealous of her. You know I'm mad about you, but Candy is the most important person in my life. This is difficult for her. You have to understand and make allowances for her. She's only seventeen. It's an awkward age. She's just a child, really.'

It was a phrase Shalom was to become very familiar with over the following months – years even.

Since then, any thoughts Shalom had had about winning Candice over were well and truly knocked on the head. She supposed it was better this way. At least she knew where she stood. The battle lines had been drawn, and if Candice wanted to play it that way, that was fine by her. Shalom knew she had a fight on her hands, but whatever it took, she was *not* going to let Ossie's daughter come between them.

Anyway, soon they'd have a baby of their own, and that would change everything. Ossie adored children. He'd always assumed he'd have a large family and now she would give him another chance at fatherhood. Not that she had any intention of having a brood – one, maybe two, and that would be it. A boy and a girl would be nice, she mused. Her mother was usually right, she reflected, and she said it gave a woman a whole different standing in a relationship when she was the mother of her partner's child. And if Candice didn't like it, well, she'd just have to get used to the fact. It was positively ridiculous the way she expected to be babied by her father. And Ossie was as bad, still calling the girl Princess as if she was six years old.

'For heaven's sake, stop calling her that,' Shalom had said in an unusual burst of irritation not so long ago, after another hostile encounter with Candy.

Ossie had looked astonished. 'But it's what I've always called her. It's just habit, that's all.'

'It sounds pathetic. She's a grown woman now, I bet she hates it. I've seen her friends sniggering when you do it.'

'Oh,' Ossie sounded hurt. 'I didn't think . . . yes, I suppose it would be embarrassing. I must try to remember not to.'

'Come here, darling.' Shalom had immediately wound her arms around him. 'You're too good – that's your problem.' She kissed him and began to unbuckle his belt, feeling him grow hard at her touch. 'Little girls grow up,' she said in a cute baby voice, 'but never in their daddy's eyes.' She opened her blouse to reveal a low-cut balcony-style bra that her breasts threatened to escape from at any moment. Ossie groaned and bent to lick the nipple she exposed. 'Come to bed, big guy.' She pulled away and led him by the hand, laughing softly.

As Ossie followed her eagerly into their plush bordello-style bedroom, Shalom wriggled out of her jeans and draped herself provocatively on the bed. Seconds later he was on top of her, inside her, thrusting intently as she gazed, breathless and adoring, into his eyes. When he came, she held him, cradling his head against her breasts, and smiled.

The battle might have gone to Candice, but Shalom would win the war. After all, as Candice had rightly pointed out at that first meeting, she was sleeping with her father.

As strategies went, it was a pretty foolproof one, and Shalom knew just how to keep a man happy in that respect.

'No potatoes for me, Gran, thanks. Just eggs and bacon.'

'What? None of my special-recipe sauté potatoes? Are you sick?'

'I'm fine,' Candy assured her, 'I'm just cutting back a bit. Eggs and bacon are fine. Protein is good,' she said knowledgeably.

'You're not on one of those awful diets, are you? Ruinous to the hair and skin, you know.' Jennifer dished up the eggs and bacon on plates and added her special potatoes to all but one.

Charlotte was out at a committee meeting and Candice and her pals, Emma and Katy, were having a late breakfast with Jennifer.

'Nope. I've just been training at the gym.'

'Training for what?'

'Training – you know, working out, getting fit. That's all.'

'I must say you *are* looking well. And now that you mention it, yes, you've definitely got slimmer.' Jennifer passed the plates over.

Candice was pleased. The personal trainer she had signed up with was putting her through hell, but he was worth every tortuous minute if it meant losing weight and getting in shape – and she was. Even Gran had noticed now.

'Of course in my day,' Jennifer sat down at the table, 'nobody needed to diet. Food was a luxury we had to do without.'

'Gran grew up in Gloucestershire when the war was on,' Candice explained.

'Didn't have have to do any of this keep-fit nonsense either. No petrol. We had to cycle or ride everywhere. Lot to be said for it.'

'Was it as romantic as it looks in all those old movies?' Emma asked wistfully.

Jennifer smiled. 'I used not to think so, but now, well, when you get to be my age, everything looks better in retrospect. It did make situations and people more intense, I think.'

'Gran was proposed to lots of times, weren't you?'

'Oh, I had my admirers, to be sure, but I only had eyes for Flinty. Until I met your grandfather, of course.'

'Flinty was Gran's first fiancé, wasn't he?'

'Yes. It was love at first sight for both of us. I was only sixteen and I had snuck out with my sister to a local dance. I thought with my lipstick and powder I looked very grown up, but really I was just a terribly innocent and excitable young girl.' She paused, remembering.

'Go on.'

'Well, once we got into the hall, there were all these wonder-fully good-looking men everywhere – Yanks, of course. All the girls were terribly keen on them, but I found them a bit forward, really. I was terribly shy, you see, and I suppose I looked older than my sixteen years. I was still awfully skinny, but even at that age I had quite a bust. Good bosoms, you know – all the Wilding women did – runs in my side of the family. Candice, bless her, takes after her father's side.'

Emma took a gulp of her Buck's Fizz and tried not to splutter as Katy caught her eye.

Candice watched them, daring them to so much as smile, her 34A measurements being the cause of much resentment on her part.

'Anyway, where was I? Well, a few of them surrounded me, and my sister was swept off, and a rather pushy chap asked me to dance. I was brought up never to refuse an invi-tation to dance, terribly impolite, unless the chap in question was drunk – which this chap clearly was. Didn't like the look of him anyway – smarmy type.'

'What did you do?' Katy was agog.

'I said, "No, thank you very much, I'd rather not. I think you've already had too much to drink."'

'Then what?'

'He didn't like that at all. Clearly wasn't used to being turned down – he became quite nasty, really. As I'm always telling Candice, and you girls should take note, origins will out.'

'What do you mean?' Emma asked.

'It means that someone's background and upbringing will always show through eventually, however much a person may try to suppress or avoid it. No avoiding the genes.'

'Anyway, what happened?'

'He looked me up and down, then said, "You're right, honey, I must be drunk. Who'd want to dance with you? I've seen better legs than yours on a piano."'

There was a gasp from the girls.

'To which I retorted, taken aback though I was, "And I've seen a better face than yours on a clock!"'

'Ohmigod!' said the girls, gasping with laughter.

'Quite. Then I heard this wonderful deep voice say, "Stand back, please, I'll handle this," and the owner of the voice stepped in and punched the Yank's lights out.'

'Brilliant!'

'Yes, he was, rather. Anyway, that was how I met Flinty, all six foot four gorgeous inches of him. Blond, blue-eyed and cheekbones I'd have killed for. We corresponded for four months. I only saw him on leave once, when he proposed and I accepted. Then the letters stopped and I received word from one of his squadron that he'd been killed in action over Germany. I had to come clean and tell my parents, who'd had no idea of my secret romance. I don't think I came out of my room for weeks.'

'What did you do?'

'What everybody else did – I got on with things. There were so many girls and women mourning lost lovers and husbands. The war was over, it was a time of huge upheaval, everyone had to help each other – it was the only option.'

'So how did you meet Candy's grandfather?'

'Over a horse.' Jennifer chuckled. 'It was all because of dear old "Fruity" Nesbit. He was one of the gang in London – you know, a chum. I was about twenty-two, an apprentice at Sotheby's. Fruity was terribly well off and his family had a flat in Cadogan Square. One night, we were all a bit squiffy, and someone found a bottle of peroxide in the cleaning cupboard. One of the chaps dared him to dye his hair blond, and by the end of the night his hair was flaxen. His parents came to town the next day and it didn't go down at all well with his father. He threw a complete fit, said he was going to have him sent out to Malaya to work on the plantations. Poor old Fruity did a runner and caught the mail boat to Ireland. A few of us went over for a weekend to console him, and he was having the most wonderful time hanging about the race-courses and gambling and he asked me to look over a horse he was thinking of buying so down we all went to Kildare to this lovely stud farm. As we watched this three-year-old being put through his paces, I was aware of this chap behind me talking, and then I realised he was talking to me!' Jennifer paused for effect as the girls listened, enthralled.

'What did he say?' asked Emma.

'"He'll fall at the first fence, mark my words – won't stay the pace, just like his predecessors – and I'll wager most of your suitors too." That was dear old Jeremy,' Jennifer laughed. 'Cut straight to the chase. I was intrigued, of course, and, luckily for me, he looked as nice as he sounded. We fell madly in love and were married six months later.'

'That's so romantic,' Katy sighed.

'You must miss him,' Emma ventured.

Jennifer smiled. 'Yes, I do miss him, of course I do, but he's around, you know. I can tell when he's around. The dogs know too. Animals are more finely tuned than we are. Just because someone dies doesn't mean they're not keeping an eye on you.'

As if to illustrate the point, Bonnie and Clyde emerged from under the table and began to bark, tails wagging.

'It's time for their walk. It's important to keep to a routine,' Jennifer said, getting up from the table.

'We'll clear away the dishes, Gran,' Candy said.

'Thank you so much for breakfast, Jennifer,' Katy and Emma said.

'It was a pleasure to have you girls. I hope I didn't bore you with all my talk of the past.' Bonnie and Clyde sat quivering with excitement as Jennifer produced their leads.

'It's much more exciting than anything that's happened to us so far.' Katy sounded glum.

'You never know what's around the corner.' Jennifer set off with the dogs, walking stick to hand. 'Cheerio, girls – and don't tell your mother there was Buck's Fizz with breakfast, she'll lecture me about how I'm setting you a bad example.'

'Bye, Gran,' Candy called after her.

'Are you really sure about this Candy?' Emma asked after they were sure Jennifer was gone.

'Of course I'm sure.'

'What time's your appointment?'

'Two-thirty.'

'Chinese dentist time,' quipped Katy.

'Very funny,' Candy said, giving the table a final wipe. 'Come on, let's go back upstairs. Dad got the *Sex and the City* movie downloaded for me ages ago. Anyone for cosmos?' she laughed as her friends followed her.

6

P.J. was woken by the unusual sound of Bones barking downstairs. Even more unusual was that it was bright outside. He checked the clock: 9:30 a.m. He sat up with a start. He must have overslept. And then he remembered – it was Saturday and there was no surgery. All the same, he was usually awake hours before this. No wonder poor Bones was barking, he must have been dying to get out for a pee, and being the well-trained animal he was, he'd rather explode than make a puddle on the floor, particularly if Sheila were to come across the evidence and find him responsible. P.J. couldn't say he blamed him.

That was it! No wonder he had slept in. Sheila had left yesterday to go on a weekend pilgrimage to visit some religious shrine or other and the house was blissfully quiet, apart from Bones protesting from the kitchen. Normally Sheila didn't believe in time off and came in on Saturday, just as she did every other day, to keep hearth and home pristine for her beloved employer. In fact, because she didn't have her surgery duties to distract her, Saturday was the day she got down to the *really* thorough cleaning assault.

P.J. had long since become used to being roused from a reasonably pleasant dream or slight hangover stupor by the strains of the industrial-sized hoover Sheila wielded outside his door. *Errmm, errmm, errmm* it would drone until it seemed as if it was right inside his head, and P.J. would give up any hope of returning to sleep for a well-earned lie-in. What would happen if he were ever to bring a woman home didn't bear thinking about. 'Sorry, hon,' he'd imagine saying as a noise to wake the dead began any time around seven a.m. – from the hoover outside the door, to the clatter and banging of windows and floors being attacked, to pots and pans being brandished. 'The good news is, there's a cooked breakfast waiting for us downstairs.' And then he and his lady friend would stroll downstairs, hungry after a late night of love-making, saunter into the kitchen and he would say, confidently, with a look that brooked no nonsense, 'Sheila I'd like to introduce my lover, Mrs X, and honey, this is my mad housekeeper, Sheila.' The fantasy, for some strange reason, always stopped there.

But today P.J. stretched lazily before leaving his comfortable bed. Today, there would be blissful peace with not a single soul to bother him. He would have to make the most of it.

Downstairs, he released a grateful and forgiving dog into the garden and set about making coffee and toast. He was about to retreat upstairs, cup and plate in hand, when Bones bounded back inside looking dismayed that he was about to be abandoned again.

P.J. relented. 'All right,' he said, grinning, as he jerked his head towards the kitchen door. 'I won't tell if you won't.' Bones dashed past him and shot upstairs, where, as he fully expected, P.J. found him looking both adoring and guilty as he sprawled on the bed.

Climbing back under the covers, P.J. flicked on the television and checked the sports results. There was a Grand Slam rugby match too this afternoon, he reminded himself. Ireland were playing away, in Edinburgh. P.J. had had two tickets for the match (a gift from a patient) but didn't fancy going. These days, a rugby trip took longer and longer to recover from. Instead, he had given the tickets to Alex, hoping he might suggest going with him, which he *would* have considered. Instead, Alex had said, 'Thanks, Dad, they'll come in handy. Just in time too, a client of mine will kill for them.'

'Big supporter, is he?' P.J. had enquired.

'What? Oh no, she's a girl. But she's after a rugger bugger and apparently Edinburgh's one of the more fun away games to go to.'

'It is,' P.J. said, feeling deflated. Those tickets were like gold dust, virtually unobtainable. It wasn't that he resented them going to this girl, whoever she was, but they probably wouldn't even be used for the game. They would likely go to waste while the girls got dolled up and staked their claim in the pub or hotel of choice and waited for the boys to come back, geared up and ready for action.

He thought of all the matches he and Jilly had gone to over the years, at home and away. She had enjoyed them all as much as he had, particularly England v. Ireland, where she would insist on shouting for England even in the midst of the Irish supporters. For some of the bigger home games, they would have a pre-match lunch, eagerly attended by all their friends before setting off to the game or settling down to watch it at home in the kitchen, as P.J. would today. He thought of Jilly now, as he always did, and wondered if she could see him and what she would think of him and how he had done without her.

He was lonely. He let the thought roll around his head for longer than the usual millisecond he allowed it. He knew Jilly would definitely not want that for him. They had discussed it on several occasions, even before she had become ill, that if anything were to happen to either of them, they would each want the other to find happiness with someone else, never dreaming for a moment that the unthinkable occasion was so much closer than they could have possibly imagined.

'Just as long as you know that if the bedposts are rattling in protest, it's me from wherever I'll be watching – and not your new lover,' P.J. had grumbled, joking.

'I wouldn't want you to be on your own – really,' Jilly had said seriously. 'You wouldn't do well. I'm not saying you wouldn't cope,' she added, seeing the look of objection on P.J.'s face. 'But you're a man who *needs* a woman, it's what you're made for – and some very lucky woman out there will need you too.'

'The only need I have right now,' he had retorted, tired now of the mournful nature of the conversation, however theoretical, 'is for my gorgeous, sexy wife to attend to her conjugal duties – immediately.' He climbed on top of her and kissed her lingeringly. 'I'll give you rattling bedposts,' he had laughed, coming up for air.

P.J. smiled, remembering, then jumped as his elbow was firmly nudged, and Bones (who had been edging artfully up the bed towards his master) thrust his big face under his arm and snuggled down beside him, sighing happily, his head resting on P.J.'s hip.

'Looks like you're my only prospect for bedroom company, mate.' He ruffled his dog's head. 'I mean, who on earth would take us on?' he asked as Bones yawned widely. Thirty seconds later, they were both asleep.

He was awoken for the second time that morning by his dog. This time, Bones was licking his hand assiduously. 'What the . . .?' P.J. began, then collapsed back on the pillows again. Good Lord, it was ten to twelve; he'd been asleep for almost two hours. He leapt out of bed, hit the shower, skipped shaving and dressed speedily. 'Come on, fella, it's time we got some fresh air. I'll take you for an extra-long walk now, then we can veg out and watch the match. How about that?' Bones hurtled downstairs ahead of him and by the time P.J. reached the hall was already sitting with his lead in his mouth, his tail thumping eagerly against the floor.

Outside, the bracing January Saturday was clear and bright. P.J. inhaled the crisp air and felt himself revive. He really must try and get more exercise, he thought, but somehow there just never seemed to be enough time. A daily stroll or two to the park with Bones just didn't do it – his waistbands were beginning to feel particularly tight these days.

Inside the park gates, he let Bones off the lead and headed for the riverside so that he could throw Bones's favourite rubber toy into the water. He was laughing at Bones, who, soaking wet, emerged up from the riverbank, shook himself heartily, panted heavily and did his typical Labrador victory parade before replacing the toy at his master's feet. P.J. was bending down to pick it up when he heard a clipped, accented and very disapproving voice.

'You're an absolute disgrace!'

P.J. straightened himself up and looked around, expecting to see a naughty child being reprimanded, but the park was quiet. The voice came again from behind him, louder this time.

'You there! Yes, you!'

P.J. wheeled around to see an immaculately turned-out elderly woman leaning on a park bench, regarding him with derision. She was wearing a green padded Barbour jacket, tweed herringbone skirt, green Hunter wellingtons and what he'd bet was a Hermés headscarf tied elegantly under her chin. She looked like a slightly taller and more glamorous version of the Queen – and just as forbidding. As she brought a dog whistle to her lips, two white and tan Jack Russells hurtled out of the undergrowth, raced to heel and sat at her feet obediently.

'I'm sorry,' P.J. looked around again, perplexed, checking if there was some mistake, 'but are you talking to *me*?'

'I certainly am,' the woman said. 'I don't see anybody else around, do you?'

P.J. walked towards her slowly, wondering if she was a bit of a loony. Perhaps she wasn't meant to be out alone or needed directions home – but then, the dogs were obviously hers.

He tried again. 'You were saying . . .?'

'You heard perfectly well: you're a disgrace.'

'Might I enquire why, exactly?'

'That unfortunate creature belongs to you, I take it?' She pointed a walking cane at Bones, who was lying down, gnawing happily at his toy.

'That's my dog, yes. What is unfortunate about him, I have no idea. Do you have some kind of objection to my owning one?'

The woman snorted. 'I should think so. Look at him! He can hardly walk, never mind run. The poor animal is obese. It's outrageous to let a dog get that fat. I've a good mind to report you. I'll have you know I'm very well connected, and the animal-rights people would take a very dim view of this, a very dim view indeed. When was he last at the vet? Surely he or she must have said something to you?'

'Not that it's any of your business,' P.J. was counting to ten, slowly, 'but Bones has regular veterinary check-ups. He's in perfectly good health.' He was embellishing the truth a bit on this last point, as his vet had pointed out (tactfully, mind you) that Bones was very, very overweight.

'Bones!' The woman showed the first signs of mirth and laughed heartily. 'Well, that's surely a misnomer.'

On hearing his name, Bones came over to investigate and sniffed at her with interest.

'Sit!' she commanded. And he did, responding immediately to the authority in her tone, although he looked worriedly towards P.J.

He was rewarded by an examination worthy of a Crufts judge. 'Just as I thought,' the woman proclaimed, examining his teeth. 'Magnificent dog. Beautiful head. Damned fine pedigree, I'll wager.'

'Well, now that you mention it, his grandfather, or maybe great-grandfather, was a field champion, actually,' P.J. said, vaguely remembering his pedigree papers lodged in some long-lost pile of paper in his office.

'What's the matter with you?' She looked perplexed, then held out her hand. 'Jennifer Searson. I live across the square.'

'You do?' P.J. took the proffered hand and shook it, feeling decidedly wary.

'Number 42.'

'I thought that was . . .' P.J. trailed off.

'Yes, it used to be Ossie Keating's house, but it's my daughter's now – actually, it always was. I live in the basement. Converted flat. Suits us both.'

'How do you do. I'm—'

'I know who you are. You're that doctor chap everyone's always talking about.'

'Is that so?'

'I must say, it's pretty typical.'

'What is?'

'Physician heal thyself and all that.'

'I'm not sure I follow you.' Definitely early Alzheimer's or dementia. P.J. was mentally running through possible diagnoses.

'You're clearly no stranger to the knife and fork yourself!'

For once, P.J. was lost for words.

'And if I'm not mistaken,' Jennifer continued, giving him an unapologetic once-over, 'and I rarely am, Doctor, you're a good-looking man if you'd care to keep yourself in any sort of shape. Can't bear people who let themselves go to seed. Shows dreadful lack of character. But no need to inflict your lack of discipline on this fine animal. Is this the only walk he gets?'

'Well, sometimes we get out in the morning.'

'Sometimes? And for a stroll like this? That's not good enough.'

'Bones and I are perfectly happy with the arrangement. Now if you'll excuse me, Jennifer, it was very nice meeting you.' P.J. made to walk away.

'He'll be dead before the year's out,' she called after him. 'Mark my words. Then you'll be sorry.'

P.J. stopped in his tracks and turned around. It had been a long time since he'd lost his temper, and when he did, he was fearsome. He didn't want to do it now – she wasn't worth it.

'I'll tell you what,' she said, oblivious to his rising blood pressure. 'My daughter takes these two,' she indicated the Jack Russells, who were now racing around with Bones, who was doing his best to keep up, 'three times a week to Sandymount Beach for a proper run, an hour at least. I'm sure she'd be glad to take Bones along. Three months of proper exercise and you won't know him. He'll love it. What do you say?'

Before P.J. had a chance to reply, she continued.

'Monday, Wednesday and Friday, seven a.m. sharp. That too early for you to have him ready?'

'Certainly not.' For some inexplicable reason, P.J. felt it imperative to rise to the challenge.

'Jolly good, then. I'll tell her to pick him up on Monday. Come along.' She blew again into the whistle and her dogs dashed back to her, leaving Bones looking deflated.

'Cheerio, Doctor!' And with that she was off, although P.J. noted the limp and the grimace she fought to conceal. She was probably in a good deal of pain with that hip, he deduced, but not as much as he'd have liked her to be in. Shaking his head, he threw a few more balls for Bones, then made for home himself.

'Holy Mother of Divine God,' he said aloud. 'What do you make of her?' He looked at Bones, who was, now that he cared to admit it, panting alarmingly and plodding along rather slowly. P.J. was suddenly overcome with guilt. 'I have let you get appallingly fat, old chap. The old bat was right, we do need to shape up. But that's all about to change – you'll hit the beach and I'll hit the gym. And,' he reflected mournfully, 'I expect we'll have to take a look at our respective diets, too.'

And then another thought hit him. If the mother was anything to go by, the daughter was *bound* to be a complete harridan. Oh well, who cared? He would have Sheila hand

Bones over and reclaim him. Sheila would be able for any amount of them.

With that potentially awkward encounter resolved, P.J. set off for home feeling considerably better about the forthcoming arrangement.

Carla sat in the small baroque-style church and closed her eyes, letting the uplifting strains of the choir wash over her. She certainly hadn't intended on going to mass – she couldn't even remember the last time she'd been to church at home in New York – but for some reason it had seemed like a good idea this Sunday. In one of the guidebooks she had read, she remembered the church being described as a gem, and it didn't disappoint. Built in the gardens beside and behind number 87 St Stephen's Green, the church was the work of the late Cardinal Henry Newman. Known locally simply as University Church, the correct title was in fact Our Lady Seat of Wisdom. Carla smiled at that – she could sure do with a bit of wisdom.

She had woken up that morning at eight o'clock in the little one-bedroom basement flat she had rented in Wellington Square and had known immediately that she wouldn't get back to sleep. It was one of those dark, grey, misty January mornings and already a light drizzle was trailing against the window. Despite the weather, Carla had suddenly felt the need to get out – anywhere. She pulled on her sweatpants, trainers and a top, put on a baseball cap and set off. Walking briskly, she reached her destination, Sandymount Beach, in about twenty minutes, and once she was down on the sand, she began to run. That was something she hadn't done in a while either, and she felt the better for it. At home, she used to run at least three times a week, sometimes more.

Home. That's why she'd had to get out. If she'd stayed one more minute in the flat, she would have been tempted to pick up the phone and dial home, and that was the one thing she was not going to do. Not yet, anyway, not even when she was feeling this homesick – *especially* not when she was feeling this homesick. Looking around her, she wasn't sure whether the general greyness helped or not. The sky was grey, the sand was grey, and the sea, or what she could see of it, the tide being so far out, appeared to be grey as well. But it wasn't New York grey. Still, it felt good to get out, to run, and, good to watch other early souls out and about, walking their dogs or playing with their kids.

Afterwards, she picked up the papers on her way home and, after a long, hot shower, settled down to read them. Except she couldn't settle. That was when she'd decided to go into town, go to church and afterwards meet Liz for a pizza. Liz was her neighbour and shared the flat across the hall with another Slovakian girl. They were both studying hotel management and had jumped at the chance for an exchange year in Dublin.

Pino, her usual companion, was on duty and Astrid was away for the long-promised weekend in Vienna with Rollo, so instead of relaxing at home on her one Sunday off in the month, Carla found herself back in town, sitting in a church of all places.

She closed her eyes now and remembered all the times she had gone to mass with her mother, father and three brothers. The ritual had always been the same for as long as she could remember: her mother singing, making pancakes in the kitchen, chasing them to get clean and dressed, and her father, drinking coffee and saying without fail from behind his newspaper, 'You can't beat real Italian coffee, nothing like that dishwater the Americans swallow.' And then they would set off in their Sunday best, all of them in the car, the boys – Marco, Paulo, Bruno – and herself, squabbling in the back.

After mass, they would return home and her mother and one or more of her mother's many sisters would gather in the kitchen to prepare the wonderful lunch that could include anything from eight to eighteen friends, neighbours and various relatives and, of course, the parish priest, Father Barbero. They would eat and talk and laugh and argue long into the evening, until Carla would climb onto her father's knee and fall asleep. Later her mother would put her to bed and read to her, telling her stories of when she had been a little girl in Italy. Carla never tired of these stories and eagerly looked forward to the time when, as her mother promised, they would go to Rome, just the two of them, to shop and sightsee and visit family. Only it never happened that way.

One Sunday, everything changed.

The Sunday her mother had complained of feeling dizzy before mass and then had collapsed on the floor with a sickening thud. The Sunday she had been rushed to hospital in an ambulance and Carla had been rushed to her room and kept there, watched over by her fretful aunt. The Sunday when Father Barbero came over and the other, younger priest. When the house was full of people, but everyone was crying, not laughing. The Sunday her mother died. The Sunday that had been Carla's eighth birthday. When everything had changed for ever.

After that, she had never liked Sundays much. Oh, life went on. The old brownstone house was always full of people, and her three older brothers grew up and so did she. Her father didn't remarry. He didn't have to, really. Carla's many aunts and uncles made sure he was never alone, and that seemed to be enough for him. He threw himself into the family business, and, one by one, her brothers joined him. Except it was Carla who outshone them all.

At first, she had gone along with her father's wishes. She had worked hard at the private convent school she attended, and, despite her protestations, she had gone to a prestigious finishing school in Switzerland, where she perfected her French, learned how to arrange flowers and recognise a good painting and listened politely at the cookery classes, just about managing to hide her monumental disinterest.

When she returned home, her father had her career all mapped out for her – an apprenticeship with Gerard Matteus, the renowned gemologist, after which she could take her pick of positions in any firm of jewellers, or indeed consultancies, in New York, or wherever she chose.

It was then that she put her foot down. Carla wasn't interested in diamonds, sapphires or rubies. She understood what her father was trying to do – provide his daughter with what he imagined to be the most glamorous, feminine and sought-after career any girl could want. But like many a father before him, Antonio Berlusconi had underestimated his daughter.

Carla's passion was, not unnaturally, food. From the age of thirteen, she had cooked competently and efficiently, helping with and sometimes preparing the weekly Sunday lunches and evening dinners, quickly finishing her homework so she could join the productive, comforting atmosphere of the kitchen, fitting in seamlessly and learning effortlessly from her aunts, father and various household cooks. By fifteen, she was scouring New York's food markets the way other girls scoured flea markets, creating and collecting recipes and then constantly improving them, instinctively knowing just the right ingredient or twist to add that vital *ooomph* to a dish. By eighteen, her aunts were standing back and learning from her.

At first, her father thought it amusing, touching. Of course he was glad, proud even, that Carla was such a good cook – it reflected well on him, seeing as he ran the most successful chain of Italian restaurants in New York. But as a career? Certainly not. He had no intention of allowing his only daughter to engage in the fiercely competitive, fiendishly aggressive and downright cut-throat world of the kitchen. That was the arena in which her brothers would compete and carry on the family tradition. So far, two of them were doing very well, and the other, Paulo, who failed to show the family flair in the kitchen, had become an accountant, also vital to the family business.

Carla begged and pleaded, to no avail.

'I will not have my daughter working like an immigrant pauper in some hellhole of a kitchen,' Antonio fumed. 'Why can't you just *try* the gemology apprenticeship – for me?' he tried cajoling.

'Because I don't even *like* jewellery – I never have!' Carla screamed.

'Forget the jewellery then! Think of the career, the people you'll meet from educated, aristocratic backgrounds. Men who appreciate the finer things in life, who show finesse, discernment – not some idiot, arrogant chef who will work you to the bone just for the pleasure of it, especially because of who you are!'

'Don't worry,' Carla had replied scathingly, 'they can't all be like you.'

'How dare you!'

'Very easily – just watch me.'

After that particular scene she had packed a suitcase, and, with the help of the money in the savings account her mother had left her (for the shopping trip to Rome) she had caught a flight to Paris, stayed in a hostel and from there had done her research. Within a week she had secured her first position in the kitchen of her choice.

She started off as a plongeur, washer-up and general dogsbody, but within a year she was the most requested sous chef in the kitchen. After Paris came Switzerland, then London, where working under an infamous French establishment chef, she was part of the team that obtained the restaurant's third Michelin star.

She went home once a year, and her father eventually accepted defeat. Six months after that, she was back. A year on, heading up the kitchen at the trendy new M Hotel, she was listed among America's top five chefs to watch in *Time* magazine.

Her brothers were not altogether happy. The family business was doing well and they were due to expand and add another restaurant to the chain, this time in Manhattan. Carla saw her chance. She had always dreamed of running her own restaurant.

'Let me head it up, Papa,' she begged her father. 'Berlusconi's needs a newer, modern flagship. I know I could do it.'

Her father hemmed and hawed and finally agreed to at least consider the idea. 'Let me talk to your brothers.'

They were adamantly against the idea.

'So what?' Carla cried. 'It's what *you* say that goes, Papa. What does it matter what they think?' she fumed. 'Marco has always been threatened by me, and Bruno's a lazy chef.'

'That's no way to talk about your brothers.'

'It's the truth! You know it is.'

'What if it is, Carla? Is that so bad? Why must you be so . . . so driven? You're nearly thirty now.'

'Twenty-eight.'

'Exactly! Don't you want to find a nice man, settle down, have some *bambinos*?'

'I want a restaurant of my own. And if you won't help me, I'll do it without you.'

'Carla,' he reasoned, 'please, this is your *family* you're talking about, your own flesh and blood. Nothing is worth creating friction and bad feeling between family. Besides,' he gestured helplessly, 'if you won't do it for me, at least think of your mother – think of what she would have wanted.'

'She'd have wanted me to have a fulfilling life of my own – that's what she would have wanted, not to be running around after a household of selfish men all my life like she did!' She got up, pushing her chair back angrily from the table. 'You can shove your restaurant! And tell my brothers they're welcome to their out-of-date, third-rate brand of dining. The word on the street is that Berlusconi's is in trouble. When was the last time you checked the figures, Papa? Is Paulo as good an accountant as Bruno is a chef?

If I were you, I'd make sure the books weren't the only thing being decently cooked in the *family* restaurant.'

'Now you have gone too far, Carla.' His voice was quivering with anger. 'My sons would never be responsible for such a dishonourable act.'

'Is that so?' Carla looked pityingly at him, her arrogant, handsome, pig-headed father, too proud to even contemplate that his sons could be letting things slip, withholding vital information, that they would be too afraid to admit the truth to him.

'Just remember that you heard it from me first. I could have turned things around for you. Good luck, Papa. I hope you work things out.' She began to walk away.

'Come back here! I haven't finished talking to you.'

'We have nothing more to say to each other, Papa. Say goodbye to my brothers for me – neither they nor you will be hearing from me for quite some time.'

'Where are you going?'

'What's it to you?'

Truthfully, Carla had had no idea what she was going to do. She was shocked at her brothers' resentment and at her father's lack of support for her and his total disregard for her wishes, despite all her hard-won achievements. Everything had to be on *his* terms – which meant, as usual in her family, that the men got to run the show, even if it was turning out to be a very lacklustre production.

She handed in her resignation with regret at the M. Carla knew she had to get away from New York again, away from her family and their antediluvian, masochistic behaviour.

She never really knew what made her choose Dublin. Perhaps it was because she had not one drop of Irish blood in her, no long-lost relatives, no ancestors, no roots. She simply knew that one night she found herself in an Irish hotel in Manhattan called Fitzpatrick's, where her friends were meeting other friends, visiting from Ireland. When she mentioned that despite all her travels throughout Europe she had never been to Ireland, not even when she had been living in London, outrage was expressed. Instructions were issued, addresses written down, Guinness and oysters extolled, poetry and pubs eulogised, *craic* mightified, and suddenly it had all seemed like a very good idea. A week later she had a one-way ticket on an Aer Lingus flight to a city where nobody knew her, and better still, where nobody knew she could cook – there was something wonderfully liberating about that. She called it her year of being invisible – a gap year in more ways than one. She rented a small flat, got herself a job as a waitress and settled in to forgetting all about drive, ambition and career advancement.

That had been three months ago and she hadn't phoned home once, except to leave a message to say she was safe and was taking a year out to travel. But it still got to her – or rather, *they* got to her – even across all the miles.

Rousing herself from her thoughts, Carla realised that mass was over. The priest said the final blessing and people began to file out of the church. She waited a minute, until the church was almost empty, and went over to light a candle and to say a silent prayer to her mother. Sometimes she missed her more than ever. Perhaps it was because today was Carla's birthday, and this was probably the closest thing to a celebration she was going to get.

She'd have loved to be able to talk to her mother about how lonely she got sometimes.

It was odd, but when she felt very lonely, the only person who sprung to her mind was Dom. If she was with him, she wouldn't be lonely. But since the 'incident', he was assiduously keeping his distance and Carla made sure to be equally aloof around him, even though she knew she was being stupid. What would her mother tell her to do? What would she say to her? *Oh Mama, I'm falling for a guy that doesn't have the slightest interest in me apart from a drunken kiss which he clearly regrets, since he can barely look me in the eye any more. And all because I threw myself at him. I'm a mess.*

Outside, the rain had stopped and she walked quickly across the Green and onto nearby Dawson Street, into the pizza place where she was meeting Liz. Inside, it was jammed, although Carla quickly spotted Liz waving to her through the throngs of people from a table at the back.

'*Ciao, bella*,' she grinned as Carla sat down. 'Red okay?' she asked, pouring Carla a glass. 'It's that kind of Sunday, don't you think?'

'Perfect,' Carla agreed, feeling suddenly more cheerful. 'God, it's nice to be waited on for a change,' she said as the pizzas arrived.

'So, how's Dublin's smartest eatery?'

'Exhausting.'

'I'm looking forward to the DVD,' Liz grinned.

'What DVD?'

'Pino says he got a friend to copy the footage from that Tudor party you were at. He says you look adorable in it! He's having us all around next Thursday for a private viewing.'

'It was something else, all right. Unbelievable. Oh shit,' Carla muttered, shrinking back in her chair.

'What?'

'I've just seen someone.' There was no mistaking the blonde, blow-dried hair and the smiling, determined expression, head bent towards her dining companion as she talked intently while signing the bill.

'Who?'

'Oh, it's nothing,' Carla brushed it off. 'Just someone I work with and would rather avoid. It's okay, she looks as if she's just about to leave.'

And she did – walking briskly through the tables and towards the exit, giving a frosty smile to the manager who held the door open for her. There was no mistaking Tanya, but it was who she was lunching with that interested Carla.

It was Eric, Dominic's accountant, and he was looking anything but happy.

Carla felt her professional antennae vibrate. Something was up, and she'd bet her bottom dollar it had to do with Tanya and her cavalier attitude to entertaining her friends at Dominic's. Few established restaurants, let alone a new one, could cope with all that comping. Despite what had happened between them, Carla suddenly felt a wave of concern for Dom. He was so good at what he did, so trusting – was it possible he was unaware of what Tanya was doing?

'I have to say something to Dom,' Eric persisted as he scurried to keep up with Tanya's lengthening strides. 'It would be remiss of me not to. I've only held off this long because you asked me not to, but really, Tanya, he needs to know. Something has to be done.'

'Just one more month, Eric, that's all I'm asking. Four weeks. That won't hurt – can't hurt – surely? Dom has a lot on his plate right now, if you'll excuse the pun,' she smiled. 'I'm sure even you have noticed that his parents' marriage is under quite a lot of strain at the moment. He really doesn't need any extra concerns right now. Anyway, it's nothing I can't take care of. A few more reviews, a mention or two in the right columns . . .'

'Tanya, this is way beyond the bounds of playing PR games. Dominic's is in real trouble. I don't think you're quite grasping the fact.' Eric was frustrated, his small, thin mouth pursed in disapproval. 'As for Dom's parents, well, Cici herself is responsible for quite a large chunk of the deficit, not to mention you and your PR chums.'

Tanya had grasped it all right. 'Look, I have a plan. There's always a way round these things if you just keep calm and think laterally. If you tell Dom now, he'll just go into a spiral of panic and then we really will be in trouble. Just a month, that's all I'm asking.' She flashed him her most beguiling smile. She had no intention of letting Eric ruin her plans.

'Well . . .' Eric was reluctant. 'I hope it's a plan that ends in four zeros, because that's what it's going to take to get him out of the red. One month, Tanya, that's all I can promise. After that, it'll be out of my hands.'

'You won't regret it,' Tanya beamed and kissed him on the cheek. 'You'll see.' She waved goodbye to him as she slipped into the taxi at the head of the queue on the Green.

Once she was home, Tanya switched on the gas fire and slipped into her favourite cashmere hoodie and lounging trousers. She thought about ringing Dom and then decided against it. He was lunching with his father in the Royal Irish Yacht Club, and although he had invited Tanya, she had encouraged him to take the opportunity to have a good man-to-man talk to his father and find out what exactly was going on with him and Cici.

'I mean, it's ridiculous, Dom,' she had said to him last week when they were heading upstairs after a late night in the restaurant. 'Moving into the mews, living at the bottom of the garden and carrying on as if she was a – well, certainly not a wife and mother of three, not to mention pushing fifty.' Tanya couldn't help the nasty little jibe escaping. Her own mother was the same age and had followed Cici's 'career', as she snidely called it, since her arrival in Ireland all those years ago, when she had snared one of the most eligible bachelors in the country seemingly overnight.

'Hmph,' her mother had said. 'No wonder they got married in Rome. It was the talk of Dublin at the time. James Coleman's parents were *not at all* happy about their son marrying an Italian showgirl.'

'Was she really a showgirl?' Tanya had asked.

'She claimed she was an actress – well she would, wouldn't she? But no one here has ever seen or heard of any films she was in.'

'Please, Tanya,' Dom said, 'not now. I have no idea what's going on with my mother, and I'd say Dad knows even less. But I'd really rather not think about it at the moment, if you don't mind.'

Tanya knew when to back off. 'Of course, lovey, I'm sorry. It's absolutely none of my business. It's just that I hate to see your dad so, well, helpless, and he seems so desperately unhappy.'

'That's probably because he is,' Dom sighed. 'Look, like I said, I really don't want to talk about it – she's probably just throwing a few parties, taking a bit of space. You know what she's like. It's not as if she's having an affair or anything, is it?'

Tanya chewed her lip. 'Look, I probably shouldn't say this, but you know what this town is like, and in my business, well, I get to hear more than most people. I'm sure there's nothing in it, but . . .'

'But what?' Dom was frowning.

'Like I said, I'm sure it's nothing, but Cici has been seen around a lot with Harry McCabe. I've seen them myself, lunching in Dominic's at least twice. People are beginning to talk.'

'Harry McCabe!' Dom exclaimed. 'But he's only . . . he can't be more than—'

'Your age,' Tanya finished. 'Exactly.'

'That's impossible.' Dom looked horrified for a moment.

'I'm sure you're right, babe. I'm sure it's just gossip, but if your father gets to hear of it – or perhaps he already has – it won't help things.'

'No,' Dom agreed, 'it certainly will not. I'll have lunch with him on Sunday, sound him out, find out what's going on.'

'I think that would be a very good idea.' Tanya looked sympathetic. 'It can't be easy for him, poor man.'

Now, at home, sitting with her feet curled under her on the large modern sofa, Tanya cursed Dom's mother for her appalling timing, never mind behaviour. And as if that wasn't bad enough, now she had this financial mess in the restaurant to worry about too. At this rate, marriage would be the last thing on Dom's mind, even though they had been getting on better than ever these past few months. Tanya had made sure of that. She frowned, lost deep in thought. Things were not going her way. Indeed, they appeared to be conspiring against her. But that was ridiculous. That was the way losers thought, and whatever else she was, Tanya was not a loser. Still, for the life of her, she couldn't think what to do. *Make it happen*, the voice whispered in her mind. *Take control*. But how?

She loved Dom, of course she did. Who wouldn't? He was handsome, charming, funny, kind and thoughtful. But it was more than that. She didn't just love Dom, she loved everything he represented, everything he was a part of – everything, in short, that she wasn't. It was something Dom couldn't possibly understand, even if she had been able to find the words to explain it to him. How she longed to be a part of his world – that cultivated, rarefied world of careless elegance and throwaway, confident remarks that were the product of enviable educations and glamorous backgrounds, unimaginable advantages that the people upon whom these blessings were bestowed seemed to take for granted.

But Tanya never would. She would enjoy every hard-won, exquisite minute of belonging to that world, precisely because she knew what it was like to look in at it from the outside.

She often tried to remember her dad. Sometimes she thought she could. If she looked at a photograph for long enough, sometimes she thought she could remember his face, his smile. Sometimes she thought she remembered his smell, a vague combination of tobacco and aftershave, or his voice, a comforting, gravelly reassurance, but then she would wonder if it was all in her imagination.

When she asked her mother about it, she was bitterly

dismissive. 'I'm not surprised you can't remember him – he was never around,' she had laughed.

'But he must have been, some of the time at least,' Tanya persisted.

'Not in my version of events, sweetheart. He was working, or so he claimed, and when he wasn't working he was on the golf course. Both pastimes were followed by a stint in the pub – *she* encouraged it, of course. It was because of her he remortgaged the house – to pay for *her* expensive tastes. You and I didn't warrant such consideration.'

'But he must have had some decent qualities,' Tanya pressed. 'I mean, you married him, didn't you? There must have been something.'

'He was charming, I suppose,' she admitted grudgingly. 'In the beginning. Attractive and charming – weak men often are. But he lied to me, pretended he was much more successful than he actually was. I had no reason not to believe him initially.' She grimaced. 'Then even the lies became third rate. By the time I decided to find out just how bad things were, he had conveniently run off with his secretary to America. Such a cliché. I don't think that man ever had an original thought in his head. Then, of course, I was left with the whole pack of cards tumbling down around us.'

Tanya knew the rest of the story by heart. It had been recounted many times, with varying degrees of anger, bitterness and contempt. To listen to her mother, you'd think that *she* was the only one who'd suffered, who'd gone to superhuman lengths to salvage any sort of home and upbringing for her young daughter. Not that Tanya denied it – she knew she had an awful lot to thank her for – but sometimes she felt as if her mother almost relished the delicious victimisation of it all.

Tanya had known since she was very little that something was amiss in her family. It wasn't just that she didn't have a daddy, and when other children asked her, as they did, she would say, as she had been coached to, 'My daddy lives in America. He has a very important job there and I fly over for holidays to see him.' That usually inspired equal measures of intrigue and awe, followed closely by enquires about Disneyland and whether or not she had been.

'Of course I have,' she would say and would relay in impressive detail descriptions of rides, roller coasters, castles and queues. For a child who had never been there and wasn't likely to go, she knew more about it than many of its bona-fide visitors. But she had watched numerous videos of it, mesmerised by the one and only letter she had received from her absent father, in which he had promised to come for her and take her for a special holiday in America and they would go, just the two of them, to Disneyland. That the invitation never materialised, just as her mother predicted, year in and year out, made the fantasy somehow all the more important to her, and so she would embellish it in minute, exquisite detail until it was so vivid, so word perfect, she almost believed it herself.

That was when she had been very young.

When she got to be about ten or twelve, she merely said, if asked, that her parents were divorced and that her dad lived in Florida. By then she had gathered, without ever having the matter properly explained to her, that her father had not only been absent, but somehow had been *lacking*, even in the short time he had lived with her mother, when she, Tanya, was a baby. She sensed a certain triumph in her mother, that this lack, having been diagnosed like a case of measles or mumps, had indeed manifested itself in such a noteworthy and lasting legacy. All Tanya knew, though, despite the clucking reassurances of her mother's few family members and female friends, was that her father, however unreliable and lacking he may have been, had left her – and much, *much* worse, had never once come back for Tanya.

After that, everything else had been easy: living in a smaller house in not nearly as nice a neighbourhood or not having new, up-to-date clothes like the other girls in her class. She had learned later that the nuns at the exclusive convent day school she attended had reduced her school fees considerably upon learning of her mother's predicament. She worked hard and was reasonably bright, although not terribly clever, and did well enough. Otherwise, she kept pretty much to herself. It was easier that way. She learned to dissemble, to manipulate the truth just enough to appear interesting but without arousing suspicion or jealousy. She was pleasant to the other girls, but not overly friendly or confiding, and as a result was left to her own devices, which suited her.

So when the time came and boys entered the equation, Tanya was poised and ready. At sixteen years of age, she was finally able to salvage something from the wreck that was her paternal heritage. As she grew up and into her coltish, blonde good looks, it became apparent she was taking after her father's side of the family. The gene pool, at least, had been kind to her. Now, she finally had something advantageous to work with.

Cool, disinterested and playfully insincere, she attracted guys effortlessly and just as effortlessly dispensed with their affections when they no longer suited her. Tanya wasn't interested in romance – that was for kids. She had no time for girly exchanges, analysing and poring over every minute detail of a boyfriend's text messages or phone calls. Tanya was after something much more important. She was after a life, one that had been cruelly taken from her, one that rightfully should have been hers – and she fully intended to reclaim it. She had spent far too long looking in from the outside. Now it was her turn to enter that world of wealth, glamour and society. And she had finally found the man who would help her do it.

Only he wasn't showing any signs of moving their relationship on to that vital next level. If anything, Dom seemed distracted and absorbed in affairs of the kitchen. Rollo, their chef, was having a particularly good run, and Dom, who made no secret of the fact that winning a coveted Michelin star for the restaurant was his ultimate goal and passion, was doing everything he could to humour Rollo and keep him sweet, including paying for this latest trip to Vienna for him and Astrid so they could rekindle their volatile relationship.

It was all very vexing. He should have been concentrating on keeping their own relationship on track, but of course men didn't think like that, Tanya had to remind herself. She flicked on the television and channel-hopped for a bit, hoping to find an old movie she could settle down to, when a segment of an American chat show caught her attention. *Women Who Make It Happen*, the clip was titled. She paused, remote in hand, watching idly as a housewife from Virginia related how she had turned her hobby of making accessories for shoes into a multimillion-dollar business. This was followed by the presenter introducing a more romantic angle to the discussion.

'Women everywhere,' she began, smiling broadly, 'will identify with my next guest, Cindy, who was fed up waiting for her boyfriend of eight years to propose, so when a leap year came around, Cindy leapt at her chance!' Cindy, it turned out, had proposed to her boyfriend, who had responded with a resounding yes and was on the show to share the story, along with their four picture-perfect children, of his wife's 'management' of the commitment issue.

'That's what I love about Cindy,' her rather sappy-looking husband gushed. 'When she wants something, she sure as hell goes after it till she gets it. In my case, I just thank my lucky stars she did.' The camera pulled out as they kissed and their four kids giggled nervously. But Tanya was sitting up straighter now.

It wasn't such a bad idea, she thought. Not ideal, of course, not by any means, but where did ideals ever get a girl?

And this year *was* a leap year. She pulled her diary out of her handbag – the twenty-ninth of February was a Friday. Naturally, Tanya would have preferred if Dom had taken matters into his own hands and organised a romantic and thoughtful setting in which to surprise her with the longed-for request, but if he wasn't going to get around to it, she would. It was as simple as that. Otherwise, God knows what would happen. With Cici acting so inappropriately and now Eric, the accountant, being such a pain in the neck, if something wasn't done about things, and done quickly, well, things could take a very different turn altogether, and Tanya was not going to allow *that* to happen.

She *had* considered, very briefly, getting pregnant. It was the obvious thing to do, really, and Dom adored children. He was brilliant with them whenever he was around them. Being half Italian helped, she supposed, but whatever it was, they appeared to adore him too. He could play happily with them for hours, thinking up new and ridiculous games that made them shriek with delight. He would make a wonderful father.

That was another thing that featured highly on her list of necessary qualities in a husband. She would not subject a child of hers to what she had gone through. Having an avail-able, hands-on, devoted father would be vital – particularly since she was rather afraid of becoming a mother herself.

It wasn't that she didn't *like* children; she just wasn't very comfortable around them. She wasn't sure what exactly was required of her. She supposed it was because she was an only child and hadn't had any brothers or sisters to tumble around with, to rail and argue against. Nobody had ever picked her up (that she could remember) and swung her around to delighted, excited shrieks or cuddled her or chased her around the garden playing tag or hide and seek.

But something made her recoil from simply getting preg-nant. It was such an old trick. After all, it wasn't as if she wouldn't make Dom a wonderful wife. She shouldn't have to trap or persuade him into marriage, just hurry him up a bit, make him see what a fabulous opportunity was under his nose, and might not be there for much longer if he didn't get his act together. A leap-year proposal gave her the perfect opportunity. She would make sure it would be whimsical rather than pushy. It would be rather endearing, in fact, if she handled it the right way – and that was the only way *to* handle it. She would leave nothing to chance. It would have to be absolutely perfect, and she had four weeks to make sure it was.

7

'I'm thinking Audrey Hepburn in *Roman Holiday*, Anita Ekberg in *La Dolce Vita*, and of course lots of Sophia Loren.' Erin, the art director, rifled through the racks of clothes brought by the stylist before setting off to prowl around the mews for the umpteenth time. 'Fantastic,' she muttered, alighting upon room after tastefully decorated room. 'It's perfect, just perfect.'

Wanda, the make-up artist, was methodically laying out the tools of her craft. Bob, the photographer, and his assistant were busy setting up shop in the corner of the sitting room, and perched in splendour in the middle of it all, sitting on a stool wearing a red silk robe with a head full of curlers while two hairdressers circled her, working their magic, was Cici.

It was only eight o'clock in the morning, but already the mews looked like a film set with all these people scurrying around, checking the light, steam-pressing already pristine clothes and barking instructions into mobile phones. Cici was loving every second of it. She hadn't enjoyed anything as much in almost thirty years, not since her last (well, her only) movie in Rome, when she had been just eighteen, the year before she had come to Dublin and met James. It had only been a small part, a walk-on part as a waitress, where she got to take a surly detective's order in a small café and be swatted on the behind by his dining companion as she turned away. She had been discovered by the producer of the same movie, a small, fat, balding individual, in a men's clothes shop, where she worked behind the counter, and he had approached her, telling her to come to the audition. He had handed her his card and told her to be at the studios at seven a.m. sharp. He had then proceeded to breathe heavily down her cleavage when she auditioned, declaring she was perfect for the part. The director predicted she would be the next Sophia Loren, and Cici, in a daze of unimaginable excitement, had rehearsed her one line religiously, and after fifteen diligent takes, completed her dramatic debut. In a cruel stroke of fate, her part was axed and she ended up on the editing floor instead of the silver screen. The movie went on to become a resounding flop, and her fledgling career likewise. Despite numerous auditions and a genuine talent, Cici was proclaimed to be either too similar to Sophia Loren or not enough like her – too old or too young, her breasts too big or not big enough. A few uninspiring television commercials followed, and eventually even those parts dried up as hordes of thinner girls with longer legs and frail, fragile looks became the vogue.

'You have the most amazing bone structure,' Wanda, the make-up girl, was saying now as she expertly applied foundation with her blending brush. 'And your skin is really unbelievable—' She had been about to add 'for your age', but stopped herself.

'Thank you, darling,' Cici purred. 'I'm afraid I cannot take any credit for either. I was simply lucky enough to have good-looking parents,' she laughed.

She closed her eyes and let Wanda chat away as she worked, only half listening, and tried to quell the fluttering in her stomach every time someone mentioned Harry's name, which seemed to be frequently. So far, there had been no sign of him, but he had said he'd be there at some stage during the day. Cici rather hoped it would be *after* her hair and make-up had been done.

She had done the interview earlier in the week with him, also at the mews, where he had arrived punctually at three o'clock, leather satchel slung over his shoulder, from which he produced a notebook, digital recorder and bottle of champagne.

'You shouldn't have!' she said as she took it from him, although she had plenty in her fridge, already on ice.

'Let me open it,' he said, twisting the cork from the bottle until it gave way with a satisfying pop. 'To you, Cici,' he said, raising the glass she had filled, 'and to an intriguing and I hope revealing interview.' His eyes locked with hers.

'I'm all yours,' she said playfully. 'But you must promise not to twist anything I say – I know what you journalists can be like.'

'Not a word, I promise,' he grinned. 'I can't think of a single thing I would alter about you. Now let's get started.' He switched the recorder on, sat it on the table in front of them and leaned in towards her. 'If you want to stop at any time and take a break, just say so.'

But she hadn't. He made it easy. Talking to him, recounting her early life in Rome, then her impressions of Ireland, of living in Dublin and making the inevitable adjustments that followed, her life had sounded glamorous, exciting. She had her three lovely children, and of course had been a stay-at-home mother, but Cici had never lost sight of the fact that she was first and foremost a woman. She couldn't help it, it was in her blood – she thrived on attention, particularly from men. Luckily, in the circles she and James mixed in, a full and busy social life had been part of the package. There was never any shortage of parties to attend, where she had always been openly admired, and she had cut a dashing figure on the fashion circuit, her dark, exotic colouring and bold, frequently flamboyant style making her the darling of Dublin's couturiers. One of them even referred to her as his muse, and, although flattered, she refused to favour only his creations, as most women would have done, preferring to play one designer off against the other at whim.

James had always been a thoroughly generous husband in that respect, and a significant monthly allowance was deposited in her bank account without fail, which she quickly became accustomed to and took for granted. So far, six months out of the family home and living in the mews, the same arrangement seemed to be holding up. She had been worried about that and had assiduously avoided any reference to things financial, counting, as always, on James's innate sense of gentlemanly fair play. Thinking of him now, she felt another flicker of guilt. Any time Harry's beautiful, sensual face floated into her mind, James's questioning, confused and bewildered one would appear and hover insistently behind it. It was spoiling everything.

In the interview, she had taken great care to skirt around the issue of her marriage, and Harry had diplomatically allowed her to. How was it he had referred to her? *A woman on the brink of discovering a new phase in her life, glorying in all her many and accomplished dimensions.* Cici had liked that enormously, although she wasn't quite sure what it meant. But then, if she was honest, she wasn't quite sure about anything at all any more.

'Why? Just tell me *why*,' James had pleaded, his face paling, that awful evening she had told him after dinner, when she had dropped her bombshell.

'I need some space, James.' She had rehearsed the speech so often, but now, in the presence of his awful bewilderment, it deserted her, failing to sound as reasonable and plausible as she had anticipated. 'I need to . . . to find myself, to figure out what I want from my life, from myself . . .' She had trailed off.

'But why can't you do that here?' He was aghast. 'Take a holiday, go on a retreat, whatever you like, Cici, travel around the world if you must, but moving out – I don't understand.' He had sat down suddenly, as if all the energy that had been keeping him upright had suddenly been sucked from him.

'I'm so sorry, James,' she said lamely, 'it's just something I have to do.' And she had fled from the room and into one of the many other, now empty bedrooms, where she had lain that night, tossing and turning, hearing him eventually climb the stairs and go into their bedroom, where he had softly closed the door.

Why?

That was the million-dollar question, of course, the one she had wrestled with day after day and night after night. She didn't know why. She just knew that she needed to explore, to test one last time, to push the boundaries, to have one more go – before it was too late. How *could* she explain? How could she put into words what she didn't understand herself? That no matter how confident she thought she was, how comfortable she had always been with her looks, with her life, that recently another, wheedling, pleading, some-times sinister voice had been whispering to her. A voice that told her she was losing it – that every day, a little bit of her was slipping away. A new wrinkle would appear and have to be fought, a favourite dress or outfit would no longer look appropriate on her or give her the required boost or lift that she so depended on. One day, she would enter rooms full of people chattering, laughing, watching, where heads would turn to check her arrival, but their gaze would no longer linger on her, enviously and admiringly, quite the way they once had. The prettier, fresher, younger girls, glossy and dewy in their beauty, who wordlessly assessed her, then returned their attention to their partners, triumphant and confident that she, Cici, would not distract them the way she once would have.

How could she explain this to James? Poor, straightforward, honourable James, who would no more have understood what she was talking about than she did herself. 'But I adore you, Cici,' he would have said, laughingly. 'You know that.' And she did, of course she did. But she needed more than that.

What the exact nature of that 'more' was, she didn't know, but she did know she needed to get away from these horrid, stealthy, undermining feelings and remember what it was to inspire passion, to inflame a heart and mind, to command attention, before – the thought occurred with increasing terror – before it was too late and the chance slipped away for ever. Before she felt tempted to turn into one of those pitiable women who succumbed to surgery and endless, relentless dieting and exercise until they looked as desperate and whittled away as the empty emotions inside them.

Just for a little while, she reasoned. Just a little while to have one last adventure, one last bite of the cherry, and perhaps then she could resign herself to the onslaught of invisibility, of old age, of expanding waistlines and settled folds on her skin, of warm, kindly glances instead of longing, lingering eye-to-eye exchanges. In a little while, but not just *yet*.

'Okay, everybody,' Bob, the photographer, called out. 'Let's go with the *Roman Holiday* shot first. Kerry?' He turned to his assistant. 'We're all set up, right?'

'Sure are, just waiting for hair and make-up.'

'Ready in five.' Wanda held up her hand, spreading her fingers wide.

Cici marvelled at how calm they all seemed. Bob Clarke was an über-hot English photographer with an über-hot temper if his well-known impatience wasn't immediately pacified. Yet Wanda and the rest of the team refused to be flustered and just grinned and kept on rigorously doing what they were doing. Just listening to Bob, never mind looking at his thunderous expression, was enough to make Cici quiver. But the team from *Select* were obviously used to this – after all, it was what they did for a living. All the same, Wanda told Cici, when Erin, the art director, had heard they were getting Bob Clarke for the shoot, she'd almost passed out with disbelief.

'It was Harry who swung it,' Wanda whispered. 'I don't think anyone else could have. Bob's incredibly hard to get hold of these days, and he charges an absolute fortune.'

'What do you think persuaded him?' asked Cici, intrigued.

Wanda shrugged. 'Who knows? Ireland's still hot at the moment, and there was talk that Bob has his eye on a new young model here he saw cast in a stocking ad. Harry also managed to get *Vibe* magazine to commission Bob for a fashion shoot in Connemara, so two birds with one stone and all that.'

'He certainly went to an awful lot of trouble.' Cici pressed her lips together to seal the just-applied lipstick before Wanda blotted it with a tissue.

'When Harry wants something, he usually makes sure he gets it.' Wanda dusted a final veil of powder over Cici's face and proclaimed her done.

'Great,' Cici said, although she felt a sudden shiver of apprehension as what Wanda said ran through her – or was it anticipation?

Before she could decide, she was hustled into a pretty V-necked shirt, a tightly belted swirling cotton skirt and flat pumps and ushered outside, where a bright red 1950s scooter stood, polished until it gleamed. Philip, the male model who was Cici's foil for the shots, stood in a beautifully tailored single-breasted suit, looking tall, dark and handsome, just like Gregory Peck, but unlike Mr Peck, he had a sulky, bored expression. Understandable, really, thought Cici, feeling vaguely amused, considering he was probably twenty-five years younger than her. How awful, she thought, to be a male model, all that standing around doing nothing, and then the girls got all the good shots! Mind you, when Bob appeared and looked through his lens, Philip suddenly perked up and a bright, friendly smile quickly transformed his sullen appearance.

'Okay.' Bob was in command as a respectful hush descended

on the small gathering. 'Cici, on the scooter, Philip, you too – behind her, that's it. Arms around her waist. Somebody spread that skirt out a bit! That's it.' He was still looking through his lens intently. 'Now Cici, lean back into Philip, that's it, and look back up at him.' Cici did as she was told, looking flirtatiously at Philip, who, to be fair, looked straight back at her with camera-ready lust. 'Great,' Bob enthused. 'Chin down a tad, Cici, and a hint of a smile, that's it, good girl.' And he was off, moving around them, bending and arching as the camera whirred and clicked, taking shot after shot.

'Good work, guys, we're done. Let's move on to the Sophia set-ups now, then we can break for lunch.'

Cici clambered off the scooter and was ushered off to make-up again. She was shocked. She'd had no idea just how much work went into setting up a photo shoot and was already feeling quite tired. Apart from that, it was absolutely freezing. Not that that seemed to count. The light was good, and that was all that mattered – to Bob, at any rate. The crew were well equipped with coats, gloves and woolly hats, but she and Philip had to stand for as long as it took in the outfits for each shot. The next set was to feature her dressed as Sophia Loren in her famous movie *The Fall of the Roman Empire*, which meant a whole new backdrop was set up outside in the courtyard patio. This was achieved by the placement of some fake Roman columns and steps and three amazingly convincing pieces of painted scenery, the arrangement of which looked as if it would take some time, particularly as Bob was a maniacal perfectionist.

In the meantime, Cici was back in wardrobe and make-up, dreading slipping into her next outfit, which was an elegant white Grecian-style evening dress that plunged and draped around her in all the right places, but in this cold, she might as well be standing stark naked. She hoped her nipples wouldn't be too obvious through the thin material; they were standing to attention already.

Wanda must have been reading her mind, as she instructed Cici to raise her arms, then deftly arranged her breasts with the aid of two stick-on patches that supported them from underneath. 'Tricks of the trade,' she grinned, applying nipple tape as the final touch. 'There. You're respectable.'

'God, I used to think I'd enjoy modelling,' Cici grimaced. 'I had no idea it was such awfully hard work.'

'Nobody does,' agreed Wanda. 'Not until they actually have to do it – or at least until they get to work with models. I can't say I'd enjoy it myself. Rather be on this side of the camera any day. Glamorous it is *not*. Still, very few models ever get to work with Bob. Most of them would give their right arm to. If nothing else, you're going to have a fantastic portfolio of shots to show off.'

To who? Cici found herself suddenly wondering.

'Pity your girls aren't here, or your son,' Wanda continued. 'Bob's a control freak while he's on the job, but he would have taken some great family shots afterwards – no chance you could get any of them here? It's such a shame to miss the opportunity.' She was deftly applying a thick layer of eyeliner along Cici's lashes and winging it up and out dramatically.

'No, unfortunately not,' Cici murmured. 'My girls are both abroad this year and my son, Dom, never leaves his restaurant for a moment.'

'Never mind. They'll get even more of a surprise when they see the spread.'

'Yes, I expect so.' She smiled, although inside her stomach lurched uncharacteristically. Cici hadn't actually told anyone about the shoot. She wasn't quite sure why. She was sure her girls would be thrilled for her, and Dom . . . well, you never really knew with sons, they could be so proprietorial about their mothers. And as for James . . . Cici swallowed. It wasn't as if he was a regular reader of women's magazines, but he would hear sooner or later. Someone was bound to mention it to him. She would tell him, of course, at an appropriate time, when she could casually drop it into conversation. She wouldn't think about that just yet.

'Okay people,' called Kerry, Bob's assistant. 'Take your positions please, models!' She smiled at Cici. 'You look beautiful, Cici. You really are a dead ringer for her – it's incredible.'

Cici had to hide a grin when she saw Philip dressed as a gladiator – he could have given Russell Crowe a run for his money any day.

'Philip,' Bob barked. 'Stand next to the column, that's it, and put your foot up on the step. Cici, I want you seated at his feet, looking up at him passionately. And . . . that's it, let's go, lovely.' And he was off again. Forty-five minutes later, Cici was blue with cold and trying not to shiver. Finally, thankfully, it was over.

'Okay, lunch break,' Kerry announced. Cici hadn't thought about food, but now she found she was starving. Rushing back inside, she pulled on a fleecy robe and tried to regain sensation in her limbs, which were completely numb. Lunch, she was pleased to see, had been taken care of by a local catering outlet, and the current gofer on *Select* had collected some very welcome food. There was wine too, although no one had the nerve to pour any while Bob was still in working mode. Cici helped herself to some steaming lasagne and salads and tucked in.

It was after lunch, when the team were still chatting over coffee, that Erin whispered something in Bob's ear and led him away from the table. They disappeared for a few minutes and then came back, looking pleased and hopeful.

'Cici,' Erin began, 'we've had an idea, a change of plan, if you'll allow it?'

'What's that?'

'The next shots, the *Dolce Vita* ones, we were just going to do them down here, in the sitting room.'

'Yes?' Cici listened expectantly, wondering what was coming next.

'Well, that was before we knew you had that wonderful sunken bath up there,' Erin went on excitedly. She was referring, of course, to the magnificent marble creation in Cici's master en suite that resembled a small swimming pool, with a mural of Venus rising from the waves painted on the surrounding walls. 'If you wouldn't object, Bob and I thought that if you wore the black velvet dress, you know the strapless, boned one, and we did the shoot with you standing in the bath, full of water and bubbles – you know, like the fountain shot in the movie – well, it would be just fantastic.' She held her breath.

'It'd be totally cool,' Bob nodded emphatically.

'I don't see why not,' said Cici, thinking that whatever else transpired, at least she could make sure the water was hot. These fashion people were odd, but as long as it got things over with quickly and she didn't have to be cold again, she would have agreed to almost anything.

'Brilliant. We'll get the lights rigged up straight away.' Kerry flicked open her mobile phone to tell the lighting technician.

'And just who is going to pay for that Valentino original that's about to be destroyed?' Valerie, the stylist, asked archly.

'Don't worry about it, Val,' beamed Kerry, 'I've cleared it with Harry. He thinks it's a great idea. He's on his way over now.'

Once again, Cici was led away to hair and make-up. Philip, having served his purpose in the former shots, was finished for the day and allowed to go. Cici envied him. Really, this was too tiring. She would go out of her mind if she had to do this sort of thing every day.

Wanda went to work quickly, cleansing and reapplying a lighter, beige-toned base and the palest of pink blushers to add a slight flush to Cici's cheeks. Pale pink lipstick, which she never, ever wore, was applied, and then the *pièce de résistance* – the long, ash-blonde wig, which completely transformed her. It was quite extraordinary. She wriggled into the black velvet strapless creation with the full skirt, and only then turned to look at her reflection. It showed off her spectacular curves to perfection. She really could be Anita Ekberg in the famous movie.

'Well,' she said, shaking her head, 'I don't know what to say. I feel as if I've had a whole body transplant.'

'As bodies go, Cici, yours is pretty delectable.' Val, the stylist, arranged the boned bodice of the dress one final time. 'I'd give anything to have breasts like those. Come on upstairs with you. After this, we're done.'

It was rather surreal to walk into her bathroom, which was now full of people, and see the mysterious blonde beauty who looked out at her from the mirrors. Lights were being adjusted and readjusted and the huge wide lighting umbrella angled and coaxed into position. Kerry was handing Bob a succession of lenses, which he was trying and then discarding, frowning, looking through the frame, lost in concentration. When he looked up and saw her, he gave a long, low whistle. 'This is just about as good as it gets. You look *fantastic*, Cici. Good job, Erin, and great hair and make-up.' He was all business again. 'Watch out for steam, people, make sure that water isn't too hot. Okay, Cici, into the bath, please.'

She was helped into the foaming mass of bubbles by Kerry, while Val helped hold up the hem of the dress above the water. 'I still can't believe we're doing this. It's sacrilege. Once it's soaked, that's it.' She shook her head.

'Okay, let the dress go,' Bob instructed. 'Now Cici, hoist the skirt up at the front, that's it, and let's see those legs of yours. Run your other hand through your hair, okay, fantastic.'

And it was. Cici felt faintly ridiculous, but she could tell from the expressions on their faces as the rest of the team watched intently that they were more than pleased with what they saw. She kept moving as instructed from pose to pose, gradually becoming more daring as Bob encouraged her, flattering her, coaxing her, and soon it seemed there was just her and him, working seamlessly, effortlessly as the room full of people ceased to exist.

'Okay, just a couple more, we're nearly there. I want you to kneel down, Cici, let the dress billow out behind you. Val, would you get that? Good, good. Now lean in towards me, you can hold onto the marble edge. There, yes, good, just a bit more, Cici, I want to get lots of cleavage for this one. Wanda, get that wisp of hair, would you? Okay, now grab a handful of bubbles and hold them out in the palm of your hand as if you're going to blow them straight into the camera, that's it, come on, you can look naughtier than that, Cici. That's it. Great.'

Cici thought her shins were going to crack, kneeling as she was on the hard marble, but she did as she was told and finally was allowed, with help, to stand up.

'Last one, promise. Don't move, Cici. Stay right where you are.'

She had been about to clamber out of the bath, thoroughly fed up now with a soaking wet, heavy velvet dress clinging to her.

'Okay, turn around, back to me, that's it. Val, unzip it, would you? I want a nice open V down to the waist. Actually, make that down to the bottom of that very gorgeous spine. Don't worry,' he grinned as Cici threw him a look of alarm. 'Come on, Cici, nothing wrong with a naked back. This will be very tasteful, trust me.'

Bob found himself getting quite turned on as he looked through the lens. He recognised a great shot when he saw it. It was tasteful, all right. Christ, Cici had almost hand-drawn perfect proportions, and the sensuous curve of her back against the unzipped bodice of the dress that fell open to just above her bottom was framed perfectly. Tasteful, definitely, but also wonderfully, almost unbearably erotic.

'Okay, that's it, guys. It's a wrap!' Bob finally called it a day. 'Good work, everybody. I think we're all going to be very, *very* pleased with the finished results. Well done, Cici,' he smiled warmly at her. 'I know that can't have been easy for you. Now you know why good models are so highly paid!'

She stepped out of the bath, helped again by Wanda, who took her hand, and with her other hand, she held the unzipped bodice of the dress to her breasts, covering them as best she could. She looked up, and it was then that she saw him, lounging in the doorway, a half smile curving his mouth. His eyes held hers, boldly, as he flashed her a look of what could only be described as pure, unadulterated lust.

'Hello, Harry.' Bob had only just noticed him as well. 'Didn't see you there. Very good day, very good indeed. Productive. Got exactly what I wanted. I'll be in touch next week, when we can look at the contacts.'

'Good stuff.' Harry was upbeat, professional, congratulating everyone on a job well done. 'I look forward to seeing them.' His eyes roved around the sumptuous bathroom, taking in every detail. 'Just thought I'd stop by and make sure everything was going to plan. As it is,' he checked his watch, 'I can see you've all managed admirably without me.'

'There's some delicious grub downstairs that we hardly made any inroads into, and wine, of course,' Erin said. 'Come and join us for a drink. I'll just pour some glasses downstairs.' She made for the door.

'Love to, but I'm afraid I can't stop.' He made a face. 'Got to do an interview with Rick Waters at his place in half an hour. I was really lucky to get him. Better make tracks, you guys have a good time – looks like you've earned it.' And without so much as a backward glance, he was gone.

Cici suddenly felt as deflated as the wet dress that clung to her.

While everybody was clearing up, lights were taken down and equipment put away, Cici went into one of the other bathrooms to take off all the make-up and have a long, hot shower. She was absolutely exhausted. They had started at eight that morning, and it was now half past five. How did these people do it, day in and day out? Feeling hugely relieved it was all over, she dried herself off and hurried back to her bedroom, where she slipped into her favourite jeans and pulled on a soft white V-necked sweater. She didn't bother with make-up, just ran a brush through her hair, twisted it and pinned it up and went downstairs to join the others, who, by the sounds of it, were beginning to unwind and let their hair down. Someone had found a Cuban mix CD and, over it, the sounds of raised voices and laughter filled the mews.

'Come on, Cici, where's your glass?' Erin was proffering a bottle of white wine. 'After all, you're the star of the show.'

She found one and held it out to be filled. 'If I'd known what terribly hard work it would be, I wouldn't have volunteered my services quite so eagerly,' she laughed. 'Oh, by the way,' she said to Val, who was putting away the clothes used on the shoot, 'I left the dress upstairs, in the smaller bathroom. It's hanging on the back of the door. I meant to bring it down and completely forgot.'

'No worries, Cici, I'll get it in a jiffy.'

'Thanks, Val, that would be great. I really feel my legs would give way for good if I had to go back up those stairs again. Kneeling on the marble bath floor has done them in.'

Soon, everything was packed up, and after an hour or so they had polished off what was left of the food and had drunk most of the wine. 'Here, take it with you, I insist,' Cici said, forcing the remaining bottles on Val, Kerry and Wanda, which were eagerly accepted. 'I have tons more in the fridge, really.' People began to filter out, saying warm farewells. Even Bob had let his guard down and done some hilarious imitations of supermodels he had worked with.

'I'll be in touch when I have something to show you,' he promised Cici, kissing her on both cheeks.

It was only eight o'clock, and closing the door behind them, Cici sat down, turned on the television and poured herself a glass of wine. She was relieved it was over and rather apprehensively excited about the results, which she would not be privy to for another couple of weeks at least. Now, without the cheery company of the crowd that had just left, she felt suddenly rather glum. She watched a couple of soaps, put on the dishwasher and at nine-thirty decided it might be time for an early night. She had a good book that she was enjoying, and the long day had left her feeling weary.

She was just about to go upstairs when the doorbell rang. She jumped. Who could it possibly be at this hour? James, maybe, she wondered, suddenly fearful. Perhaps he had seen all the cars and comings and goings and would be demanding to know what was going on. It wouldn't be any of her friends, or even Dom; they would always have rung first to check if calling around suited her. She waited for a moment while the bell sounded again. Oh sod it! She would just have to go and find out who it was.

He turned around as she opened the door and gave a slow, wide grin. 'I was about to give up on you,' he said, standing there as if it was the most natural thing in the world.

'Oh,' she said, momentarily taken aback. 'Well, I'm glad you didn't.'

'May I come in?' He had a suit carrier and his satchel was slung over his shoulder.

'Of course. It's, er, just that I wasn't expecting anyone. It's a bit of a surprise.' Cici stood back to let him in.

'A nice surprise, I hope?' His eyes roved over her. 'They've all gone?'

'Yes, yes, a while ago.' Cici felt flustered. 'Can I get you a drink?'

'I'll have whatever you're having.' He looked at the empty glass on the table beside where she had been sitting on the sofa.

'Oh, I can do better than that.' She moved towards the kitchen. 'How about some champagne? It's chilled.'

'Great.' He put down his bags and followed her, taking the glass she held out to him while she poured one for herself.

'Well,' he said, watching her, amused at the slight tremble she tried and failed to conceal as she poured the fizzing liquid, 'aren't you going to ask me why I'm here?'

'Should I?' she countered, smiling, brushing past him and back into the sitting room. She hoped she sounded amused, confident, although her heart was thudding alarmingly. 'How did your interview go – how was Rick Waters?' she asked, trying to sound nonchalant, although her voice sounded distinctly high pitched. She was nervous, unsure of herself, alone with Harry now for the first time – *in her house*. The thought both excited and terrified her.

'It went well, but he's not nearly as fascinating a subject to interview as you are. In fact,' he said, following her, 'I wound things up early so I could come back and see you.' Without warning, he hooked a finger into the waistband of her jeans, pulling her up in her tracks as she wheeled around.

'Harry, what?'

He kissed her then, suddenly, briefly, one hand hooking around her neck, pulling her into him, his tongue slipping into her mouth deftly, easily, perusing her.

'Harry, really!' she protested, pulling back and laughing nervously, putting her glass hurriedly on the mantelpiece. He did the same, but not before he took a swig of his drink. Then he was kissing her again, sharing it with her, as the sweet taste of champagne trickled into her mouth, his tongue lazily exploring, searching, demanding.

She pulled away. 'Harry,' she laughed, 'really.'

'Yes, Cici. Really.' He was definite, looking down at her intently. He took her upper lip between his own and sucked it lightly, then pulled back, leaving her desperately, foolishly wanting more. 'I've brought something for you,' he said, smiling enigmatically.

He made his way over to the door, where he had left the suit carrier lying against the wall.

She had wondered about that – what did it mean? God, was he planning on staying the night? Suddenly she wasn't at all sure what to do – it was all so unexpected. *No it isn't*, the small voice was whispering to her, scornful, taunting. *You've been wanting this to happen since you first laid eyes on him.* But now, she felt panicked.

He opened the suit carrier and took out something long and black, throwing it over his arm and turning towards her with that slow, lazy smile again. 'Put it on.'

'What?' For a moment she was confused, and then with a flash of comprehension she understood and panic gave way to even more panic and then sheer, and rather shameful, excitement.

'But – but—' she flustered, gazing, transfixed, at him. 'It's still wet.'

'Exactly,' he said. 'I watched you earlier. That shot in the bathroom was the sexiest thing I've ever seen. Now I want a repeat performance, but this time, just for me. Go on. You know you want to.' His eyes challenged her. He handed it to her, followed by the long blonde wig. 'Put them on, for me, and I'll see you upstairs. I'll be waiting in the bathroom.' He walked past her and up the stairs, confident, certain that she wouldn't disappoint him.

For a moment she was paralysed, standing there with the dress and wig lifeless in her arms. She could stop this right now. She could laugh and tell him he was out of his mind to think that she had the slightest interest in collaborating with this ridiculous carry-on. And then she remembered the look in his eyes, heard his voice again. *You know you want to.* And she did.

She undressed then, hurriedly, pulling off her jeans and

jumper with trembling hands, throwing her bra and panties aside carelessly, and slid into the heavy black velvet once again. She zipped it up as best she could, although she couldn't quite manage the hook at the top – but that didn't matter. Then she pulled on the wig, fixing it in the large mirror over the mantel, pulling down a tendril or two so they curled under her chin, just as Wanda had done earlier, while the rest fell in a heavy sheet down her back. She was momentarily shocked again at the sensual, blonde vision that looked back at her, mockingly, tauntingly, daring her to bring her to life. And then, very slowly, she took a few deep breaths and, holding the skirt up carefully, made her way upstairs.

He was waiting for her, just as he had promised, leaning against the mirrored wall, his arms folded, wearing a slightly amused expression. The vast sunken bath was already full, mountains of foaming bubbles rising and falling gently in frothy peaks. A thin layer of steam filled the room, making the atmosphere humid and sultry, coating the mirrors in a fine mist. He turned and wrote on one now, lazily tracing the words. *You are so, so sexy*.

She gasped, trapped suddenly in his gaze, shivering with desire, waiting, anticipating his next delicious instruction.

'Get into the bath.'

And she did, letting the skirt drop, watching it billow out, feeling its weight dragging at her, the water and bubbles caressing her bare legs.

Still he looked at her, then slowly came over and stood at the edge of the bath.

'Turn around.'

He unzipped her, tracing a slow finger all along her spine, until the dress fell away and she was completely naked. He kissed her then, on her neck, her shoulders, his cool hands stroking her, and finally turned her around to face him.

'God, you're beautiful.' He began to open his shirt and pull off his jeans, and suddenly she was helping him, tugging urgently at buttons, belts and zips. Marvelling at him, standing there before her, taut, sculpted, impossibly lean and so . . . *young*, his golden skin covered with a dusting of burnished, copper hairs.

'Come,' she said breathlessly, wanting him now, unable to be separate from him for a single moment longer. Then he was beside her, kissing her hungrily, laughing as a sea of bubbles flew up around them, displaced by their urgency. 'Lie down,' he commanded, and she did, giggling as her new blonde hair trailed around her and he slid down beside her, pulling her on top of him until she straddled him, giddy now and helpless with desire.

'Cici,' he murmured, reaching up to stroke her face and trailing his other hand slowly, tantalisingly along her thigh. 'You are every man's living, breathing fantasy. You are a *goddess.*'

And she believed him, understanding in that instant that she had always known it, had always been waiting, hoping, *longing* to hear those very words uttered.

Then, in that languorous, luxurious, erotically charged moment, the fantasy became real.

8

It took much, *much* longer than she thought it would. How did anyone sit through this every, what, two to three weeks? It was so incredibly boring. If she hadn't had her phone and her iPod with her, she'd have gone mental.

'Are you absolutely sure about this?' the colourist, Tracy, had asked her, sounding concerned. 'It's a rather drastic change, and not exactly what I'd have recommended for your skin tone. Your own hair is really lovely. If you're bored with it, we could just take it up a shade, or maybe I could add a few copper and caramel highlights, much better for the condition too.' She ran her fingers through Candy's hair, but her client had been adamant.

'No. I want it exactly like *that*. Exactly.' She held open the magazine and pointed to the photograph of Shalom, attending the opening of some new yoga studio.

'But,' Tracy tried again, 'the girl in that photo, well, she's older than you, and her style is, well, sort of flamboyant.' She struggled to find the appropriate words. 'Wouldn't you rather get something more natural-looking? And it's going to be very time-consuming to maintain. You'll need your roots touched up every two to three weeks, conditioning treatments, too. It'll be expensive,' she warned.

'Look, you're supposed to be the hottest salon in Dublin.' Candy was getting impatient. 'Are you going to do as I ask or not? Because if you're not, I can easily go somewhere else.'

'Of course,' Tracy backed down. 'Whatever you like, love.

I'll be back in a moment, just have to mix up the colour. Tea or coffee?'

'Coffee, please,' snapped Candy. 'And don't call me love.'

Bloody hell! This was one snotty little bitch she was saddled with for the afternoon. Tracy shook her head as she walked towards the cupboard where the range of colour mixes was kept. She had seen her come in, looking surly and discontent before she had barely set foot in the salon, wearing designer jeans tucked into platform boots she could barely walk in. Her handbag, too, was D&G and would have cost the better part of Tracy's monthly salary. She didn't look more than eighteen or nineteen either, despite her uppity manner. Just to be sure, Tracy decided to have a word with the manager, Gary, before she committed herself. She didn't need some outraged mother coming in gunning for her, accusing her of ruining her daughter's virgin hair.

She interrupted Gary and explained the situation, nodding discreetly in Candy's direction, where she sat in her chair, reading a magazine.

He looked over at her and shrugged. 'Go ahead, do what she wants. She can obviously afford it. Anyway, you've done your best, pointed out all the obvious reasons not to, haven't you?'

'Course I have. She wasn't interested. Got quite stroppy, actually.'

'Well then, we've been responsible about it. If she wants to be a bleached blonde, then we've got to carry out her instructions. The customer's always right, remember?' he winked at her.

'Righty-oh. Just thought I'd run it by you.'

'You did the right thing,' Gary nodded. 'Good luck. I look forward to seeing the finished result.'

'Just five more minutes,' Tracy said and checked the colour. 'Then we'll get you shampooed.'

Thank God for that, Candy had wanted to scream. She had already read every magazine in the place, and looking at the vile-smelling purple goo on her head was beginning to make her feel sick. Instead, she smiled pleasantly and said thank you. It would all be worth it in the end, she reminded herself. She checked her watch. It was a quarter past five and she'd been in there since two-thirty. Her dad was picking her up at six-thirty outside the Shelbourne Hotel as she'd instructed him. She had decided to spend the weekend with him and Shalom and she had left her weekend bag in the hotel, where she could pick it up after her hair appointment. He'd been caught off guard when she had suggested it to him on the phone last week, just as she had known he would be, but he was pleased too. Her sudden change of tack would have come as a surprise, particularly since she hadn't been speaking to him – not since that awful, awful night more than two months ago. But Candy had been doing a lot of thinking lately, along with Katy and Emma.

She'd done everything she could, but her dad had still chosen Shalom. He'd left her and Mum and gone to live with *her.*

'Maybe he prefers blondes,' Katy had quipped, and that's when the idea began to take hold. Clearly the kind of woman a man wanted looked like Shalom did, and not like her mother. After that, it had all seemed easy.

They had decided that there was no point in Candy fighting with her dad about Shalom or the new baby. Instead, it was much easier to work the situation to her advantage. Anyway, Candy was tired of spending so much time with her mother and Gran. They were great, of course, but she needed a bit more freedom now, more room to manoeuvre, particularly in light of recent events. Since her photo op at the Tudor party, Candy had got a taste for celebrity – now people recognised her. She'd had her photo taken on a few other occasions at openings and fashion shows she had gone to and decided she liked it. Emma and Katy were right, she reflected, even if they could be a bit of a pain at times. She would start being nice to Shalom, the stupid cow. It wouldn't do any harm, and perhaps just the opposite. She would start by imitating her sense of style. That would show her dad that she understood, that she could see why he left. She would become like Shalom, the kind of woman men looked at and wanted – and she would make sure that no man ever left her like her father had left her mother.

After her shampoo and conditioning treatment, another, younger girl set about blow-drying her hair. When Candy sat back down in front of the mirror, she got quite a shock. Even totally wet, just patted with a towel, her hair was, well, quite *white*. Against her pale golden brows and eyelashes, it made her look very different.

'It's a big change, isn't it?' the stylist said, a wide grin on her face as she began to wield the hairdryer and brush.

'It's exactly what I wanted,' Candy said pertly, studying her magazine and avoiding interaction.

'You'll have to rethink your make-up and get your eyebrows and eyelashes tinted, otherwise you'll look like a bit of a ghost, won't you?' She seemed pleased with the observation.

'My father's partner is a make-up artist. I expect that'll come in useful. That's her there.' Candy pointed to the photo of Shalom she had used as an earlier example.

'That's your dad's partner?' The girl's mouth dropped open. 'Wow, she's like a celebrity, isn't she? I've seen her photo loads of times.'

'Yes, I expect you have.'

'Didn't know she was a make-up artist though.'

'Well, I think that's what she was. She wears enough of it. Did a bit of part-time modelling as well, underwear and stuff. Anyway, she doesn't have to work any more, now that she's with my dad.'

'What, is he loaded or something?'

'Yes.' Candy allowed herself a grin in the mirror. 'Totally loaded.'

'Some people have all the luck.'

The traffic wasn't too bad for some reason, Ossie thought, as he cut across town in his new Bentley, heading from Christchurch towards Stephen's Green and the Shelbourne Hotel, where Candy had told him to pick her up. It was dark, of course, and cold, and people were scurrying into buses or the Luas to make their way home after a bleak February day.

He had been taken completely by surprise to get her phone call. She'd been refusing to take his calls ever since the party, and it had been worrying him greatly. Charlotte had told him to give it time, that she would come around. Shalom had been impatient with him at first and then downright cross and told him to let her stew.

'Stop ringing her, Ossie, you're playing right into her hands. That's exactly what she wants you to do. Can't you see? If you stop ringing and pleading with her, then she'll get a wake-up call and stop treating you so unfairly. *Then* she'll be on the phone quick enough.'

He hadn't been able to heed either set of advice and had been thoroughly miserable about the whole situation. Guilty, too; enormously guilty. He couldn't believe how insensitive he'd been about announcing Shalom's pregnancy the way he had, that awful night at the party. What had he been thinking? He had tried once or twice in the weeks leading up to it to mention it to Charlotte on the phone, but every time something in her voice, or something in his heart, had stopped him. Then on the night itself, when he had seen Charlotte looking absolutely radiant in that magnificent period outfit she had worn, talking and laughing with old friends . . . he just hadn't had the heart to say anything. The words he had rehearsed so often just didn't seem to ever be appropriate. Then when he made his speech at the top table and was about to skirt around it, Shalom had prodded him, quite hard actually, and whispered to him sternly. Talk about being between a rock and a hard place! So he had blurted it out – and the rest was history. Of course he was thrilled about the new baby, but it seemed to Ossie that before it had even arrived in his life, things were becoming distinctly problematic.

For starters, there had been Candy's extreme reaction. It had genuinely startled Ossie, quite apart from the awful pie-throwing incident. Ossie had thought that Candy would have been thrilled to have a new little brother or sister on the way. It was Charlotte he'd been worried about. But Charlotte had taken the news calmly, bravely even, and with her usual magnanimous generosity had congratulated him and Shalom and wished them well. He wondered, briefly, how she really felt about it, considering everything they – well, *she* really – had gone through, all the doomed pregnancies Ossie could hardly bear to remember, even now.

Charlotte was extraordinary, really. He felt another swift stab of guilt. It must have been so hard for her when he left her for Shalom. But at the time he'd been having such fun, light-hearted, naughty, giddy fun, the kind of fun that made him forget all the pain and sorrow that he couldn't fix. It had lain there between him and Charlotte and grown until it had become a chasm he could no longer even think of broaching, let alone closing. Shalom had made him feel young and carefree again, and the sex, well, of course it had been amazing. Not that sex with Charlotte hadn't been wonderful – it had – but that had all seemed so long ago. Towards the end, the sadness seemed to even follow them there, in their most intimate moments, until eventually they avoided each other more and more.

With Shalom, everything seemed possible again. It was like being given a second chance. A second chance to spoil

someone, to be irresponsible and not have to exist with that
mantle of vague misery that seemed to always be there when
he was with Charlotte.

It wasn't that she ever said anything or blamed him in any
way; nothing could have been further from the truth. But
despite Ossie's great success and wealth, he always felt he
was something of a disappointment around Charlotte's crowd,
particularly her parents. He always felt he had to prove something. And Jennifer – what a mother-in-law! He'd actually
become very fond of her over the years. She was a tough old
bird, no doubt about it, but she had a good heart and a great
eye for horses. They had spent many a happy day at the
races, he and Jennifer, and returned home a little squiffy and
almost always considerably richer. She was incredibly know-
ledgeable and interesting too, and he had learned a lot from
her. Underneath her brusque manner, she was kind and
perceptive.

Like that time at Royal Ascot, when he had had his first
runner, a wonderful three-year-old called *Johnny Come Lately*,
who had, totally unexpectedly, won the Gold Cup, beating
the Queen Mother's horse, the out-and-out favourite, by a
nose and a half. Ossie, in an uncharacteristic fit of nerves,
had almost been paralysed with fright at having the cup
presented to him by the Queen.

'What's the matter? Got stage fright, Ossie? Surely not!'
Jennifer had grinned evilly at him. Then said, with her usual
forthrightness, 'you don't want to be intimidated by that lot
– they're just a bunch of blow-in Germans, remember? Had
to change their name from Saxe-Coburg-Gotha to Windsor!
The ones you want to watch out for are the dukes – proper
aristocracy. Speaking of which, there's Nottingham now! Oi,'
she had called out to a portly looking man with a remarkably weather-beaten face, 'Biffy! Over here.'

The tall man in immaculate tails and silk top hat had
peered at her, and then shouted joyfully, 'Jennifer, I don't

believe it – good God you look wonderful, haven't changed a day!'

Then Ossie and Charlotte had been presented with the wonderful trophy (Charlotte looking utterly beautiful in a Bellville Sassoon shell-pink silk suit and a wonderful matching hat) and the Queen had congratulated Ossie heartily. After that, they had all gone back to Biffy's, or rather the Duke of Nottingham's, ongoing picnic in Car Park One, and got very drunk. He had even met Princess Diana, who had been looking very beautiful, and very pregnant. "Far too neurotic,' Jennifer had whispered to him, covertly, nodding in the Princess's direction, decidedly squiffy by this stage. 'Just like her mother. *Always look at the mother*, Ossie,' Jennifer had counselled. 'That's what they say, you know, *look at the mother before you take on the daughter*. Although in your case, better not look too closely, eh?' and they had both roared with laughter. It had been one of the best days of his life.

He never would have imagined all those years ago, on that first disastrous meeting with Charlotte's parents, that he would ever have got on so well with them down the road. And he had. He'd been genuinely saddened when Jeremy, Charlotte's father, had died, and even now, if he was honest, he missed Jennifer's outrageous remarks and remorseless good company more than he would have ever imagined.

His first meeting with Shalom's parents, on the other hand, couldn't have been more different. It had taken place a month or so before he had managed to get Candy to agree to meeting Shalom (and what an awful day *that* had been), when Shalom had pronounced it was time she introduced him to her parents, who, she claimed, were a bit worried about her and this mysterious man she was involved with who never seemed to materialise. Although Ossie could have done without it, he admitted that it was unfair for Shalom not to be able to produce her 'boyfriend', as she referred to him, to her parents.

So he had gone along good-humouredly that night in August, wearing a casual blue linen suit and a more colourful shirt than normal, a rather deep pink that Shalom had bought him earlier that week and which Charlotte would have cringed at. He felt peculiarly uncomfortable in it. Pulling up in his Bentley outside the small terraced house on the north side of the city, Ossie had felt, as well as seen, more than one net curtain twitching at their arrival.

They had been welcomed with open arms (literally) by Bernie, Shalom's mother, who, Ossie had been alarmed to find, was clearly about the same age as he was, give or take a year or two. She was also quite large, very made up and very blonde. She wore a tight white denim skirt, a sequinned cerise top with a deep V-neck that showed off a rather disturbing amount of deeply tanned cleavage and high-heeled bright pink shoes. Her father, Dessie, had been less effusive, looking uncomfortable and slightly sweaty in a clearly unworn shiny suit and un-polished, scuffed shoes with suspiciously high heels.

Bernie had grabbed the two bottles of good red that Ossie had brought and clearly forgot about them, as they never reappeared. Dinner was lukewarm stuffed peppers and chicken Kiev – 'Marks & Spencer's best!' Bernie had proclaimed cheerily. 'I can't be expected to cook as well. After all, I'm the businessperson in this family.' It had passed easily enough, served in the lean-to kitchen extension. Bernie, Ossie learned, had her own hairdressing salon in the local village. 'Wouldn't want to be relying on him,' she nodded at Dessie, who ignored her, tucking into his food. 'He never lifts a finger. Got no ambition and never did, did you? Of course, his bad back did for him. He was doing well in Bus Éireann up until then, weren't you, love? He had a nasty incident in one of those buses, didn't you, Dessie?'

'Shower of ungrateful gobshites,' Dessie said with con-siderable feeling, coming to life suddenly. 'Give 'em a life's work and they let you go without so much as a year's salary.'

'Ahem,' Bernie cleared her throat warningly. 'Wine or beer, Ossie?' she asked brightly.

'I'll, ah, have a Heineken, thanks,' Ossie plumped quickly for beer in favour of the Spanish plonk open on the table. 'Have you been away?' Ossie enquired politely. 'You have a very good tan.' This was true, although Dessie's fleshy face looked pale and pasty.

'Dear me, no!' trilled Bernie. 'God knows I'm due a holiday, but summer's my busiest time. I just go on the sun bed every day, works a treat, although I'm planning to get away to Gran Canaria in September with the bingo club.'

Dessie took his leave immediately after dinner. 'Can't hang about, got an appointment,' he winked. 'Nice to meet you, Ossie.'

Ossie jumped to his feet. 'Yes, yes, delighted to meet you too, er, Dessie.'

'Hope our Sharon's looking after you?'

'Shalom,' Shalom interrupted. 'My name is Shalom. You know that perfectly well, Dad.'

'Yes, yes, very well, very well indeed,' Ossie smiled. 'She's a credit to you both.'

'Looks like she's taken to the high life, too. Hope you can afford her – if she's anything like her mother, only the best is good enough,' he laughed heartily before disappearing out the door.

Shalom had been livid.

'Don't mind him,' Bernie had said. 'Appointment, my arse! He's off to the pub to meet his cronies.' After an hour of listening to Bernie's incessant chatter, Ossie rather wished he could have joined him.

After that official introduction, Ossie had been relieved not to have to meet them on a regular basis. Shalom, it appeared, was more than happy to spend time alone with her mother and met up with her frequently, often popping into the hair salon for a chat. Other than birthdays and Christmases, Ossie managed to claim business appointments. 'It's just nice for them to know you, darling, and see what good care you're taking of me,' Shalom had told him. *In-laws!* Ossie thought to himself. *Who needed them?*

Then there was the other little problem. Shalom had, not very discreetly, been dropping large hints that a marriage proposal would be timely. 'We'll be a proper little family now, darling, and Mummy and Daddy are a bit old-fashioned about things like that,' she had said, more than once. 'I think they're expecting an announcement any day soon.'

For some reason, this had thrown Ossie into a dilemma, one he wisely kept to himself. He had told Shalom many times, right from the very start of their relationship, that he wouldn't be getting married again. He had done it once, and that was all there was to it. Shalom had never seemed to mind or be put out about it. 'Of course, Ossie,' she had said. 'I'm so young still, it's not something I think about, really.'

Now, she appeared to be taking a different tack. He wondered why he still felt reluctant. He was happy, wasn't he? He was delighted to be having another baby after all this time – why shouldn't he take the plunge? But something, he was never quite sure what, just didn't feel right about it. There was a stubborn little voice that told him he didn't want to be pushed into anything. If – and it was a very big if – Ossie wanted to get married again, only he would decide when. All the same, it was there, like an undercurrent between them now, and Ossie knew Shalom expected a wedding – sooner rather than later.

He wouldn't think about it now. His darling daughter was spending her first proper weekend with them. He would concentrate on making it as pleasant and as much fun as possible.

He was on the Green now and pulled up outside the Shelbourne Hotel. Luckily there was a space right in front, just behind the taxi rank. He turned off the engine and waited, as Candy had told him to, in the car. He checked his watch: six-thirty on the dot, but there didn't seem to be any sign of Candy. The only person he could see was a bleached blonde girl, her curled ringlets trailing down from underneath a beaded cap, wearing tight jeans tucked into ridiculously high platform boots, talking intently into her mobile phone. She looked like a plainer version of Agnetha, from Abba fame, in her Waterloo outfit. Suddenly she began walking towards the car. For a moment he wondered if she was a young hooker and was about to wave her away, when unthinkably she opened the car door and – it couldn't *possibly* be! Surely *not*! But the voice, at least, was unmistakeable.

'Hi, Daddy!' She laughed at the look of disbelief on his face. 'What do you think of my new hairdo?'

Shalom parked her white convertible 911 Porsche Carrera and went into Bernie's hair salon. She was greeted with equal looks of awe and envy by the stylists and various clients, who had either clocked her car or recognised her from various celebrity society photos. She sat down in a vacant chair in the waiting area until Bernie had seen a client off and got one of the juniors to man the reception desk, then made a great fuss of ushering her daughter into the back staff room.

'Hello, love,' she kissed her. 'What a lovely surprise, wasn't expecting you today. Tea or coffee?

'Tea, and a muffin, if you have any.'

'Only these chocolate biscuits, pet, will they do?'

'Great.' Shalom took the cup of tea Bernie poured.

'How's our little baba?' She patted Shalom's burgeoning bump. 'Getting bigger every day.' Privately, Bernie noted, that wasn't the only thing getting bigger. Shalom's already enhanced breasts had become alarmingly large, and together with her five-month bump were beginning to form a rather solid-looking land mass. The floaty smock top she was wearing over her jeans did nothing to conceal it. Her arms, too, were losing their slenderness and she was developing a distinct double chin. Bernie wondered if she should comment and decided against it. She was bound to put on a bit of weight during the pregnancy, but still, she'd have to watch it . . .

'Didn't you have any lunch, pet?' She asked brightly as her daughter mindlessly reached for her third biscuit in as many minutes.

'Not really. I didn't feel like food. I just had a Danish or two. The baby seems to like them.'

'Well you put your feet up there and have a little rest. How's Ossie? I hope he's spoiling my girl rotten?'

'It's not Ossie that's the problem,' Shalom scowled. 'The daughter's arriving today to stay for the weekend. I told him I wasn't up to it, not in my condition, but he wasn't having any of it. Said he was picking her up and we'd all have great fun together.'

'The daughter!' Bernie's mouth settled in a grim line of disapproval. 'I thought he wasn't talking to her. Proper order too, after that disgraceful outburst of hers.' Memories of the offending newspaper coverage came flooding back, when more than one client, not to mention the staff, had been found sniggering over the pictures. 'I don't know how he can allow her in the house. Did she even apologise to you?'

'Are you joking? All she had to do was pick up the phone to him and he was ecstatic. He's playing straight into the little madam's hands. I can't believe it.' Shalom's lip wobbled petulantly.

Bernie stirred her tea and thought quickly. No point in fanning an already incendiary state of affairs, not when they'd come this far. 'Look, it's you he's with, pet, not her. So what if she has to visit the odd time? She's what, twenty?'

'Going on six.'

'Whatever. Maybe she's had a change of heart. Just be nice to her. Forget all about the other horrid business and offer to give her a make-up lesson. God knows she could do with one if those pictures were anything to go by. She'll love that. If it all gets too much, just say you're not feeling well and go to bed. In a few months he'll have forgotten she exists, he'll be so besotted with *your* baby.'

'I hope you're right,' Shalom said darkly.

'Course I am, pet,' Bernie said chirpily. 'When have I ever been wrong about Ossie? I know what a man like that wants, and he's got it in you. Then, when the baby arrives, maybe a bit before it even, I'll come and stay to help out. He or she is going to want Nana Bernie there!'

'Oh, would you, Mum?' Shalom brightened. 'I hadn't thought of that. It would be great. And there's loads of room in our house – I even get lost in it still,' she giggled. 'Although of course there'll be nannies and things, even though we've got loads of staff already. Ossie's determined I'm not to have too much to do – I couldn't cope on my own, you know.'

'Of course you couldn't. Who'd expect you to?' Bernie was indignant. 'But all those foreigners must be annoying, under your feet all the time, and nobody knows how to make your favourite smoothies like I do, do they?'

Shalom shook her head and smiled ruefully. 'I do miss our little chats, Mum.'

'So do I, pet, but like I said, I'll make sure I'm there to help out, and your father can manage perfectly well here on his own. If not, he can get up off his arse and make himself useful for once in his life. He could help out in the garden or do a bit of driving for Ossie – he'd probably even put him on the payroll, wouldn't he?' Bernie's eye's lit up.

'Maybe.' Shalom wasn't so sure about that.

'Anyway, if Ossie's moving family members in on a weekend, it's only right you should have yours around you now and again for a bit of moral support – that's all there is to it.'

'Oh, Mum,' Shalom smiled gratefully. 'I don't know what I'd do without you.'

'Hopefully, pet, you won't ever have to. Another biscuit? Oh dear, they're all gone. Never mind.'

'What do you think?' Candy did a twirl in her matching underwear, a new lacy thong with a cute little diamante decoration at the back and a black and red push-up padded bra. Her skin was a deep tan and her nails and toes had been manicured and painted a deep rouge noir.

'Wow, you look amazing. You've really lost weight since you've been going to that personal trainer,' Emma said.

'The spray tan makes all the difference, Shalom says. And you only have to have it done once a week to keep it up.'

'Your hair is just wicked. It makes you look really sophisticated, *much* older.' Katy was in awe.

'Are you sure you don't want her to do your make-up too? She said she would.'

'Um, no thanks, we'll just watch if that's okay?'

'Whatever – she's just getting all her gear together now.' Candy pulled on a short satin wrap and tied her hair back in a ponytail.

The weekend was going well. On Friday, they had gone out to dinner in the posh new Ritz-Carlton Hotel, and Candy had been chatty and pleasant, asking all about the baby and telling Shalom that she was so excited and couldn't wait to have a brother or sister.

'It was just a bit of a shock that night,' she ventured, smiling sheepishly at her dad. 'I overreacted a bit, I'm afraid.'

'That's all water under the bridge, isn't it Shalom?' Ossie had looked meaningfully at her. 'Shalom and I are just delighted you've decided to spend a bit of time with us, Princess – aren't we, Shalom?'

'Delighted,' murmured Shalom, taking a sip of water. She couldn't take her eyes off Candy's hair, which was rather spookily like her own.

'If it's all right with you, Daddy,' Candy continued, 'I thought

I might go shopping tomorrow. I need some new gear to go with my new look. I was wondering, Shalom, if you'd come along and help me choose some stuff. If we went in the morning, Daddy, you could meet us for lunch?'

'I think that's a great idea, don't you, Shalom?'

'Er, yes. Yes, of course.'

'Great,' Candy beamed. 'Then, if you don't mind, I thought Katy and Emma might come around about four o'clock. I'm going out with them to a party and I told them it would be fine if they came around and we could all get ready together, then you and Shalom can have a nice evening to yourselves.'

'Of course they can,' Ossie said. 'I'll make sure Eddie is available to drive you. Just let me know what time you want to leave and he'll drop everyone home after as well. You must promise me, Prin— I mean, Candy – that's the only condition. I won't have you taking any lifts from anyone, not even your friends – it's too much of a risk. And there's no guarantee you'll get a taxi if you're late.'

'Of course not, Daddy, you have my word.'

'I'm starting with a slightly warmer base, girls, because of Candy's new hair colour, and of course because it's a night-time look as opposed to daytime.' The girls watched intently as Shalom got to work. 'Now I'm mixing a bit of bronzing cream with the foundation on my hand, see? That's a good tip.' Another layer of bronzing powder was whisked over Candy's face and then some more 'contouring' under her cheekbones and 'shading' for the sides of her nose. 'Now a bit of blusher. I think we'll go for quite a dramatic look, and some highlighter on the cheekbones and just under her brows, see?'

They were riveted.

'Now, smoky eyes, I think.' She began wielding a dark navy shadow over Candy's lid and in the socket, and with a kohl liner pencil began outlining and emphasising her eyes, followed by three coats of mascara over a few added false lashes. She then applied a spice lip-liner and lipstick, which managed to change the shape of Candy's mouth completely, followed by a heavy gloss, which completed the look. Shalom stood back to admire her handiwork. 'Okay, take down your hair, Candy, and have a look. What do you think, girls?'

Transformation was too small a word.

'Unbelievable,' said Katy.

'Awesome.' Emma shook her head.

'Perfect,' said Candy.

Half an hour later, they were ready. They popped their heads around the door into the vast television room with the giant screen where Ossie and Shalom were watching a movie. 'Bye, Daddy, bye Shalom. See you later – don't wait up!'

'Bye Mr Searson, bye Shalom,' said Katy and Emma. 'Thanks so much for letting us get ready here.'

'Not at all, girls,' said Ossie, looking a bit shell-shocked. 'Have a great time.'

He was having trouble taking in the very made-up young woman in the tight top revealing the top of a very obvious bra and the very short skirt, who sounded like his daughter but looked decidedly different. Beside her fresh-faced friends, she looked much older.

'Bye, girls, have a great night,' Shalom smiled at them.

As the front door closed behind them, Shalom snuggled down beside Ossie on the sofa. 'She looks great, doesn't she?'

'Yes, it's just a bit of a shock, that's all.' Ossie struggled with unfamiliar feelings. 'She looked a lot . . . older.' He sounded worried.

'Darling, she is almost twenty-one. All girls her age have to experiment with different looks. Anyway, it's what she wanted. You have to let her grow up sometime, you know. At her age, I was really into my make-up too.'

'But the other two looked just the same as ever, just . . . prettier.' He sounded miserable.

'Katy said her mother would kill her and Emma said she was allergic and had to stick to her regular make-up. Candy's lucky to be able to have someone like me to show her how to work a look.'

'I'm sure you're right.' Then a thought struck him. 'Of course, it's obvious what she's doing,' he grinned. 'She's imitating *you*. She's obviously impressed with how glamorous you are.'

'I'll take that as a compliment.'

'I imagine it's just a phase,' Ossie reassured himself.

'What's that supposed to mean? You like the way I look, don't you?'

'Of course I do. I just think . . .'

'What?' A sharp note had entered Shalom's tone.

'It was just a bit of a shock, that's all.' Ossie wisely decided to say no more on the subject.

'I think it's a real improvement,' Shalom proclaimed. 'She looks hip and funky now, just like a girl her age should. You don't want her dressing like Charlotte, do you? That's not what men like, boys neither, and that's what it's all about at Candy's age. They'll be queuing up for her now.'

Ossie felt a twinge of worry, and something else, something he couldn't quite articulate. All he knew was his fresh, freckle-faced, silky-haired daughter had somehow morphed into a stranger – a very tarty-looking stranger. He couldn't deny anything Shalom had said; it made sense, in a way. She was probably right. He was just having a hard time seeing Candy grow up. It was just that he'd never imagined her growing up quite like *that*.

9

Dominic's was buzzing with every table in the house already claimed or waiting for the few remaining diners to be seated. Alex checked with the desk and was told his lunch guest was waiting in the Chameleon Bar, as instructed, and had arrived about fifteen minutes ago. Although Alex was absolutely punctual (it didn't do to appear *too* eager), he had correctly guessed that Frank Casey, one of the managers of Eurocorp, would be there well ahead of him. He had kept tabs on his career since their schooldays, when diligent, plodding Frank, not a star on the rugby field, or indeed any sport, had devoted himself to his studies and obtained a good degree in commerce and economics from University College Dublin, and through sheer determination and application had carved out a surprisingly successful, if uninteresting, path in finance and now held quite a covetable position with one of the substantial European banks that had set up shop in Dublin during the past ten years. A country boy at heart, Alex deduced that Frank would be suitably impressed and, with a bit of luck, distracted by the glamorous surroundings of the hip restaurant. As far as he could remember, lunch for Frank usually consisted of a sandwich at his desk, even when his position and indeed salary could have afforded him a prominent table at any restaurant of his choice.

Alex checked his watch – two minutes to one exactly. Perfect. He had been lucky to find a parking space almost right outside the restaurant and had carefully manoeuvred his precious red Ferrari into it, enjoying, as always, the envious and admiring glances it attracted. That car meant a lot to him, not just because of its brand name, but because of everything it represented, everything that Alex had fought and struggled for. It almost, but not quite, made up for all those other, awful years . . .

Lately, Catherine, his wife, had been suggesting he change it for something more suitable for a young couple expecting their first child. She was right, of course, they did need something more suitable, so he had surprised her and traded in the baby Mercedes he had bought her for her last birthday for a Range Rover Sport. 'Plenty of room for all of us now,' he'd proclaimed, delighted at his creative solution to the problem.

'Oh my God, Alex,' she had gasped, astonished as he led her to the front door and told her to close her eyes. 'It's gorgeous, but are you sure? I mean, can we really afford it? It seems a bit excessive, that *and* your Ferrari.'

'Of course I can afford it.' He had been rather annoyed at the question. 'The company's doing brilliantly. Anyway, in my line of business, it's important to keep up a high profile. People are hardly going to trust me with their investments unless I look like I'm doing well myself, are they? Particularly since I'm the same age as a lot of their kids.'

P.J.'s reaction to his car had been rather different that day last year when he had called around in the brand-new Ferrari to his father's house in Wellington Square on the pretext of picking up some post for his sister, Bella, who he was seeing the following in week in Florence, where she was studying.

'Hi, Dad,' he had said, moving past him into the hall and perusing the tray of mail that sat on the hall table. 'What do you think of my new set of wheels?' He nodded towards the gleaming red machine that sat in the driveway beside P.J.'s ten-year-old Jeep.

'I dread to think what that does to the gallon.' He shook his head. 'Ten? Eleven, maybe?'

'That's not why anyone buys a Ferrari,' Alex had snapped, irritated that P.J. had actually been spot on at eleven miles to the gallon.

'No, I shouldn't imagine it is. Well it's very nice, very . . .'

'Obvious?' Alex's mouth tightened. 'You think it's flash, don't you? Why don't you just come right out and say it?'

'Because I wasn't going to,' P.J. replied lightly. 'Actually, I was going to wish you all the best with it, happy driving and all that, if you'd care to give me the opportunity.'

Just then, Sheila had come up to see what the commotion was about. 'Jesus, Mary and Joseph, what's that?'

'It's my new car, Sheila.'

'It looks like a spaceship.'

'Come on, I'll take you for a spin,' Alex said, deliberately excluding P.J. from the invitation.

Sheila looked anxiously at her watch. 'I'd love to, really I would, but I've only just started cleaning the oven – the stuff has to be left on for fifteen minutes exactly.'

'I'll have you back in ten.'

'Just let me get my gloves, I wouldn't want to catch anything.'

Minutes later, Sheila and he were cutting quite a dash, swishing out of the square and onto the main road, Sheila clutching tightly onto the passenger handle. 'How do you stand the noise of it?' she shouted as the engine roared into life.

'It's part of the attraction,' Alex grinned. 'Sort of like your hoover. It's meant to sound like that.'

'Oh, right.'

Alex had a soft spot for Sheila, despite her idiosyncrasies. He identified with her driven sense for orderliness, and even as an awkward teenager had appreciated the rigorous predictability her presence had brought to their home. At least with Sheila, you knew that if it was Monday, it would be shepherd's pie for dinner, that Wednesday was laundry day or that on Thursday afternoon there would always be freshly baked scones on offer. Alex had liked that. He liked the reassurance of that comforting, methodical presence in a household and indeed life which for him had become unwieldy and unpredictable.

Plucked from his safe, familiar American schooling and surroundings at thirteen, Alex had been deeply suspicious and later resentful of the unexpected move back to Ireland. Deposited in his father's (and indeed grandfather's) alma mater, Blackrock College, Alex was to learn that an awful lot was expected of him – a lot, he quickly discovered, that he couldn't deliver. For starters, he loathed rugby, a veritable religion at the school. 'Another O'Sullivan,' the form priest had boomed with delight on his first day, as Alex had sat conspicuously at the front of the classroom, where the only free desk was left (Jilly had been late getting him off and had then lost her way, making him later still). 'Excellent! Remember your father and grandfather well, played for Ireland,' he informed the rest of the year, who were sizing Alex up with interest. This was only half right. His grandfather had indeed played rugby for Ireland, whereas P.J., although he had captained the school team and had been a noted star, had turned up for the Leinster trials still drunk from the previous night and had been sent off in disgrace, to much hilarity. It was a story he (and his friends) still told with relish, although Alex wanted to scream every time he heard it. 'No doubt you'll be carrying on the family tradition,' the priest continued. 'We'll be expecting great things from you, O'Sullivan.'

The great things had never materialised, at least not on the rugby field, and Alex had even given up competing in tennis, which he'd been good at. Seizing on his inability to fit in, the other boys had quickly started teasing him about his Texan accent, his apparent studiousness and his small, skinny frame. He was quickly christened the Milky Bar Kid from the TV spots about the goody-goody child cowboy who distributed the white chocolate bars, and from then on, life, as far as Alex was concerned, became miserable. It wasn't that he was bullied as such, but he was definitely not one of the crowd. He didn't understand their accents, their humour or their blinding obsession with rugby. For the first time in his life, Alex couldn't play by the rules and refused to try to learn these new, confusing ones. Instead he threw himself into studies, which he excelled at, and kept pretty much to himself.

Jilly asked him occasionally if he'd like to invite some friends around from school, but he always made an excuse. Instead, he made friends with a couple of kids down the road and a French boy whose father was a diplomat and who seemed to find these Irish boys as perplexing as Alex did. He never divulged his misery to his father. He already felt like too much of a failure, but admitting it to his outgoing, multi-talented, popular father would have been the ultimate defeat. Instead, he shored up his misery, gritted his teeth and vowed that one day he would show them all.

And the day did come. His qualifications were first-rate and he was considered to be a financial whizz-kid. In Catherine, he had married an exceptionally pretty, clever girl, also with a background in finance, and last year he had bought his Ferrari. There was something about it that had just been the icing on the cake. Alex was quite good-looking, tall and thin with reasonably broad shoulders, dark hair and eyes and pale skin. Girls had never been a problem. It was other men who never seemed to rate him. But pulling up in a Ferrari changed all that that and made up for all the years he had spent feeling painfully inadequate. Soon he would have his first son or daughter. He was excited and proud of that, and no matter what happened, he or she was going to have the perfect father. He would make sure of it.

'Frank!' he greeted his old school friend heartily. 'Great to see you. Let's go straight to our table. Hope I didn't keep you waiting? Just had to park the Ferrari.'

'Ferrari?' Frank's eye's opened wide. 'Crikey, business must be good then.' They sat down at their table and Alex ordered drinks. 'Couldn't be better, actually, things are going really well. In fact, that's what I wanted to talk to you about.'

'Oh yes?'

'The new development, the one in Sheffield – I might need your guys to up the investment just a tad,' he smiled reassuringly. 'Absolutely nothing to worry about, just a few punters taking longer than usual to get their acts together – you know what you bankers are like!' he laughed easily.

'How much?' Frank wasn't laughing quite so easily.

'About ten per cent.'

'Hmm,' Frank was reticent, although the very pretty waitress who came to take their order had got his attention. 'I'll have a word, Alex, that's all I can say. Things are tight at the moment. It's the same for all of us.'

'Of course.' Alex quickly ordered the day's special. 'But this one's a sure win. You'll be sorry if you get left behind.'

'Like I said, I'll have a word.'

The rest of lunch passed in discussions of shares, portfolios and interest rates. Alex was hard pushed to remember when he had been more bored. Bankers were all the same – they lacked any vision or imagination, always wanted a safe bet. But that wasn't the way you made big money. You had to stick your head above the parapet and take the bullets when they came, and when you managed to avoid them, reap the rewards of your timing.

'Thanks for lunch, Alex.' Frank sat back while Alex signed the bill. 'I've been wanting to come to this place for ages, I've heard a lot about it. Best food I've had in a long time.'

'You're welcome, Frank, good to see you. Remember to let

me know by next week, will you? Otherwise I'll have to approach some of my other clients – they're queuing up.'

'I'll be in touch.'

They went their separate ways, Alex's stomach churning in a most unusual manner, which had absolutely nothing to do with the lunch he had just consumed.

Dom felt vile. It had started at about ten o'clock that morning, when his eyes began to sting and his throat felt ominously scratchy. By four o'clock he had a throbbing head and his limbs felt like lead. He was also beginning to perspire profusely. It was Friday, and as always there would be a full house, but by four-thirty he knew it was a losing battle. He was rarely sick, and on the few occasions he succumbed to the odd cold, he usually managed to fight it off or at least weather it, but this was something more sinister. There was a particularly nasty flu virus doing the rounds and it had clearly decided to seek out his company. So weary and weak he could hardly walk, he gave in and went up to his apartment above Dominic's and collapsed into bed, reminding himself to ring Tanya and apologise for cancelling the late dinner date they had arranged at her place. Once a month, Dom allowed himself a Friday night off, and although he would be in the restaurant to greet clients, he would leave at about nine or nine-thirty, when one of the many other capable members of staff would be in left in charge. This evening, Astrid had briskly stepped into his place and happily agreed to begin her duties earlier than previously arranged, ordering him straight to bed and saying she would have Rollo have his special-recipe chicken soup sent up, which everybody knew had enormously cura-tive properties, due in no small part, Dom had heard on the grapevine, to rather generous amounts of some magic ingredient that was bracingly alcoholic. Dom had declined the offer, saying the thought of any kind of food made him feel infinitely worse. Agreeing to notify the kitchen if he had the slightest requirement, he had made his escape. Now he just had to give the bad news to Tanya.

She was going to keep the whole thing very low key, simple, not in any way premeditated, as if the idea had just popped into her head. They often had a late-night supper at her place, so there would be nothing unusual in that. She made sure she was looking her best, but that was a pretty much constant discipline anyhow. She had thought about setting up the whole romantic dinner thing. Although she would be far too nervous to cook, she could have ordered something gorgeous from many of the designer grocery stores that catered to the thousands of young, busy people like herself, leading demanding, executive lifestyles. And then she reminded herself – tonight was about Dom, not her, and he liked nothing better than a takeaway from their favourite Indonesian restaurant. That was the easy bit. Rehearsing what to say and, more importantly, how and when to say it was proving to be a minefield. If she overdid it, she would appear at best silly, at worst desperate. If she was too light-hearted, he might think she was joking and then the moment might be lost for ever. Her mind was spinning with various scenarios, so much so that she was brought back to earth with a bump when she realised that she had just chewed through the nail of her little finger, painted a delicate frosted caramel. She cursed rather vehemently, which was most unlike her. Really, she would have to pull herself together.

Just then, her phone rang. She almost didn't pick up. She really wasn't in the mood for chatting to anyone, especially her mother, whom she hadn't confided in, although she knew she would have endorsed and heartily encouraged Tanya's choice of action. For some reason, she preferred to keep the whole idea to herself. The only thing that needed to be broadcast was the result itself. The manner in which it would have been achieved would remain her and Dom's little secret.

She checked the number that flashed on her screen. Oh God, it was Dom. Please, oh please, she thought, don't let him be cancelling – not tonight of all nights.

'Hi sweetie, how are you?' She answered the call in her brightest voice.

'Awful,' he croaked. 'That's why I'm ringing. Tanya, I'm sorry, but I really can't make it this evening, I've got this awful flu that's going around and I can barely stay upright. I'm afraid I wouldn't be much use to you, never mind any company.' He broke off as a fit of coughing took hold of him.

'You poor, poor darling, you do sound dreadful. Don't move, I'm coming right over.'

'No, really,' he wheezed, 'there's no need. You've no idea, this thing's a real bugger. I'd hate for you to get it, and, like I said,' another fit of coughing began, 'I'm really feeling pretty vile. I'm just going to crash out.'

'Nonsense,' Tanya said crisply. *Don't panic*, she told herself, *do* not *panic*. She searched for exactly the right blend of sympathy and matronly firmness. 'You can't possibly be on your own when you sound like that. I'm coming straight over. What would happen if you collapsed or couldn't breathe or something? I'll sleep in the spare room even, but Dom, sweetie, I wouldn't have a minute's peace of mind here knowing you were lying there that sick and weak. Don't worry about a thing. I'm on my way.'

She clicked off her phone.

Even if Dom had had the strength, which he didn't, he wasn't given a chance to dissuade her.

Damn it anyway, she thought. What was it her assistant had said to her that morning? Something about Mercury being retrograde, upsetting the best-laid plans and all that. Tanya wasn't superstitious – she was on a mission, and it would take more than an uncooperative planet to get in her way. She felt in her jeans pocket and reached for the little piece of paper she had been carrying around all week. *Who makes it happen?* It read. *I make it happen.* And she would. She couldn't afford not to.

Astrid was happy and refreshed after her weekend with Rollo in Vienna. They'd had a wonderful time visiting her home and meeting her parents, who had approved of him greatly. Now, at the end of her first week back, she was happy to take on the extra Friday night shift as front of house and even happier that Tanya was nowhere in evidence, poking her nose in where it wasn't wanted and breathing down everyone's necks. Astrid had informed Rollo of Dom's sudden illness and, as she knew he would, he insisted on whipping up his famous chicken soup, even though Dom had shuddered at the thought of eating anything. She would just go and check on things in the kitchen and make sure everything was going according to plan.

Dom lay in bed feeling sicker by the minute. His head ached, his limbs ached and now he was in the grip of escalating waves of nausea. He *really* didn't want to see anybody. He had dosed himself with Paracetamol and only wanted the blessed oblivion of sleep. He was just about to drop off when he heard Tanya's key in the door. The sound of it suddenly irritated him profoundly. Although he had pushed the thought to the back of his mind (he had so much else to deal with, after all), he'd lately been regretting giving her a key so easily. Normally he was reticent about such things, but it had made sense at the time, especially when Tanya had been overseeing the decoration and organisation of his flat. She'd been quite adamant about it, actually, and he had to admit he would never have got around to it without her. It was just that lately she'd taken to popping in and out at any time of the day, or indeed night, that suited her, and now he wasn't sure it had been such a good idea. That was the trouble, Dom reflected, just as his teachers always told him at school – he never really thought things through or considered the implications. Much as he hated to admit it, Dom now felt he would rather have his key back, but he was in no condition to have that particular conversation now.

'Only me, sweetie,' she called from the hallway.

God, his head ached. Even his ears hurt, which was ridiculous, and the *click clack* of Tanya's heels on the wooden floor and the scratching of her overnight wheelie case seemed to penetrate every hair of his head. When she came in, he tried to smile weakly. He knew she meant well, but . . .

'Poor darling,' she cooed, sitting down on the edge of the bed beside him, 'you really do look rough.' She smoothed his hair back from his damp forehead. 'I'm just going to get settled and then I'll come and take your temperature. You're burning up, you poor pet.' She smiled determinedly. 'Then I'll decide whether or not we need to call the doctor.'

'No. No doctor,' it was a croak, but Dom's scowl was unusually bad-tempered, Tanya thought. 'If I'm not feeling better tomorrow, maybe. Please, Tanya, I just want to be left in peace.'

'Well, all right. I suppose you've every right to feel grumpy, Mr Bear Head. But we'll see what the thermometer says anyhow.'

One hundred and three degrees, said the thermometer.

'That's it, I'm calling the doctor.'

'Tanya, I couldn't stand it. Look, it's just the flu,' Dom muttered. 'Tomorrow, if I'm not better, then . . .'

'You really are being awfully silly – and stubborn,' she frowned. Then she had a brilliant idea. 'Don't worry, darling, I'm just popping downstairs for a moment, there's something I have to check on.'

It was Friday night and the chances of getting a doctor were zero to none – not for hours, anyway – but she was almost sure she had noted a booking for tonight in the name of P.J. O'Sullivan, for a party of four. He was the famous doctor and a regular at Dominic's, knew Dom's parents too. With any luck, he'd be in the restaurant now. She was pretty sure the booking had been for eight-thirty. It would be the perfect opportunity.

Dinner had been Catherine's idea. She had mentioned it to P.J. when she called him on the phone to check how he was doing, as she and Alex hadn't seen him in a while.

'Great idea,' he had proclaimed. 'Let's do it this Friday, I'll book Dominic's. Does eight-thirty suit?'

'Perfect.'

'And I'll bring Sheila, if that's all right? If she doesn't have a hot date, that is,' he chuckled.

'What could be a hotter date than dinner with you, P.J.?'

'My son is a very lucky man, Catherine.'

'And I'm a very fortunate daughter-in-law,' Catherine smiled down the phone.

'How is Alex, by the way?' P.J. enquired. 'He wasn't in great form last time I had lunch with him.'

'Oh, he's fine. A bit stressed with this deal and so on, but he'll enjoy a night out. It'll do him good. He's been working too hard lately.'

'Good. Well, I'll look forward to seeing you both.'

'See you Friday then.'

P.J. put the phone down thoughtfully. No wonder Alex was stressed, as Catherine had put it. The property market was in free fall and the banks were clamping down. It certainly wasn't a good time to be a developer, and that luxury hotel, spa and golf complex that Alex was putting together didn't appear to be moving ahead as it should. Not that he was an expert in the property business, but P.J. heard a lot through his patients, and a lot of them who were in property were having to tighten their belts considerably, and they were the big guys. As for the others, a lot of them were folding under the pressure. He just hoped Alex wouldn't be one of them.

He sighed. He had tried to advise him, but Alex would never listen to him, always took offence. It was almost as if he was waging some personal battle between them, determined he would win – that he would somehow 'show' P.J., when all P.J. had ever wanted for him was that he be happy. He had a lovely, pretty, clever wife and a new baby on the way. He had everything any young man could possibly want, didn't he? Yet Alex always seemed to be dissatisfied, resentful in some way. Still, P.J. thought, looking on the bright side, at least he hadn't invested anything in Alex's latest scheme. Things weren't looking too good on that front.

'Why the bloody hell Dominic's?' Alex had stormed, flinging off his coat as he came in on Wednesday evening and going into the kitchen to pour himself a drink.

'What's the matter with you?' Catherine had asked. 'Why *not* Dominic's? We always go there. You love the place, we all do – it's the best restaurant in Dublin.'

'I'm sick of it, that's why. And I don't particularly want to go out on Friday. I've been working my ass off, it's been a bitch of a week and if anybody had bothered to ask, I was looking forward to spending a quiet night in with my wife.'

'Well it's all arranged now. Your father's booked a table, and,' she continued firmly, despite the thunderous expression her husband was wearing, '*I* would like to go out on Friday. We haven't been out for ages, Alex, and I'm tired of being cooped up in the house here waiting for Junior to arrive. You're out there meeting people, having lunch wherever you please. I haven't been to Dominic's in ages.' There was an unusual edge to her voice. 'It'll be fun.'

Alex sighed. 'Sorry, babe, I didn't mean to have a go at you.

I'm just tired, that's all. And I really don't fancy a night out with Dad throwing his weight around, doing his utmost to hold court in any restaurant. But if that's what you want, I'll be on my best behaviour. I wish it was just you and me, that's all.' He came over and put his arms around her.

'It'll do us good to get out, and it'll be good for your dad too. Oh, he's bringing Sheila.'

'Is he? Oh good,' Alex brightened. 'If she's at the table, then even Dad will be upstaged.'

Catherine laughed, but she was really very worried. Alex was becoming even more touchy than usual, snapping and taking imaginary offence at the slightest thing, although he was always immediately remorseful afterwards. She also knew he wasn't sleeping. She was awake herself at night a lot with the baby, both of them tossing and turning, and more than once she had awoken to find Alex's side of the bed empty and, calling softly to him, had found him downstairs, poring over figures in his office, or worse, the time she had found him with his head in his hands, a large brandy beside him.

He had always been rather highly-strung and sensitive, but he was clearly terribly stressed. She hoped it was just about the baby's fairly imminent arrival. Alex was such a perfectionist, he would want every eventuality planned down to the most minute detail for his new son or daughter, preferably for the next twenty-one years. But life wasn't like that, Catherine knew. You couldn't plan or protect people – even your own family – no matter how much you wanted to.

All the same, they needed to sit down and have a good talk about it all – and Alex's development scheme. He had been unusually evasive about it when she had asked him lately, saying everything was just fine, though the banks were being a bit of a pain, but investors were queuing up. As an accountant, and a good one, Catherine had a good grip on such matters. It was just that with Junior's arrival growing ever closer, figures, except her own expanding one, were far from her mind. And when she did try to make sense of them, they didn't add up at all.

Alex sat down beside Catherine, determined to relax and to try to chat and vaguely follow the plastic-surgery programme she was watching with interest. It seemed to him almost as surreal and grotesque as his week was proving thus far – and it was only Wednesday. Why Dominic's of all places, and this Friday? Of all the bad luck. He would rather die than be seen in there and have to smile and meet and greet that arrogant twit Dom as if nothing had happened. And it wasn't as if he could explain to Catherine, tell her what had transpired, not with the baby nearly due, and certainly not with all the other, far more worrying scenarios that could follow . . . it didn't bear thinking about.

He'd thought it was such a brilliant idea – and it was. More importantly, so did the banks – it was what had sold them on the Royal Alexander Golf and Health Resort. The deciding 'hook' was that he would get Dominic's to open a second restaurant there. It was already proving a crowd-puller in Dublin and it was widely tipped to win a Michelin star any day now.

So he'd approached Dom. He knew him vaguely; their families lived on the same square – their parents would have been contemporaries and Dublin was such a small place anyway, socially speaking. He had asked him to meet him for a drink, said he had something he wanted to seek his opinion on. Dom had agreed, as he knew he would, and Alex had suggested meeting in the Royal Dublin Society, where he was a member. *That should impress him*, Alex thought. Those posh Glenstal Abbey boys loved going to all of their various clubs. And Dom had been there on the dot of six-thirty as arranged, looking casual and effortlessly elegant beside Alex's very carefully thought out and rather stiff outfit. Alex had ordered drinks, and then, barely able to contain his enthusiasm, had set out his proposition to Dom, who listened carefully while Alex spread the proposed plans for the resort on the table in front of them.

'One hundred and twenty acres, just forty minutes from Dublin,' Alex was explaining. 'Hotel, golf course and spa – it's going to be world-class, the best in the country. It would be a fabulous chance for you to expand, wonderful for your brand.'

'Expand?' Dom had looked at him quizzically. 'How exactly do you mean?'

'Another Dominic's, of course.'

'Sorry, Alex, let me stop you right there.' Dom had been startlingly deliberate. 'I assumed you were interested in some sort of restaurant or catering facility, naturally, but another Dominic's is out of the question. Dominic's is a one-off. There's no question of me lending my name to anything else. It would dilute the brand, not bolster it. I'm not interested in a chain or any kind of expansion, as you put it. I'll happily advise you, or indeed explore the option of setting up something different, but I'm afraid Dominic's is off the board.' He had finished his drink and thrown Alex a charmingly regretful smile. 'I'm sure you'll have any number of celebrity chefs taking your hand off for the chance to open with you. If I can be of any help whatsoever, I will be. Let me know. Now I must rush, restaurants don't run themselves.' And he had left – just like that – leaving a seething Alex in his wake.

Arrogant prick! He might have known, Alex ranted to himself. Thought he and his bloody restaurant were too good for him. What had he said? *Diluting the brand.* What a joke. Dom was nothing more than a spoiled rich kid. What the hell would he know about brands? That had been yesterday, and Alex didn't know how he was going to break the news to his investors, or the banks. Sod Dom, he didn't need him or his stupid restaurant. There were, as Dom had pointed out, plenty of celebrity chefs who would jump at the chance to open a restaurant in the resort. Except it wasn't any number he had wanted, it was Dominic's.

And now he had to go into the blasted restaurant with his father, of all people, and act as if he was having a good time, when he'd rather starve than be seen in the place.

Tanya made her way downstairs and into Dominic's. She had a quick word with Astrid, who was on the desk and looked none too pleased to see her, and walked discreetly towards the table where P.J. and his group were sitting. The clientele that night, she noted, could have been her own handpicked selection of Dublin's crème de la crème. To her right, the Tánaiste was dining with her husband while to the left was a large table of businessmen headed by Dublin's best-known financier. In the corner, two members of Viper, looking unusually groomed and spruced up, were dining with their respective wives. Approaching P.J.'s table, she quickly appraised his fellow diners. There was his son, Alex, and a very pretty pregnant woman, obviously his wife. P.J. was there, of course, and a very strange woman sitting beside him. She could have been anywhere between forty and sixty and was wearing a charcoal-grey dress with a collar buttoned right up to her chin. Around her neck was a set of rosary beads that she fingered regularly, and her face was completely devoid of make-up. She glared at Tanya as she approached, almost stopping her in her tracks. And was that . . .? Surely not, but yes, she appeared to be wearing plastic surgical gloves. Perhaps she had some strange skin condition. She sat bolt upright in her chair and was eyeing the cutlery suspiciously. Tanya quickly approached P.J. from his other side and bent down to whisper in his ear. Luckily they were between courses.

'What's that?' he listened. 'Of course, right away.' He stood up to follow her.

'I'm so sorry,' she smiled apologetically at the surprised

faces, 'we have a little emergency, and it's so fortunate to see we have a doctor in the house. I won't take him away for long, I promise.'

'I really do appreciate this, Dr O'Sullivan. The wine and any drinks you've had will be on the house, naturally.'

'Not at all,' said P.J. as he followed her out and up the stairs to Dom's apartment. 'I wouldn't hear of it. You're quite right to come and get me. One can never take any chances. I'm delighted to help.'

'Dom, sweetie,' Tanya called to the covered shape in the bed of the master bedroom, 'there's someone here to see you. I'll wait outside, of course,' she murmured to P.J. 'The bathroom's just there if you need to wash your hands.' And she discreetly closed the door behind her.

'Dr O'Sullivan!' Dom croaked. 'What on earth?'

'A happy coincidence, Dom. I was having dinner downstairs, and please, call me P.J. I hear you're a bit under the weather?'

'No, I'm fine, really. It's just this flu that's going around.' He struggled to sit up.

P.J. washed his hands briskly and returned with the medical bag he had retrieved from the car on the way up.

'Well, let's just have a look at you old chap. Never hurts, you know.'

Fifteen minutes later, P.J. emerged and found Tanya waiting in the sitting room.

'How is he? I was so worried.'

'He'll live,' P.J. grinned. 'He was right, it's just a dose of this horrid flu that's doing the rounds. He's doing the best thing he can, plenty of sleep, plenty of fluids, a couple of Paracetamol when he needs them. Call me tomorrow and tell me how he's doing. He should be right as rain in forty-eight hours, if a bit weak, but nothing a bit of TLC won't take care of,' he winked at her.

'I'm so relieved. I was afraid it might have been something

serious. That was so kind of you to come and check on him. Let me show you back down.'

'You go and tend to your patient, I can see myself out. Mind you, I suspect he won't be much company tonight. Probably best to let him sleep and sweat it out.'

'Yes, yes, of course. Thank you again, Doctor. I – we're really most grateful.'

'Pleasure,' said P.J., looking forward to getting back to the sirloin of beef he had ordered.

Dinner was going very well. P.J. rejoined his table and smiled as he listened to the good-natured banter.

'What was it you ordered, Sheila?' Alex asked.

'What I always order. Chicken. Plain and roasted, nothing fancy.' She looked disapproving as a selection of dishes were brought to the table the minute P.J. rejoined them. Nestling under their silver covers, the table waited in anticipation as the immaculately choreographed waiters lined up and, with military precision, whipped the covers off to reveal and then distribute the art-directed array of wonderful food.

'Bon appetit.' They faded away in perfect unison.

'Thank you,' everyone said, salivating at the delicious-looking concoctions. Even Sheila's roast chicken breast seemed to have acquired a wonderful caramelised luminosity, and the fresh green runner beans and mashed potatoes were arranged in a meticulous design that even she couldn't fault.

Alex was in good form for a change, although he had looked strained on the way in, but once he had sat down and had a good look around, he seemed to suddenly cheer up. Clocking the financier at a nearby table, the restaurant suddenly seemed to meet with his approval again.

'No sign of Dom,' Catherine, said. 'Must be his night off.'

'No indeed,' P.J. said. 'That's who I was just called away to check on. He's feeling thoroughly miserable, poor chap, got this awful flu that's going around. Nothing serious though.'

Pity, thought Alex. He turned to P.J. 'Enjoying the wine, Dad? I think it was a good choice, don't you? A client of mine imports it.'

'Excellent choice, Alex. It's going down a treat.'

'Good,' Alex said, resolving to sit back and enjoy dinner. Now that Dom was out of the way, there was absolutely no reason why he shouldn't.

'To your very good health, everybody,' P.J. said, raising his glass.

In Dom's apartment, things were not going according to plan at all. Time was running out for Tanya. It wasn't just the matter of timing, of it being the twenty-ninth of February and a leap year, the acceptable time for a woman to propose marriage – there was the other, considerably more pressing matter of her financial situation. Her credit-card bills were huge and there was no way she could pay them. Tanya didn't just want to get married to Dom – she needed to, particularly before he discovered how freely she had been dispensing favours to her friends and contacts. But what else could she do? It had been the only way. Dominic's had been her major account – it had been a real coup to win it – and naturally she had had to give it her all, at the risk of neglecting her other, considerably less important, clients, who despite what she had intimated to Dom were pretty low-rent stuff. And if she was representing Dominic's, she had to look the part. Tanya couldn't afford designer clothes, but she liked wearing them. What she couldn't buy, she borrowed. She simply developed a close relationship with one or two designers, who were only too happy to loan her outfits or evening dresses for a special occasion if she guaranteed them a good table at the now impossible-to-book restaurant – and an appropriate discount on the bill.

Then there had been the decoration of Dom's apartment. Tanya had chosen only the best of everything, and it didn't come cheap. She had been loath to bring the matter of bills up to Dom (it was so unromantic), and she had simply managed to stall for a while and pay a few crucial amounts here and there by persuading Eric to advance her the cash from accounts, assuring him that Dom would settle up with her later.

Now, though, she was beginning to panic. She hadn't always been a spendthrift, not until she had started earning money, and even then, in the beginning, she had been careful. But then she would get the craving, the compulsion to purchase something lovely and relish the warm, comforting glow of satisfaction it gave her. It was the one area of her life she couldn't seem to keep under the rigorous control she managed otherwise. When Dom found out what the whole lot had come to, he would flip. Maybe even dump her. She took a deep breath. That wasn't going to happen.

She had left Dom to sleep as he'd requested, rather brusquely actually, after P.J. had left. She had felt pretty miffed that he hadn't exactly thanked her for her Florence Nightingale display of wifely concern. But then, that was men for you; they were always a nightmare when they were sick. Since then, she had been in the sitting room trying unsuccessfully to watch television. Now it was nearly eleven o'clock and she was beginning to panic. What disastrously bad luck for Dom to be sick tonight of all nights, February the twenty-ninth – D-Day. The day she had planned and prepared for so assiduously. But Tanya was used to life throwing her curve balls. She had negotiated them before and she would do so now. There simply wasn't any other option. It was far from ideal, but on the positive side Dom was weak and vulnerable. Even if romance wasn't on the menu, he would have to appreciate her obvious devotion to him. Taking a deep breath, she dabbed some more perfume on her wrists and at her neck, then got up and softly opened the door to his room, which was in darkness.

She flicked on the lights. 'Dom, sweetie?' She went over to him and sat on the bed. He was out for the count, breathing deeply, his mouth relaxed. She looked at him, thinking how handsome he looked, even sick as he was, his aquiline profile resting on the white pillow, accentuating his dark skin and hair, his sensual lips, ridiculously long eyelashes and strongly curving brows that made him seem like something carved by Michelangelo. She felt his forehead with her hand. It was still damp, but definitely cooler than it had been. His temperature was obviously dropping.

'Dom, darling,' she said, a bit louder this time, leaning in close to him, willing him to wake up.

'What?' He woke with a start, then struggled to sit up. 'You gave me a fright. I thought I might be in Casualty.' He rubbed his eyes, looking like a confused little boy. 'Why are all the lights on?'

'I just wanted to check on you, make sure you were all right.'

'Well I was. I was having rather a nice dream, actually.'

'Dom, there's something I need to say . . . to ask you.'

'What, now?' He gave a low groan. 'Tanya, can't it wait? I'm really not—'

'Dom, listen to me.' Her tone was sharper than she intended, but it was now or never. Her heart was thudding alarmingly and she felt like she would faint if she didn't get the words out.

He looked at her searchingly. 'What is it? What's so important? Has something happened?' He sounded worried. 'God I feel sick,' he moaned, collapsing back on his pillows.

'Dom, you know how much I love you, don't you? How we love each other?'

'What?'

She took his hand in hers and looked at him tenderly. 'I love you, Dom, more than anything in the world.'

'Tanya—'

'Just listen, Dom. I love you so, so much, and that's why, because it's February twenty-ninth . . .'

He was looking at her strangely.

'Because it's, um, a leap year, you know . . . I'm asking you to marry me. Dom, will you? Marry me? You're everything I've ever wanted in a husband, a life partner, and I would be so honoured to be your wife. I'd love and cherish you just like I'm doing—'

A look of comprehension mixed with something else, something urgent, flitted across his face, then he flung the covers off and almost pushed her out of the way.

'Dom!'

'Sorry, Tanya,' he spluttered, 'I think I'm going to be sick.' The bathroom door slammed behind him.

When he reappeared ten minutes later, looking pale and drawn, she was still sitting on the bed. 'Are you all right?' she whispered, fear suddenly seeping into her very bones.

The silence as he climbed back into bed was screaming in her ears. 'For God's sake, Tanya,' he croaked, 'can't you just leave me alone? We'll have to talk about this, but not now.'

She knew she should stop, back off there and then, but she couldn't. 'But you only have to say yes, Dommie, just one little word.' She felt her heart constricting.

'This isn't the time or the place, Tanya. Please, don't do this to yourself.' He looked chalk-white now.

And then she heard a discreet cough, and a knock on the bedroom door. Tearing her eyes from Dom's distraught face, Tanya's head snapped up to see Carla standing in the bedroom doorway, with a bowl of something steaming that smelled delicious.

'Excuse me,' she said, 'but the door was open. I did knock, but no one answered.' She chewed her lip awkwardly. 'Rollo sent this up. We were all so worried about you, Dom.'

Tanya mustered every ounce of self-control she had and forced herself to smile brightly. She got up and walked over to the door. 'Thank you, Carla. I'll take that.' She took the tureen of soup from her. 'You can tell everyone there's no need to worry. Dom's just got a bad bout of flu, but he mustn't be disturbed for the next forty-eight hours by *anyone*. Doctor's orders,' she said firmly. 'Thank Rollo, of course, it was very thoughtful of him.' She stared at her hard, watching Carla pull her glance away from Dom, who was looking right back at her. 'You can go now, Carla. Dom needs to rest.'

'Of course,' said Carla. 'Goodnight.'

'Thank you, Carla,' Dom croaked as he cleared his throat. 'That was kind of you, I appreciate it.' He gave her a heart-breaking smile.

'Not at all, I – we're concerned about you. I hope you feel better soon.' And she was gone.

'I take it you're not hungry,' Tanya said, turning back to him, her voice tight.

'No, I'm not. You have it. I'm going back to sleep. We'll talk tomorrow,' he said wearily.

'Fine. Sleep well,' she said and closed the door behind her. Her hands were beginning to tremble, the spoon rattling against the tureen. This was not the way it was supposed to turn out. And that bloody Carla, sneaking in, sly and specu-lative. How much, if anything, had she overheard? In a sudden fit of spite, Tanya poured the chicken soup down the kitchen sink. She couldn't look at it. Not now, not tomorrow. She didn't think she could ever eat again. Her stomach was clenched in a hard, terrifying knot of fear.

IO

It was out, on newsstands everywhere, right on the front rack. There, on the front cover of the March issue of *Select* magazine, blowing a kiss to the camera with the stunning black velvet dress billowing around her in the water, was Cici, leaning out of her marble bath, surrounded by bubbles and looking very seductive indeed. *Ireland's Sexiest Woman* was the cover line that blazed across the shot.

After she had recovered from the shock (and it had been a shock), Cici had been thrilled and delighted, although it was very naughty of Harry not to tell her. The photo shoot she had done, along with the other five women featured, was also, unbeknownst to her, a competition of sorts, and a handpicked group of judges had voted her the winner. It was now official. According to *Select* magazine, Cici Coleman-Cappabianca was Ireland's sexiest woman.

She had received an advance copy a week before the actual magazine was on sale to the public. It had arrived courtesy of a special courier and she had taken the large brown envelope and bouquet of magnificent flowers inside, wondering what the occasion could be. When she opened it and saw the cover, she had to sit down. There was a note, of course, in Harry's now familiar scrawl: *Just sharing what I knew the minute I first set eyes on you with the rest of the country. Your adoring, number one fan, Harry.*

She had smiled then and flicked through the rest of the article. She had to admit it read well, and Bob's shots were fabulous, the best one, of course, being the one of her with her back to the camera, the bodice of the dress falling away in a perfect V to reveal her wonderful curves. It was quite simply stunning, very sensual, yet utterly tasteful. All the same, Cici had a sudden shiver. What would James think of all this? She'd better tell him before someone else did, but how? He was bound to hear. She chewed her lip. James wasn't keen on publicity of any kind, even at the best of times. Normally she would have discussed something like this with him, sought his opinion, but it had all happened so quickly. She wouldn't think about it now. She would call him up in a couple of days and tell him.

To be fair, James had been behaving impeccably. He never rang or pestered her about a decision. He had given her her space as she had requested, and every month, her personal account was topped up as usual. Cici couldn't help feeling terribly guilty about that. It wasn't as if she was running the family home any more. She assumed their housekeepers were taking care of groceries, flowers and so forth, much as they did when she had been in residence, but at least she had always supervised everything. And cooked. Cici loved to cook. She had often thought she was happiest in the kitchen, with her family around her, all laughing and bickering and helping out with the chores, just like any family. She felt a pang thinking about it. Poor James. He must be so lonely. With Dom gone and the girls away, no matter how well the house was run, it must be awfully empty there just on his own. Well, they had plenty of good friends, she reasoned. Not that she had heard from many of them lately, she mused. They were probably all horrified at her behaviour, at putting James through this seemingly unnecessary and painful separation.

But lately she'd been too busy to even think about it. She was simply having too much fun. Harry was like a drug to her. She knew she was in denial about the whole thing, that sooner rather than later she would have to take responsibility for her actions, but somehow, even when she tried to force herself to think about it, her mind would wander and take a delicious detour away from the highway of harsh decisions and down one of the many scenic back roads, meandering through romantic, sensual encounters with Harry, where she could bask in his adoration of her, which appeared to be utterly genuine and without guile. It was like discovering an age of innocence, a time gone by filled with love letters, notes and flowers left hidden in places where she would later find them and, of course, long, languorous hours of lovemaking.

With Harry, Cici found herself discovering her body anew, as if resurrecting some wonderful instrument from a hidden place and relishing it, appreciating it as it came to life in the hands of a talented, eager musician. And they did make sweet music together. How could they not? With Harry, nothing was ever rushed or perfunctory. He believed in setting the scenes as carefully as he embraced the act that followed.

They never went to his place. What was the point? Quite apart from the fact that Harry had temporarily moved back into his father's house while he was searching for a place of his own to buy.

'Dad's on his own in the old place and he enjoys having me there, particularly since Mum's gone,' he had told her. Harry's mother, Cici learned, had died tragically when he was just fifteen. After routine surgery, a post-operative infection had set in, and weak as she was, she was unable to fight it despite the desperate efforts of the hospital staff and every cocktail of antibiotics imaginable. Other than relating the incident, Harry rarely discussed her.

Poor boy, thought Cici with a rush of tenderness. It must have been terrible for him. Boys were so attached to their mothers, and at that awful, in-between age, so unable to relate to them or untangle their own inarticulate, confused emotions.

Thinking of which, Cici realised, she hadn't heard from Dom in the past week or so. She must ring him, have him to dinner or at least drop in for a drink – if she could prise him away from the awful Tanya. Cici didn't like Tanya. Neither did her girls, who had discussed her with their mother at length. James had thought her perfectly charming, but then, James was a man. He wouldn't understand or pick up the subtle signals long ingrained in the feminine psyche that alerted women to a predatory female. Not the man-eating kind; that wouldn't have bothered Cici in the slightest. They were open and straightforward. No, it was the closed, carefully composed ones who appeared harmless and innocuous on the surface and almost always harboured inner complications and turmoil, visiting unwarranted anxieties and tribulations on hitherto carefree and untroubled families and relationships. As far as Cici was concerned, Tanya might as well have had Trouble tattooed on her forehead with a capital T, and she was patently wrong for Dom. Cici sighed. There was absolutely nothing she could do about it. She would just have to sit back and hope against hope that her only son would discover the fact for himself. Knowing Dom, that wouldn't necessarily be any time soon. Much as she adored him, Cici was not oblivious to each of her children's various shortcomings, and Dom's, in the emotional arena at any rate, was quite simply laziness, a very dangerous laziness that might just lead him into a long-term relationship that would be very hard work indeed – for all of them.

She checked her watch and hurried upstairs. Harry would be arriving in a little under an hour, and she felt the familiar rush of excitement. She would just have time for a quick shower and shampoo. Undressing quickly (only to get redressed and then undressed *again*), she padded over to her dressing room to wonder, with delicious anticipation, what outfit she would wear to greet him.

Flicking through her racks of clothes, Cici thought they seemed unusually crowded. She was meticulous about her wardrobe and always made sure to get rid of something old whenever she acquired a new item of clothing. Several charities had done very well out of this sensible, ordered habit of hers. Now she was perplexed, until, reaching the end of the rail, the reason for the crowding revealed itself. There, at the left-hand side of the rack, were four hangers of Harry's suits and jackets, and beneath them, on a shelf, were two stacks of neatly folded shirts, jeans and underpants. Her own tops, which had been kept there, had been moved to another, already occupied shelf to the right. She shook her head and smiled. How sweet. He obviously wanted to leave some spare clothes there, which was entirely reasonable and sensible, she supposed. But she had never noticed him bringing them in, and he had never mentioned it to her. Well, that was men for you. When did a woman's shelf space or clothes, for that matter, ever take precedence over other, more important matters? All the same, she would have liked him to ask her first, as a matter of courtesy.

She reproved herself. Really, how old-fashioned of her! She was turning into an old nag, just like those women she despised. Young people never thought about such things or considered anything other than the urgency of the moment. Wasn't that what she loved about Harry? His spontaneity, his exuberance and how he made her feel? She would have to learn to be flexible, unconcerned, to go with the flow. She would mention it to him later, playfully, when she was lying in his arms, drowsy, happy and sated.

'James?' Angela, his long-time PA, popped her head around the door of his office.

'Yes?' He looked up from the papers he was studying. 'What is it?'

'I thought you'd want to see this, although you probably have already.' She held the magazine out to him. 'It's wonderful. I'm sure you've all been so excited about it,' she continued tactfully. 'I was in town at lunchtime and I thought I'd pick it up for you, it's only out today. Cici must be thrilled.

Do tell her I think she looks amazing, won't you? I'll bring you in your coffee in just a mo,' she said, smiling, and left the magazine on his desk, closing the door behind her.

Phew, she thought. *Poor James.* He had never said a word about his wife leaving him, but it was the talk of the office, particularly since Cici had been spotted on more than one occasion around town with a tall, blond, handsome and decidedly younger man, young enough to be her son, people were saying. Angela shook her head. She couldn't believe it when she'd heard the rumours. Cici and James had been one couple she would have bet her life on lasting the distance. They had always seemed so happy together. James adored his gorgeous, glamorous, Italian wife and made no bones about it, and she had appeared to return that adoration. And they made, or *had* made, such a handsome couple. It was a shame. Just went to show you never could tell. And now, with that magazine out and Cici being proclaimed Ireland's sexiest woman, well, that would really put the cat amongst the pigeons, Angela thought. She had guessed, shrewdly and correctly, that James probably had no idea about it, but already the office was humming with the latest gossip. Angela had thought it only fair to let him know as discreetly as she could. She hoped it wouldn't cause any trouble. She was desperately fond of James and had worked for him now for almost fifteen years. He was looking wretched, poor man. He had lost weight and looked pale and tired. Probably wasn't sleeping a wink. Still, it wasn't her place to ask any intrusive questions. These things sorted themselves out sooner or later.

He had resisted for as long as he could. Now, draining his coffee, James took a deep breath and picked up the magazine. Looking at the cover, taking it in and perusing the main article inside, and the other seemingly endless shots of Cici, the outside world receded and eventually stopped altogether. All that was real, or rather, weirdly *surreal*, was that he appeared to be sitting in a chair, holding a magazine in his hands, reading about the woman he called his wife as she related her life to another man. A man who, by all accounts (James was kept updated on events), she was seeing on a regular basis. A man young enough to be her – *their* – son. He looked earnestly at it, studying the pictures in a kind of daze. He admired their beauty, *her* beauty, as if the woman in them were a stranger. And so she was – to him at any rate. This wasn't the warm, exuberant, loving woman he knew. This wasn't the mother of their children, who had looked after them, loved them, and him. This was a stranger who talked about her life as if he didn't exist, as if their family had somehow been some obscure accident of fate. This creature in her blonde wig, her make-up and her witty, throwaway expressions was someone he didn't know. She certainly bore no resemblance to his beloved wife.

He wasn't jealous. James had always celebrated Cici's beauty, had always willingly shared her company and time with whoever she chose to bestow it on, even when he longed to be alone with her. All the endless trips, parties, house guests – he had allowed her anything her heart desired. He would have, *could* have put up with anything – but not this. This was too much. Not the publicity itself – that was the least of it – but the awful, twisting, unrelenting pain he felt. To have to stand back, silent and unobtrusive, while he watched his life, *their* life, their *family* for God's sake, disintegrate.

He had done his best for the past six months, he really had, hoping against hope that she would get this thing out of her system, that it was all some midlife crisis that would burn itself out. But he couldn't take it any longer – the sympathetic phone calls from friends, the knowing glances. James Coleman was a patient man, a kind man and a surprisingly intuitive man. He was also a brilliant man, ruthless in business when he had to be, and he did not suffer fools gladly. And that was what he felt himself to be now, in a sudden, blinding flash of admittance. He had sat back and played the waiting game for too long. Now it was time for action, however deeply unpleasant that action might be. It was time for him to talk to Cici, to confront her and sort this awful mess out with as much dignity as could be mustered.

With a sigh that came from the very depths of his being, James picked up the phone. He never entered the fray without making sure of the rules of the game. It was what had got him to where he was today.

'James,' his old friend and solicitor, Malcolm Stokes, boomed into the phone. 'What corporation are we taking on this month?' he chuckled.

'I'm afraid this isn't a business call, Malcolm.' James didn't bother with niceties. 'I wish it were that simple. I need you to get me the best divorce lawyer in the country.'

As soon as he had made the call, he felt immediately better. At least he was taking action, however ghastly and painful the consequences might be. Then, with another sigh, he made another reluctant phone call.

'Mike?'

'James, good to hear you, thought you'd slipped off the radar altogether,' his understanding and abandoned golf partner said.

'Mike, you know that charity ball you and Janet invited us to?'

'I do.'

'I'd be delighted to join your party. Unfortunately, I will be joining it alone.'

There was a beat.

'Marvellous!' proclaimed Mike. 'That's great news, James, Janet will be thrilled. I'll email you the details. See you Friday.'

In his office in town, Mike put down the phone and immediately rang his wife.

'Excellent news, Janet. James is joining our party after all.

No, not Cici. He's finally appearing to see sense at last. I was beginning to seriously worry about him.'

'Is it true?' Sophia asked Dom from the small apartment she shared with two other girls in Florence, both studying art history like her.

'Yes, I'm afraid it is,' her brother sighed as he heard the bewilderment in her voice.

'But why? How?'

'Who knows? She won't discuss it with anyone. She moved into the mews saying she wanted space. Now she's Ireland's sexiest woman and is having an affair with some guy who's barely two years older than me.'

'Eeeuuuuw.'

'Exactly. Although,' Dom added ruefully, 'I can't exactly sit in judgement, since I was even younger than Harry when I had my little liaison with the *comtesse*.' Dom fully understood now how hard it was to be on the other side of the older woman/younger man divide. He'd been the younger man several times and had been taken aback at how upset and angry his lovers' sons were about their mothers' affairs. Now he understood why.

'Dad has been as patient as he can be,' he continued, 'but now he's had enough. He's already talking to lawyers.'

'I can't believe it. I have to talk to her, make her see sense. She must have gone mad.'

'I wish you luck.'

'She'll listen to me, she always does.'

'I wouldn't be too sure, Sophia. Anyway, it's better you know. It's the favourite topic of conversation in Dublin at the moment, or so I'm reliably informed.'

'Poor you. How are you anyway?

'I'm fine.'

'And Tanya?'

'She's fine too.' There was a pause.

'And? Come on, Dom, this is your sister, your intuitive, wonderfully perceptive sister.'

'Tanya and I have split up.'

'Oh, Dom. I'm sorry.' Sophia fought to keep the glee from her voice. 'But none of us thought she was right for you, you know – just think of all those gorgeous women out there who'll be queuing up for you.'

'Funny,' Dom sounded glum. 'That's exactly what some woman said to Dad last week.'

'It's a man's world,' Sophia said knowingly. 'No amount of post-feminism is going to change that.'

'You could have fooled me. You've been out of Dublin for too long,' Dom grinned.

'You know what they say in Rome . . .'

'What?'

'"The world is old". Nothing happens that hasn't already happened before and will happen again. You just have to roll with the punches.'

'Tell me about it. I gotta go. Take it easy, Sis.'

'Bye, Dom, and don't worry. I'll talk to her, get her over here, see what's really going on. *Ciao*.'

Sophia put down the phone thoughtfully. So it was true. She knew something was up when her mother had moved into the mews, claiming it was just so she could have a little change of scenery while she was working on renovating the interior. Sophia just assumed her parents had had a row and were taking time out to cool off. Then she had begun to hear the rumours, the veiled questions from friends mentioning that their parents hadn't seen Cici and James out and about as usual, coupled with her father's evasiveness on the phone the few times she had brought it up. Now she understood. But another man? A younger man – much younger. Ugh! What had got into her mother? Everybody, even Sophia's friends, always commented on what a handsome couple her mum and dad made and how happy they seemed. What the hell was going on?

Florence was beautiful in March but today she felt unseasonably cold. Grabbing her long cardigan and pulling it on over her T-shirt and jeans, Sophia headed out to meet her friends at the local café for a glass of wine and a slice of pizza. She thought about texting her younger sister, Mimi; last time she'd heard from her, she was in Buenos Aires, doing South America. Then she thought better of it. What was the point? It would only upset her. She would call her mother later that night and get her to come over to Rome for a couple of days, for a bit of shopping and to catch up. Then she would find out exactly what was going on.

P.J. was up bright and early, ready to set off for the gym. He hated to admit it, but he was actually enjoying getting fit again, and the results were beginning to manifest in a very satisfactory manner. He had already lost a stone in a month and was feeling fitter and more energetic than he had in years. His personal trainer, Pip, a strapping young South African, had been putting him through his paces three times a week and was pleased with P.J.'s progress.

'Muscle memory, P.J.,' he told him, weighing him and taking his measurements. 'We might forget what our bodies can do, but they don't. The fact that you played so much rugby, even if it was a long time ago, will stand to you. Your muscles remember all that training, and as long as you put the work in, which you have been doing, it can be surprising how quickly the body responds. Well done, mate. We'll increase the weights next week, concentrate on some explosive lifting and intensive interval training, and you'll be back in shape in no time.'

'Whoa!' P.J. was alarmed. 'I'm not as young as I used to be. I'm not sure I like the sound of all that.'

'Nonsense, you're well able for it. Your body won't change unless you force it to. That's what you're paying me for, isn't it?' Pip had grinned.

All the same, P.J. thought, catching sight of himself in the bathroom mirror, it was gratifying to see the beginnings of some impressive muscles again. Just then, the doorbell rang. He checked his watch; it was ten to seven. He'd better make tracks or he'd be late, and Pip didn't take kindly to being kept waiting. Hurrying downstairs with his gym kit, the doorbell sounded again, this time longer. Who could it be at this hour? He hoped it wasn't an emergency, and where was Sheila? He opened the door and found himself face to face with a very good-looking woman.

She smiled and held out her hand. 'Dr O'Sullivan, I presume? I'm Charlotte Keating.' Seeing the perplexed look on his face, she added, 'I'm here to collect Bones for his walk?'

'What?' P.J.'s manners deserted him as confusion was replaced by something else, a curious feeling, one he couldn't quite get his head around. Then he remembered himself. 'Of course! You must be Jennifer's daughter. Come in, please.'

She stood in the hall, looking amused at his obvious confusion. 'I hope I'm not disturbing you. I'm a few minutes early, but I like to set off before the traffic gets too heavy.'

Just then the kitchen door opened and Bones hurtled up, a considerably slimmer Bones, P.J. had noticed of late, followed, hot on his heels, by Sheila.

'Oh, Mrs Keating,' she said. 'I'm so sorry, I didn't hear the bell. I was hoovering, you see.'

'Not at all, Sheila, I've just arrived. Dr O'Sullivan let me in.' She reached down and put a lead on Bones, who sat obediently and looked adoringly at her. P.J. could well understand why.

'Well, then, we'll be off, right Bones? Nice to meet you, Dr O'Sullivan.'

'P.J., please.'

'I'll have him back at the usual time, Sheila. See you later.'

'Er, just a moment,' P.J. heard himself saying.

'Yes?' she turned questioningly.

God, he had never seen such beautiful, enormous brown eyes. 'You're going to the beach?' He cursed himself for sounding like a halfwit.

'Yes, we always go to Sandymount Beach. Is that a problem?'

P.J. could feel Sheila's eyes boring into him with disapproval.

'I was just after a bit of exercise myself. Would you mind if I joined you?'

'Aren't you off to your gym?' Sheila said accusingly.

'I was,' P.J. smiled at Sheila, 'but a bit of fresh air is what I need, now that I think of it.' He thought he saw a twinkle in the big brown eyes.

'I'd be delighted,' Charlotte said.

'Good,' P.J. said, dumping his kit under the hall table. He would text Pip to cancel his workout. He'd earned some time off anyway, and it wasn't as if he wouldn't be exercising. Walking was the best exercise of all. He recommended it to his patients all the time. And he would be doing it, if appearances were anything to go by, in the company of a beautiful and very charming woman.

'There's a pile of wellies in the back of the car,' Charlotte said, loading Bones into the rear of the station wagon, along with the two Jack Russell terriers P.J. recognised from his meeting with Jennifer. 'I'm sure one of them will fit. Pity to spoil those new trainers of yours. It can be a bit mucky if it's been raining. Do you go to the gym a lot?'

'Only in the past month.' P.J. settled himself into the passenger seat. 'I was very out of condition, you see, out of practice.'

'You look pretty fit to me.' She glanced at him, manoeuvring the car out onto the road.

P.J. had to stop himself from staring at her, this apparition who, astonishingly, lived across the square from him and who he had never set eyes on.

'Let's just say I'm a work in progress,' he grinned. 'Rather like Bones here,' he added, listening to his dog panting glee-fully in the back. He sounded as excited and eager as he felt himself.

Candy loaded her parcels into the brand-new, black, two-seater BMW convertible that was an early twenty-first birthday present from Ossie and slid in behind the wheel. She was exhausted. Two and a half hours at the hairdresser (again), just to have her roots touched up, then lunch in town with Emma and Katy (although they'd had to rush back to lectures) and some enthusiastic shopping had left her drained. Being a glamorous girl about town was hard work, but def-initely worth it, she thought, tilting her head back to get another look in the rear-view mirror at her shiny, platinum hair. It was amazing the difference it had made. Since she had gone for the complete colour change, she had also had extensions added. Now she and her waist-length platinum ringlets and catwalk-worthy make-up were turning heads. It was true, she decided. Blondes definitely did have more fun. Men were looking at her now, properly – younger ones, older ones and a good few in between, but not as much as they were going to. She had almost, but not quite, finished her transformation. She had lost weight, not too much, and thanks to her regular workouts with her trainer had toned up nicely, enough to be slim but not skinny. Her new look was sophis-ticated. She looked much older and worldly, with quite a Paris Hilton vibe going on, actually. There was no sign of the gawky, rather insecure young girl that had looked back at her from mirrors in the past. She had been well and truly left behind.

Not that things had been easy of late; quite the contrary, in fact. But no pain, no gain, Candy reminded herself. It had been difficult, much harder than she could have anticipated, standing her ground. She still didn't like to think of her mother and grandmother's faces when she had appeared back home that fateful day four weeks ago. Even after a couple of vodka and tonics with Emma and Katy to bolster her resolve before facing the music, Candy had been taken aback. Jennifer's expression alone had been thunderous, and that was before the storm had broken.

She had come back in the evening after her weekend with her dad and Shalom and gone into the sitting room where Charlotte and Jennifer were watching *Gone with the Wind*.

'We're in here, sweetheart,' her mother had called, hearing her come in the front door. 'Have you eaten? There's plenty left over if you haven't.'

When she walked in, there had been a stunned silence.

Jennifer had been first to speak. 'Is that a wig you're wearing under that cap?' she asked, looking curiously at her.

'No, Gran, it's not,' Candy had said, glaring at her, feeling her courage deserting her as she looked from her gran to her mother's comprehending and distraught face.

'Oh, Candy.' Charlotte's hand flew to her mouth. 'Your hair, your beautiful hair. What have you done?'

'What does it look like I've done?' she snapped. 'I've gone blonde, that's all. It's not a crime, is it?'

'But those clothes,' Jennifer spluttered. 'That frightful make-up. You can't possibly be serious. She's not, Charlotte,' Jennifer went on disbelievingly. 'It's a fancy dress or something, isn't it – she's having us on. You've come from a party, is that it?' Jennifer was looking at her as if she had grown antlers.

'I was at a party last night, yes.' Candy wandered over to the drinks cabinet and poured herself another vodka and slimline before sitting down and crossing her legs. 'But this has nothing to with that. This is my new look, and if you don't like it, you'll just have to get used to it.' She took a sip of her drink, enjoying the drama she had unleashed.

'Your father's behind this, isn't he?' Jennifer sounded mutinous.

'Don't be ridiculous, Gran. Not that it's any of your

business, but he and Shalom think I look fabulous. Shalom did my makeover for me, in fact. She was very good to me all weekend. She's not nearly as bad as I thought she was. She's quite nice, in fact. You were right, Mum, I just hadn't ever given her a proper chance. The three of us got on very well, actually.'

Candy wasn't sure why she was deliberately imparting this spiteful and not altogether true information to her mother, but seeing the look of pain on Charlotte's face and feeling Jennifer's simmering outrage were making her feel strangely elated, powerful, even.

'Well,' said Jennifer dryly. 'That explains a lot.'

'Please, Mother.' Charlotte had recovered her power of speech. 'Let's not talk about this now.'

'She looks like a tart. A cheap, trashy tart. Look at her!'

'Mother.' Charlotte threw her mother a warning look, but it was too late.

'If you won't say it, I will.' Jennifer's face had turned puce with rage. 'If you've any sense, Candice, you'll wash that clownish muck off your face right now and go straight into a hairdresser first thing tomorrow and get that awful platinum blonde toned down. It makes you look like an old woman.'

'The only old woman around here is you!' Candy said nastily. 'You're completely out of touch, and so are you.' She turned on Charlotte. 'Look at you both, sitting in here. This place might as well be an old folks' home. You need to get over yourselves, get with the programme – and you need to get a life, Mum. Gran is having a very bad influence on you. At least Dad and Shalom know how to have a good time. What would either of you know about what's fashionable now? You're both stuck in some weird time warp. Well, you're not going to drag me into it. I think you're both sad, the pair of you. No wonder Dad left you, Mum! What man would possibly want you? You're no fun, and you're not going to turn me into some pathetic replica of you either,' she ranted. 'I've seen how it works. Men want a girl who's fun and who looks hot, and if you don't like the way I look, then that's too bad. I don't have to stay here, you know.' And then she'd fled from the room, run upstairs and slammed her door.

She was furious, furious and horribly confused and upset. Not because of the rumpus she had caused – she had been prepared for that – but what had shocked her, frightened her, was that she had made her mother cry. Tears had suddenly begun to slide down her face, even though she had tried to hide them. Candy had never seen her mother cry, not even when Dad had left. She had always been calm and controlled, annoyingly so. Now, seeing her like that, so openly upset and hurt, was making Candy feel very strange indeed. But she couldn't think about that now. She would think about it tomorrow – wasn't that what Scarlett O'Hara had said in the movie they'd been watching?

She had to get out. She couldn't stand another minute of this place, of her mother's silent reproach and Jennifer's equally vociferous disapproval. What did they know anyway? Candy suddenly felt very tired. She had never had a row with her mother, not really, not like this. She got out of her new clothes and flung them on the floor, then went into her bathroom and ran a hot bath. Taking off her make-up (it took ages to do it properly, with all the different oils and cleansers Shalom had made her buy), she peered at her face in the mirror. Devoid of make-up, she was unusually pale, her white-blonde hair making her look almost ethereal. She twisted it up into a knot and slid into the comforting bubbles, closing her eyes. She hadn't meant for things to turn out like this, to say what she had to her mother, but she had to stand her ground. She was almost twenty-one, for heaven's sake – a sussed and savvy young woman. If her mother and gran couldn't see that, at least her dad could, and did. And that was all that mattered, wasn't it?

11

'You have to talk to him, Charlotte, it's as simple as that.' Jennifer was firm. 'Put a stop to this nonsense once and for all.' They sat in her kitchen beside the bright red Aga after a Sunday lunch of roast lamb that had seemed terribly lonely without Candy.

'It's not that simple, though, is it?' Charlotte sipped her glass of red miserably as she looked across the table at her mother. 'I mean, she's almost twenty-one. She has a mind of her own and we know what she thinks of me – I can't see her listening to anything I say.'

'That's not the point and you know it. She's playing you off, one against the other. It's textbook behaviour for children of divorced parents. I've seen it many times on all those American chat shows, and whatever age she is, and whatever you may think of her, Candy is just a very mixed-up young girl in many ways.'

Charlotte was all too well aware of that fact. She had hardly slept since the awful row. The sight of Candy's hideously dyed platinum hair had dismayed her, but she had felt powerless to say anything. Candy was so like Ossie; that was a major part of the problem. She did exactly what she wanted and up until now had got away with it. Charlotte still felt so guilty about the divorce and the effect it had had on Candy. She knew she felt hurt and betrayed and in some confused way was trying to win her father's attention and love. Charlotte just desperately hoped it was a phase she might grow out of.

'She blames me for her father leaving,' Charlotte said quietly, 'and maybe she has a right to.'

'That's piffle and you know it. Whoever she blames for it – and I don't think even Candy is aware of who that is – you and Ossie are allowing her to turn into a complete monster.'

'You think I don't see that?' said Charlotte angrily. It was so simple for her mother, who saw something wrong and fixed it, never thinking about the sensitivities underneath the hard shell that Candy had put up to hide the vulnerable centre. She'd be devastated if Charlotte told her she looked like a slapper. Jennifer was always blunt, and Charlotte herself had suffered the consequences over the years. She'd always vowed to be a different kind of mother. Now she didn't know anything, except that bawling Candy out wasn't going to help anything.

'Well, what are you going to do about it?' Jennifer prodded.

'I don't see what I *can* do. Since she's moved in with her father, it's up to him and Shalom, I suppose, and what they're prepared to put up with under their roof. What I say isn't going to make an awful lot of difference.'

'That's where you are very wrong.' Jennifer poured some coffee. 'Let's leave Candy out of this for a moment. She's seeking attention, particularly from her father. That's as plain as the nose on her face. Ossie won't see that, but he *will* listen to you, Charlotte, I know he will. He has huge respect for you, whatever may have transpired since your marriage, and he *will* listen to you, particularly with regard to your daughter.'

'I don't see what I can say, really.' Charlotte chewed her lip. 'I mean, imagine it: "Hello, Ossie, I'm very concerned our daughter is turning into a carbon copy of your girlfriend and it's freaking me out and it should be freaking you out."'

'Don't be ridiculous,' Jennifer scowled. 'Of course that's not what you're going to say. Ossie will see that quite clearly for himself. It just might take him a while to acknowledge it.'

'And in the meantime he encourages it?'

'I didn't say that. We have to move carefully here. Candy's well-being is at stake and that's all that matters. As dear Jeremy would have said, she's difficult to load, but it's nothing we can't resolve if we keep our heads.'

Charlotte grinned despite herself at her mother's turn of phrase, 'difficult to load' referring to a highly strung horse who required a lot of coaxing into a horse box. 'That's rich coming from you, Mummy. As I recall, it was you flying off the handle that sent her storming off to her room and now she's gone.'

'I'm sorry about that, but I'm not sorry for what I said. Every bit of it was the unvarnished truth, and Candy needed to hear it. She *does* look like a tart.'

'Much as I hate to agree with you, you're right. But I can't say that to her.'

'Mark my words, whatever you say or don't say, Ossie isn't going to like it.'

'According to Candy, he already does.'

'That's nonsense – he's just humouring her. No father wants to see their daughter trussed up like a cheap hooker.'

'Mother!' Charlotte protested. 'There's no need to go quite so far.'

'There's every need, Charlotte, which is why you have to talk to him. You have to make him realise what he can't quite admit to himself – that he's made an awful mistake with that Shalom creature. Men have terrible double standards, Charlotte. Just because he may be having sex with Shalom doesn't mean he'll want his own daughter to turn out like her. Quite the opposite, I should think.'

'It's a bit late for that.'

'It's never too late,' Jennifer smiled. 'Now how about planning something nice, something non-confrontational? Why don't you suggest having dinner with him, on Friday perhaps, just so you can discuss things.'

'I can't.' Charlotte had almost forgotten. 'Not on Friday. I already have a dinner.'

'A dinner party, how nice.' Jennifer was pleased for her. 'Who's giving it?'

'It's not a dinner party.' Charlotte was suddenly looking uncomfortable, almost shifty even. 'Just, um, dinner.'

'Dinner? With whom? Why are you beating about the bush like this?'

'Dr O'Sullivan has asked me to have dinner with him this Friday.' There, she had said it.

'Dinner! With the doctor! Charlotte, why didn't you tell me? What fun!' Jennifer exclaimed.

A wave of guilt washed over Charlotte. How could she even be thinking of going out and having fun when all this was going on with Candy? Charlotte had been thinking of nothing but Candy and had been phoning her constantly, both on her mobile and even Ossie's landline, but Candy was refusing to take her calls. It hurt more than Charlotte could have imagined.

'It will do you a world of good,' Jennifer went on. 'Candy was right about one thing, Charlotte – you do need to get out and about a bit. Dinner with the doctor's just the ticket. Wait till Ossie hears about that! He's very eligible, you know. I've heard all about him on the grapevine, a sort of modern-day Robin Hood.'

'Well, you certainly know more about him than I do. And it's only dinner.'

'That'll do for starters,' Jennifer grinned. 'Speaking of which, have you anything decent to wear, Charlotte?'

'I'm glad to see you're still your ruthlessly practical self, Mother.'

Let's go into town tomorrow, shall we? I feel like spending some money. After all, I'm a woman of considerable means, and what better way to spend it than buying your daughter a wonderful outfit for your first date in how many years?'

'It's not a date. Really, Mother, you're making me nervous.'
'That's what they all say.'

Friday evening came around as usual, harbinger equally of wonderful possibilities and doomed expectations. Dom, for one, was glad. It was their busiest night in the restaurant and he needed to throw himself into it completely, to be totally absorbed so that he wouldn't have to think about the ghastly two weeks that had preceded it. He had more or less recovered from his flu, although he still felt pretty weak, but it wasn't so much the physical symptoms that were bothering him as the emotional ones.

What a nightmare! It had all started when he had come down with the awful dose that was doing the rounds. Then the unthinkable, unimaginable drama with Tanya had unfolded. To say Dom had been surprised was an understatement. He had been pretty out of it anyway when she had sprung her leap-year proposal on him, barely coherent with a raging temperature. The whole thing had been absolutely horrific. Dom was not in the business of hurting people, but what had transpired had taken him so much by surprise that he had been more abrupt than he'd meant to be. The result had been a very angry and resentful girlfriend.

Dom sighed, thinking about it all. What the hell had got into her? The Tanya he knew had been cool, calm and always reassuringly in control, both of her career and her emotions. The woman who revealed herself that night had been on the verge of hysteria. And even before her surprise proposal, there had been the appalling incident of her approaching and interrupting a customer. That was strictly against restaurant rules – a doctor in the house was entitled to enjoy his time off just like any other guest, unless of course it really *was* a matter of life or death, as had been the case with Mrs Fitzgerald. But to drag poor P.J. O'Sullivan away from his family dinner on a Friday night on the pretext that he, Dominic, had been mortally ill – well, that had been the final straw as far as Dom was concerned. Of course P.J. had been charming about it – he was always charming, he was that kind of man, he wouldn't know how to behave otherwise – but it was a monumental black mark against Tanya for her to abuse her position like that. And Dominic had told her so in no uncertain terms the following morning. It hadn't gone down well.

After that, pointing out their basic unsuitability as a long-term couple had been relatively easy. Still, the whole thing had pulled him up in his tracks smartly, and he'd been doing a lot of thinking, taking stock of his life. But marriage? That had been the last thing on his mind. He was only twenty-eight for heaven's sake, and even if he had been contemplating it, which he hadn't, he had never, at any point in their relationship, hinted to Tanya at a long-term commitment.

Mind you, that wasn't quite how Tanya had seen things. After the tears and pleading, when she realised he was serious about ending their relationship, she had thrown the most enormous wobbly.

'You miserable bastard!' she had screamed in fury. 'After all I've done for you!' She'd picked up a silver photograph frame and flung it at him across the room. Ducking quickly, he had just avoided it. That was when he had asked her to leave, instantly, telling her that he would have anything else of hers sent around to her apartment – and there wasn't much, he had been relieved to see, just the few items of clothing and toiletries she had left in the spare room. The whole incident had left Dom feeling shaken. Women! He would certainly avoid them for the foreseeable future. His restaurant was what was important to him now and he would focus on that.

That was when he had got the second, much nastier shock. Eric, his accountant, had rung him, requesting an urgent meeting. When Dom had seen him, coming into his office at the back of the restaurant, his lips pursed and acting unusually twitchy, he had immediately known that something was wrong. And it was. Dominic's was almost twenty thousand euro in the red. That was when Dominic had *seen* red.

'What the hell were you thinking?' he had said through clenched teeth, looking at the figures that laid it all out in black and white. 'Why didn't you let me know about this immediately?'

'I did try.' Eric was white. 'But Tanya was adamant that you shouldn't be told about it just yet – that you had, um, rather a lot on your plate, so to speak. She wanted a little more time.'

'What the hell has Tanya got to do with it?' Dom demanded. '*I* employ you. You're *my* bloody accountant – you should have come to me.'

'You, um, didn't seem all that concerned with accounts,' Eric had protested. 'I did try to approach you once or twice.'

'Not hard enough.'

'Tanya is a very persuasive girl, Dom. She gave strict instructions that you were not to be disturbed by any of this, that it was more important to get the restaurant up and running and keep the positive reviews coming in. I did say I was going to give her a little more time and that was all.'

Dom sighed, suddenly feeling terribly weary. 'Well, Tanya is well and truly out of the picture now, Eric.'

Eric coughed politely. He had heard, of course, from the staff; it was the talk of the restaurant. 'It's not quite as bad as it seems, Dom. If you stop all the comping and the free-bies and maybe cut back on a few areas in the kitchen, with the staff, we should be able to turn it around in a few months.' He looked sheepish.

'At the expense of Dominic's,' Dom said, chewing his lip. 'This situation should never have been allowed to develop, Eric. I'm very, very angry.' And he was, but truth-fully, Dom knew he was the one at fault. He had been carried away by the enormous success of Dominic's, by their wonderful clientele and the constant rave reviews they were getting and had made the biggest mistake that a restaurateur could make – falling for his own publicity at the expense of hard economic facts. Now he was going to have to pay the price.

'Leave it with me for a few days,' Dom said. 'I'll have to get my head around this, talk to the bank, consult with a few people before I make any permanent decisions. And from now on, you talk to me and to me only – got that?'

'Absolutely.'

It had been a huge wake-up call for Dom, and a timely one. But things could have been worse. At least the situation was redeemable, although it would take a lot of hard work. But he had been lucky – it wasn't too late. He could turn things around, he knew he could. His restaurant was the over-riding passion in his life, and he was going to make sure nothing, but nothing interfered with that.

He checked the bookings for tonight. It was a full house, a lot of their regulars and a few high-profile names, a politician bringing a party with a visiting dignitary and a well-known actor booked under his code name. It was a good mix for a Friday night. Dom headed to the kitchen to give a sterner than usual pep talk. He had been lackadaisical of late, but that was all about to change.

Striding across the restaurant floor, he couldn't help noticing Carla, busily polishing tables. She looked up and for a second their eyes met, although she immediately resumed her study of the table. Despite himself, Dom felt the same powerful surge of attraction followed by the embarrassing but delicious memory of their encounter in the bedroom that night at the party. If he was honest, it was never very far from his mind.

Carla was tired and her arms ached. She had been busy keeping busy, which was all she did whenever Dom was around. All the same, despite the tension that was evident and the speculation amongst the staff that there was some kind of trouble afoot, there was an air of general elation at the news that Tanya was gone.

Carla had seen Eric coming out of Dom's office looking pale and had shrewdly guessed that Tanya's comping and whatever else she had been up to had come to light. Dom's face when he strode past her and into the kitchen confirmed her suspicions. He looked absolutely furious. She remembered someone trying once to scam her father in New York and the resulting furore. She felt sorry for Dom – it was every restaurateur's worst nightmare. She was glad, in this instance, that she was on the other side of the kitchen doors. Stress levels in any restaurant were always worst in the kitchen.

'You can almost see your reflection in that table, Carla.' It was Astrid, coming over to chat. 'There's no need to look so busy now that the wicked witch has gone.' She grinned evilly. 'Isn't it a lovely surprise? Even I couldn't have expected such a rapid exit for our manageress.'

'Tough for Dom, though.' Carla paused in her polishing.

'Nonsense, he's much better off without her,' Astrid proclaimed. 'Speaking of which, he could hardly keep his eyes off you just now. I think he fancies you.' She raised a speculative eyebrow.

'Don't be ridiculous.' Carla felt herself blushing.

'What's ridiculous?' Astrid demanded. 'You'd make such a cute couple. I'm surprised it never occurred to me before.'

'I'm a waitress, Astrid. Dom is my employer,' Carla said patiently, hoping she didn't sound as flustered as she felt. And then, not sure why, she lied, 'Besides, I've met someone. I'm seeing him tonight as a matter of fact.'

'Astrid?' Dom came out of the kitchen and called to her. 'You're wanted inside, Rollo wants a word with you.'

'Coming, Dom,' she said, walking towards the swing doors, then turning back to Carla she called, 'Enjoy your hot date tonight, I'll want all the details tomorrow.'

Nothing in Dom's expression indicated that he had heard the comment, but he couldn't not have. Yet again, Carla wished she could keep her big mouth shut for once in her life.

It's not a date, it's not a date, it's not, it's not, it's not. Just dinner, that's all, dinner with a nice, friendly, educated, entertaining (and oh, all right, very attractive) man. Someone who lived across the square. Someone who would be a friend, someone nice to talk to, good company and her own age group. No ex-wife, no strange habits and someone who had, by all accounts, a steady, reliable career and had asked her to have dinner with him. What was the big deal? Oh, God, was it a date? She was going on a date with a man when her daughter was in a crisis, all because her ex-husband had fallen in love with a phony bleached blonde. And now Candy had moved in bag and baggage with her father and Shalom.

For a moment, despair threatened as Charlotte wondered what Candy was doing – was living with Ossie and Shalom what she wanted? Maybe she was having so much fun she never even thought about her mum. Had she lost her lovely, headstrong, mixed-up daughter for good? She dragged her mind away from the unthinkable and focused on the job at hand.

Charlotte was uncharacteristically nervous. What would she talk about? How did one behave these days on a date? The questions and possibilities were flying around her head. And worst of all, what should she wear? At least that was a practical problem, one she could apply herself to and concentrate on.

The shopping trip with Jennifer had been productive, if nerve-wracking. They had gone into town early and headed for Brown Thomas, and in the end Charlotte had come away with several new outfits, although Jennifer had been miffed when the assistant had looked at her blankly when she had announced she wanted everything on approbation, saying, 'I've had an account in this shop since 1950.'

'There's no need, Mummy,' Charlotte had said. 'I can always come back and exchange them if they're wrong, and I'm pretty sure we've made some good choices.'

'Yes, but you never know until you get home, do you? Things can look quite different in front of your own mirror. The lighting in these places is designed to make *every-thing* look nice. And why is everybody foreign?' she whispered loudly. 'None of them speak proper English, it's disgraceful.'

'They speak perfect English, Mummy. Now let's get out of here and go have a nice lunch.'

'Good idea.' Jennifer was flagging and her hip was killing her, although she had managed to try on three lovely suits and purchased two of them.

Charlotte had lingered briefly at the designer jeans section they passed, thinking of how she used to love taking Candy shopping. It seemed ages ago since they had, and now Candy certainly didn't want to go with her. Even if she did, Charlotte reflected, she would probably want some awful-looking stuff, if her new image was anything to go by. She was probably going shopping with Shalom these days, and that made her feel even worse. What was she to do? Was it better to let Candy work it all out herself, or should she confront her more persistently? But maybe that would drive her even further away.

Now, appraising herself in the mirror, Charlotte had to admit she looked well. She had opted for a soft, black, knitted wool dress that moulded her willowy figure perfectly, with a nice V-neck that was low enough to be interesting without being obvious. The dress came to just below knee length and looked very well with the black opaque tights and her new black suede, high-heeled boots that fit like gloves. A wide black leather belt with a large silver buckle completed the outfit. It was elegant, but definitely casual. She had had her hair trimmed and blow-dried and it fell in soft waves around her face to just below her shoulders. Her hairdresser had persuaded her to leave it longer than usual, saying, 'It suits you this length, and you've got the hair for it.' And she had been right. Actually, she felt rather glamorous for a change. If only she didn't feel so ridiculously nervous. When her mother came into her bedroom, she jumped.

'Only me!' Jennifer grinned. 'I must say you look very nice, Charlotte, very nice indeed.' Jennifer sat on the bed and regarded her approvingly.

Charlotte smiled at her, despite her nerves. Jennifer was in her evening attire of her favourite quilted dressing gown, gold elastic-heeled ballet slippers and full make-up, although she had pin-curled her hair and had her hair net on.

'Do you ever take your make-up off, Mummy?' Charlotte asked, shaking her head. 'I don't think I've ever seen you barefaced. I bet you even sleep in it.'

'If you mean do I use all those insanely expensive cleansers and potions, no, I do not. Nothing wrong with my Pond's face cream and a good facecloth. Make-up was my generation's armour. There's nothing you can't face if you've got your lipstick and powder on. In moderation, of course.'

'I wish I didn't feel so nervous.'

'What on earth are you nervous about?' Jennifer demanded. 'He's a nice chap, isn't he? I think you'll have a good time.'

'It's been so long, I suppose.'

'All the more reason to enjoy it. Actually, I'm envious of you.'

'What?' Charlotte was startled. 'Why?'

'Why do you think?' Jennifer looked mulish. 'I'm only seventy-five. I'm not in the grave yet, you know. I'd love to be going out to dinner with a nice man to a lovely restaurant. I like men's company – always did. Not that I don't enjoy all my women friends, but there's nothing quite like the excitement of getting ready and dressing up to go out on a nice date, is there? Be honest.'

There it was, that word "date" again. Charlotte quailed inside and then felt immediately remorseful.

'You're right, Mummy. I *am* looking forward to it. I just feel out of practice.'

'It's like riding a bicycle; it'll all come back to you. I'd swap places with you in a jiffy.'

'Oh, Mummy.' Charlotte sat down beside her on the bed. 'I'm sorry. How selfish of me. I never realised.'

'No one does,' Jennifer said ruefully. 'Not until you're in the same position yourself. I know I'm an old woman, really, but I'd love to have a nice man friend to go out to dinner with occasionally, have a bit of fun with, you know. People think because you're a certain age, or a widow, that all that sort of nonsense goes out of your head – and it does, most of the time. But inside, part of us always remains a young, hopeful girl. I know that sounds ridiculous, but it's true.'

'It doesn't sound ridiculous at all,' Charlotte hugged her. 'You've been wonderful, so brave, and you must miss Daddy dreadfully.'

'Oh, it's not so bad. I'm just feeling a bit maudlin, that's all,' she said, returning to her usual brisk self. 'And be careful, Charlotte, you'll ruin your make-up.'

'Oh God, there's the doorbell.' Charlotte looked alarmed.

'Well go on, hurry up.' Jennifer gave her a prod. 'Have a lovely time, and don't talk about your divorce or your lack of a social life.'

'I have a very full social life, by any standards.' Charlotte was indignant.

'You know what I mean,' Jennifer replied ominously. 'And if he asks you out again, which he will, tell him you're not free for at least a week – that you're inundated with suitors.'

'Really, Mummy, now you *are* being ridiculous,' Charlotte laughed. 'I'd better go. Will you be all right?'

'Of course I'll be all right. Aren't I always? And Charlotte?'

'Yes?' Charlotte paused at the top of the stairs.

'You look lovely. You're a very good-looking woman. I don't think I ever told you that – not properly. He's damned lucky to be taking you out to dinner. Now get going.' She waved dismissively at her.

'Bye, Mummy, see you later.'

'I hope not – I shall be fast asleep with any luck, with or without my make-up. We'll catch up tomorrow – or whenever.'

It was pathetic to feel this nervous. It was only dinner. Only getting into a taxi, going to a restaurant, picking up a knife and fork and eating and talking, like normal people did every day of the week. All the same, P.J. wished someone would answer the bloody door. He felt very peculiar standing there at the top of the steps in his new suit, and a very nice new suit it was. He had treated himself to it as part of his new slimmer image. His tailor had been impressed, not just at the long-overdue visit from his long-time client, but at his new, improved measurements. 'Well, well, well, P.J.,' he had said. 'You're an inspiration to the rest of us. You're a fine figure of a man – I haven't seen you looking so well in years. It'll be a pleasure to kit you out in a few new suits. You'll be a grand advertisement for me.'

And it had been fun. He'd commissioned three. The one he was wearing now was an elegant, dark navy, single-breasted number, with a bright red lining, just for fun. He was glad now he hadn't worn a tie, just a crisp, white, open-necked shirt. He fingered the collar now, chewing his lip. He'd give it thirty more seconds, then he was out of here. He wondered if he'd got the day wrong. He was capable of anything, but he was sure he had said eight o'clock on Friday. At the bottom of the drive, the taxi waited patiently.

Suddenly the door opened, and there she was.

'I'm so sorry, I don't think I heard the bell the first time,' she said breathlessly. 'I hope I didn't keep you waiting?' She looked anxiously at him.

'Not at all,' he grinned, taking in the vision that stood in front of him. 'But I was just about to lose my nerve. It's been a long time since I've, um, asked anyone out to dinner.'

'Oh,' Charlotte sounded relieved. 'Me too. I almost had to have a drink for Dutch courage.'

P.J. thought it best not to divulge that he had almost cancelled out of nerves. 'You look fantastic,' he said truthfully. 'I ordered a taxi, shall we go?'

'Absolutely,' Charlotte beamed. 'Just let me make sure I have my keys before I close the door. I'm a bit flustered.'

Just then a voice floated down from upstairs.

'Charlotte?' P.J. recognised Jennifer's voice, calling loudly.

'Yes, Mummy?'

'Remember, no sex on a first date – I don't care how old you both are.' It was followed by a throaty chuckle.

'Oh, God.' Charlotte put her hands to her face. 'I do not believe she said that. The woman's a witch.' She closed the door, and then they both began to laugh.

'She's quite a woman, your mother,' said P.J., taking her arm as they went down the steps and to the taxi, where he held the door open for her as she slid in, then got in himself around the other side. 'If you have half her spirit, it should be an interesting evening.'

'I must apologise for her – she's incorrigible.'

'She's only having a bit of fun,' P.J. grinned, 'and isn't that what life's about?'

'You're right,' Charlotte agreed, 'it is, and I for one haven't been having nearly enough of it.'

'Me neither,' P.J. said. 'What about we start making up for lost time then? Tonight, fun will be on the menu, first and foremost.'

'You're on,' said Charlotte, rising to the challenge. And

suddenly she didn't feel nervous at all, just comfortable, and a little bit giddy.

'Good,' said P.J. approvingly, and then to the taxi driver, 'Dominic's restaurant, please, and don't spare the horses.'

Further across town, in the Mansion House ballroom, James Coleman was also having a surprisingly good time. He had been dreading going to the charity ball alone, even if it was in the company of his good friends Mike and Janet. But despite his misgivings, the evening was proving very enjoyable. Their party of ten were a lively bunch and included, seated to his left, a beautiful, recently divorced blonde whose husband had been involved in a less than desirable paternity suit with a young Danish actress. The tabloids had had a field day with what was widely referred to as the Danish Pastry Affair, and his wife, a former model, had sent him packing. James remembered meeting her a couple of times over the years, although not at such close quarters, and was finding her to be charming and amusing company. She appeared to be equally captivated by him. By the time the band started up, James found himself asking her to dance and they were cutting quite a dash on the floor. Around the ballroom, people were watching and commenting with discreet interest. As the grapevine went into action, more than one available, and many other *not* so available women, felt a definite thrill to hear that it was true: James Coleman was almost certainly on the market again.

One person was not having a good Friday night. In fact, it was the worst Friday night of her life. In her (borrowed) flat off Stephen's Green, Tanya sat in her living room in semi-darkness, the television on but muted. As a series of pictures flitted across the screen, she watched, numbly, as people moved, conversed and went about everyday, normal actions as she sat, alone and silent. It had been more than two weeks since the unspeakably dreadful night of her leap-year proposal to Dom. How she had managed to get through it, she didn't know – sheer, automated habit had got her up every morning and into the shower. The face that she looked at as she applied her make-up had looked the same, but surely could not belong to her. She felt as if nothing did, or ever had. She had done the bare minimum at work, avoided her mother and finally, the equally dreaded and desired weekend had arrived, where at last she could be left alone and could lock herself in her flat and stop the pretence that life as she knew it could possibly continue in any realm of normality.

How could she have done it? How could she have been so abysmally, profoundly stupid? What could have possessed her? How could she have blown her romance, her life, sky high? The questions as much as the memories tormented her. Up until then, everything had been just fine. She was sure it had. If only she had waited – if only she had played it cool – if only she had got pregnant – *anything* at all except the disastrous action she had taken that had unleashed this unimaginable result. And she had planned it all so carefully – but not carefully enough. She hadn't asked herself the un-answerable question of what she would do if Dom turned her down because it was unthinkable to her. She couldn't, wouldn't, contemplate such a thing. But then fate had inter-vened, the fate she had fought against every single day of her life, and now, just as she thought she had triumphed, it had caught her out. And no matter what she said or did or how many times she thought things over from every conceiv-able angle, there didn't seem to be a single thing she could do about it. She had lost him. Dom Coleman-Cappabianca was gone from her life.

Even her money problems paled into insignificance. She may have been broke, but Dom was special – he would have looked after her, taken care of her, she knew he would have.

Putting her head in her hands, Tanya sobbed and sobbed.

It didn't make her feel any better, but it did make her feel calmer. And then she felt something else, something so real, so all-consuming it almost took her breath away. It was pure, unadulterated, primeval rage, and it coursed through her, wave after wave of it. This was something she could relate to, could allow herself to feel, unlike the dreadful, bereft feeling of loss and emptiness, which she could do nothing about. This was palpable, this rage. It would motivate her, inspire her to function, to act. Did Dom Coleman-Cappabianca think he could dispose of her, abandon her without so much as a backward glance, turn her out of his apartment, take away her key? Tanya laughed out loud, the sudden sound almost shocking her. Tomorrow was another day, and she was going to make that bastard Dom pay for robbing her of her dreams, her life. He would rue the day he ever crossed her.

She sat up straighter and turned on the lamp beside her, then flicked the remote until she found the shopping channel. Her mother was right – all men *were* bastards. But there was always something you could do to cheer yourself up. For Tanya, that was shopping. So what if her credit cards were nearly all maxed out? She deserved to buy herself something. She didn't need to splurge – just a little present or two for herself, it always made her feel better. She needed it now more than ever.

12

April was Cici's favourite time of the year in Rome. She was shown to her suite in the chic Hotel de Russie on Via del Babuino and sat down gratefully on the bed, kicking off her shoes. It was so good to be back. She would have a quick shower, then spend the day shopping and wandering around before meeting Sophia. Her daughter was coming down from Florence that evening and they would spend the time catching up and having a good heart-to-heart. She couldn't wait to see her and to hear all her news. On the phone, Sophia had sounded concerned, but Cici had reassured her that everything was fine, really, that she would explain things to her when she saw her.

Truthfully, things were very far from fine – which was another reason Cici was glad to be out of Dublin and back in her native Rome, even if it was only for two all-too-brief days. It would give her time to think. It had been so much fun in the beginning, but now, facing the facts she knew she would have to face sooner or later, Cici could see that her fling with Harry was just that – a fling. A delicious, exciting one to be sure, but it had no future, none at all. He would see that too, she was sure, when she explained that they would just have to remain friends from here on out. For now, though, she wouldn't think about it – she would enjoy Rome and its delights and cherish the short time she would have with Sophia.

Cici adored her children. They were everything she had hoped for and more, bright, kind, funny and generous. Even

Dom hadn't been judgemental about it when she had dined very obviously several times in his restaurant with Harry. If it had bothered him, he had never said so – although it must have, she thought with a stab of guilt. And that lovely young waitress who had served them, what was her name? Oh yes, Carla – Cici had noticed Dom gazing at her several times. She was sure he fancied her, and if the lingering looks Carla had thrown in his direction were anything to go by, the feeling was certainly mutual.

Cici smiled. Carla reminded her of herself when she was younger, and she would be a far better girl for Dom than the awful Tanya. Thank God that was over – or so Sophia had told her on the phone. Cici had wisely said nothing to Dom about it – one never knew with young people. She hoped it *was* over, but what if they got back together? She sincerely hoped not, but in the meantime she would keep her opinions to herself. After all, it wasn't as if she had any right to advise anyone on their love life at present. But all that was about to change. She would sort things out calmly and with dignity on her return home.

She would break things gently to Harry when she got back to Dublin. He would be upset, of course, but he would understand, see the sense of it. After all, he was a brilliant journalist, a writer – he knew how the script went. And there would be no shortage of young, eager girls to console him. She smiled rather sadly, thinking of it, but it was the only way. She had just wanted a bit of fun, really, one last, naughty love affair. Hadn't she said at the very outset that she had been good at pretending? And he had entered into the whole spirit of that fun.

The past six weeks *had* been fun, she thought, allowing the powerful jets of water to sluice over her as she washed off the flight, but when he had begun to move his clothes in and then, to her horror, had set up a fax machine in the spare bedroom, and then that rather awkward moment when he had suggested she give him a key . . . well, she had known that it was time to put a stop to things. The weekend away had come just in time to avoid the 'we need to talk' conversation, but she was sure that he had guessed, and being the delightful, well-mannered young man he was, he would take it all in his stride.

Lately, too, she'd been missing James. This had surprised her. Not because she didn't love him – she did, hugely – but because she had assumed they'd drifted apart the way so many couples did even in the midst of being so together. James, she often thought, was married to his work and golf had become his mistress. That was true from a certain perspective, but from another, truer one, she realised how that very togetherness, however mundane it may seem, had a physical presence of its own. She missed his quiet, thoughtful, determined devotion, his unstinting support for whatever she did, particularly in this case, which he didn't, couldn't possibly, understand, and which must be so terribly painful for him. But it was all she had needed, this trial separation, this foray into irresponsibility, this last taste of freedom, of things forbidden. She wondered what he was doing now and smiled, thinking of him. He had been so strong and clever, really, to leave her alone as she had asked of him. There had been no pestering phone calls, no demands to know what she was doing and with whom, no nasty manipulating or turning the children against her, which he could so easily have done. She had worried about that. She knew she was pushing it being seen around town with Harry, but no one could prove anything. James was definitely not the type of husband who would have her watched or spied on. He was far too much of a gentleman and had too much integrity, an integrity that she very much respected him for.

James, she realised, as she had suspected that night in the Horseshoe Bar so long ago, was a man in a million. She just had to tell him that, and she would, repeatedly. She would make it up to him. She would tell him how wrong she'd been, how easily and stupidly she had trifled with their marriage, their family. She knew now, without a shadow of a doubt, that that was the only thing that meant *anything* to her, that wonderful, extraordinary unit that she and James had created, that had been, that *was* her strength, her raison d'être for all those years when she had thought herself to be slipping away, becoming invisible – now she knew it was the only tangible thing that made her what she truly was: a wife, a lover, a mother. The most affirming roles to the feminine psyche – the ones that no career, no amount of freedom, publicity or celebrity could possibly provide – and she had taken them so much, so shamefully, for granted. She belonged with James, with her family. Every fibre of her being told her so.

Feeling calmer and happier about her decision, she dressed quickly, slipping into a cool pink linen trouser suit and a pair of flat black patent Tod's she could traverse the cobbled streets in as comfortably as possible. The phone, when it rang, startled her.

'Señora Coleman-Cappabianca?' the voice from the front desk enquired.

'Yes?'

'There is someone to see you in reception. Shall I say you will come down?'

'Of course, I was just on my way. Who is it?'

There was the slightest pause. 'I am instructed to tell you it is a surprise.'

'Oh, I see.' Cici smiled into the phone. Sophia must have arrived earlier than she'd anticipated. She had probably caught an earlier flight. How wonderful. Now they could go for a lovely long lunch. 'I'll be down right away. I'm leaving now.'

Catherine placed the tiny wicker chair in the corner of the newly decorated nursery and almost laughed aloud. It was so small! Ridiculous, really, like a doll's chair, but she had been unable to resist it when she had come across it in the village shop. It was a brightly coloured pink and blue, with a bit of yellow thrown in for good measure. Set in the corner, it looked adorable. She tried to imagine a little person sitting in it and shook her head. Bending down to move it ever so slightly to the left, she felt the first sharp twinge. Startled, she gasped and straightened up, rubbing her back where she had felt it. Gosh, if labour pains were a lot worse than that, then she really wasn't looking forward to it. She focused instead on the excitement, just under eight more weeks, and it wouldn't be a minute too soon. She was fed up now and dying for the pregnancy to be over. She felt tired now almost all the time, and she was bored too. Wandering downstairs, she decided to make a cup of tea and watch some lunchtime TV, anything to take her mind off things. Alex was away for the day in London, talking to some bank or other, and he had been even more tetchy and jumpy than usual. Actually, it was a relief not to have him around. He was beginning to make her more nervous than she already was.

She was three steps from the bottom when the next pain hit her, harder and swifter, almost taking her breath away. She grabbed the handrail for support and suddenly felt frightened. It was a false alarm, surely. It couldn't be happening – not now. She was only thirty-three weeks, babies weren't supposed to arrive until forty. She got to the kitchen before another band of pain contracted around her middle, almost doubling her over with the force. Reaching for her mobile phone, she quickly called an ambulance. Oh please, please, let this not be happening, not now when Alex was away, when she was alone. She dialled Alex's number, but it went to voicemail. She left a brief, breathless message. Then she called P.J.'s surgery and prayed for someone to answer.

'Dr O'Sullivan's surgery,' Sheila's clipped tones answered.

'Oh Sheila,' Catherine gasped, the phone trembling in her hand. 'Something's wrong. Tell P.J. the baby's coming and

Alex is in London. I've called an ambulance, but – ohhh,' she groaned as another contraction hit. 'Please, just tell him.'

Almost crying with relief, she managed to open the door to the ambulance crew. 'My bag,' she cried, 'it's upstairs, in the front room.'

'Don't worry, love,' said the paramedic. 'We'll have it in a jiffy.' He helped her to a chair as she groaned again. 'How far along are you?'

'Thirty-three weeks.' She looked stricken.

'We'll have you there in no time. Just try to relax. Tom,' he yelled to his colleague who had run upstairs to get the bag, 'make it sharp, looks like we have an early arrival here.'

'Oh God. My husband – he's not here.'

'Don't you worry, love.' He helped her into the ambulance. 'We'll get in touch with anyone you need to call. Which hospital is it?'

'Holles Street,' she gasped.

'We'll have you there in no time. Right, Tom, Holles Street – full steam ahead,' he nodded at the driver jovially, although Catherine could see the seriousness in his expression. As the sirens started to wail, tears began to roll down Catherine's cheeks. She had never felt so frightened in her entire life.

P.J. was writing a prescription for anti-anxiety medication to a very charming, if neurotic, twice-divorced woman who had been a patient of his long before her first marriage, when the phone on his desk rang.

'If only all men were as understanding as you are, Dr O'Sullivan,' she beamed at him adoringly, 'I'm quite sure the divorce rate would halve overnight.'

'Excuse me please while I take this.' He tried not to sound impatient, but Sheila knew never to interrupt him mid-consult – not unless it was serious. However, 'serious' to Sheila, if she was having one of her days, could mean that he wasn't hustling patients through on what she considered to be a time-efficient schedule. Though that hadn't happened in quite a while.

'I see. Right.' His voice was grim. 'Cancel all patients for this afternoon, we'll reschedule for tomorrow.'

'An emergency?' The divorcee looked simultaneously hopeful and impressed.

'Yes, I'm afraid so, one I must attend to immediately. Sheila will see you out.' He terminated the visit abruptly, handing her the prescription.

'Oh,' said his patient, sounding disappointed. 'Yes, of course. Good luck with it.'

'I should think we'll need quite a bit of that – and thank you.' P.J. stood up as she left the room, then he grabbed his phone and strode out of the surgery, leaving Sheila to give the few waiting patients the bad news.

Cici took the lift down to reception and strolled towards the front desk.

'Ah, Señora Coleman-Cappabianca,' the concierge smiled, 'your guest is outside, in the terrace. Champagne is already on its way.'

Champagne! Well, it *was* a quarter past twelve, Cici supposed, although it was rather unlike Sophia to order it. She wandered outside, where her gaze drifted to one of the occupied tables in the shade of the umbrellas that were dotted around the famous terrace, and then her smile froze as the champagne arrived and was duly set down and poured. It wasn't Sophia who raised a glass to salute her – but Harry.

He stood up to greet her, his face alight, but suddenly Cici was gripped with foreboding. This was going to be difficult. *Look on the bright side*, she told herself. At least she was alone. Imagine if Sophia had been with her, which could so easily have happened. She would have to play this carefully.

'Well,' she said, allowing him to kiss her on the cheek and hug her, 'this is certainly a surprise.' She sat down and took a much-needed sip of champagne.

'A good one, I hope,' he grinned playfully. 'I couldn't resist it. Well, that's not quite the truth,' he looked at her meaningfully. 'Actually, I couldn't bear the thought of being without you for a whole weekend, and you in Rome, alone . . . I just had to.'

'Harry,' she began gently.

'I thought maybe we could stay on for a while, together, you know, when your daughter goes back. I told them to leave my luggage in your suite.'

Oh, God. This was worse than she could possibly have imagined. Cici bit her lip. 'Harry, darling Harry, I'm afraid that is impossible, and it wasn't a good idea at all for you to come here.'

'What do you mean?' He looked surprised. 'Nothing's impossible. I'm here, aren't I? I'm looking forward to meeting Sophia. Isn't that her name? We can all have a lovely time, then when we're alone . . .' He reached over to stroke her cheek and suddenly she felt a spasm of anger. How dare he follow her here? How dare he spoil a weekend she had planned with her daughter?

'Harry,' she said sharply, 'listen to me.' She had his attention now. He slouched back in his chair, his face sulky and (how had she never noticed this before?) unattractively child like. 'I told you I was coming to Rome to meet my daughter to catch up with her, do some shopping. I never in a thousand years dreamed you'd follow me here. It's unthinkable.'

'Why?' he asked, a sneer lacing his voice. 'Why is it so unthinkable?' He looked at her speculatively. 'You've done a lot of unthinkable things with me, haven't you? As long as they're on your terms, you seem to find them perfectly acceptable. *More* than acceptable, I would go so far as to say.'

He smiled nastily, while Cici, almost lost for words, felt a slow blush creeping up her neck and flooding her face. She wasn't sure if it was induced by mortification or rage. She tried to keep her temper.

'Be reasonable, Harry. I'm here in Rome to see my daughter.'

'So you've said.'

'If I had wanted or thought it appropriate for you to be here, I would have asked you to be here. This,' she waved her hand, 'is totally inappropriate.' She took a deep breath. 'It's out of the question for me to introduce you to Sophia. She doesn't even know about you.'

'Us,' he corrected her. 'She doesn't know about *us*.' He was leaning in towards her now. 'There are, in case it has slipped your memory, Cici, two of us in this relationship.'

'Not any more.' The words escaped her before she could stop them.

'I'm sorry?'

'So am I, Harry. I never anticipated this, but then, you never gave me a chance to.' She took a deep breath. 'I'm afraid I'm going to have to ask you to leave.'

'To leave?'

'Yes, Harry, to leave. I didn't want to have this conversation, certainly not here, and certainly not under these awful circumstances, but you leave me no choice.'

'And what if I don't?'

Cici felt her throat constrict as a fresh wave of panic gripped her. She mustn't let him see it or sense how flustered she was – no, make that frightened. 'Then you will be making things unnecessarily awkward for yourself.'

'For myself?'

'Yes, Harry, for yourself. There was no need for any of this. If you had only talked to me, consulted with me—'

'Consulted!' He almost spat the word as he stood up, pushing the chair back angrily. 'I have to consult with you?

The woman who threw herself at me, begged me, pleaded with me, night after night? "More, Harry, oh yes, Harry, don't stop, Harry,"' he mocked her.

'Please,' she whispered, bringing her hand to her mouth. 'Please don't do this.'

'What's that, Cici?' He put his hand behind his ear. 'I didn't quite hear you – a little louder, please. You were asking me something. Sorry, *begging me*, weren't you? You appear to be very good at that at least.' He came around and leaned into her neck as she recoiled.

'You don't understand.' She was almost sobbing now. 'You should never have come here.'

'Don't worry,' he hissed at her, his eyes blazing. 'I'm going. But you haven't heard the last of me. Nobody, least of all some pathetic, middle-aged woman whose husband can't even be bothered to fight for her, tells me what to do.' He laughed a hard, bitter laugh. 'He was probably glad I took you off his hands for a while.'

'How dare you!'

'Very easily, Cici. Who do you think you are, anyway? You're just a sad woman pushing fifty, desperate for some young flesh. You're all the bloody same. Don't think you're any different. You disgust me!'

And with that he strode away, attracting not a few interested glances to their table in his wake.

She sat there, stunned, immobile, and then remembered where she was – in public. Anyone at all could be watching. Summoning all the acting talent that had failed to get her to the silver screen in the past, Cici regained her composure, at least outwardly, sat back in her chair and took another sip of champagne. Never had it tasted quite so bitter. As if on cue, the waiter arrived with the bill to sign. 'Señora,' he placed it discreetly in front of her, then gestured questioningly at the empty glass opposite her. 'Take it away,' Cici said, signing her room number with a flourish, although she felt as if she might faint. What the hell. A wasted bottle of Krug was the least of her worries.

P.J. parked his car in an almost legitimate space opposite the National Maternity Hospital. Who cared about clamping at a time like this? He had called Alex, of course, who had left his meeting in London immediately and was desperately trying to make his way to Heathrow and get the first flight he could. P.J. had told him not to worry, that he was on his way to the hospital.

'Thanks, Dad.' Alex was grateful. 'I really appreciate it.'

'Don't worry, everything will be fine, I'm sure of it. Holles Street has the best neonatal staff in the world. Whatever happens, Catherine and the baby will be in the best possible hands.'

'Ring me the minute you know anything.'

'Will do.'

Now P.J. ran across the road and in through the doors of Holles Street and was instantly transported back to earlier times, when Alex, his own son, had been born.

'Catherine O'Sullivan?' he asked at the front desk. 'She's a patient of Dan Collins. I'm her father-in-law, Dr P.J. O'Sullivan. She was admitted about an hour ago?'

'Just a moment, Dr O'Sullivan, I'll check for you now. Take a seat.' P.J. waited for what seemed like an interminable amount of time with other excited or weary relatives. Just then, the girl he had spoken to approached him. 'Catherine is in the recovery room. I spoke to Dr Collins's registrar and you can go down now, they're expecting you.'

Getting out of the lift and walking down the corridor, P.J. immediately recognised Dan Collins talking to one of his staff. He looked up as P.J. approached. 'P.J.,' he exclaimed, smiling, 'good to see you.'

'Dan, we're all worried sick. What's the story?'

'It all went very well.' He patted his old friend on the back reassuringly. 'We did an emergency section. Catherine's coming around now but she's very groggy. The baby's in neonatal intensive. Why don't you go in and see her, then I'll take you over.'

P.J. went over to Catherine and pulled up a chair. 'Hey,' he said, taking her hand. 'Hello, Mum, how're you doing? You gave us all a fright.'

Her eyes fluttered open and she smiled. She was still very out of it. 'P.J.,' she murmured. 'The baby . . .?'

'It's all right, Catherine, everything will be just fine. You just need to rest now.'

'Alex?' she whispered.

'He's on his way. He should be here in a couple of hours, he's at Heathrow.'

'But my baby . . . where?'

'The baby's in neonatal,' he told her, leaving out the 'intensive'.

'Will you . . .?'

'I'm going there right now. You just get some rest. I'll be right back.' She was already fast asleep.

It was only when he rejoined Dan and they made their way over to the hushed area of neonatal intensive care that P.J. stopped in his tracks. 'Dan, I forgot to ask – boy or girl?'

'Congratulations, Granddad,' he smiled, 'it's a boy!'

As the doors opened and they were allowed in, P.J. felt his throat constrict that his first grandson, Alex's boy, would have to make his foray into the world in such a tenuous, precarious manner.

'Don't look so worried, P.J.,' Dan said. 'He'll have the best possible care here, you know that. He's thirty-three weeks, a little earlier than we'd have liked, but he'll do fine, just you see.'

P.J. looked down at the tiny figure in the incubator and shook his head. Around him, the highly trained team were working in their quietly efficient manner. He was already on a ventilator and a drip was being inserted into his scalp. It was all routine procedure, nothing P.J. hadn't seen a hundred times before, but now he felt so completely helpless. He felt a huge rush of affection for this little chap who couldn't be held by his parents and was struggling so bravely all alone.

'Come on, old chap,' Dan said quietly. 'Let's get back to Catherine, she'll need someone to be with her. They'll keep a good eye on him here.'

'I know they will,' P.J. said, reluctantly tearing himself away. 'It's just all been a bit of a shock.'

They were almost at the door when P.J. noticed one of the nurses look back sharply in the direction of the baby's incubator. He followed her glance to the Registrar, who was bending over and checking the drip on his grandson. His expression had changed from one of concern to urgency. He looked up and beckoned. 'Over here *now*, guys, *quickly*. Looks like we've got a bleeder.'

'Come on, P.J.' Dan was sympathetic but firm as P.J. froze. 'They know what they're doing. Go back to Catherine, I'll keep you updated. *Go.*'

Cici had returned to her suite as nonchalantly as possible, although inside she was frantic. Passing reception, there was no sign of Harry, and she hoped against hope that he had gone and hadn't somehow wangled his way into the room. She opened the door slowly. There were no signs of anything untoward. Just to be sure she checked everywhere – cupboards, bathroom, even under the beds. Then she reproved herself. This was madness! Of course his luggage wasn't here! All the same, she felt terribly nervous. She wondered if she should phone him, then decided against it. Really, he had behaved appallingly. He knew full well that she had come to Rome specifically to catch up with Sophia, have a heart-to-heart and do some shopping. She had never even hinted that he should join her.

She sat down on the bed suddenly, putting her face in her hands. She had seen another side to Harry now, a rather unpleasant, unnerving one. His reaction hadn't been in any way apologetic or even conciliatory. He had been livid the moment he realised she was serious about asking him to leave, livid and unnecessarily vicious. His hurtful remarks were still reverberating in her head. The whole thing had left her shaken. But it was a lesson, she told herself, a good lesson, and thank God Sophia hadn't been around to witness it. She would never allow such a near miss to happen again.

Pulling herself together, she left the suite and took the lift down to reception, where she left strict instructions that she was expecting her daughter to join her that evening at about seven o'clock and that she alone was the only visitor she would be entertaining. The man at the front desk told her he understood completely and informed her that her previous visitor had left and taken his luggage with him. Harry seemed to have gone on his way.

Feeling considerably better about things, Cici left the hotel and paused for a moment, deciding where to go. Instinctively, she turned left, strolling up Via Babuino, hardly noticing its discreet art galleries, exclusive antique shops and furnishing stores, heading for her favourite stomping ground of the Spanish Steps and Piazza di Spagna. Absorbing the sights and smells of her native city, she began to feel better, its familiar, bustling ambiance restoring her with every step. She checked her watch; it was a quarter to one. Suddenly she discovered she was ravenously hungry. She grinned to herself – drama always had that effect on her. She needed lunch, and she knew exactly where she was going to go. Turning right into Via della Croce, she made her way to her favourite restaurant, Fiaschetteria Beltramme, the hugely trendy place for fashion and media people in Rome. As Cici walked past a queue of ordinary mortals and tourists and into the interior that could have passed for an Italian grandmother's front room, she was welcomed instantly in a similar fashion by Toni, one of the long-time staff. 'Señora Cici!' He rushed over to her, beaming from ear to ear. 'How wonderful to see you. You are dining alone?'

'Yes, Toni, just a table for one, if you can fit me in?'

'There is always a table for you here, Señora,' he said warmly, showing her to what she knew was one of the most enviously coveted tables in the house.

'Thank you, Toni,' she smiled up at him as she slid into the chair. 'It's good to be home.'

James heard his mobile phone bleep twice and saw he had a message. He knew who it was from too. He opened it, smiling. He wasn't used to receiving messages. He mostly used his phone to make or take a quick call whenever needed, but lately, his phone had been the bearer of some very nice, and for a change, endearing, communications. It was from Sarah, the beautiful blonde divorcee who had been quite unabashedly chasing him since they had sat together at the charity ball. James was finding it quite disconcerting, really, but in a very nice way. *Dinner at my place tonight? 8:30? Do say yes. Longing to see you! Sarah xx*

James thought about it for a minute, then texted back. *Love to!* He put his phone back in his pocket and smiled. Why not? He didn't have any other plans for the evening.

He thought about Cici. He knew she was in Rome and that she would be meeting Sophia for some mother–daughter catching up. He could just imagine the pair of them hitting the shops. He was almost caught by a swift pang of regret, but with enormous self-will told himself he was doing the right thing. The papers had gone out today. On her return, Cici would discover that he had decided to file for separation and divorce.

He gave a deep sigh and forced himself to concentrate on the sales figures in front of him, suddenly very glad of the surprise dinner invitation. Sarah was amusing company, and she had been through the mill herself over the past year or two and understood the ravages a prospective divorce unleashed on someone. He was looking forward to dinner with her. At the very least, it would take his mind off his own immeasurably sad domestic situation.

P.J. was suddenly overcome with tiredness. Sitting in his kitchen with Bones at his feet, he realised he hadn't eaten since breakfast. He decided to throw on some pasta and open a bottle of red. What a day! Poor Catherine. She'd been terribly upset, not unnaturally, at the turn things had taken. Thank God Alex had got back, though, and once he had turned up and rushed to her side, Catherine had burst into tears of relief and, P.J. supposed, sheer exhaustion. He had left them alone then, and his good friend Dan Collins had been marvellous, sitting with them and explaining everything to them and taking them to see their newborn son. Charlie, they were going to call him. They were a proper little family now, the three of them. P.J. felt quite emotional just thinking about it. Seeing her face light up as Alex had come into the room, concern and love written all over his face for her, P.J. was thankful that his own son clearly had a wife who adored him, as he did her. It was what every marriage – every family – should be.

Thinking of family, he suddenly remembered. In the midst of all the drama, he had clean forgotten to tell his sisters, and indeed his own father the news that he was a great-grand-father. It was only seven-thirty, P.J. checked, not too late to ring him. At eighty-five years of age, Charles O'Sullivan was still in good health, if a little frail. His wife, Maureen, P.J.'s mother, had passed away three years ago after a series of strokes. Charles still lived in their small regency villa just ten minutes from Wellington Square in the care of two full-time

Filipino carer nurses. It was a perfect arrangement, as Charles made no secret of the fact that he would hate going into a residential home, preferring to take his chances and go 'with his boots on', as he put it, in the comfort of his own home. P.J. was in the happy position of being able to help him to do so, financially at any rate. His father was under the illusion that he was paying for the nurses entirely from his own capital resources – if he had known the true cost of employing them, which P.J. contributed to considerably, he would have keeled over on the spot. He answered the phone now in the less robust, but familiar tones, which by turns had both comforted and terrified P.J. as a young boy.

'Dad, it's me.'

'P.J. How nice to hear from you.'

'Are you sitting down?'

'I rarely do anything else these days,' he chuckled. 'As a matter of fact, I'm just reading the *Medical Times*. Why do you ask?'

'Well, the good news is you've just become a great-grandfather. The bad news is that makes me a grandfather.' P.J. grinned at his end.

'How marvellous! Congratulations, P.J., I'm so pleased. But I thought, or am I being dopey, the happy event was still some weeks away?'

'No, you're spot on, Dad. The little grey cells are still as efficient as ever. He's a preemie, arrived at thirty-three weeks. Dan Collins was looking after Catherine, did a wonderful job.'

'It's a boy then!'

'It certainly is.'

'Well, well, well, another O'Sullivan. With a bit of luck he might even be a rugby player, eh?'

P.J. paused. 'I'm not so sure about that, Dad.'

'What? Why?'

'He's a bleeder,' P.J. explained. 'The tests came back late this evening, Von Willebrand's.' P.J. knew his father realised the implications. 'They were alerted when they put the drip in.'

'Of course, of course,' his father tutted. 'Oh dear, that must have been worrying for Alex and Catherine, poor things. But just as well they know. It's easily treated and monitored these days, the drugs are first rate. Shouldn't affect the little chap at all, they'll just have to be careful with surgery and dentists, of course. But I see what you mean, contact sports probably aren't a good idea. Still, we must be thankful for small mercies. At least he made the trip here safely. When can they take him home?'

'All going well, Dan Collins thought two weeks.'

'Good, good.' Charles sounded thoughtful. 'Von Willebrand's certainly isn't in our side of the family – you realise that, don't you? Jilly must have been a carrier and not known it – unless Catherine is, of course.'

'Yes, I was thinking that.' P.J. rubbed his chin distractedly.

'Well, I'm sure they're doing the full profile of tests. Marvellous what they can pinpoint these days. Medicine has come so far since my time. All the same, you should all get yourselves tested. There's Bella to consider, she should know if she's a carrier.'

'She's coming home next week. I'll discuss it with her, but right now she's just over the moon about having a new nephew.'

'How wonderful. I'm looking forward to seeing her. Do give her my love.'

'Oh, and Dad?' P.J. saved the best bit of news till last. 'They're calling him Charlie, after you.'

'Well, well, well, how very kind.' P.J. thought he heard tears in his voice. 'Tell them I'm delighted, absolutely thrilled and delighted. In fact, I'm going to have a small glass of whiskey the minute I put the phone down.'

'In that case,' P.J. smiled, 'I won't delay you.'

'Thank you for ringing, P.J., I appreciate it, and congratulations again. It's quite a feeling becoming a grandfather, isn't it? I remember the day well myself, one of the proudest moments of my life.'

'Goodbye, Dad. Bella and I will see you when she's home.'

'I shall look forward to it.'

As P.J. put the phone down, he was lost in thought. His attention was captured by the pasta he had put on, which was now boiling over, water cascading and spitting onto the cooker. Rushing to turn down the gas, the unsettling, unarticulated thought that had begun to surface in the back of his mind was, for the present moment, forgotten.

He was just about to tuck in when his phone rang. It was Charlotte, of course. He had meant to ring her too; she was waiting for news.

'Charlotte!' he said. 'I'm so sorry, I completely forgot to call you back.'

'Never mind that.' He could tell she was smiling. 'Quick, tell me what happened.'

'It's a long story.'

'Well, are you or aren't you a grandfather?'

'As a matter of fact, I am,' P.J. said proudly. 'I have a beautiful grandson called Charlie.'

'Oh, P.J.,' she gasped. 'How wonderful. What are you doing?'

'Sorry,' he gulped, 'I was just shovelling some pasta into my mouth. Haven't eaten since this morning.'

'You mean you're sitting there on your own with a bowl of pasta when you should be celebrating?'

'Well, yes, I suppose so.'

'I've never heard anything so ridiculous in my life. Come over here right now, I've got champagne on ice and a lovely fresh salmon poaching.'

'I'd love to, if you're sure.'

'Of course I'm sure. It'll be a novelty for me. I've never had dinner with a grandfather before,' she chuckled.

'In that case, I don't see how I could possibly refuse.'

'And bring Bones if you want to, he shouldn't be left out either.'

P.J. smiled. 'We'll see you in ten.'

Cici looked at her daughter sitting across from her and smiled.

'What are you thinking, Mum?' Sophia pushed a glossy dark ringlet over her shoulder and looked at her mother speculatively as she bent to take a sip of her cosmopolitan in the stylish stemless cocktail glasses that sat in tumblers on their very own beds of ice.

'I'm just thinking how beautiful you are, and how very happy I am to be here with you,' Cici sighed.

'Me too,' grinned Sophia. 'And you look beautiful too, Mum. You always do.'

She had arrived, as arranged, at seven o'clock with a flurry of hugs and kisses, chattering ten to the dozen. After examining the suite thoroughly and proclaiming it perfect, she had taken a shower and they decided to have a drink in the bar downstairs before dining in the hotel or perhaps heading up to one of their favourite restaurants near the Spanish Steps. Tomorrow they would go shopping. Now, Cici listened happily to Sophia's accounts of university and her student life in Florence.

'Let's have another, shall we?' Sophia suggested as the waiter came to take their glasses.

'Why not?' smiled Cici. 'It's been far too long since we've chatted like this. I could listen to you all evening. Tell, me,' she asked, 'have you heard from Mimi?'

Sophia nodded. 'She's having a brilliant time. She's in Buenos Aires right now. Her Facebook accounts are scintillating,' she grinned.

'I dread to think what she's up to.'

'Oh, nothing much, just a lot of partying and sightseeing.' Sophia chewed her lip, thinking of the phone call from

Dom and wondering if she should broach the delicate subject that was her parents' marriage. 'Mum, I don't mean to pry, but what's going on with you and Dad? It's just that Dom was talking to me and he seemed worried.'

'There's nothing to be concerned about, darling.' Cici was immediately consumed with guilt. She knew her children knew about the temporary separation, but other than that, both James and she had agreed not to say anything further on the subject. 'Daddy and I needed this time apart. Sometimes couples do, just to, well, reassess things.'

'I don't think Daddy needed it.' Sophia looked at her mother astutely. 'It's just that everybody always thought you and Daddy were so happy together.' She bit her lip anxiously. 'Aren't you?'

'Oh, darling.' Cici was flooded with remorse. 'Of course we were – *are*. I think this time apart was a good thing, really I do. And yes, you're right, I'm sure Daddy wasn't keen on the idea, but he's been wonderful, very understanding. He's allowed me my space, and I realise now that that was all I needed, just a bit of time on my own to have a little look at the world again, see what it feels like to be myself again and not just somebody's wife or somebody's mother.'

'So you're not getting a divorce then?'

Cici put down her drink and looked at her incredulously. 'A divorce? Of course not. Whatever put that thought into your head?'

Sophia thought it best not to mention what Dom had said. Perhaps he'd got it wrong. Maybe Dad had just been angry when he'd been talking to him.

'It's quite the opposite, actually,' Cici smiled ruefully. 'I've realised in the past few weeks just how much I love your father, and I'm going to tell him so the minute I get back home, and every day after that too.'

Sophia smiled. 'That's more like it, Mum. I was beginning

to think you'd taken leave of your senses. You'll never find another man like Daddy, you know.'

'I do know, darling. And I'm going to make it up to him, I promise.'

'Good,' said Sophia, finishing her drink. 'Now let's go for a stroll and find somewhere lovely to have dinner.' She felt a lot better after talking to her mother. Dom had obviously got the wrong end of the stick, which was typical of him. And this Harry person he had spoken of clearly didn't figure in her mother's plans at all, thank God. She hadn't even mentioned him to her. Linking her mother's arm in hers, they walked out of the hotel and decided to stroll to Piazza di Spagna.

'Isn't it brilliant that Dom has broken up with Tanya?' Sophia said. 'I couldn't stand her. There was something awfully sly about her.'

'I must say I couldn't warm to her at all,' Cici agreed. 'Poor girl, though. I'm sure she's terribly upset.'

'Not as upset as we'd be if Dom had married her,' Sophia said emphatically.

'Perish the thought,' Cici laughed.

'You know,' mused Sophia, 'I always thought Dom would go for someone more, well, passionate, sensual. A bon viveur, someone who loved their food, loved life and wasn't afraid to show it. Someone like—'

'Us, you mean?' Cici finished for her, laughing.

'Exactly.'

Sophia was right, Cici thought, that's exactly the type of woman Dom needed. And she was right under his nose – because those were the very words she would have used to describe Carla. Although she didn't know her well, it was the impression Cici had of her from the restaurant, and it wasn't for nothing all the staff and customers were mad about her too.

They strolled along happily, pausing on the Via Condotti

to admire the wonderful wares in the traditional designer clothes shops, where Sophia spotted and fell in love with a fabulous handbag. Cici, delighted to be on happier ground as regards her family, immediately insisted on purchasing it for her. 'I want to, *cara*,' she insisted when Sophia protested at the price. 'A beautiful handbag for my beautiful daughter. Now come, let's eat.'

At the top of the street, they entered the Piazza di Spagna, quirkily described as being shaped like a crooked bow tie, which it was, and surrounded by houses painted in muted shades of ochre, cream and russet. It was crowded, as always. Ahead lay the Spanish Steps, and to the right, another little tucked-away restaurant that Cici favoured. They found a table easily and were seated with welcoming smiles by the waiters, who were happy to escort them to one where they could see and be seen easily.

'I'm ravenous,' Sophia said as the waiter arrived and poured the wonderful Barolo from Tuscany that Cici had ordered.

Cici raised her glass. 'To family,' she said, smiling fondly at her daughter.

'I'll drink to that,' Sophia retorted warmly.

They had finished their meal and were just planning their shopping itinerary for the following day over coffees when a voice interrupted them.

'Cici, darling. And this gorgeous creature,' he said, his eyes roving over Sophia appreciatively, 'must be Sophia. I'm *so* sorry I'm late, but I only got away from my meeting just now. I hope you've ordered something delicious for me.'

As she looked up in utter disbelief, Cici saw Harry, who swiftly pulled up a chair from the table beside them and sat down, smiling confidently.

'Allow me to introduce myself. I've heard so much about you,' he said to Sophia, whose coffee cup had frozen on its way to her mouth. 'Harry McCabe.' He signalled to the waiter for a glass to be brought and helped himself to some wine.

For once in her life, Cici was lost for words, too horrified and shocked to take in the scene that was unfolding before her.

Sophia, on the other hand, was not. She looked disbelievingly from one to the other, and then, ignoring Harry, she turned on Cici with a horrified sob.

'Mum – how could you? How *could* you?'

'Darling, please,' Cici protested in vain while Harry sat there, looking calmly interested.

'I don't believe this.' Sophia looked at Harry with loathing.

'I'm sorry,' he enquired innocently, 'have I said something to upset you? Your mother assured me you were looking forward to meeting me, and I was – and indeed *am* – very much looking forward to meeting you.' He appeared bewildered and rather hurt.

'Harry!' Cici wanted to scream but her voice emerged as a whisper. She reached out to put a comforting hand on Sophia's arm, but it was too late. She had jumped up from her chair and was looking at Cici as if she were a stranger.

'You set this up!' she cried. 'Both of you! You never wanted to see me at all, it was all just a horrid excuse to introduce your – your lover boy to me.' She almost spat the words, then she ran from the table and pushed her way through the crowds, tears running down her face, and disappeared down Via Condotti.

Somehow, Cici found her voice. She looked at Harry, fury blazing from her eyes, but he remained smilingly unperturbed. 'You vicious, horrible, nasty human being. How could you?' she asked incredulously. 'What have I ever done to you to deserve this?'

'I did warn you, Cici,' he said calmly, though onlookers from neighbouring tables were beginning to take a distinct interest in them. 'I don't take kindly to being dismissed on a feminine whim. You treated me very shabbily back at the hotel. Now I'm afraid you're going to have to face the consequences.' He smiled infuriatingly.

'You're a monster. I don't know what I ever saw in you.' Cici was rigid with shock. 'I despise you.' She pushed her chair back and stood up from the table, pausing only to pick up Sophia's new handbag, which she had left behind.

'What a fickle creature you are,' he said nastily, watching her carefully. 'One minute it's James you don't want, the next minute it's me.'

'Don't you dare bring my husband into this – or any of my family.'

'Why not? I can do pretty much exactly as I please, Cici. You see, I don't have a wife or children, for that matter, to answer to. You, on the other hand, do. But I'm very disappointed in you Cici, very disappointed indeed.' His mouth was set in a thin line and his eyes were strangely alight in his face. 'I've done an awful lot for you, and you're really quite extraordinarily ungrateful.'

'Stay away from me,' she hissed, 'and stay away from my family.'

'Or what?' he asked blithely. 'It seems to me that you're finally out of your depth. You shouldn't have messed with me, with my affections. And now it seems there's really not a lot you can do about anything, is there? While I,' he said as he brought his glass to his mouth and took a drink of wine, 'can do exactly as I please.'

She had heard enough. She wouldn't listen to another word from this insane man who looked and sounded like Harry, but couldn't possibly be him. Fleeing the restaurant, Cici ran to the nearby taxi rank and flung herself into a car. 'Hotel de Russie,' she gasped to the driver. As the car pulled away, the tears began, and even then, she kept looking behind her, out the window, as if Harry could materialise before her yet again, determined to ruin everything she held so dear.

Reaching the hotel, she paid the driver, put on her sunglasses to hide her ravaged face and quickly went inside.

The man behind the front desk coughed discreetly as she tried to hurry past reception to the lift. 'Señora?' he queried.

'Yes?'

'Your, er, most recent guest, she has departed.'

'What?' Cici was aghast.

'She checked out just ten minutes ago and left instructions for me to inform you of her change of plans.' He seemed apologetic. 'You have just missed her.'

'Oh – oh, I see.' Cici forced a smile. 'Thank you so much.'

'Will you be expecting any other guests?'

'No, I won't, thank you. And I'm afraid I've had a change of plan myself. I need to get on the first available flight to Dublin. Will you arrange that immediately please?'

'Right away, Señora.' He seemed disappointed.

She fled to her suite, locked the door and sat, immobile, on the bed. She hardly noticed the tears streaming down her face. She was suddenly cold and began to shiver. What in the name of God was going to happen now?

In number 42 Wellington Square, P.J. had just finished some delicious poached salmon and asparagus, washed down with a particularly nice bottle of white. He and Charlotte were sitting in her kitchen. Bones had joined Bonnie and Clyde in their basket and was now snoring loudly. 'Thank you, Charlotte,' he said. 'I can't remember when I had a nicer piece of salmon, or a nicer evening, for that matter.'

'It has been nice, hasn't it? I'm so glad you came over.'

'So am I.'

And it *had* been a lovely evening. He had arrived over as instructed, with Bones, and they had celebrated his new-found status as a grandfather with some ice-cold champagne and not a little hilarity, although Charlotte had been concerned to hear about the baby.

'It's not serious,' P.J. reassured her, 'not in Charlie's case. It's just a mild bleeding disorder. It often doesn't even show up until much later in life, when one has to have surgery or dentistry. In a way, they're lucky he's been diagnosed now. It means they can keep an eye on him.'

'What about Alex and Catherine? Do they know yet how he inherited it?' Charlotte was curious.

'They'll run all the usual profile of tests. We should find out in a few days.' P.J. yawned. 'If Alex has it, I must say I'll be surprised, although it's perfectly possible. I do remember him bruising quite a lot as a youngster, now that I think of it, and getting a lot of nosebleeds, but most small boys do. I'm afraid we doctors are always rather dismissive of our own children's symptoms. Comes with the territory. We're notorious for being unsympathetic to family members unless something's life-threatening,' he grinned. 'I must get myself tested, just out of curiosity.'

'As long as little Charlie isn't in danger, then that's all that matters.'

'You're right – and he's not. All going well, they should be able to bring him home in about two weeks.'

'Poor Catherine. How awful to have such a worrying time with your first baby. I can't imagine. Candy, thank God, was robustly healthy when she arrived, and even then demanded relentless attention. Come to think of it, she's been doing that ever since,' she smiled ruefully.

'Why only Candy?' P.J. enquired. 'Didn't you want any more kids?'

'It's a long story.'

'I'm not in any rush.' His eyes were warm as he topped up their glasses.

So she told him all about the fall she'd out hunting, about her first miscarriage and the four that had followed in the intervening years. He listened attentively, never once interrupting her.

'I can't imagine how devastating that must have been for you.'

'It was,' she said quietly, 'and for Ossie too. He – that is, we – had always wanted a large family. But it wasn't to be. Except . . .'

'Except that Ossie gets to have another chance with someone else,' P.J. finished the thought for her. 'It's horribly unfair.'

'Yes,' she smiled sadly. 'It did seem unfair at the time, but that's life. You men can go on reproducing forever. It's not so easy for us women.'

P.J. sighed. 'Life isn't fair, that's for sure. When you're in my line of business, you come across a lot of people who've been dealt unfair hands. You just have to make the best of the good stuff when it comes along.'

'You're right, of course. And I have Candy – or at least I used to,' she said, sighing. 'She's moved in with her dad for a bit. There was a disagreement. She needs some space . . .' She trailed off, thinking of all the recent drama with Candy, but she didn't want to say any more about it – not yet – although she felt she could have told P.J. anything.

'Tell me about it,' P.J. said wryly, shaking his head. 'My son Alex thinks I come from another planet. I should go.' P.J. checked his watch. 'It's late and I'm keeping you up. But thank you, I really can't think of when I've spent a nicer evening.' He paused. 'That's not entirely true, I can – it was the last time we had dinner together.' He smiled.

'Oh, P.J.' Charlotte went a little pink. 'What a nice thing to say – I think so too.'

'Do you want me to go?' He held her eyes, hopefully. 'I *could* stay . . . that is, if Jennifer doesn't appear to chase me out.'

'My mother is safely in bed in the basement. Which is where I should like to keep her locked a lot of the time.'

'Then I think we should go to bed too . . . what do you say?' P.J. took her hands in his, hardly believing what he was suggesting, but they had to broach the subject sometime, and it felt right to do it now, to stay, and not right at all for him to go back alone across the square and end this lovely, warm and comforting evening.

She hesitated for only a second. 'Yes. Let's go upstairs.'

So he followed her, holding her hand, as she led him up to her bedroom, and he took her in his arms and bent to kiss her, marvelling yet again at the softness of her lips, and how they yielded so perfectly to his.

While she was in the bathroom, P.J. quickly discarded his clothes, putting them on the sofa that sat across the foot of the large double bed. He kept on his boxer shorts and snuck a quick peek at himself in the mirror before slipping in between the cool cotton sheets. All that training had paid off. He wasn't looking half bad. Either that, or the wine was affecting his reflection. All the same, he was nervous. He knew it was ridiculous, but it had been so long, over five years, since he had made love to anyone. He had almost forgotten what it felt like. He hoped he would remember what to do.

When she emerged, naked, from the bathroom, her dark hair in a cloud around her shoulders, smiling nervously at him, she took his breath away. Her figure was stunning, slender and gently curvaceous in all the right places. When she slipped in beside him he pulled her close, breathing her in. 'You are so beautiful, do you know that?' he said, stroking her hair back from her face and looking into the depths of those huge dark eyes.

'Oh, P.J., I know it's silly, but I – well, I haven't – you know – it's been a while.'

'Me too,' he murmured. 'All the more reason to enjoy it. Let's just take it slowly, hmm?'

So they did. Wonderfully slowly. And he hadn't forgotten, he realised, and neither had she. And even if he had, his body was reminding him, urging him on, in the most deliciously memorable way.

It was true, he thought, losing himself in her kiss, in her

wonderful, arousing caresses. There were some things you never forgot. Just like riding a bicycle – except much, *much* nicer . . .

Would the night *ever* end? Cici had tossed and turned miserably, alternating between tears and terror, completely unable to sleep. Now, at six o'clock in the morning, she gave up trying and hauled herself out of bed, feeling like death warmed up.

She had been unable to get back to Dublin the day before, as she had so desperately wanted to. The two flights had been completely full. She could have gone back via London, but she couldn't have stood hanging about in Heathrow, and it wouldn't have got her back that much earlier. Instead, she was on the lunchtime flight today. Only six more hours, six interminably long hours, and she would be at Da Vinci Airport, hopefully about to board a flight for home.

Home. The word reverberated in her mind. After Harry's hideous stunt yesterday, she doubted if she would have any kind of home at all to return to. She certainly seemed to have lost a daughter. Cici had been trying Sophia's phone incessantly, but it had been turned off – she couldn't even leave a message. Thinking of her, her heart constricted again. She would never, as long as she lived, forget the look of bewilderment and betrayal on Sophia's face when Harry had turned up.

And then she would think of him, of Harry, and be gripped with an anger so devouring it threatened to consume her, the raw, primal anger of a mother thwarted in protecting her vulnerable, innocent child. Then she would relapse into fear. Where was he now? If he had been capable of setting up that spiteful scene he had pulled off so successfully, what, if anything, would his next move be? The questions tormented her. She desperately wanted to talk to someone – anyone – but who? Sophia wouldn't take her calls. There was no point in calling Dom, who would no doubt be on the receiving end of Sophia's version of events. And James . . . oh God, if only James were here. If only she could talk to him and explain, he would know what to do. No matter how awful things were, he would fix them and make them better. She thought about calling him, even now, and held her phone in her hand. All she had to do was punch in his number, but her fingers began to tremble so violently she abandoned the task before even attempting it.

What would she say? 'Please, James, come and get me, my insane lover is trying to destroy me and our family.' Just thinking about it made her blood run cold. If James knew, if he got to hear about Sophia and what had happened, he would be incandescent with anger. And what's more, she knew he would have every right to be. He would never forgive her, *could* never forgive her, and she didn't blame him. She was a wicked, selfish, irresponsible woman who had risked her marriage and family for a series of cheap thrills, thrills from which she now not only recoiled, but whose memory, and that of their instigator, left her reeling with nothing but shame and awful, chilling foreboding.

She passed the hours with gritted teeth, forcing herself to have a massage in the spa, followed by a blow-dry in the hairdresser's. When the masseuse had commented on how tense her muscles were, Cici had wanted to relieve that very tension by punching her. Instead, she had muttered something about stress and willed the girl to revert to silence. The hairdresser hadn't been much better. A chatty, cheerfully gay coiffeur had regaled her about her resemblance to Sophia Loren and his obsession with her and Cici had wanted to kill him. But still she smiled and murmured encouragingly, comforting herself with the thought that she would soon be on her way.

The hotel staff bade her a respectful farewell, and at last she was in the taxi, on her way to the airport. She had never wanted to get out of Rome so fast in her life. She never wanted to see the place again.

The flight, thank God, was on time. Boarding it, she tried Sophia's number one last time before switching her phone off. At least this time it went to voicemail. 'Please, Sophia,' Cici begged. 'Please ring me, *cara*, I have to explain to you. I beg you, ring me. What happened was a terrible thing – it wasn't how it looked, I promise you. I had no idea. He – Harry – followed me over. I would never, never—' She was cut off. She hung up miserably.

The flight, too, seemed interminable, although they landed on schedule in Dublin in the midst of a gently rolling mist. Cici reclaimed her case from the baggage carousel, and before getting a taxi, stopped in the airport shop to pick up some fresh milk and a couple of magazines. Once she was home, she didn't want to have to go outside her front door. Not now.

'Wellington Square, please,' she told the driver.

'Been anywhere nice?' he asked cheerily. 'Hope you've had better weather than you left behind.'

'I'm sorry, I'm very tired.' She leaned back and closed her eyes, not caring if she sounded rude. Thankfully the traffic was light, and they made good headway. Safe in the assumption that the driver wouldn't engage her in further conversation, which she would have been incapable of, she opened one of the magazines. Leafing idly through its pages, she barely registered the new colourful summer fashions or the many smiling, handsome couples that stared out at her from various glamorous functions. Until one photograph caught her eye. She looked again, carefully, blinking, squeezing her eyes shut and opening them again. But there was no mistaking it. No mistaking the handsome face, the dark hair greying at the temples, swept elegantly back from the aristocratic brow, the mouth she knew so well relaxed in a wide, happy smile. It was James. *Her* James. And beside him, looking equally happy, her head thrown back and laughing, was – oh, God, it was Sarah de Burgh, the fabulously beautiful, fabulously wealthy, blonde, *divorced* Sarah de Burgh. They had been attending a ball in aid of the Grosvenor Foundation, held in the Dorchester Hotel in London. Cici closed her eyes again. She thought she was going to pass out, or at the very least be sick. Thankfully, the taxi pulled up at Wellington Square, outside her house – James's house.

'You all right, love?' The driver handed her her case. 'You look a bit peaky. I could give you a hand in, if you like.' He seemed genuinely concerned.

'No, thank you, I'm all right.' She tipped him generously. Trailing her case on its wheels along the side path and down to the mews, she took a few deep breaths. *Just keep breathing*, she told herself. *You're almost home, almost inside.* She twisted the key in the lock, and mercifully the door opened. She dragged her case inside, shut the door and pulled up the blinds, which had been left drawn, blinking as her eyes adjusted to the late afternoon sunlight streaming through the window. Then she turned towards the mirror over the mantelpiece and froze, her hand flying to her throat. There, scrawled in bright red lipstick, was one solitary word. *Whore*, it screamed at her.

For a very long moment, she stood stock still, like an animal transfixed, then cold, hard reasoning tugged at her brain. She hadn't given Harry a key, she was sure of it, but she had left one out for him on one or two occasions. He must have had it copied. How could she have been so stupid? But now was not the time for recriminations. Moving as if through a bad dream, she forced herself to walk through the house, upstairs, wanting with every step to flee, to escape, but to where? To who? This was something she had got herself into and now had to get herself out of.

'Hello?' she called hesitantly, her voice sounding eerily

unreal. Upstairs, she went into each room, methodically, and there it was again, on the mirror in her bedroom and in the bathroom. *Whore*. That appeared to be the extent of the damage.

Searching everywhere, in the cupboards (at least his clothes were gone; he must have taken them) and under the beds, Cici realised, relief flooding through her, that she was alone – at least for the moment. Then fear gave way to anger and she picked up the phone. 'Get me the number of an emergency locksmith,' she instructed directory enquiries. Then she went downstairs, found some glass cleaner and a cloth and proceeded to wipe away the horrible evidence of Harry's vitriol.

By the time the locksmith arrived, the mews looked as it always had. She felt better having taken action. She might have been naive, but this was nothing she couldn't sort out. She had to believe that – had to. One step at a time. The locks would be changed and Harry would never set foot in her home or her life again.

While the locksmith went about his work, Cici unpacked, put on the washing machine and changed out of her travelling outfit – normal, sensible actions, even if they were undertaken by a woman who felt anything but.

Satisfied that her new locks were installed and working, she put her set of new keys carefully away, turned on the alarm and ran a hot bath, forcing herself to think as she sank into the soothing water. She would meet with James as soon as possible, tomorrow, hopefully. Tell him how sorry she was, how she had lost sight of everything, even herself. She would move back into their beautiful home and make everything right. They would sell or rent the mews and she would put this terrible part of her life behind her. He would understand and forgive her; he'd never been able to resist her. Getting out, she patted herself dry, slipped into a cashmere top and lounging trousers and suddenly found she was hungry. She went downstairs and fixed herself a light supper and poured herself a glass of wine.

Turning on the television, more for background noise than anything else, she wandered over to pick up the post that had gathered while she'd been away. There wasn't much. A few mail shots, a couple of bills and one rather official-looking letter, addressed to her, here at the mews. She was intrigued. She hadn't had her mailing address changed. Any post was dropped down to her from the main house by the housekeeper. She finished her supper and, curling up on the couch, took a sip of wine, finally beginning to relax. She opened the letter, barely registering the title and company address of the sender. She didn't need to – the first line after *Dear Mrs Coleman-Cappabianca* had got her attention. *We are instructed by our client, Mr James Coleman, of 15 Wellington Square, to inform you of his intention to initiate immediate proceedings for formal separation followed by divorce.* Numbly, she allowed her eyes to follow the neat, computerised script, advising her to consult with and appoint a family-law solicitor of her choosing and have them contact and enter into negotiations with Mr John O'Carroll, of McGregor, O'Carroll and Lawson, at her earliest convenience.

Cici felt the room spin around her. Clutching the letter, she seemed to be unable to move, watching it as it began to tremble in her hand. It couldn't be true, it *couldn't* be. There'd been some terrible mistake. James would never do something like this – not without telling her, warning her. And then she heard the small voice of truth whisper in her head. *You didn't exactly talk to or warn him when you decided to turn his life upside down.* That was the real truth, she knew, just as she knew that McGregor, O'Carroll and Lawson were the most feared divorce lawyers in the country. And John O'Carroll, the leading partner, was not known as 'The Rottweiler' without good cause. She sat there, stunned and suddenly very, very frightened.

13

'That was . . . you are . . . *amazing*,' said Candy, collapsing back on pillows that had seen better days. Beside her, Josh hauled himself upright, and leaving her in bed, made for the tiny kitchenette.

'So they tell me,' he quipped. 'Wanna beer, babe?' He opened one for himself.

'No, but I'd like you back here and right beside me as soon as possible.' She smiled in what she hoped was a provocative fashion as she watched him walk back towards her, his thin, hungry-looking body and slightly bandy legs seeming impossibly attractive to her. His skin was pale, his hair long and dark and when he looked at her, which wasn't often enough, his slanting cobalt blue eyes seemed to see right through her. She wasn't so keen on the wispy goatee he allowed to ruin his sensitive mouth and finely chiselled jaw, but it was a small flaw in the overall perfection.

Candy had never met anyone like Josh, and she certainly hadn't ever known anything approaching the skills he was capable of in bed, or indeed out of it. She smiled as he got back in beside her and watched him as he lit a joint, inhaling it slowly. Candy had only had a few boyfriends, nothing serious, just part of the crowd she used to hang around with, and Robbie, who her parents had loved because they knew *his* parents and he was a talented horseman, tipped to pick up an Olympic medal in the three-day eventing. Though he was awfully nice and really good fun, his aptitude in the saddle sadly wasn't matched anywhere else. Apart from a few fairly tame attempts at drunken fumblings on Robbie's part, Candy really hadn't understood what all the fuss was about sex.

That had all changed when she met Josh, and it had all been quite by accident. Her mother's new boyfriend (ugh!) or whatever she called him, that stupid doctor, had invited her mother and her to a Viper concert, the coolest band on the planet.

As the end of their latest world tour, they were wrapping up in Dublin with a mega-hyped performance and were threatening to take a break for quite some time after that, so tickets to the show in the Royal Dublin Society were almost impossible to get hold of. P.J., however, was doctor on stage at any, or indeed all of the venues they played at, if he so chose, worldwide. Apparently, they had all been mates from a million years ago.

Candy couldn't stand him. For starters, he called her mother *babe* or *hon*, and worse still, she even seemed to like it. When she was around P.J., her usually calm, aloof mother became like a pathetic, simpering teenager. If she hadn't seen it with her own eyes, she wouldn't have believed it. They were embarrassing, the pair of them. Even her father and Shalom were past that sort of stuff.

She had only gone to the concert with them because Emma and Katy had been so impressed. She had demanded that they be included, thinking that would put a fly in the ointment, but P.J. had said he would see what he could do and had been able to produce another pair of tickets. Not only that, but they were in the VIP area. Katy and Emma had almost fainted when they'd heard that. And better still, since P.J. was technically on duty as doctor on stage, they all got to go backstage and meet the band afterwards and go to the after-concert party to end all parties. Though she was grudging in her acknowledgement, even Candy had to admit it was a pretty cool gig, and one that was to prove very exciting for her, for it was that electric, unforgettable night that she met Josh.

'What's a gaggle of cute little schoolgirls like you doing in the VIP area then?' he had asked, his mouth curving in a lazy smile, aiming the remark mostly at Emma, who looked incredible in tight pink jeans and a floral smock top.

'We're not schoolgirls and I'm here with my mother,' Candy had retorted, flicking back her platinum ringlets. 'What's it to you?'

'Nothing really.' He turned to her and gave her a once-over, not seeming very impressed at all. 'Daddy with the band then?'

'Don't be ridiculous. My mother's with a – a friend. And my father is a property developer. You've probably heard of him,' she added for good measure, 'Ossie Keating.' There, that would put the arrogant jerk in his place.

'That figures,' he said, infuriatingly.

'What do you mean?'

'Poor little rich girl – it's written all over you, love.'

Candy was speechless with anger, but Emma and Katy had been reduced to helpless giggles. He grinned at them, then held out his hand by way of introduction. 'Josh McIntyre, video director.'

'Wow,' breathed Emma, 'you, like, shoot all the video footage?'

'And direct it. You're cute,' he added, 'want to be in a video? We could do some test shots sometime.'

Now it was Emma's turn to be speechless. 'Give me your numbers,' he instructed, although he hadn't so much as looked at Candy.

Nonetheless, she found herself offering her phone number to him along with Katy and Emma.

'I'll be in touch. Better not tell your mother, though,' he winked at Candy. 'Parents can get twitchy about their little darlings being filmed.' And then he had walked away, leaving them staring after him.

'Wow,' said Emma again. 'D'you think he was serious?'

'Doubt it,' Katy said. 'Anyway, he's, like, really old. Thirty-five maybe?'

'He's cute,' Candy said, her head tilted to one side. 'Really cute.'

Emma and Katy exchanged looks and shook their heads.

Candy was smitten. For a whole week after that she dreamed about him every night. She could hardly eat.

When he rang, she couldn't believe it. And it was *her* he rang – not Emma or Katy, but her.

'Meet me,' he said and mentioned a pub she didn't know, but pretended she did.

She agreed to meet him readily – too readily. She didn't tell Katy or Emma, and she most certainly didn't tell her mother. She wasn't really talking to her and had been avoiding all her invitations for coffee or dinner. Anyway, her mum had got a boyfriend now – if even *she* could get a man, then it was about time she had a love interest herself. Instinctively she knew both her mum and dad would have hated Josh, but so what? They didn't exactly consult her about their choices, did they?

He never took her out, not properly, not to dinner or anything, and when they met, those few initial times in obscure pubs (he had even stood her up once or twice), he had let her pay for the drinks. She'd been shocked, but automatically did what he told her. This was obviously the way the girls he went for behaved. She had never met anyone like him and had no idea how to play things. Sometimes he seemed miles away, as if he was in his own world. Other times he openly admired other girls, which infuriated her, although she pretended she didn't care. And then other times he would be kind and sweet to her. Like the first time he had invited her back to his flat. It was small, much smaller than she had imagined. She had assumed he lived in a smart chrome and black leather infested apartment, filled with boy toys and gadgets and a huge TV. What she found was a pokey one-bedroom flat with a rather flea-bitten carpet. It was in the city centre, she supposed, although in a less desirable part than she would have expected – but what did she care? She was inside the front door, at home with him – that was all that mattered, wasn't it? He told her to undress, and she did, quaking with excitement and apprehension, then feeling vulnerable and exposed as he made her wait, looking at her appraisingly from every angle. Then he had made love to her, slowly and carefully, until lying on the scratchy acrylic rug in front of the fireplace she writhed beneath him, breathless with excitement. Candy had never had a proper orgasm, not like this, and she was hooked, instantly. She only had to look at him and she was aroused, and in the weeks that followed, he made sure she had plenty of them.

It had been Josh's idea for her to get her boobs done, although she'd been toying with the idea for quite some time. But now she had a good reason to go ahead with it. 'You should do something about those,' he had said, tweaking a nipple playfully one afternoon when they were lying in his bed.

'What?' She'd been taken by surprise, not altogether pleasantly.

'Have your boobs done, love. Those aren't tits, they're fried eggs,' he had laughed.

'Don't you like me the way I am?' Candy had chewed her lip.

'I'd like you a whole lot better with a pair of 34Ds.'

'Well,' she said doubtfully, 'I had been thinking about it, but I thought maybe a B or C cup, not a D.'

'Why not? If you're getting them done, you might as well get your money's worth. And I know a good surgeon. He might even give you a discount. I send a lot of girls to him.'

'What girls?' Candy looked shocked.

'Models. Relax,' he laughed at her. 'In my line of business, girls are always getting stuff done – they have to, otherwise they don't get the jobs.'

'Oh,' Candy said, feeling better about it. 'Of course, I see.'

And the more she thought about it, the more it seemed like a good idea, so one day she picked up the phone and made an appointment to go for a consultation at the clinic Josh had recommended. She met with the surgeon, who wasn't very nice at all – he was rather brusque and spoke very little English. But she had gone ahead and had booked herself in for the breast-augmentation procedure two weeks from then, and told Ossie and Shalom she was staying with Emma for the week to check out a few courses she was thinking of doing.

She had felt miserable coming around from the anaesthetic. Katy and Emma were sitting exams, so they couldn't be with her. She hadn't told her parents, or even Shalom, who had clearly had her own breasts enlarged. And Josh, although he had assured her he would be there when she went into theatre and came around, hadn't even visited, saying he was on an important freelance gig. So she had come to, feeling nauseous and vulnerable and as if her chest was about to explode. 'What do you expect, love?' the clinic nurse had said cheerfully – a little too cheerfully. 'You've gone from a 34A to a 34D – those puppies are bound to be making their presence felt.' She had grinned as she refused to give Candy any more painkillers. 'Doctor's orders,' she'd said, then had left.

Candy had burst into tears. The next day, still feeling horribly tender, wearing bandages and a support bra, Candy and her new breasts were hustled into a taxi and she was taken back to Josh's place, where she arrived to an empty and very grim homecoming. Suddenly she wanted to be at home, to have her mother with her, or at the very least Emma and Katy. At least they could have examined the surgical results in combined awe. But she was here, alone in Josh's shoddy and, more to the point, empty flat. For a second, she thought about calling her mum. She thought of the time she'd had her tonsils out when she was ten, and how wonderful her mum had been to her, bringing her up ice cream and taking care of her when she was feeling miserable. But she couldn't back down now. Fighting back tears, she crawled into the unmade bed. She couldn't even curl up – she had to lie propped up on support pillows and hope for sleep. It was a more likely prospect than company, she realised.

It was late when Josh finally got back, and Candy was relieved to see him.

'Hey, baby!' He greeted her with a kiss, smelling of beer, which made Candy feel nauseous all over again. 'How're my girls?' He looked impressed at the size of her new chest.

'They're in agony,' she said, although just looking at Josh made her feel better.

'Poor you. Never mind. Think of the fun we're going to have playing with them, eh?' he grinned. 'Brought back a pizza, fancy some?'

'Maybe just a teeny bit.'

'Good girl. Heat it up for us, would you? I need to take a shower.'

'Sure,' Candy said, struggling to get out of bed. If she had thought the clinic unsympathetic, she certainly wasn't going to be treated like a recovering patient here, she thought miserably. Still, it would all be worth it in the end. She had a fabulous new figure, and a fabulously sexy man to enjoy it with, someone who needed her and wanted to be with her. A sore chest for a few days was a small price to pay.

It was late, but once Dom started, he wasn't going to stop until he worked all this out, even if the figures were beginning to swim in front of his eyes. Sitting in the back office, he poured another glass of Chianti Classico and realised he was almost three-quarters of the way through the bottle. He didn't care. His restaurant was in trouble and it was all his own fault for taking his eye off the ball. Since that awful day when Eric had broken the news about the accounts, Dom had been grappling with the situation every which way. Now he was going to have to pay the price and let people go and he could hardly bear it, especially when all the team had worked so hard to make Dominic's the success it had become, at least as far as appearances went. It was still the most popular place in town to eat, and the food was superb, although Dom couldn't help noticing, going through the books, that Rollo had been extraordinarily wasteful and unnecessarily extravagant a lot of the time. That would have to change. He was racking his brains, trying to work out how he should approach the whole thing, when he heard a noise and the door was pushed tentatively open.

'Oh, I'm sorry.' It was Carla, looking surprised to see him there. 'I left my phone behind. I don't have a landline so it's my only form of contact with the outside world – I get worried if I don't have it on me,' she gabbled. 'I saw the light on and just wanted to check everything was all right.'

'I wish I could say it was,' Dom smiled at her, pleased at the unexpected company.

'What's wrong?' She looked concerned.

'How long have you got?'

She shrugged, smiling back at him, looking very Italian. She reminded him in that moment of his mother and sisters, and suddenly he wanted to tell her everything.

'I'm not rushing anywhere.'

'Then would you join me in a drink? I think I might need to open another bottle anyway, there doesn't seem to be quite enough in this one.'

'I'll get it, you stay there.' She returned with a bottle and another glass, then opened the bottle expertly and poured two fresh glasses. 'Chianti is still my favourite,' she smiled.

'Reminds me of so many long Sunday lunches from a very long time ago.'

'Tell me about yourself, Carla. I really don't know anything about you.' Dom caught her eye and looked at her quizzically.

'You first,' she said. 'You tell me what the problem is, and then I'll tell you about me.' She pulled up a chair and sat down opposite him.

An hour and a half later, they had gone over every possible permutation. Dom had been astonished at Carla's grasp of the business.

'My family runs a restaurant – that is, my father and three brothers run it – but I know how it works,' she said, not quite telling the whole truth but not lying to him either. She was still cautious, still not sure how much, if anything, she should tell him.

'How come you're in Dublin?' he asked, not unnaturally.

She shrugged. 'It was a spur of the moment thing. There was a fight – a family thing. I needed to get away, have some space, so I decided to take a year off and Dublin seemed as good a place as any.'

'That bad, huh?'

She smiled. 'Families. Can't live with them, can't kill them, but I do miss them all – especially Dad.'

'What about your mum?'

'She died when I was eight.'

'I'm so sorry.' His eyes were full of sympathy.

'Yeah . . . well.' She changed the subject quickly. 'Speaking of mothers, yours is a beauty. She seems like fun too. She's always nice to me when she's in the restaurant.'

Dom's face clouded. 'They're always lovely when they're not your own,' he said wryly. 'They're splitting up, my parents.'

'Oh, I'm sorry. I didn't know.'

'Neither did we till quite recently. I thought my parents had the happiest marriage on the planet. Apparently Mum had other ideas. I'm sure you've noticed she hasn't been dining here with my father.'

Carla nodded. 'I know. That must be tough.'

'It's certainly weird to see your mother taking up with a guy half her age.'

'Is it serious? I mean, your mum and this guy?'

Dom shrugged. 'Who can tell? She's like a different person these days. She looks like Mum, sounds like Mum, but she's sure as hell not behaving like Mum. She used to be great – you'd have loved her,' he said without thinking.

'Maybe she's just going through some stuff – you know, trying to find herself. It's tough for a beautiful woman to face getting older.'

Dom seemed surprised. 'Maybe you're right,' he said thoughtfully. 'I never thought of it in that light.'

He looked at her, and as their eyes met all the past awkwardness and embarrassment melted away. But suddenly Carla was frightened. This was getting personal, and Dom had wanted business advice, not a lecture on families. It was time to get back to the subject in hand.

'You can lose two waiters, that's it,' she proclaimed. 'You are front of house. Astrid or I will take over when you can't be there. She won't ask for much of an increase, and it's cheaper and easier than hiring someone new.'

'And you?'

'I'll do it as a favour,' she grinned. 'Then you'll owe me one.' She paused. 'The real problem is Rollo. That's where you have to cut back.'

'I can't let him go – the restaurant depends on him, on his reputation.' Dom looked worried.

'That's only partly true. And maybe you won't have to let him go, but you can ask him to take a cut in salary. Explain the situation, and if he won't agree, then he'll leave anyway.'

'Then what will I do?'

'Let's worry about that when we come to it,' Carla said, yawning. 'The kitchen is running like clockwork anyway. If they have to, the sous chefs will manage without an executive chef for a little while. You can go in and shout at them in the meantime.'

'It's almost midnight,' Dom said, looking at his watch. 'Thank you for listening to me, and for your advice. I hate doing it, but it's the right thing to do.'

'We work in a precarious business,' she said, clearing away the glasses and the second bottle. 'It's always touch and go.'

'Speaking of going, it's far too late for you to be off out there on your own. And it's a horrible night.' It was: a wind had got up and rain was driving against the window. 'Why don't you stay the night in my place?' he heard himself saying. 'It's only upstairs, and as you know, I have a spare room. I promise I'll behave, though to be honest, I'd like very much to misbehave with you.'

She coloured slightly. 'I could get a taxi,' she ventured.

'You could.' Dom was moving towards the window and looking out at the lack of cars on the street. Then he paced back and was standing in front of her. 'But don't you think that would be silly when you can just grab a bed upstairs?'

'I – I don't know what to say.'

'Then don't say anything.' He moved closer, and then his arms were pulling her to him and his hands were moulding around that amazing bottom. And she wasn't pulling away. Then he bent his head and did what he had been longing to do ever since he had done it the last time. He kissed her, slowly and thoroughly, and as she kissed him back, he thought he had never tasted anything quite so delicious.

Carla never made it to the spare room. They barely made it upstairs. Shedding their clothes, they clung to one another, hungrily discovering each other's bodies long into the night. When she awoke, sometime towards dawn, in a tangle of limbs, Carla extricated herself gently, propping herself up on an elbow and looking at Dom's beautiful face as he lay sleeping. She slipped out of bed and padded to the kitchen to get a drink of water, suddenly thinking again of her family, her father. He had always told her she would know when she met the right man – now she knew what he meant. He would be happy for her, happy she had finally found him – although possibly not quite so happy that she was in bed with him and had had such abandoned sex with him *before* marriage. She smiled at the thought and went back to the bedroom, where she slipped in beside Dom and snuggled up to him, breathing him in and kissing his shoulder as he stirred briefly in his sleep.

'*Cara*' was the word he murmured as he hooked his hand around her thigh. Italian for *darling*.

Carla had never felt so happy.

James Coleman was sitting very comfortably in the spectacular drawing room of Sarah de Burgh's mansion that looked out over Dublin Bay. She had just given a most enjoyable dinner party for fourteen people and had entertained them all impeccably. She really was a charming hostess, James thought, smiling at her as she topped up his glass of red. The others had all left, Sarah's housekeeper was clearing up in the dining room, and it was just the two of them now, enjoying a nightcap.

'You look beautiful tonight, Sarah,' he said truthfully as she joined him on the sofa. And she did. The black dress she wore was elegant and showed off her superb figure, which she obviously kept in meticulous shape. Her blonde hair was loosely waved and her blue eyes shone in the firelight. Her skin, too, was beautiful, pale and luminous. No wonder she had been Ireland's most successful model. As far as James could tell, she hadn't changed a bit. Plus she was charming and kind. James wondered why on earth her husband had been mad enough to leave her – although naturally he didn't say so.

'I really enjoyed this evening, it was wonderful. You went to an awful lot of trouble,' he said, smiling as she leaned against him and wrapped his arm around her shoulders. He had been seeing quite a bit of her, and was becoming more and more fond of her, but . . .

'A penny for them?'

'I should go, it's late. I'll call my driver.'

'Oh, Jamie, don't be such a spoilsport,' she pouted prettily, then giggled. She was a little tipsy, and so was he. The selection of wines had been first rate and he told her so.

'Then stay and have another glass.' She slanted up at him, then pulled back and sat up. 'James?'

'Er, yes?' He didn't have to ask; he knew what was coming next. He cleared his throat awkwardly.

'Don't go – there's no need to. Stay here. You can leave in the morning,' she said huskily, leaning in to kiss him. He had kissed her before, of course, many times – but nothing more. It wasn't that he didn't want to sleep with her, it was just that it felt like crossing a line of some sort, one there would be no coming back from, and part of him, an irritatingly reluctant part of him, just didn't feel ready for that.

'Please?' she said, batting those huge blue eyes. 'I really don't want to be alone tonight, and I don't think you want to be either, if you're honest.'

'I'm sorry, Sarah.' He stood up. 'I really do have to go, I have a terribly early start tomorrow,' he lied. 'Another time, I'd love to.'

'When?' she asked, petulantly. 'All you've ever done is kiss me – is there something wrong with me? Something unattractive?'

'Sarah, darling, you know perfectly well you're beauty personified. Look, it's late, we'll discuss this another time. I really must go.'

'Of course you must.' She smiled suddenly, but her eyes were hard. 'That's what all you men do, isn't it? Go, eventually.'

'Sarah,' James gestured helplessly. 'It's just not the right time. It would spoil things between us, and I don't want to do that.'

'What *do* you want?' The question hung menacingly in the air. Sarah folded her arms and regarded him, her many diamonds glinting on her fingers and wrists. 'You're still in love with that wife of yours, aren't you?' she said bitterly.

'Really, Sarah, this isn't the place or the time.' He suppressed a flash of anger.

'So you keep saying.' She was hurt now, and angry. He couldn't say he blamed her.

'I'll call you tomorrow.' He bent to kiss her cheek, then let himself out and called his driver to meet him on the road outside. Loosening his collar, he took a deep breath. He must be mad. He had one of the most beautiful women in the country offering herself to him on a plate and he had turned her down. What the hell was the matter with him?

Back inside one of the most beautiful homes in the city, one of the most beautiful women in Dublin was asking herself the very same question. What the hell was the matter with James Coleman?

He was charming, considerate, handsome and very, *very* rich – and he hadn't so much as made a move on her, apart from kissing her – very well, actually, perhaps too well. It was driving Sarah mad. And they made such a wonderful couple, all their friends were saying so – they were the talk of the town. She knew he had feelings for her; he was too gentlemanly to waste her time otherwise. She looked at herself in the mirror, at the outfit she had taken so much time selecting, at her appearance, which she'd gone to so much trouble with. She looked great, she knew she did – everyone was always telling her she looked ten years younger than her forty-eight years. And she was rich too, so no one, least of all James, could accuse her of being after him for his money. And it had given her ex-husband something to sit up and take notice of! He'd had to take another look at her, through the eyes of another man – a man even more successful than he was in many ways. Sarah had loved showing him that she wasn't on the scrap heap just because he had thrown her aside in favour of a younger, more likely racier, model. Word on the street was he was put out, jealous even. Well, it served him bloody right.

Still, Sarah flung her clothes off angrily. Just what, exactly, did he have to be jealous of? It had been four weeks now, more or less, since James had been asking her out, and although she knew he was embarking on a painful divorce, it really shouldn't stop him from moving their relationship on a bit, particularly in the bedroom. Why was he hesitating? She assessed her naked body in the mirror critically. Didn't he fancy her? Was that it? Wasn't she sexy enough? Alluring enough? Was it because she had already been abandoned by one man? Used goods? A series of debilitating questions began to crawl around her mind – the needy, unanswerable questions of the abandoned wife or lover. *Why me? Why am I not enough?* Beautiful as she was, and the envy of most women who knew her, Sarah de Burgh went to bed lonely yet again and cried herself to sleep.

14

'**B**ella!' P.J. swung his daughter off her feet as she fought her way through the waiting crowds at Arrivals to meet him.

'Hey, Dad!' she laughed. 'You're looking good.' She was impressed. 'You're half the man I left behind.'

'I wasn't *that* bad,' P.J. protested, taking her case and leading the way out to the car park.

'I know, I'm only teasing. But you *were* out of shape. That trainer of yours must be good, you're looking really fit.'

'And you look as beautiful as ever.' P.J. regarded her proudly. She was beautiful in a natural, unaffected way and was becoming more like her mother every time he saw her. She was tall and slim, and her long, golden blonde hair hung in waves down her back. Her skin was golden too, with a smattering of freckles across her nose and cheeks. Her smile could light up a room. 'How's college?'

'It's great.' She slid into the car while P.J. stowed her case.

'Hope all those Italian men aren't distracting you from your studies?'

'Actually, I've met a very nice English guy, we've been seeing each other for a couple of months now. You'll like him – his name's Tim.'

'Any chance of meeting him?' P.J. raised an eyebrow.

'Sure, I'll bring him home one of these days, or you can always come over for a visit – you could even bring your girlfriend.' She looked at him wickedly.

'What – I – who?' P.J. spluttered.

'It's okay, Dad,' Bella grinned. 'The Wellington Square network has gone into action. There's not a lot those sash windows miss. Actually,' she continued, 'it was Sophia Coleman-Cappabianca who mentioned it. She's in Florence too, you know. We all meet up quite a bit, the Irish crowd. When I was talking to Sheila, she confirmed it.'

'Sheila!' P.J. was shocked.

'Don't worry, Dad, she approves. So do I, by the way. It's time you got out there again, had another female friend. It's what Mum would have wanted, she told me so. And if this friend of yours . . .?'

'Charlotte.'

'If Charlotte is good enough for Sheila, then she must be a very special woman.' Bella looked mischievous.

'She is. I'd like you to meet her, if you want to.'

'Of course I would. I'm looking forward to it.'

'Good.' P.J. was pleasantly surprised.

'But I'm dying to meet my new nephew. How's he doing, little Charlie? Alex is so uncommunicative, and I didn't want to upset Catherine by asking any awkward questions. Tell me everything.'

'He's doing fine, he's a terrific little chap.'

'Oh, that's great, I'm so pleased. Is he . . . will he be all right?'

'He *is* all right! He's fine, he just arrived a little early, gave us all a bit of a fright.'

'But this Von Whatsit?'

'Von Willebrand's. It's not a big deal, really. It's a fairly common, and luckily in Charlie's case, mild bleeding disorder. It often goes undetected, actually. It shouldn't be a problem or restrict his life in any way. Contact sports probably aren't a good idea but apart from that, surgery and dentistry are the only things to be careful with, and the drugs these days pretty much take care of that anyhow.'

'Isn't it an inherited thing?' Bella looked concerned.

'Yes, it is.'

'And?'

'Alex is the carrier, all the tests have confirmed it. Catherine was negative.'

'That means . . .' Bella chewed her lip.

'Yes, sweetheart.' P.J. was sympathetic, seeking to reassure her. 'It means you could be a carrier too. If you want to, we could have the tests done while you're home.'

'Definitely.' Bella looked worried. 'I'd want to know. Might as well find out as soon as I can.'

'It's really nothing to worry about, honestly, and just because one sibling has it doesn't mean another will. Anyway, there's someone else who's dying to see you,' P.J. said, changing the subject. He couldn't bear to see Bella looking so worried.

'Who?'

'Granddad, of course. He's beside himself with excitement. I told him we'd call around tomorrow, if that's okay? Maybe take him out to dinner?'

'That would be lovely, Dad, I'm dying to see him too.' Bella smiled as they pulled into Wellington Square and drove up to number 24, where she leapt out of the car and ran up the steps. She had no sooner reached the top when the door opened and Sheila stood there, in her working outfit of a buttoned overall and a shower cap on her head, which she had recently taken to wearing. Her face was scrubbed and red, as always, but when she set eyes on Bella, it almost cracked in two with smiles. 'Well, well, well,' was all she could say.

'Sheila!' Bella hurled herself at her and threw her arms around her, and Sheila tried to look disapproving.

'Now, that's enough of that. You know I'm not a tactile person,' she said, patting Bella gingerly on the back with her surgical gloves.

'Oh, look!' cried Bella, 'it's Bones, darling Bones! A much slimmer Bones!' And then there was a lot of people tripping

over one another as Bones raced to bring Bella as many
retrieving gifts as he could find to welcome her back.

'Will you look at that dog,' said Sheila. 'He's got an envelope in his mouth now, he's been at the post tray. It could
be something important.' She tried to catch him, but Bones
was hurtling about with delight at his beloved family member's
return.

'A bill, with any luck,' said P.J., lugging Bella's case inside.

'I have the dinner on,' said Sheila. 'Seven o'clock, on the
dot?' She tapped her watch.

'Why seven, Sheila?' P.J. asked innocently.

A look of alarm crossed her face. 'It's always at seven.'

'I know that – I was just checking.' He grinned wickedly
at her.

'Pay no attention to him, Sheila, he's winding you up,' said
Bella.

'He never does anything else. How you ever became a
doctor, I don't know. You should have been a comedian,' she
scowled as she retreated to the safety of the kitchen.

'You're appalling,' Bella grinned at him.

'Nonsense. She loves it. Fancy a drink?'

'I'd love one.'

'Good. So would I, and we have exactly twenty-three and
a half minutes to enjoy one before dinner.'

'It's good to be home, Dad,' said Bella, giving him a hug.

'Good to have you home, sweetheart.'

Tanya was in the hairdresser's and was so angry she could
hardly sit still.

She had walked the long way around, of course, as she
had been doing ever since the débâcle, so she would pass
Dominic's and might have a chance of running into Dom
either going into the restaurant or coming out of his apartment. So far, she had managed to do neither. Occasionally
she would sit at the window seat in the small coffee shop

across the road and monitor the situation discreetly over a skinny cappuccino. Then, this morning, she had seen *her*.

Tripping out gaily at eight o'clock, practically luminous with delight, from Dom's apartment, Carla had run around the corner and into the restaurant. She was followed a respectable five minutes later (Tanya had waited, and watched) by Dom himself, looking equally chipper. Tanya had thought the cup in her hands was going to break, she was clenching it so tightly. *How could he? How could he?* It was all her fault, of course, the scheming little bitch. Tanya knew she'd been dying to get her claws into Dom the minute Carla had sashayed past her in the restaurant, wiggling that bottom of hers. She had always known she was trouble. *And what was she doing here anyway?* Tanya mused, suddenly intensifying her speculating. There was something odd about it all. Sure, Carla was all New York attitude and Italian gesturing. Rollo adored her and so did Pino – make that most of the staff. But still, there was something about her that didn't add up. She was too cool, way too sure of herself to just be a waitress from the Bronx. All Tanya's instincts were screaming that there was a story there somewhere, and she was going to get to the bottom of it, whatever it was. She sure as hell wasn't going to sit back and let Carla walk off into the sunset with her boyfriend.

Because that's what he was, Tanya reminded herself. Dom was hers – and no one else's. She had ordered him from the universe and the universe had obliged. This awful misunderstanding they had had was merely a test to see how badly Tanya wanted him. She had read about things like this happening. Tanya wasn't giving up – not now. She'd sooner die.

'All right, love?' queried the colourist, looking at her strangely in the mirror.

'What?' Tanya snapped.

'You were miles away. I was just asking have you got any nice holidays planned?'

'Yes,' answered Tanya. 'As a matter of fact, I do. I was just thinking about my honeymoon.'

'I didn't know you were engaged.' Her eyes widened.

'I'm not. Not yet.' Tanya smiled up from her magazine. 'But it's only a matter of time.'

'Yes?' James was more brusque than usual, but he was developing a healthy respect for the phone, particularly since picking it up seemed to elicit some rather intense reactions these days.

'James? John O'Carroll here. Is it a good time? If it's inconvenient I can always call you back later.'

'No, no, not at all,' said James, recognising the brisk voice of his family-law solicitor. 'Go ahead.' He tried to sound pleased to hear from him, but his spirits began to sink.

'Well, James, this is a very unusual situation I find myself in.' There was a long pause.

'I'm all ears, John.'

'You're going to find this hard to believe, James, as I did, but you see, the thing is, you're not really married at all.' Now the pause was audible. 'Hello? James, are you there?'

'Yes, yes, of course I'm here. Would you mind repeating that?'

'You heard me! I could hardly believe it myself, old chap – you must be the luckiest man alive! That marriage ceremony in Rome . . . well, it turns out there's a loophole – a very significant one, actually. You didn't fulfil the residency requirements. The religious ceremony was genuine, of course, but legally, here in Ireland, I'm afraid it doesn't qualify at all.'

'Are you telling me . . .' James was processing every syllable. 'Are you saying that the woman I exchanged vows with, have lived with for thirty years, have had three children with – are you telling me that this . . . this *loophole* gives me an out?'

'Well, I wouldn't say that, exactly, but it sets a precedent, a very interesting precedent, point of law and all that. Of course, we'd have to be careful how we presented it – wouldn't want to come across as callous or opportunistic, but a judge, well, there's no doubt—'

'Don't even think about it.'

'I beg your pardon?'

'I said, don't even think about it.'

'But James, I don't think you understand. You see—'

'I understand perfectly, just as I hope *you* understand and are listening very carefully to me now.'

Silence.

'If you think that I would avail of such a cheap and shoddy blow as to suggest, however justifiably, that my marriage to Cici was in any way, shape or form invalid, then consider yourself off the case. Whatever has transpired – and I don't doubt your team has come up with a valid point – anyone who thinks that I would shirk my responsibilities or make a mockery of a relationship that has been the cornerstone of the better part of my life because of an unfortunate *loophole*, as you put it, is sadly misguided. Clearly you have gathered the wrong impression of what kind of man I am, but let me tell you now: I married my wife – and that is what she is – with every intention known to man, honourable or otherwise. Anything to the contrary that has come to light is an unfortunate, profoundly sad revelation, and one, I most assuredly advise you, not to be used in court, or indeed my case. Do I make myself clear?'

'Absolutely.'

James let out a long breath.

'I imagine this has come as quite a shock.'

'I'm becoming rather accustomed to sudden shocks and revelations, John. I don't know if you can appreciate that.'

'I understand completely. And may I say, your reaction is most refreshing, and there is not a hint of patronisation in that observation. You see, I happen to have an enduring marriage of my own spanning thirty-three years, which I owe, I might add, to a wonderful and, er, challenging woman that I am fortunate enough to call my wife. Contrary to popular opinion, obtaining divorce decrees for my clients gives me little satisfaction, except, of course, where there is real sadness and mutual misery.' He paused significantly. 'Despite the, er, current storm in a teacup, I suspect this is *not* the case between you and your wife. You have been quite articulate on the subject, revealingly so. You might want to consider that – or perhaps even *reconsider* your intentions.'

'I take your point, John, and thank you. But for the moment, consider yourself on the case. I haven't quite dispensed of your services yet, although your observations are uncannily astute,' James couldn't help smiling.

'You're the boss.'

'I still like to think so.'

'I'm here if you need me.'

'Thank you, John, I'll be in touch.'

'Oh, and James?'

'Yes?'

'What I've just told you . . .'

'What of it?'

'Don't dismiss it completely out of hand. It may have its uses, significantly advantageous uses if it were to be, ah, sensitively employed, if you get my drift. Just a little man-to-man advice, you understand? Or should I make that man to *woman*.'

'I hear you.'

'All's fair in love and war – you don't need a lawyer to tell you that, I hope.'

'I imagine this phone call has cost me dearly already,' said James. 'Rest assured, I shall put its content to good use.'

'In that case, I won't detain you any further.'

'Thank you, John, and I mean that.'

'My pleasure. Do let me know how things work out.'

'You'll be the first to know.'

Sensations streamed through her body. Ebbing and flowing, rising and falling, rivulets of exquisite pleasure flooded her senses. As Josh's hands roved freely over her, then inside her, searching, stroking, expertly coaxing her to the brink again and again, Candy thought she would die of pleasure. It was wonderful, it was amazing, it was . . . awfully bright. 'What's with the lights?' she gasped, squinting. 'They're practically blinding me.' She pulled away from him fractionally.

'I like to look at you, baby, you know that,' he mumbled, his mouth fastened on a nipple, eliciting another set of delicious sensations.

'Can't you turn them down? It's like a bloody operating theatre in here.'

'Quit the running commentary, will ya, you're wrecking my buzz.' He entered her swiftly, taking her by surprise.

'Oh . . . oh,' she said.

'I'm not hearing any complaints now,' he said, grinning, as he rolled off her ten minutes later.

'Oh, Josh, baby, you're the best.'

'I keep tellin' ya.'

Candy stretched languorously, basking in her post-orgasmic glow. 'Can we turn the lights out now?' she murmured, snuggling up beside him. The effects of the enormous joint he had given her earlier were kicking in and she was feeling almost comatose, if still giddy.

'Nope, we haven't finished yet.'

'You're insatiable.' She giggled. I can't take any more.'

'You don't have to – it's my turn. Now you get to do the hard work.' He told her in no uncertain terms what he wanted her to do to him.

Candy would rather have just relaxed for a while, but she couldn't help herself. If Josh was issuing the instructions, then

Candy did exactly as she was told. 'And make sure you let me know just how much you enjoy pleasuring me, Miss Rich.'

Candy hated it when he called her that, but she didn't tell him. Her tongue was employed busily and, by all accounts, very effectively elsewhere.

Later, Candy heated up the remnants of last night's Chinese. Josh lounged on the couch, flicking the remote. When she handed him a plate and a bottle of beer and sat down beside him, he looked at her appreciatively. 'You're getting quite good at this,' he grinned. 'I'll make a sex kitten of you yet.'

Candy scowled. 'Quite good' wasn't what she wanted to hear. They watched a Mad Max movie, or rather Josh did while Candy sat quietly beside him. 'Can I stay over, Josh? It's late.'

'Nope. Got an early start.'

'So what?' Candy whined. She hated leaving him, hated the way he turfed her out into the night.

'So, no, you can't stay over.' He kept his eyes fixed on the screen.

'Why not?'

'Because I say so.'

'I don't want to go.' She really didn't. She hated sneaking into her dad's house at all hours, not that he or Shalom seemed to notice, or if they did they didn't comment. She still hadn't told anyone about Josh, not even her girlfriends.

'What you want doesn't work in my world, Miss Rich.'

'Don't call me that – I hate it.' Candy stood up and picked up the plates, fearful suddenly of the tears that threatened. Why was Josh so mean to her sometimes?

'No you don't, you like it – I could call you anything at all and you'd like it. Isn't that so?' His voice was gravelly, his tone suggestive, and worst of all he was right. And he knew it.

'No, it's not so. I hate it.' Candy was petulant, but the

thought of leaving Josh and going out into the cold, windy night made her want to cry.

'Baby.' He got up and pulled her to him, stroking her hair and holding her close. 'You can stay at the weekend, maybe.'

'Promise?'

'I never make promises, baby.'

It was as good as she was going to get. Candy forced herself to smile. It was a straw, a fragile straw, but it was something to cling to.

'Okay,' she said in a small voice.

She was just at the door when he pulled a piece of folded paper from his jeans. 'Sweetheart?'

She looked up, surprised. That was a definite improvement.

'Yeah?'

'Put your name on that for me, would ya?' He grabbed a pen from the table.

'Why? What is it?' she stalled, loath to go, but hating him for letting her.

'I need a second signature. It's just a witness thing, you know, a lease for my landlord.' He smiled lopsidedly at her, making her heart constrict. She would do anything for that smile, for any sign of approval. 'Here.' He handed her the pen and pointed to where her signature was required.

It looked like a normal kind of form, but the print was very small and she couldn't really read it. She knew you should never sign anything without reading it fully, but she was tired, and Josh was smiling at her . . .

'C'mon.' He tapped his foot, irritation a heartbeat away.

She put the paper on the table and leaned over to scrawl her name. Nothing happened. 'It's empty.' She shook the pen and tried again. It was no use.

'Sorry,' she said, and then, because she couldn't resist it, 'you should have let me stay. I have a pen somewhere in my bag, but I don't have time to look for it right now – I'll have to run if I'm to get a cab out there.' She opened the door and stepped into the cold hallway, shivering. 'Bye.'

'Never mind, I'll get someone else to do it for me.' His eyes were cold behind the smile. 'See ya.'

The minute she was outside, she felt desolate. Who would the 'someone else' be? Another girl? One of the models, maybe? She should have done as he asked – and she absolutely shouldn't have made that last parting remark. She had pissed him off. Displeasure had been written all over his gorgeous face.

15

'We need to talk about Candy.'

'I was just about to ring you with that very suggestion,' Charlotte said grimly at her end of the phone. 'I take it she's still with you. I haven't heard from her in over a week. If I'm lucky I get the odd text message.'

Charlotte was seriously worried. She had left at least ten messages on Candy's phone and even several with a woman who said she was Shalom's mother when she had rung Ossie's house. Now she wondered if they had even been passed on to Candy.

'In a manner of speaking.' Ossie sounded tired. 'She comes and goes whenever she pleases. In the beginning it was all right, but now I'm pretty sure there's a guy involved.'

'Who?' Charlotte felt her anxiety rising. She'd let Ossie take care of their daughter and look what was happening.

'I have no idea. She tells me she's staying with a friend.'

'A friend! Who?' demanded Charlotte. 'Ossie, she's twenty years old, she's never lived away from home. Her best friends haven't seen her either – I rang both Katy and Emma's mothers yesterday. What the hell is going on?'

'Don't tear strips off me, Charlotte,' Ossie said defensively. 'I'm as concerned as you are. She was here last night, but not every night.'

'We'll have to sort this out.'

'Are you up to lunch? I'm free today, or whenever suits you.'

'Today's fine. You can come here. I'll see you at one?'

'If it wasn't because our only daughter is causing such havoc, I'd say it would be a pleasure,' Ossie sighed, trying to make light of things.

Candy was proving a force to be reckoned with. And how, he grimaced, was he going to tell Charlotte about Candy's boob job? She would have a fit. He paled at the thought. He hadn't noticed it himself, not until Shalom had taken him aside and pointed it out. Then, when he had looked properly, he wondered how he could possibly have missed it. But then, it wasn't exactly as if he was supposed to scrutinise his own daughter's figure, was it? When he had confronted her about it (he had tried to get Shalom to talk to her − he was embarrassed to − but she was having none of it), Candy had been quite snotty.

'So what if I have?' she had said nonchalantly. 'There's nothing wrong with a bit of self-improvement.'

'Did you discuss it with Mum?' He fervently hoped she had.

She sighed, exasperated. 'No, I didn't. I'm over eighteen, Dad, I don't *actually* have to discuss anything with you *or* Mum. I bet Shalom didn't discuss it with anyone when she had *her* boobs done − unless, of course, it was after she met you.' She had let the comment hang in the air accusingly.

Ossie had been furious but had kept his mouth shut. The conversation was heading for dangerous territory and he wasn't going to go there.

'I'll see you at one.' Charlotte put the phone down and tried to take deep breaths.

Ossie had sounded weary. Well, it was hardly surprising. What did he expect? He had spoiled Candy beyond all reckoning and now he, or rather they, were paying the price. And whatever was going on, Candy clearly had the bit between her teeth. The more she thought about it, the more furious she became with Ossie. But then, she hadn't exactly tried to stop him from spoiling Candy, had she?

Charlotte suddenly felt terribly defeated. There was no point attacking Ossie. It wouldn't get her anywhere. She would make a nice lunch for them both, then hopefully they could work this thing out.

Opening the fridge, she had a good look at the contents. There wasn't an awful lot of food, but there was a nice bottle of Sancerre chilling. She would pop out to her local deli to pick up some treats and some nice fresh bread. They would have . . . what did P.J. call it? An indoor picnic. Thinking of him, Charlotte smiled. He made her laugh. And that wasn't all he made her do. He made her feel sexy, desirable, almost wanton. He was a fantastic lover. When she was in bed with him, she became someone else entirely, and they had been spending more and more time there . . .

More importantly, he seemed to be a fantastic father. Suddenly, she wished she could talk to him about all this instead of Ossie. P.J. would know what to do.

It was about three o'clock that day when Jennifer spied P.J. walking across the road heading for number 42 with a large parcel under his arm. She pulled up in her ancient Mini Clubman and wound down her window. 'Hello, P.J., what have you got there?'

'Oh, hello, Jennifer, didn't see you. I was miles away,' P.J. grinned at her. 'It's a fine brace of pheasant a patient of mine gave to me. I've finished up early today. Bella, my daughter, is home for a few days. I was wondering if Charlotte would like them.'

'She'd love them!' Jennifer said immediately.

'Shall I give them to you to give to her?'

'No, give them to her yourself, she'll be delighted to see you. Why don't you come in now for a cup of coffee?' Jennifer nodded towards the front door before turning her car into the driveway, pulling up beside the large silver Bentley that was parked at the bottom of the steps. P.J. followed her on foot and waited as she got out of the car.

'How's the hip?' he asked.

'Super. I feel like a youngster,' she laughed.

'Let me,' he said, insisting on taking out and carrying the bags of groceries she had bought. 'Er, Jennifer,' P.J. rubbed his chin, 'I'm not sure I should come in. Charlotte appears to have company.' He nodded at the Bentley. 'Nice car.'

'Yes, it is rather. Shame about the plonker who drives it, though.' She grinned evilly. There was no need, Jennifer thought, to mention it was *Ossie's* Bentley. P.J. would find that out for himself in just a minute. In fact, it was a perfect opportunity, she reflected: nothing like two men meeting up over a mutual woman to spur on a bit of action. Jennifer was pretty sure Ossie still had feelings for Charlotte, and though she was fond of him in her own way, despite his appalling behaviour on the marital front, she felt that Charlotte was still too much under his influence. She needed to see him up against a real man – a man like P.J., Jennifer thought astutely. And it wouldn't do P.J. any harm either to see that Ossie was still hovering in the vicinity. Men were proprietorial creatures when it came to the women in their life – nothing like a bit of competition to make the chase more interesting – and Jennifer was very definite about who she wanted to win.

'Look, I really don't think—'

'Nonsense, she'd love to see you.' She looked at him meaningfully. 'We'll be arriving just in time, I'd bet my last dollar on it.'

'Well, if you're sure.' P.J. followed her first into her own flat in the basement, where he left the parcels, and then, still carrying the pheasant, followed Jennifer upstairs. Without pausing to knock, Jennifer walked into Charlotte's kitchen, where she was greeted with varying degrees of surprise.

'Mummy!' said Charlotte.

'Hello, Jennifer,' said Ossie, standing up to greet her.

'Hello you two.' Jennifer was smiling broadly. 'I've brought a visitor.' She indicated P.J., who had followed her in and was now standing rather awkwardly with his gift.

'Sorry to barge in. I thought you might like these, Charlotte, and then I ran into your mother. P.J. O' Sullivan,' he held out his hand to Ossie by way of introduction, who shook it firmly.

'Oh, how silly of me.' Charlotte sounded flustered. 'Ossie, this is P.J. O'Sullivan, you know, the doctor who lives across the road. And this is Ossie,' she said to P.J. 'My, er, my . . .'

'Her ex-husband,' Jennifer finished for her. 'Now that we've got the introductions out of the way, any chance of a cup of coffee?'

'Of course, I'll just make another pot.' Charlotte jumped up, glad to busy herself with the task. 'Please, sit down.' She indicated a chair to P.J., who was eyeing the remains of the very nice lunch and the bottle of Sancerre. 'I really don't think I should.'

'Nonsense,' said Jennifer. 'Tell him, Charlotte – we're not interrupting anything, are we?'

'Of course not.' Ossie seemed uncomfortable. 'Actually, I was just about to leave.'

'You'll do no such thing,' Jennifer insisted. 'At least have a cup of coffee with us before running off.' She managed to make it sound as if he was a naughty schoolboy.

'I didn't mean to imply I was running off.'

'Then sit down,' Jennifer smiled.

So they did. Charlotte poured some fresh coffee and handed around some homemade brownies and everyone made particularly polite conversation.

It was P.J. who eventually made the move. 'I really must go. My daughter is home on a visit and I have to be getting back. Thank you for the coffee, Charlotte.' He stood up to go. 'Good to meet you, Ossie.'

'Yes, yes,' Ossie said heartily. 'Very good to meet you too!' He thought he managed to hide his surprise very well, considering. First Charlotte was being unreasonably angry with him about Candy's behaviour and now this handsome doctor chap breezing in . . .

'Do bring Bella over before she goes back,' said Jennifer. 'We'd love to meet her – wouldn't we, Charlotte?'

'Yes, of course,' agreed Charlotte, 'but I'm sure she has a very full social calendar, Mummy. She won't want to be meeting old fogies like us.'

'Actually,' P.J. turned and looked at Charlotte from the door, 'Bella is really looking forward to meeting you.'

'Oh – well.' Charlotte was taken aback. 'That's great. I – we'd love to meet her too.'

'We'll sort out the details later.' Jennifer was sitting at the table, looking very pleased with herself.

As Charlotte saw P.J. out, Jennifer proclaimed to nobody in particular, 'He's a thoroughly nice chap, that doctor. *Thoroughly* nice. Very handsome, too, and doesn't know it either. They're the best sort.'

'He certainly seems like a nice bloke,' Ossie said. 'Widower, isn't he?'

'Yes. Lost his wife five years ago to cancer – dreadful business. Lives all on his own in that big place across the road. Very sad.'

'I remember her, now that you mention it. Blonde girl, stunning-looking. That *is* sad,' Ossie said.

Why had she done that? Charlotte banged about the kitchen in a manner most unlike her, throwing things into the dishwasher and swiping a cloth over the counter surfaces with unnecessary vehemence. Why, when she had been having an important discussion with Ossie about Candy, had Jennifer decided to roll into the kitchen accompanied by P.J. of all people? The whole thing had been excruciatingly awkward for them all – apart from Jennifer, of course, who had seemed to find it all thoroughly amusing. She had disappeared swiftly afterwards, anticipating her daughter's wrath, and was hiding out downstairs in her flat, having a little 'lie-down', as she called it.

Ossie had looked tired when he came in. They had begun as they intended, talking about Candice, agreeing that her behaviour of late had become quite unacceptable and that, as Jennifer and others had quite rightly pointed out, she was turning into a little monster.

'I don't know what to do, Charlotte,' Ossie had said, despair flitting across his face. 'She's a force to be reckoned with. I don't know where she gets it from.'

'She's like you,' Charlotte smiled ruefully, 'a chip off the old block. And she adores you. I think she's just trying to get your attention.'

'But she's always had my attention.' He seemed bewildered.

'I know that.' Charlotte took a deep breath. She would have to tread carefully here. 'But fathers and daughters have a special relationship. I'm afraid we spoiled her dreadfully, Ossie.' She looked up at him from those enormous brown eyes. 'And it's got to stop. That, and the fact that she seems determined to do whatever it takes to keep winning your attention. Take her recent, um, makeover.'

'She looks like a tart!' Ossie spoke with feeling, failing to realise the irony. 'I got an awful shock. She's ruined herself, her lovely hair, and all that awful make-up.'

Charlotte said nothing.

'Don't *you* think she looks awful?' he asked, looking concerned.

'Well, yes,' Charlotte said, biting her lip. She had refrained from screaming, *can't you see she's turning herself into the spitting image of your plastic slapper of a girlfriend? That's who she's imitating, for God's sake – that's how badly she's trying to get your attention*. Instead, she said, 'Have you tried talking to her about it? She won't listen to me or Jennifer, told us we're living in the Dark Ages.'

'I did think about it, but when I mentioned it to Shalom, she said that all girls that age are really into the make-up and hair thing.'

Charlotte fought to keep her mouth shut, but because she couldn't, *wouldn't*, remain mute on the subject, said, 'I imagine it's much easier to watch when it isn't actually your *own* daughter you're talking about.'

Ossie looked at her for a long moment, then nodded. 'You're right, of course,' he said miserably. And then, steeling himself, he told her. 'There's something else.'

'Oh God, what?' Charlotte held her breath.

'She's had a boob job.'

'What?' Charlotte gasped. 'When?'

'Ten days ago, apparently. I didn't notice, not at first. It was, er, Shalom who pointed it out. She was wearing a lot of baggy jumpers and stuff, and, well . . .' He paused, looking at the horrified expression on her face.

Charlotte put her face in her hands. 'I don't believe this,' was all she could say. 'How could you let this happen?'

'She *is* nearly twenty-one. She's not a child,' he said gently.

'I suppose you paid for that too.'

'I knew nothing about it.' Ossie looked hurt.

'No, of course you wouldn't.'

'Charlotte, that's not fair.'

'My girl was perfectly beautiful just the way she was. Poor, poor Candy,' she whispered, shaking her head. 'What next?'

Ossie looked even more uncomfortable. He had no idea what to say.

Charlotte got up to clear some dishes away. She couldn't look at him. She was afraid of what else she might say.

When she sat down again, Ossie had tried to reassure her, but it was too late. He could already see the tears she had tried to wipe away.

He had taken her hand then. 'Charlotte?'

She had swallowed, her throat constricting.

'It's not that bad, really. It's probably just a phase.'

'She's craving male attention, Ossie,' Charlotte said. 'That's a phase that can go on for a long time, with disastrous consequences for a girl – *our* girl,' she added miserably.

'I'm sorry, Charlotte, so sorry for everything. Truly, I am.' Ossie sounded equally miserable. 'I don't think I ever told you . . . that is, I don't think I ever said how much I appreciate your handling of all this, since I left. It must have been hard for you. I often think about that, and I just wanted to say I think you're pretty amazing.'

She got up then, quickly, and turned on the kettle, unsure suddenly, her normal composure deserting her yet again. 'I'm not amazing,' she heard herself saying. 'If you must know, I cried myself to sleep that night, and for a great many nights after that. I just had to keep things together for Candy, and now I wonder why. It doesn't seem to have done any good. Sometimes I think she hates me, blames me for everything. Maybe she's right.'

'Don't say that. You *are* amazing, you've always been amazing. I always knew you were too good for me, but I had hoped Candy would take after *you*, be lovely and gentle and feminine and, well, you know, posh, I suppose. And instead she has to go and take after me.' He looked wretched. 'You're right, she *is* a chip off the old block, God help her!'

And suddenly, looking at the expression on his face, Charlotte had begun to laugh. They laughed and laughed and then suddenly, hearing the drone of the chair lift, pulled themselves together as Jennifer had appeared in the doorway – followed, unthinkably, by P.J.

Charlotte had hardly been able to believe it. Of all the worst possible timing. Why had Jennifer chosen that moment to invite P.J. in? Even she couldn't be that oblivious to the sensitivities of the situation, but she certainly had appeared to be. It hadn't taken a feather out of her, and in fact she seemed to have enjoyed the whole encounter tremendously, while she, Charlotte, had cringed through it, the collective awkwardness of herself and both men almost palpable in the room.

And P.J.! Poor P.J. had looked as if he would rather be anywhere else than there. She had seen him as his eyes roved over the table, taking in the remains of the lunch and indeed the empty bottle of Sancerre that she had quickly cleared away, how he had stood looking supremely uncomfortable with his gift of the pheasant until Jennifer had relieved him of them and told him to sit down.

Ossie had looked equally uncomfortable and suddenly quite guilty, as if he were a naughty schoolboy caught playing truant, and all the while they chatted about ridiculous things like the weather and even the Lisbon Treaty while Jennifer sat back, looking delighted with herself. Thankfully P.J. had put an end to the embarrassing torment by getting up to leave. She had felt dreadful then, afraid that he would read the wrong thing into her and Ossie's meeting and that she would never see him again. But then he had said that his daughter was looking forward to meeting her, and she'd been almost speechless with surprise and delight. That must mean he had spoken to Bella about her, that she mattered to him. It must mean— *Oh, stop it!* Charlotte told herself. She was becoming ridiculous, worse than a teenager, going over every word and trying to decipher every hidden meaning behind perfectly normal conversations. It was just that when she had seen the look on P.J.'s face, the sudden uncertainty that had flitted across it before he could hide it, her heart had constricted. She couldn't bear for him to be hurt or upset. He was the one person in the world who had been kind to her and she was having such fun being with him. She couldn't have survived what she was going through these past few weeks without him.

And Ossie had certainly noticed it. Before P.J., she would have found the meeting with Ossie intimidating and depressing. She would have felt inadequate and been distraught at the thought of Shalom and their baby on the way. Instead, she had been able to be strong and confront Ossie. Or was that a bad sign? Was she being a bad mother? She had tried, she really had, in every possible way, but now maybe it was time for Ossie to take more of a fatherly responsibility than he had done to date. There was more to being a father than just doling out unlimited amounts of money – and that had been Ossie's solution to everything. As far as she was concerned, there was nothing more she could do except be there for Candy if or when she needed her.

She wondered when, or indeed if, she would hear from P.J. Should she ring him and apologise? But for what? What could she say? *I'm sorry you walked in on me and my ex-husband having lunch*? She would look pathetic. But what if he didn't ring? What if seeing her and Ossie together had put him off, given him the wrong impression? What if she never heard from him again? Charlotte put her face in her hands. She couldn't bear it. What a mess, what a stupid, stupid mess, and it was all Jennifer's fault!

'It's always much worse first thing in the morning,' the glamorous thirty-something career woman was saying. 'Particularly, funnily enough, on a Monday morning. On a Friday, I hardly have any symptoms at all. Why do you think that might be? Doctor? Are you listening to me?'

'Yes, yes, of course I'm listening, I was just thinking about what you were saying, running a few ideas through my head.' P.J. was brought back to earth with a bang. These were the kind of patients he found it the hardest to sit through. They weren't really sick at all – not in the conventional sense – just self-obsessed and wanting to go over every minute detail of their mostly imagined symptoms with a professional that they would listen to and then disregard if the forthcoming diagnosis wasn't pleasing.

The woman in question was as healthy as an ox. She had

decided she was depressed in the wake of yet another relationship break-up and, in this instance, a run-in with her boss.
P.J. sympathised greatly with both parties. He'd bet she was a
nightmare to work with or live with. Now, she was suggesting
a course of anti-depressants, which he had put her on several
times before, and P.J. was almost ready to write her the prescription just to get rid of her, but he stuck to his guns. Anti-depressants had a real and positive place in modern mental-health
issues, but they were not medicinal sweeties to be handed out
on demand, and certainly not in a case such as this, where
they would merely be masking and prolonging a personality
problem that would have to be dealt with sooner or later.

'I'm prescribing a course of CBT.' He wrote the details
down and handed them to her.

'CBT? I haven't heard of those before.' She looked pleased.
'Are they new?'

'CBT stands for cognitive behavioural therapy, which is
what I think you need, not anti-depressants. We've tried them
before and they haven't made much difference, have they?'

'But I—'

'We're talking about a behaviour pattern here, Lisa, not a
depression. That's why you'll find CBT very helpful. I've
referred you to a therapist who is an excellent practitioner.
I'd like you to make an appointment as soon as possible.'

'I'm not sure I think—'

'I'm telling you what *I* think, Lisa. That's what you pay me
for, for my professional opinion, and that's what you've got.
Now, if you don't mind, I have a lot of very sick people out
there waiting to see me.'

'Well, really!' Lisa slung her designer bag over her shoulder.
'So much for bedside manner. You're just like all the rest of
them, can't take our money quickly enough and then want
to write us off! You won't be seeing me again, Doctor!' She
flounced out of the office.

P.J. sighed. He hadn't meant to be sharp with her, but

sometimes you had to be cruel to be kind. He certainly wasn't doing her any favours encouraging her to believe her own interpretation of the matter. The girl needed therapy, it was as plain as the nose on her face, and all he could do was point her in the right direction.

He was interrupted by Sheila, carrying in a cup of tea and a muffin. 'You've a twenty-minute break,' she said triumphantly. 'Mr O'Riordan cancelled and Mrs Clancy isn't due in until twenty past, so make the most of it.'

'Thank you, Sheila, that muffin looks good.'

'Maggie O'Neill left a bag of them in. I have the rest up in the house.'

'That was kind of her.'

'I doubt kindness had anything to do with it – she's just trying to outdo my recipe,' Sheila sniffed. 'But I said I'd give you one.' She stood, waiting for the verdict.

P.J. bit in dutifully. 'It's excellent, Sheila, really excellent, but, between ourselves, not a patch on your own.'

'I thought as much.'

P.J. shook his head as she returned to the surgery. What was a little white lie when every patient between now and closing up would benefit from the beatific happiness that Sheila would radiate? Satisfied he had at least performed one good deed for the day, he set about enjoying one of the most delicious muffins he had ever tasted. It wasn't that Sheila's muffins weren't good – they were – or rather, they had been. But since she had taken to wearing those surgical gloves, all her muffins had begun to taste of rubber. It was just that neither he, nor anyone else, had the heart to tell her.

Telling, or indeed withholding, the truth, P.J. reflected, was one of life's great dilemmas. Speaking of which, it had come as a surprise to him just how rattled he'd been to see Charlotte with her ex-husband, having what had patently been a very cosy lunch until they'd been interrupted. It wasn't that he disliked the fellow – Ossie had been perfectly pleasant – he just would rather not have met him, and certainly not under those circumstances. P.J. tried to examine his feelings. Charlotte and her ex-husband were as entitled as anybody to have whatever relationship they chose with one another, and of course they had a daughter, and P.J. knew more than most people just how big a tie family was. People could say what they liked, but the old saying held true: blood is thicker than water, and rightly so.

No, P.J. didn't begrudge Charlotte her relationship with Ossie, such as it may be. It was just that he was pretty sure Ossie hadn't been thrilled to see *him*. Oh, of course he'd been polite, friendly even, a nice bloke, but P.J. had picked up immediately on the distinctly speculative evaluation Ossie had directed towards him. It was a man-to-man thing, suitor assessing suitor. And that was it – that was what had been niggling him, he realised. He had assumed, rightly or wrongly, that Charlotte and Ossie were over, ancient history. Charlotte had told him as much and P.J. had no reason to doubt her, but he had seen with his own eyes that Ossie quite clearly still had feelings for Charlotte, and he hadn't looked at all happy at meeting P.J., or indeed at hearing any of the references Jennifer had made (which had been plentiful) to his relationship with Charlotte.

The whole incident had been very ill timed, really. It was an awful pity he had run into Jennifer the way he had. Otherwise the unfortunate meeting would never have happened at all and he wouldn't be feeling so . . . what was he feeling? Perturbed? Perplexed? Uncomfortable? Yes, but there was something else, something more annoying. P.J. scowled. He was jealous. That was it, pure and simple. He was having a very bad case of the green-eyed monster, and as far as he knew there was really no cure for it. He wouldn't think about it now. It was ridiculous – at his age! What was he even thinking of?

Anyway, he reminded himself briskly, he had his own family

to be concerned about. There was Bella, for instance. She was looking forward to meeting Charlotte, she had told him so, but now he wondered about it. When Jennifer had suggested bringing her over, Charlotte had seemed to pooh-pooh the idea of meeting her, although when he had said that Bella was hoping to meet her (he had watched Ossie's reaction to that too), she seemed to be pleased. To tell the truth, she had seemed a little on edge herself. He hoped Ossie hadn't done anything to upset her. Charlotte had been through enough on that front already.

He wondered what he should do. Should he just tell Bella that Charlotte was busy, or should he suggest a dinner maybe? Either way, he would have to talk to Bella. The tests had come back, and thankfully Bella was clear – she wasn't a carrier of Von Willebrand's. P.J. had hoped as much. Interestingly enough, his own test had also come back negative, which meant he wasn't a carrier either. It could mean a number of things, but Jilly, bless her, was not there to confirm matters, or indeed be tested herself. She must have been a carrier, or else . . .

P.J. forced himself to focus on the facts in hand. What mattered was that Alex had the disorder, and his new baby Charlie too. That the rest of the family was clear was a blessing. He would talk to Bella about it this evening. She would be relieved.

And then they would have to talk about Alex.

Ossie slammed his fist on the horn. 'Look where you're bloody going, mate!' he shouted out the window of his Bentley at the guy who had sauntered across the road without looking, daring any motorist to so much as touch him.

'Look out yourself!' the guy yelled back. 'What's your problem? You're just another prick in a fancy car.' He gave him the finger for good measure.

Ossie forced himself to take a few slow breaths. He shouldn't let it get to him, but recently he was feeling increasingly under pressure, though just why, he wasn't sure. Business was tough, of course; times were tough for everyone in property, but he was still holding up, although no one could take anything for granted in the current crash. It was all uncharted waters at the moment. He truly felt for the others, the first-timers particularly, young chaps who had ventured into the market at the worst possible time, some of them up to their necks in debt. And the financial situation was dire. Still, at least that was something he could handle. His domestic situation was quite a different kettle of fish, and one which he increasingly felt less and less able to cope with.

Candy taking up residence had changed everything. Initially he'd been happy to have her stay while she took some time out and decided what she wanted to do with her life. She had dropped out of university last year where she had begun to study drama and literature and pronounced it boring. From there, she had said she wanted to pursue a career in acting, and decided a modelling course wouldn't be a bad idea to start off with. That had proved futile, and the acting career didn't seem to be materialising either, although Candy assured her father that these things took time. Time indeed, and as it turned out, a lot of it spent on his payroll. Ossie didn't even like to think about how much he had coughed up on Candy in the past couple of months. He would have to take her to task and stop her allowance, even though it upset him to have to even think about that. She would have to learn the hard way, as everyone did eventually, that she either supported herself or got back into some kind of educational system that would provide a career at the end of it. And her behaviour of late was becoming increasingly worrying.

He and Charlotte had gone over the various possibilities of what might happen, the most likely scenario being Candy being pursued by someone entirely unsuitable for her, after her, or rather her father's, money. And what if she were to marry such an unscrupulous sort? Children and an objectionable son-in-law to support indefinitely . . . it didn't bear thinking about.

Shalom was also beginning to get fed up with having Candy around and made her feelings felt on the subject. 'She's big and bold enough to get a job of her own and be paying for her own place. I was at her age,' she said.

She was becoming increasingly moody with him and incessantly reminding everybody of the imminent birth of the baby in six weeks' time. Her mother, Bernie, seemed to be visiting more and more lately. Initially Ossie had been unperturbed about this, thinking it was good that Shalom had some company and someone she could talk things over with, but increasingly Ossie was coming down to find Bernie bustling about in the kitchen first thing in the morning, when he wanted some breakfast – in peace and quiet. Listening to Bernie's shrill train of chatter and whizzing blenders of smoothies were beginning to do his head in. Shalom had even begun referring to one of the many spare bedrooms in the west wing as 'Mummy's room', and Bernie seemed to be spending more and more time in it. Why only last week he had turned away a delivery van of some ridiculous instrument only to learn from a highly indignant Shalom that Mummy's sun bed was taking up too much space in her house and she, Shalom, had told her she could keep it here for as long as she wanted. Ossie sighed. He would have paid quite an obscene amount of money to send both mother and daughter away – quite far away, actually – to get the real thing.

And then there had been that lunch with Charlotte last week. He'd been quite nervous about the whole thing, and not just about Candy. He had pulled into the driveway, parked his car and walked up the steps, just as he used to do, and had been welcomed by Charlotte, looking (he had to admit he had been taken aback) absolutely stunning in a pair of skinny denim jeans tucked into dark brown soft suede knee-high boots. Her hair hung about her shoulders in a dark cloud, and her face, her skin . . . she looked lit up from inside. Radiant. Younger too, somehow, and much more carefree. It had taken his breath away.

She had put on a really lovely lunch and they had tackled the matter of their wayward daughter. When he told her about Candy's boob job, she'd been terribly upset, as he'd known she would be. But she had been quite tough on him, he felt, unfairly so, as if the whole thing had been *his* fault. But then they'd begun to laugh, really laugh, about something silly, and he had looked at her, laughing, tears of mirth pouring down her face, and he'd wanted to leap across the table and take her in his arms. It was as if the past twenty years had been wiped away, all the tragedy, all the hurt – and then Jennifer had come in. Unannounced, of course, accompanied by that doctor chap. Handsome bloke.

It had spoiled everything. Oh, they had all sat down on Jennifer's instructions and had coffee and made small talk, but the mood had been broken. P.J., or whatever he called himself, had come over on the pretext of bringing a brace of pheasant to Charlotte (who on earth brought a brace of pheasant as a gift these days?). Ossie sighed – he'd never understand their lot. Posh people really were a law unto themselves, no matter how much money you had. Clearly he'd become quite a friend, maybe more.

Ossie scowled. He had said something about introducing Charlotte to his daughter; Ossie had picked that up right away. It had been said for his benefit, of course. Typical male behaviour, trying to stake out his territory. But what of it? Charlotte was entitled to entertain whomever she pleased in her house. There was clearly something going on between them, or if not, the doctor very much wanted there to be. Any fool could see that.

Ossie pulled into the impressive gates of Windsor Hall and

continued up the long gravelled driveway. He was in a bad mood, that was all. Who could blame him? Life got you down sometimes, that was all there was to it. Or was there? He certainly would pay no attention to the ridiculous voice that whispered in his head that he was jealous. He'd been the one to leave his marriage, hadn't he? All the same . . .

He saw Candy's BMW parked outside. That was good. She was home for a change. He remembered her mentioning something about that doctor and a concert he had brought Charlotte and her to. He would ask her casually about him and her mum. Very casually.

'Candy? Where are you?' Ossie called up from the huge square hall, his footsteps echoing on the boldly patterned Italian tiles.

Candy scowled. She was hiding out in her bedroom and hated being disturbed, especially now. It had been exactly a week since she had heard from Josh – or rather, not heard from him – and the silence was excruciating. Anything would have been better. If he had bawled her out, yelled at her, even if he had hit her she wouldn't have cared, but to leave her like this, to withdraw from her totally . . . she couldn't bear it. And he hadn't returned or even acknowledged a single one of her increasingly desperate and desolate text messages or voice messages, pleading with him, begging him to tell her what was wrong. She had cried for three whole days and nights, and now there were no more tears left, just the cold, empty, terrifying abyss she was looking into that would be a life without Josh. She wouldn't even contemplate it – couldn't. One day at a time, she kept reminding herself, just get through today. He'll ring tomorrow.

And now, just when she needed it like a hole in her head, her stupid dad was hollering for her. What the hell did he want now? Why couldn't they just leave her alone? Her mother had been hounding her with messages, and every time she had thought it would be Josh. She'd better go down, otherwise he might come up looking for her, to her room, where even he would notice something was up. Her room looked like a bomb had hit it. Clothes had been discarded all over the place and there were so many used tissues on the floor it looked like there was a carpet of snow. She pulled on some jeans, quickly ran into the bathroom and splashed some cold water on her face, rubbed in some foundation and concealer and hoped for the best.

Downstairs, she found Ossie in the kitchen. 'Hi, Daddy,' she said, heading for the fridge to get a drink.

'Hi, Princess, I was wondering where you were. What are you up to?'

'I've got the flu, I'm staying in bed. Don't come too close, I wouldn't want to give it to you.'

'Should we call the doctor?'

'No, I'll be fine, I'm just feeling horrible. If I don't feel better in a couple of days, I'll go to the doctor then.' She pulled out a snipe of champagne and held it towards him. 'Open this for me, would you?'

'Champagne? When you've got the flu?' Even Ossie looked taken aback. Candy didn't care.

'Well, you know what they say, drink plenty of fluids.' If she had her way, and she fully intended to, she would get completely smashed in the privacy of her own bedroom before the night was through.

Ossie raised an eyebrow but pulled the cork effortlessly. 'Well, go easy on it. Oh,' he paused, rifling through some papers on the countertop. 'Speaking of doctors, was it P.J. O'Sullivan who brought you and your pals to the concert with Mum a while back?'

'Yeah. Why?' Candy's antennae were up and she held her breath. Did he know about Josh? Was that what was coming next?

'Oh, nothing, just wondering. He's a neighbour of ours, that's all. Well, you know, in the old . . . in Mum's house.'

Candy looked at him strangely. 'If he's a neighbour, he's a very friendly one,' she said, taking a sip of her champagne. 'He might as well live in the place for all the time he spends in his own house.' There, that should shift any unwelcome scrutiny of her own social life at the moment. She watched as Ossie's face remained inscrutable. 'I wouldn't mind, but he brings the bloody dog too. That's part of the reason I moved out, actually.' Now she had his attention.

'Really? Well, it's nice Mum has a friend.'

Candy snorted. 'I'd say "friend" is a bit of an understatement. But yeah, she has every right to have a boyfriend – surprising it took her so long, actually.' And with that she retreated upstairs to her sanctuary of grief, where once she was behind closed doors she threw herself on the bed and feverishly examined her phone for signs of life. Seeing none, she took another gulp of champagne, swallowing the bitter, fizzing liquid. It made a change from the taste of her tears.

Suddenly she could bear it no longer. She would go to him. If she could only see him and talk to him, everything would be fine, she knew it would. She would make sure she looked great – it wouldn't take too long, just an hour or two – and then she'd drive into town and call around to Josh's flat. She didn't care who or what she found there, as long as she could talk to him.

Ossie closeted himself in his office. There was still an hour or two to go before dinner, and he really didn't want to be disturbed. There was no sign of Shalom and, better still, none of Bernie. They were probably out somewhere together.

So Charlotte and this doctor were clearly an item then. Well, what of it? It was all perfectly respectable. He was a widower and she was a – a divorcee. Why was that so hard to say? *Because you still think of her as your wife*, said the small voice in his head. And it was true, he reflected, he did. He couldn't help it; Charlotte would always be his wife. She was the one he had pursued, had exchanged vows with. How had it all gone so wrong? Did he still have feelings for her? *Of course*, was the answer to that. But was it possible that he was still in love with her? But that would mean . . . no, he would not follow this ridiculous train of thought. He was happy, happy with Shalom and a new baby on the way. Because if he wasn't . . . Oh, God. Ossie shook his head. This was the way to madness.

To distract himself, he booted up his computer and decided to run through his emails, anything to take his mind off the women in his life. There wasn't much; everything went to his head office for his secretary to screen. If anything urgent needed his attention when he was away from the office, then she alerted him. There were a couple from a few mates, a better than usual joke and one from his brother in Australia, asking when he was making an honest woman of Shalom. And then he noticed it. Marked urgent, with a red flag attached, was one from his secretary. That was strange – usually she called him if there was anything urgent. Then he remembered he'd put his phone on silent since the last meeting he'd had in town. Looking at it, there were five missed calls from her and several messages. He clicked on the email and simultaneously dialled his voicemail. Both messages began with varying degrees of urgency. 'Ossie, ring me the minute you get this,' said the voice message.

'Tried ringing, your phone's turned off. You need to see this,' the email said. Putting his phone down, Ossie scrolled down the email, which was from an unidentified address. It read simply: *Take a look at this, Mr Keating, and let me know what it's worth NOT to see your daughter having sex on the Internet.*

With a creeping feeling of dread mingled with disbelief, Ossie clicked on the attached mpeg. Before his eyes, the screen came to life and he watched three quick takes of a couple indulging in various sexual positions and activities, clearly just a sample of what was on offer in the full version. He had never laid eyes on the man, but there was no mistaking the young woman. He'd have known her anywhere. Quickly he shut the offending clip down then, feeling so angry he thought his head was going to explode, he strode out of his office into the hall. He didn't hear or seem to notice the front door open while Shalom and Bernie came in loaded with shopping bags. Ignoring them completely, he broke into a run, and taking the stairs three at a time, let out a roar of such magnitude that Shalom dropped her new D&G handbag and Bernie had to put her hands over her ears.

'*Candice*!' was the word that reverberated off the walls.

16

Cici couldn't remember when she last ate – for the past two weeks the thought of food revolted her. She hadn't been dressing either, not in the proper sense, and as for make-up, why bother? Why paint a pretty face on the outside when inside she felt beyond ugly? Where had it all got her? What was the point? Much easier to slip into her cashmere lounging suit, which then gave way to a succession of sweatpants and tops, and finally just her towel robe. Then the effort of putting on even that seemed pointless and she had just stayed in bed, venturing forth only to make an occasional cup of coffee. Her world had come to an end, so why pretend that life could be in any way normal? She had had a perfectly wonderful one, a marriage and a family, and she had screwed it all up royally. And now she was paying the price. Now she was being discarded by possibly the most loving, supportive (and now sought-after) husband that had ever existed. How could she have been so monumentally stupid? How could she have let her pathetic vanity, her ridiculous insecurities, her lack of conscience, destroy everything she held so dear? It had been sheer insanity. Now no one cared if she were alive or dead, least of all herself.

When her phone rang, she barely bothered to pick it up, particularly since Harry was still leaving the occasional nasty text message and voicemail, probably, Cici speculated correctly, under the influence of alcohol. Then, squinting over the sheets, she saw it was James. Lunging for the mobile, she tried to sound upbeat.

'Hello?' she said.

'Hello, Cici, it's me.' The voice was brusque, but it still belonged to him, that sorely missed and dearly beloved voice.

'James. How are you?'

'I'm well, thank you. I'll come straight to the point, Cici.'

Oh please, don't, she begged him silently. *No more points, no more clipped, punctuated finalities. Please, let's talk about anything else.*

'I assume you've received my, er, solicitor's instructions?'

'Yes, yes I did.' She managed to articulate the words and sound normal, when she really wanted to scream.

'Good. Well, there's something I need to talk to you about – to, ah, discuss?'

'Of course.' She steeled herself.

'I thought we should meet for lunch. Today, at my club?'

Anything could happen. She grasped the lifeline like a drowning woman.

'That would be lovely, James.'

'One o'clock?'

'I'll be there.'

'Good. Well, goodbye then.'

She hurtled out of bed. It was eleven o'clock. She had one and a half hours to try and make herself look vaguely human. Lunch was a good thing, a chance to meet and talk with her husband and hear whatever he had to say. It was a tiny ray of hope amidst the dark, all-consuming void she'd been living in since she'd opened that horrible envelope. Maybe God had answered her prayers and was going to give her the second chance she had begged Him for, even if she didn't deserve it. She could hope. There was nothing wrong with hoping.

Bingo! She'd hit pay dirt. She had just *known* there'd been something sly and underhanded about her. Well, her little fabrication was about to be blown sky high. Waitress, my ass!

Tanya had guessed as much. Carla Berlusconi was no waitress. She was, according to what the Internet had offered up, a world-class chef! It wasn't exactly what Tanya had hoped to discover about her, but nonetheless it was spectacular. The question was, why? Why on earth had she chosen Dublin – and indeed Dominic's – to conduct her incognito existence? It was probably something to do with her family's chain of restaurants in New York. But who cared? Whatever way she tried to explain or wriggle her way out of it, it wasn't going to look good. Nobody liked a spy in the camp, particularly in such a tightly knit group as a kitchen.

Tanya grinned, thinking of it, savouring the prospective shock and anger. Rollo would be outraged to be made a fool of by a woman, and one who was, by all accounts, a much more talented and acclaimed chef than he was. And as for Dom . . . Tanya's mouth curved in a smile. Who knew what the deceitful little witch's reasons were, but Tanya would bet her bottom dollar that Carla didn't have Dom's interests at heart, and Dom was passionately protective of his restaurant. To undermine it in any way would be seen as a personal attack on everything he held dear, and sneaking around pretending to be a waitress while Carla went about whatever unsavoury undercover business she was conducting would be seen as the worst kind of attack of all.

It wasn't going to go down well, but what a story. Tanya was so excited at the thought of leaking it to her press contact that her fingers were trembling as she punched in the number.

Dom was having trouble concentrating. He was trying to work out what to say to Rollo about the financial situation and how to approach asking him to take a cut in salary. He had already let two of the waiters go, and had found that incredibly difficult. Then he would think about Carla, her feisty determination and willingness to work so hard, and, more importantly, the absolutely amazing sex they were having. No wonder he was having trouble thinking about anything else. What else was there worth thinking about?

When she had stayed in his place that first night, he had woken up to find her gone from the bed, and found her in the kitchen.

'Coffee?' she had asked him, looking sheepish. 'I couldn't sleep.'

'Me neither.' He came over and dropped a kiss on her forehead.

'Would you like to try again?' he said, slipping his arms around her and pushing a stray tendril behind her ear.

'To sleep?'

'Something like that.' He had kissed her then, and it had been every bit as promising and tantalising as the night before.

'Yes,' she said, smiling up at him. 'I think I would.'

'I was hoping you'd say that.'

Since then they had been trying, not very successfully he suspected, to keep their blossoming affair to themselves – at least until they got used to the idea. It wasn't that everyone in the restaurant wouldn't be happy for them – they would – but just for the moment, they wanted it to be their own delicious secret. But they would have to say something soon, and then – Dom kept trying to avoid the awful thought – Tanya would be bound to find out. He should probably tell her, he thought, but then, they were over. Whatever way she found out, it was all perfectly legitimate – she was probably dating someone else herself by now, he reassured himself.

During the week, he and Carla slipped up to his apartment at every opportunity, and at the weekend, Dom would follow Carla to her basement flat in Wellington Square. He would have followed her anywhere, the realisation dawned on him slowly – he couldn't get enough of her.

Happily, she seemed to feel the same way about him. Neither of them had mentioned the 'L' word yet, he thought, grinning. They didn't have to. It was written all over their faces and expressed quite eloquently in many other ways, without them having to say a word.

Lunch was not going at all well. Cici had been meticulously punctual, arriving at the Royal Irish Yacht Club at five minutes to one, and had taken great care with her appearance, wearing a suit she knew James loved on her, though it felt as if it was two sizes too big – she had lost that much weight. She wasn't pleased when she looked in the mirror. She looked gaunt and drawn, with purple shadows under her eyes that no amount of concealer properly covered.

James had arrived precisely at one o'clock and they had gone straight to their table by the window. Cici had accepted James's offer of champagne but had then been dismayed when he ordered water for himself. They had chatted about the weather, business and the recession until Cici thought she would scream, she felt so awkward. But there was nothing she could say – James was calling the shots now and he was taking his time getting to whatever it was he wanted to discuss with her. What was there to discuss anyway, she thought miserably. Whether or not to go to court, or to arrange a dignified out-of-court settlement? Either way, she didn't care. She just wanted her gorgeous husband to tell her it had all been a terrible mistake and that he was still as much in love with her as he had ever been. She allowed herself this thirty-second fantasy, gazing wistfully out over the bright blue bay beneath them.

'Cici?'

'Sorry.' She was contrite. 'I was miles away.'

'My solicitor tells me you still haven't appointed a firm to represent you legally.' He looked at her patiently, but his face was unreadable.

'No, I haven't,' she said wretchedly.

'You'll have to sooner or later, and it might as well be sooner.'

No I don't, she thought. *I can lock myself away and hide in bed and never come out again and waste away and die. Why bother hiring solicitors?*

'You see,' James was toying with the salmon on his plate, 'something very unusual has come to light. About the case, that is.'

'What?' she said blankly, staring at the lamb she had barely touched.

'Well, the thing is . . . it turns out we're not actually married at all.'

Her head snapped up and she gasped. 'What?'

'That's exactly what I said.' James gave a little laugh and wiped the corner of his mouth with his napkin.

'If this is your idea of a joke . . .'

'No, I wouldn't, nor would my solicitor joke about anything this serious.'

'But what – how?' Her hand went to her throat. She could barely form the words, let alone the questions.

'Apparently we didn't fulfil the correct residency requirements in Rome prior to the marriage. While the religious ceremony was legitimate, it turns out that legally, back in Dublin, it doesn't stand up at all. So as I said, in the eyes of the legal system, we're not married at all. Extraordinary, isn't it?' James sounded thoroughly amused. 'So you see, you really must hire a solicitor as soon as possible so we can sort all this out. Then you'll be perfectly free to pursue this, er, young friend of yours – Harry, isn't that his name? – and we can all go our separate ways much sooner than we thought.' He looked pleased.

'But I don't want to,' she croaked.

'Oh really, Cici, even you must tire of playing games eventually. Don't be silly.'

'No, you don't understand. I don't want him – Harry. I want you, James!'

'Is that so? I must say you have a funny way of showing it.

Forgive me if I've lost my sense of humour, but I don't really find any of this amusing. I'll be glad to get it all wrapped up. This revelation about our marriage is a most welcome one and perfectly timed.'

'No, it's me who should beg for forgiveness,' Cici cried, the words coming out in a torrent. 'Please, James, I beg of you, give me a chance to explain.'

'Cici, don't do this. Leave us some dignity.' His voice was clipped and cold.

'I don't have any dignity! I don't want any dignity! Not if it means losing you. I love you, really I do, I've always loved you. I believe you know that deep down – you must!'

'Is that what you told Harry too?' His eyes were hard.

'No – never! I never loved him, James. It was stupid selfish, madness, but I never loved him.' She paused to draw a shuddering breath. 'But now – now I hate him! He's insane! He tried to upset Sophia. He followed me to Rome. You have to believe me.'

'Yes, I heard about that sordid little incident. Sophia was and *is* upset – upset and angry. I empathise entirely with her.'

'I'll make it up to her and to you.' She reached out to take his hand across the table, but he withdrew it. 'Harry is mad.' She began to cry, exhaustion and desolation making tears pour down her face. 'He followed me to Rome. I was going to finish with him before, but I did then, and ever since he's been threatening me and sending horrid messages to me. I know I deserve it all, I know it's all my stupid fault, but believe me, James, I have paid the price. If there was anything I could do, anything to turn back the clock and undo what I did, I would. But I can't.'

'That much at least is true.' He looked at her, unmoved.

'Please, James,' she whispered. 'Please can we go somewhere and talk properly? I beg of you, let me explain – please give me that chance.'

For a split second he seemed to waver, then he took a

breath and stood up. 'No, Cici, I'm afraid not. The only talking that will be done from here on out will be between our solicitors. Which is why I would urge you once again to appoint one. If not, I shall proceed with the divorce without you. It's your choice. I will, of course, accord you all the financial security entitled to that of any wife. We did, after all, live as husband and wife for a great many happy years – or so I foolishly thought.'

'James, please,' she said, barely audible.

'Thank you for meeting me for lunch, Cici. I'll leave you to make your own way home.' And with that, he walked away from the table and out of the dining room.

She wasn't sure how long she sat there, looking out unseeingly over the sea, grey now and bleak.

'Ahem.' It was the elderly waiter, clearing his throat discreetly as he removed her plate. 'Can I get you anything else, Mrs Coleman?'

The words plunged a knife into her very soul. *Mrs Coleman.* It was probably the last time she would ever hear them uttered.

Carla had just finished her afternoon shift and was looking forward to having a much-needed evening of pampering, including a long bath, then falling into bed – alone for a change. Dom was away for a couple of days, selecting and ordering some new wines for their increasing list. How Carla would have loved to go with him! As it was, they were tight staffed enough already. Instead, she was using the time to catch up on her sleep and beauty treatments and generally daydream. Every thought, every action, every fibre of her being was revolving around Dom. She could hardly believe what was happening and she couldn't think of anything else.

There was only one thing weighing heavily on her mind. She still hadn't told Dom the truth about who or what she was. She was scared he'd think she was sly and secretive, and then, when they had made love that first time, that amazingly wonderful time when she *should* have told him, she hadn't wanted to ruin the moment. She'd been trying to find the right time and there never seemed to be one, and the longer she left it, the harder it got. What would she say? *You know how you think I'm a penniless waitress? Well* . . . She just couldn't find the words somehow. And Dom was so kind and thoughtful. He had even said he thought she should go and see her father, that maybe they might go to New York together. She could talk about everything else with him, it seemed, but now she was consumed with anxiety about telling him the truth.

At home, she took off her coat and boots and went straight to the tiny bathroom to run a hot bath with generous helpings of aromatherapy oil. She put a conditioning treatment on her hair and sank into the silky water and wished Dom was with her. Afterwards, she did her nails and toes, dried her hair and slipped in between fresh sheets. She picked up the phone eagerly when it rang.

'Hello?'

'Hey, gorgeous.' It was Dom and her heart skipped a beat. 'What are you doing?'

'I'm in bed, having an early night for a change.'

'I wish I was in there with you.'

'Me too, although I could do with getting some shut-eye. I'm definitely sleep deprived. I got two orders wrong today, I've never done that.'

'That has nothing to do with lack of sleep, as you well know.'

'Is that so?'

'Absolutely. I'll prove it to you when I get back. Now I have to go down to this tasting dinner, which will go on for hours.'

'You're good at that.'

'Be careful, Carla, or I'll skip the dinner and stay up here having phone sex with you.'

'I'll settle for the real thing. When are you back?'

'Tomorrow, late afternoon. I'll see you then.'

'Good. I miss you.'

'I miss you too.'

'*Ciao, cara*.'

'*Ciao*. Oh, and Carla?'

'Yes?'

'I'm crazy about you. You know that, don't you?'

'Oh Dom, I've been mad about you since I first set eyes on you.'

'Sweet dreams, *cara*.' There was the briefest of pauses. 'I love you.' He hung up before she could say a word, but the warmth and smile in his voice were loud and clear.

He'd said it! Dom loved her. She had hoped, of course, dreamed of it in every waking moment, but to hear the words . . . She tried calling him back but couldn't get through, so she sent a text message instead. *I love you too – hurry home xxx*

Then she kissed the phone, bearer of such lovely tidings, and snuggled down to sleep. Tomorrow she would tell him, explain about why she had kept it all a secret. He wouldn't be cross. Dom never got cross.

It was the phone that woke her again, in what felt like the middle of the night. Fumbling blindly for the light switch, she picked it up. No number showed up on the caller display. Perhaps it was Dom again, calling from France, maybe from a landline, but it was five a.m. He was probably squiffy after his wine-tasting dinner and didn't realise what time it was.

'Hello?' she said tentatively.

'Carla?' she recognised the voice at once.

'Marco? How did you—?'

'Thank God. Listen, never mind how we got your number. You must come home right away. It's Papa – he's had a heart attack.'

'Oh my God, Marco, no!'

'Hurry, Carla. I'll meet you at JFK – just get yourself over here as fast as you can.'

'Is he — is he . . .?'

'He's still alive, but he's critical. He's asking for you.'

'Oh God, oh God, I'm on my way — I'll leave right now.'

'I'll pray you make it in time. Let me know your flight details when you can.'

She moved as if in a bad dream, methodically flinging things into a case, checking her passport, turning off lights and banging the door behind her, only just remembering to lock it. She hailed a taxi in the street and told him to get to the airport. Something in the tone of her voice and her ravaged face made even this most cheerful of Dublin taxi drivers refrain from asking if she was off somewhere nice. Instead, he nodded brusquely and drove intently through the early morning darkness until finally, the lights of Dublin Airport loomed ahead of them.

Tanya awoke with a thrill of anticipation she hadn't experienced for a long time. She didn't bother with her exercises, just showered and did her hair and make-up with even more care than usual. Donning a pair of slim black trousers and a long, slinky, black V-necked jumper, she slipped her feet into her new black suede ankle boots. Slinging her bag over her shoulder, she made for the door, took one last approving look in the mirror and headed out, humming 'These Boots Are Made for Walking'.

It didn't take her long to reach the fashionable coffee bar and deli where her breakfast companion was waiting for her.

'Just an Americano for me,' she said to the waiter. 'Well?' she asked the journalist, who was tucking into a full Irish.

'Take a look at this,' he grinned, handing her the morning edition of the paper. 'I think you'll like it.'

Tanya flicked quickly to his avidly followed gossip and entertainment column and consumed every syllable of the article. 'Excellent!' she proclaimed, shaking her head and grinning.

'You owe me one.'

'Yes, Owen, I most certainly do.'

It had been the longest three hours of her life.

The Aer Lingus staff had been kind and concerned, but the flight was full. She was on standby, and they were pulling out whatever stops they could. She rang her brother, who sounded battle-weary but confirmed that her father was at least still alive, still holding on. She had just finished the phone call when the ground hostess beckoned her to the desk. 'Good news, pet, we've got you on. You can go and check in now.'

Carla could only nod her gratitude. She couldn't speak, as tears were pouring down her face. 'Come on, love, I'll go with you,' said the sympathetic girl. 'It's your dad, is it?'

Carla nodded again and blew her nose.

'I'll say a prayer for you. Don't give up hope. Here,' she fished in her handbag and pressed something that felt like a coin into Carla's hand. 'It's never let me down yet. You'll get home in time, I know you will.'

Carla looked at the small silver medal and smiled. It was a miraculous medal, just like the one her mother had worn around her neck all her life.

'Thank you so much, but don't you need it?'

'Plenty more where that came from – my parents' house is full of them. God bless, pet, and safe journey.' And then she was disappeared into the crowds of tourists and holiday-makers all intent on making their way out of Dublin.

It was just as the flight was called to board that she remembered to call Dom. She was already on a couple of days' leave from work so there was no need just yet to call the restaurant – they wouldn't be expecting her.

She longed to hear his voice, but on the other hand she was afraid she would break down completely if she heard it, wanting him to be here now to hold her, reassure her.

She dialled his number and tried to keep her voice steady. It went to voicemail. 'Dom,' she began haltingly. 'I have to go home, to New York. It's urgent. It's my father. He's had a heart attack, and he's critical. I'll call you when I have news. I love you.' She switched the phone off as she boarded, already dreading turning it on at the other end, on the other side of the Atlantic, fearful of the devastating news it could bring her at any moment.

Back in Dominic's, they were going through the morning drill, preparing, as usual, for the lunch sitting.

The cutback in staff meant they all had to work extra hard, and everyone was feeling the strain.

In the kitchen, tempers and nerves were even more frayed than usual as Rollo was making no bones about the fact that taking a hefty cut in salary was affecting his creative instincts.

He had said as much to Astrid. They had both discussed their options carefully.

'It is only because I feel for him,' Rollo had said, shaking his head sadly. 'It was a bad day when he got mixed up with that Tanya woman – I knew she would be trouble.'

'We all did, for Dom at any rate, but I thought she was just a nuisance here. I never dreamed she would be taking liberties with the accounts. Although all the freebies – how could Dom not have noticed?'

'He is creative spirit, like me.' Rollo shook his head. 'He was building his restaurant, caring for his kitchen. His accountant is to blame.'

'But now look what's happened.' Astrid was mournful.

'I know. I told him I would stay for as long as I could on this pay cut, but only because I don't want to see him go under. I can't do it for much longer, Astrid, maybe a couple of weeks. Already I have had two offers after making discreet enquiries. And I think soon, I would like to go back to Italy.'

Astrid's face fell. 'To Italy?'

'Yes – home, to Italy.' He took her hands and grinned. 'But only if my Astrid comes with me.'

'Oh Rollo,' she beamed, all thoughts of Dominic's travails forgotten. 'Of course I will.'

It was Paddy, the kitchen porter, who saw it first. He'd been sitting in the staff room having his tea break and had paused when mid-mouthful he saw the headline. DOMINIC'S DISH OF THE DAY, it read, followed by a subhead. *What will debonair restaurant owner have to say?*

The article went on to speculate about 'riveting revelations' that sexy J-Lo look-alike Carla Berlusconi, a waitress who was a favourite with staff and clients alike, was, in fact, none other than an undercover plant. She was herself an acclaimed and talented chef who had worked in several single- and double-starred Michelin restaurants before heading up the kitchen at the famous M Hotel in New York.

Carla, it was pointed out, was the daughter of Antonio Berlusconi, head of the famous New York chain, noted for his aggressive expansion technique in taking over key restaurants and adding them to the family business. Clearly the beautiful Carla was on an undercover mission here in Dublin to glean the information needed before Dominic's presumably became the chain's first Irish flagship. Watch this space . . .

The article was accompanied by a shot of Dom, looking gorgeous at a polo match, and one of Carla, at work in the restaurant, plates in hand, looking stressed and cross. It had clearly been taken by a mobile phone. There was also a shot of Tanya, looking immaculate, with a sad smile on her face. She was quoted as saying, 'Unfortunately Dominic's is no longer a client of mine. In light of certain inexplicable discrepancies I no longer felt I could consciously represent them in my capacity as PR consultant, so I terminated our contract. Therefore I have no comment to make.'

Paddy almost choked on his morning pastry. Grabbing the

paper, he dashed onto the restaurant floor, gesticulating wildly. 'C'mere, lads, get an eyeful of this!'

They just about got through lunch.

No one could believe it, least of all Rollo, who was roaring and banging about the kitchen like a bear.

'To think I have offered my services practically for free to this – this idiot! And all the time he has a spy under his nose!'

'It's not Dom's fault.' Astrid shook her head. 'She's my friend, and even I had no clue. I can't believe it.'

'What does he think he's running? A restaurant or a TV reality show? What is she doing here? Why is she pretending to be a waitress?' Rollo was becoming more and more angry the more he thought about it, especially when he thought about how much he really did like Carla – or rather, *had* liked her. He had depended on her, confided in her. How could she ridicule him like this? And her credentials – they were even better than his! It was completely intolerable. 'Tonight.' He banged his fist on the counter. 'I will do one more night here – that's it. Then I go. I will not be humiliated like this by anyone. I don't care if it's not Dom's fault – he should know what's going on in his own restaurant – know his own staff, for God's sake! For all we know he could be part of it. He's probably in on it himself.'

17

Dom, as it turned out, wasn't in on it.

When he wandered into the restaurant at six-thirty that evening, he was smiling, happy and eager to get to work, especially to talk to Vincent, the sommelier, about the successful trip to the Loire and the fantastic wines he had selected. He was also counting the minutes until he could get away and go to Carla's place. He was so lost in thought about her, about how he had told her that he loved her and that she had texted back that she was in love with him too, that he failed to notice the strained, subdued atmosphere he walked into.

'Hello, Dom, how was your trip?' Astrid asked and smiled wanly.

'Great, thanks.' He headed for his office. 'How were things here?'

'Oh, fine.'

'Good. Tell Rollo I'll be in to see him in a mo.'

'Er, Dom . . .'

'Yes?'

'Have you, um, heard from Carla?'

He looked at her strangely. 'Why?'

'You need to see this.' She handed him the morning's paper, open at the offending article. 'I'll, uh, be in the kitchen.' She backed away discreetly.

For a moment he stood there, perplexed, as the combination of the shots of himself, Carla and Tanya – *Tanya?* – fought with the headline and subhead. Then, still reading, he went over to a table, sat down and studied it carefully. When he had finished, he looked up. The room was empty. Everyone had clearly retreated to the kitchen.

It was only then that he reached for his phone, which he had forgotten to turn back on after the flight. Sure enough, there were a couple of messages. The one from Carla, from last night, one or two texts and one telling him he had three voicemail messages in his mailbox. He dialled the number and listened, a myriad of emotions fighting for expression. One was from his mother, asking him to phone her, another was from his mate Paul, and then the one he really listened to, from Carla. 'Dom,' it began, 'I have to go home, to New York. It's urgent—' and then the rest of the message broke up. He listened to it again, replayed it twice and then deleted it, put his phone back in his pocket and headed for the kitchen to face the troops. He had never felt so foolish or betrayed in his entire life.

This was the woman he loved, who'd been sleeping with him, and all the time she had been keeping this huge secret. He'd never dreamed Carla was like that. Tanya, maybe, but Carla? And yet, if she was Antonio Berlusconi's daughter, why not tell him, and why flee back to New York? There could only be one reason – and it was staring at him in black and white.

The flight took for ever. Strong headwinds were against them, which meant a possible five hours turned into seven. Thankfully, Carla had a window seat, and the man beside her read assiduously, so she was free to put on her head-phones and pretend she was listening to music or watching a movie. Of course, she could do neither – her mind was either racing or numbly frozen. She couldn't eat, either, so there was no whiling away the interminable hours. She tried to sleep, but found that every time she closed her eyes, another memory would float to her consciousness. She didn't need or want to watch the in-flight movie – she had one of her very own playing in her head.

Her father smiling as she, Paulo, Marco and Bruno helped their mother decorate the enormous Christmas tree.

Her father laughing and looking on proudly as she managed unsteadily to ride her first bike.

Her father ageing overnight, his grief palpable, at her mother's death.

And then the picture she had always shut out, that he always joked about, now almost unbearably painful to contemplate, of her on her father's arm, at some unknown time in the future, as he walked her down the aisle.

He couldn't . . . it wasn't possible – it would be too cruel. He had to make it, had to at least hold on until she got there and could tell him how sorry she was for everything and tell him how much she loved him. Tears began to roll down her face. She silently prayed: *If you're up there, please let me see him, let me talk to him one more time. Just one more time.*

'Where the hell is she?' Paulo paced the floor of the small private hospital room.

'How do I know?' retorted Marco, running his hands through his hair. 'She got the flight, that's all I know. She should be here any minute.'

'Any minute could be too late.' Paulo shook his head.

'Don't say that.'

'Why did she have to go away? Why couldn't she have just—'

'Coulda, shoulda, woulda,' Bruno looked at him. 'What's the point?'

They lapsed into silence, the only sound the bleeping of the monitor that told them their father's heart was still beating, although he hadn't spoken since last night, when he'd lapsed into unconsciousness. The nurse came in to check on him.

She looked at them sympathetically and shook her head. 'No change.'

Rollo was as good as his word.

He stayed for one night and one night only. There was no talking him round. Not even Astrid could persuade him. His ego was badly bruised, and fond though he was of Dom, he refused to stay on. Once the article had been published and the press in general got wind of the news, other journalists were soon on the scent of a good story and the phone had been going all day. It was infuriating, but they had to answer it in case it was a reservation. Several tabloid journalists had actually called to the restaurant hoping for a comment or revealing shot, and tempers and patience were fraying. Dom tried Carla's phone again and it went to voicemail. He knew it was churlish, but he couldn't help it. He left one message. *Nice one, Carla, you really pulled it off. I may have meant nothing to you, but I thought at least your colleagues would. I hope it was worth it.*

A patient of P.J.'s in property rang him with the news. 'I thought it was your boy, and thought you'd want to know before it's general knowledge.' Only minutes later, Catherine called him, in tears.

'P.J.,' she said, fighting to control her voice. 'I'm going to my mother's and I'm taking Charlie with me. It's Alex. The banks have pulled the plug and he, well, he's sort of lost it, really. He won't talk to me, to anyone. He told me to go, that we were better off without him.'

'I've just heard about it. I'll go over and try and talk to him.'

'I don't think he'll talk to you of all people. Sorry,' she gulped, 'I didn't mean it like that. It's just he's so defensive where you're concerned.'

'I hear you,' P.J. said. He understood all too well what Catherine was trying to say.

'But I'm really worried about him. He's not himself, and—'
She broke into fresh sobs. 'Oh P.J., I'm so scared. I don't
want to leave, but he won't listen to me, and I have to consider
Charlie.'

'You're doing the right thing.'

'Will you ring me when you – if you . . .?'

'Of course. Let me know when you've got to your mum's
– just text me.' P.J. put down the phone. What else could he
say? Of course Catherine was worried – he was worried
himself. More than worried, if he was honest. He should have
seen it coming, and maybe he had. Some day, somehow, he
had always known this situation was going to blow. The question was – how high?

It was only seven-thirty when he reached Alex and
Catherine's place, but the house was in darkness. Catherine's
car was gone and only Alex's red Ferrari sat in the driveway.
P.J. got out of his jeep and rang the doorbell.

Nothing.

He took out his phone and called Alex's number, but it
went to voicemail. He left a message anyway, knowing how
unlikely it was that Alex might listen to it. 'Alex, it's me, I'm
outside. Let me in will you? We need to talk.'

Still nothing.

He sighed, but his heart quickened. He had to get into the
house. Alex was in there – he was sure of it – but what if he
had done something stupid? What if he couldn't cope with
this débâcle, this debt? What was it he had said to Catherine?
That she and Charlie would be better off without him? P.J.
fought to keep calm in the face of escalating panic.

He could call the Fire Brigade, he could call an ambulance, but it appeared the one person he couldn't call or talk
to was his own son.

Sod this! he thought with a sudden surge of anger. *I'm
getting in, whatever it takes.*

He thought about breaking a window, but then that would

cause a furore and the neighbours might get involved. He assessed the front door critically. It was solid oak. It was unlikely, even with the best of intentions, that he could shoulder it like they did in the movies. And even though he had powered many a scrum, he wasn't as young as he used to be. In the end, he decided to give it one more try, and opening the letterbox, bent down and yelled through it.

'Alex, I know you're in there. If you won't let me in, I'm going to make my own way in.'

Still silence. Now he was scared. There was nothing for it; he would have to break in. He thought one more warning was only fair. 'Fine. If that's the way you want it, Alex, I'm coming in.'

He was just about to force or break a ground-floor window when the door opened. Wheeling around, P.J. regarded the figure who looked back at him. He resembled Alex, a thinner, gaunt-looking Alex, but it was the face, the unreadable expression in his eyes, the curl of the mouth that were unfamiliar.

'I suppose you've come to gloat,' Alex said. 'Well, do come inside, Father dear. So tacky to have to make a song and dance on the doorstep, although we all know how you love an audience.'

P.J. realised immediately that whatever else, Alex was well and truly drunk. He stood there, swaying slightly, in a pair of well-worn jeans and a stained sweatshirt, his feet bare, his face unshaven.

'I will come in, Alex, if that's all right.' P.J. walked past him and into the hall. 'I'd like to talk to you.'

'I suppose Catherine has been on?' Alex smiled and arched an eyebrow. He closed the door and then headed towards the sitting room. 'I told her to go. Better off without me, Charlie and her. Can I offer you a drink . . . Father?'

'I'll have whatever you're having.' P.J. thought he'd need it.

'Of course you would – it's whiskey.' Alex waved the almost empty bottle in the air. 'I seem to have made quite a dent in it.' He reached for a tumbler and poured what was left into it. 'Cheers,' he said, handing it to P.J., then pulled another bottle from the press and proceeded to top up his own glass.

'How much have you had?' P.J. asked him levelly.

'Pretty much enough – on every front.'

'I can understand that.'

'Can you? Can you really?'

'Look, Alex—'

'I'd rather not, actually, if it's all the same to you. I've looked at it every which way and it – my life – seems pretty much screwed.'

'I want to help.'

'I'm sure you do. How noble.'

'Alex, I know—'

'You don't know anything. How could you?' He laughed bitterly. 'You've always got what you wanted, haven't you? School hero, rugby star. Got the career, got the girl, got all the adoring patients. How could you possibly know what it's like to not measure up?'

'Alex, can we just—'

'Just what? Talk? Make it all better? The answer to that is no. I don't want to talk, and certainly not to you. Frankly, you're the last person on earth I want to see right now.'

P.J. had a sharp intake of breath.

'Not so nice, is it, to be on the receiving end? How embarrassing for you, the great Dr P.J. O'Sullivan, to have a son who's such a sap, such a failure.'

'Shut up with this self-pitying drivel. You may hate the sight of me, but you're my *son*. I'm your *father*. We're family – we'll work this all out.'

'Actually,' Alex took a swig of his drink and smiled pityingly at him, 'that is where you're wrong – for once in your life.' He waved an admonishing finger at him. 'You see, this may come as a shock, but you don't actually know *everything*.'

P.J. sighed. He wasn't going to get anywhere – not with Alex in the state he was in – and yet he couldn't leave him alone, not like this. Even if he was the last person on the face of the earth Alex wanted to see.

'Contrary to your opinion of me, Alex, I'm actually quite well aware of that.'

'I beg to differ, P.J. – otherwise you wouldn't be referring to me as your son.'

'What?'

'You heard me.'

'What do you mean?'

'Just what I said. I am not your son. You are not my father.'

For a moment – a long moment – everything slowed down. P.J. opened his mouth, then closed it.

'What? Lost for words? That's a first.' Alex's eyes were hard. 'Maybe *you* could kid yourself for thirty-odd years, but I won't. I'm pretty sure you know, maybe you've always known, but the tests at any rate must have provoked an inkling of curiosity. Not on our side of the family, is it? Von Willebrand's? Catherine's neither.'

'Alex, that doesn't prove anything. Just because—'

'Shut up.' Alex was quietly derisive. 'She told me. Maybe she never told *you*, but Mum told *me*.' He looked P.J. in the eye. 'Funny what people confess to on their deathbeds, isn't it?' he said matter-of-factly, but his expression was bleak. Then realisation dawned. 'Don't tell me – how extraordinary. You really *didn't* know, did you?' Alex regarded him with something approaching amusement.

'Know what, exactly?'

'That there was someone else, shortly before you. Some other guy. She said she couldn't be sure initially, but the timing was right and apparently I'm the spitting image of him. She showed me a photo. He tried to contact her when he heard she was getting married to you, but by then she had set off for Ireland. I guess it must have weighed on her conscience. Or maybe it was the morphine at the end. Who knows? She said not to say anything to you, that it would – what were her words? Oh yes, that it would break your heart. That no father had ever been more thrilled with a son than you when I arrived. Ironic, don't you think? So you see, P.J., she was thinking of you right until the end. It didn't bother her that she might be upsetting me, her own son. It was always about you.'

'You can't be sure,' P.J. began.

'Oh stop it, will you? Bella agreed to have the DNA tests done while she was home. We are not, as I suspected, full siblings, which pretty much confirms Mum's story. Sadly, she's not around to fill in the details. Just as well, really. At least she doesn't have to see what a mess I've made of things. But the day she died, she took with her any hope I had of ever really fitting in. I know she loved me,' he said, looking defiantly at P.J. 'It's just that you were always in the way. You always took too much from her – there was never any left for me. Now I understand why. She was guilty, trying to make it up to you – even if she never told you. You must have known.'

'No.' P.J.'s voice was flat. 'I didn't.' True, there had always been the sliver of possibility, but it hadn't mattered. Now he didn't know what to say. He looked at the son who had always been a stranger to him and wanted to reach out to him.

'So you see, it's a wasted journey you've come on, P.J. I am not your son and there's no need for you to be here.'

'You're my son in every way that matters, Alex,' P.J. said quietly. 'I know we're very different people, and maybe I haven't been the kind of father you needed, but Mum was right about one thing – no father was ever more thrilled by your arrival, and whether or not you are my biological son makes no difference to me whatsoever. Perhaps I wasn't very good at showing it, but I have always loved you, always been proud of you and your achievements.' P.J. realised with every word he was saying that it was the truth.

'More importantly,' he continued, '*you* now have a son, a family of your own. Listen to me, for them if not yourself. I want to help, Alex.'

'There's nothing you can do.' Alex stood up, almost shouting. 'I've lost everything. I'm ruined. That's how good a husband – a father – I am.' He broke down, sobbing hoarsely. 'Go on, go – get out of here.'

P.J. looked at the stooped figure, the shoulders heaving with grief and defeat, and thought his heart would break. 'I'm not going anywhere, Alex,' he said quietly, going over to him. He removed the glass gently from his hand, then he put his arms around his son and held him as he collapsed against him and cried his heart out.

'I'm sorry,' Alex whispered hoarsely when he drew breath.

'So am I, son, so am I.' P.J. wiped his own face. 'Come with me – I don't think you should stay here and you certainly shouldn't be on your own.'

'Where are we going?' Alex asked anxiously, reminding P.J. of the small, uptight little boy he had once been.

'Home, son,' P.J. put an arm around his shoulders. 'We're going home.'

18

'Carla! Thank God.' Her brothers hugged her.

'How is he?' she whispered, almost afraid to look at the body lying so still in the bed, hooked up to machines.

'No change. He lost consciousness last night,' Marco said gently. 'Go sit with him.'

'We'll leave you alone for a little while. We've been taking it in shifts and I could do with something to eat,' Bruno said. 'We'll be in the canteen if you need us.'

Carla could only nod miserably, not trusting herself to speak.

'Come on,' Paulo said to his brothers, nodding towards the door. 'Call us if there's any change.'

'Papa,' she whispered, sitting down on the small chair beside the bed. 'It's me, Carla. I'm here.' She took his hand in hers. 'I'm here, Papa,' she said again, tears rolling down her face. She brushed them away angrily. She would not cry now – she would pull herself together, for him. 'I'm so sorry, Papa, for all our stupid fights.' She bit her lip. 'Please wake up. I need to tell you some things. I need to talk to you. I need to tell you I love you.'

The nurse came through the door quietly, and taking in the scene, slipped out again, equally quietly. No matter how many times she saw it, she never got used to watching family or lovers as their hearts broke, as they begged a loved one not to take leave of them.

Her brothers came back after half an hour. They sat through the night, talking, crying and laughing softly around the bed, lost in memories and recalling happier times.

Once or twice, Carla went out to check her phone. There were no messages. She had checked it, of course, immediately after arriving in JFK, terrified of bad news, that she might have been too late, but there was only a weird voice message from Dom, sounding accusatory. She had hardly bothered to listen to it, she was so desperate to get to the hospital. There had been another message from Astrid, asking her to ring her. Not a word from anyone about her father, enquiring as to how he or she was. At the time it hadn't really registered with her, but now, in the small hours of the night, it bothered her. Didn't Dom care? He hadn't sent so much as a text message. Carla was too upset to give it much thought, but all the same, it hurt. She tried his phone again, but he didn't pick up – it went straight to voicemail. She didn't leave a message. Because nothing mattered, she reminded herself, nothing mattered at all, as long as her father regained consciousness.

No one had ever seen Ossie so angry, not even Charlotte. When he had rung to ask if he could see her to talk about Candy, he had been abrupt and uninformative. She had duly agreed, wondering what Candy could have done now.

When he arrived that evening, she had been shocked. He was so angry he could barely speak. After making coffee and listening to his halting account, she could understand why. Worse still was watching the offending mpeg. Ossie hadn't wanted her to see it, but she had insisted.

'She's my daughter too, Ossie.'

'Not so's you'd know it,' he said grimly. 'I'm warning you, it doesn't make pleasant viewing.'

'I'd rather know the worst,' she said weakly.

After that, they'd had a drink and a very long talk about what to do.

Candy was frightened.

It took her a while to figure out she was scared, because

she had become so used to doing exactly as she pleased, causing maximum drama at maximum expense – generally everybody else's. But she had never experienced her father's anger – never even seen him angry, come to think of it – until that moment when he had roared her name so loudly the roof almost shook. He had barged into her room and told her in an ice-cold voice to get herself down to his study now.

'I'm going out.' Candy had looked at him as if he was stupid.

'You. Downstairs. In my study. *Now.*'

Candy's mouth dropped open.

He had looked at her strangely then. Something had made her obey him and not reiterate the fact that she was going out – indeed *had* to go out – to find Josh. She dropped the brush she had been about to put through her hair and heard it rattle on the dressing table as she left the room. Downstairs, he had all but propelled her into his study and closed the door. Candy would never forget the hideous moments that followed.

'Go over to my computer,' he commanded in a voice she had never heard before.

'What?'

'Do as I say.'

Candy walked over to the vast mahogany desk and stood behind it.

'Sit down.'

She did, wondering if her father had taken leave of his senses, only this dangerous, sinister tone he was using was making her very uneasy.

'Open the email in my inbox.'

Again, Candy did as she was told. Something about sex on the Internet? What was this?

'Read it. Carefully.'

Take a look at this, Mr Keating, and let me know what it's worth NOT to see your daughter having sex on the Internet.

Still she didn't get it. Was this some sort of joke?

'Now click on the attachment.'

She thought she was going to pass out. She sat there, frozen and sick, unable to speak. Eventually she managed to whisper, 'What are you going to do?'

'I'm going to think very carefully about this, Candice,' he said in the same strange, measured voice, 'and about you. You are going to do the same. As for the kind of people you are . . . mixing with . . .' He let the words hang in the air. 'Well, you can see what they think of you.' That hit her like a blow. 'You will go to your room and stay there. You may go down to the kitchen to eat, but consider yourself under house arrest. You will hand over your phone and laptop and have no access to phones or computers of any kind. I have my best security people on this, and if you so much as attempt to send out one text message, all hell will break loose. Do I make myself clear? Now get back upstairs to your room and stay there until you hear from me again. Your mother will have to be told about this. I imagine she'll have something to say about it too.'

'Please,' she whispered, 'not Mum.'

'Don't think it gives me any pleasure, Candice. I can only imagine how horrified and hurt she's going to be, but she must be told. Your behaviour leaves me no alternative. Your appalling carry-on may not only have destroyed your own life as you know it but is going to cause enormous distress to a wonderful mother. Whatever about you, she doesn't deserve this.'

That had been two days ago. She had stayed in her room – she couldn't even think about facing anyone – but today she had been faint with hunger and had tiptoed downstairs to get herself some breakfast. Shalom was in the kitchen when she got there. Neither of them said a word. Even Shalom looked shocked and uncomfortable. She avoided making eye contact and appeared relieved when Candy took her mug of tea and slice of toast upstairs with her. The silence had been deafening.

It was like awaiting execution, Candy thought, shivering.

And then came the summons. From outside her door, she heard her father's voice.

'Candice, you will come down to my study now. I want you there in no less than three minutes.'

Suddenly Candy wanted her mother. She wanted her calm, forgiving, loving presence, even though she was so filled with shame and self-loathing. She hardly dared think what her mum would make of this. Why hadn't she stayed at home with her and Gran? None of this would ever have happened. Why had she come to this awful house? Now she couldn't even phone her mum. And why, oh why, had Josh done this to her? For that was who was behind this – that much was clear. All she had been to him was an opportunity to blackmail her wealthy father. How he must have laughed at her. Running to the bathroom, she was horribly, violently ill.

She ran a facecloth quickly over her face, and with trembling legs made her way downstairs to her father's study. The door was closed. She knocked tentatively.

'Come in.'

She opened the door slowly and her throat constricted. In front of her, looking more wretched and upset than even *she* felt, was her mum, sitting beside her father on the large sofa. There were dark circles under her eyes and she had clearly been crying. She was sitting very straight and her hands were folded in her lap. Looking at her, Candy wanted simultaneously to flee the room and throw herself at her feet and beg for forgiveness, but she could barely meet her eyes. Her father, on the other hand, looked white-faced and grim, but sat with his legs stretched out, his feet crossed. He appeared to be deep in thought. Nobody said a word.

Candy closed the door behind her and waited, unable to drag her eyes from the floor.

After what seemed like an eternity, her father got up and strolled towards the window, then turned to face her. Finally he spoke. 'Your mother and I have given this distasteful matter a lot of thought and we have finally come to a decision.'

'What are you going to do?' she whispered, her eyes flitting from Charlotte's distraught face to Ossie's impassive one.

There was another pause and then he said, 'We're not going to do anything at all, Candice. You are.'

'What?' She looked astounded.

'You got yourself into this ugly mess, and you should get yourself out of it.'

'But how?' She paled.

'That's for you to figure out. You know this chap, we don't. And frankly, I have no intention of meeting him or entering into any sort of negotiations with him or his kind. You can tell him that for starters.'

'You mean you won't help me? You won't stop him from putting that . . .' she faltered, looking bereft.

'It's your life, Candice,' Ossie continued, 'as you are so fond of reminding us all. Now I suggest you go back to your room and figure out what your plan of action is.'

'But I – but he wouldn't take my calls.' She looked about six years old.

'I can't say I'm surprised,' Ossie continued in the same cold, matter-of-fact tone. 'What did you expect?'

'Mum?' It was a heartfelt plea as Candy looked imploringly at Charlotte, and it broke Charlotte's heart, but she had promised Ossie – no giving in.

'Oh, Candy,' Charlotte said, shaking her head helplessly, her face etched with grief. 'What have you done?'

'Go back to your room,' Ossie commanded, the first signs of tiredness entering his tone.

'I'm sorry,' Candy whispered. 'I'm so sorry.'

'I'm sure you are, but that's not a lot of help to anyone now, is it?' he said. 'Now go.'

So she did, creeping upstairs and back into her room.

She wasn't to know that the second she left the study, Charlotte broke down and sobbed while Ossie held her and tried to comfort her. 'It's only a scam,' he said, 'not serious blackmail. I'm pretty sure about that. But it's no harm for her to get a wake-up call.'

'But if it gets out . . .' She shook her head. 'Candy'll be ruined. It's unthinkable.'

'Let's not assume the worst just yet.'

'But I can't leave her like this, Ossie. Let me take her home, at least. She looks so shattered.'

'We've already decided,' Ossie said gently. 'It's time for me to do what I should have done years ago. The chips are down, now Candy and I will have to pick them up together. I know this is tough for you, but really, I'd prefer if you'd leave her here with me. There are a few new ground rules I need to enforce.'

'All right,' Charlotte agreed, sniffing. 'I'd better go.'

Ossie saw her to her car. From her bedroom window, Candy watched her mum's car pull away, then she crawled into bed and cried her heart out.

P.J. sat down at the kitchen table and opened a bottle of red. He was all done in. Bones, lying in his bed beside the Aga, lifted his head momentarily to watch him pull the cork, then stretched languorously, thumping his tail a few times before drifting back to sleep. Sheila popped her head around the door. 'Is there anything I can get you before I go?'

'No, Sheila, I'm grand, but thank you for everything this evening – you're a trooper. Join me in a drink?'

'As you well know, I'm a Pioneer.' She looked at him sternly. 'But I will have a cup of coffee with you before I turn in.'

'Of course,' P.J. smiled. 'How silly of me, I genuinely forgot. I must be getting old. You don't mind if I do?'

'After the day you've had, you're entitled to whatever you want,' she said briskly, 'but you're looking tired. Don't sit up too late.'

'I won't.' He sipped his wine while Sheila put on the kettle and clattered a few cups and saucers for good measure. She was upset too, he could tell.

He had brought Alex back an hour or so ago, a very weakened and feeble Alex, and Sheila had got a shock when she saw him. But she had immediately rallied and acted as if it was the most natural thing in the world that P.J. should bring his thirty-year-old son home, ask Sheila to make up the bed in his old room, then help him upstairs and undress him and put him to bed as carefully and tenderly as if he had been ten years old. Then he had given him a shot of sedative and sat on the bed beside him until Alex had fallen into a deep sleep.

Only then did Sheila see the tears he quickly brushed away. 'I'll take his clothes and put them in the wash,' she said quietly, picking them up off the floor. She hesitated for a second, then said, 'Will he be all right?'

'I think so, but he's been through a lot recently. He's been under a lot of strain. I'm going to keep him sedated for a couple of days and see how he is after a good rest. Then we'll take it from there.'

'What about Catherine and little Charlie?' Concern flooded her face.

'They're with Catherine's mother.'

'Don't tell me she's left him?'

'No, not at all. He told her to go, said she and Charlie were better off without him.'

'He never!' Sheila's hand went to her mouth.

'He's lost the business, Sheila. He wasn't himself. He's been under a terrible strain and carrying it and a few other loads all by himself.'

'Aren't they lucky they have you to turn to.' Sheila shook her head wonderingly.

'I didn't do enough. I should have seen this coming.'

'Now don't you go blaming yourself. You're a wonderful father – everybody says so.'

P.J. smiled ruefully. 'What would "they" know?'

'Well, I know it.' She was firm.

'Thank you. As I'm always saying, I don't know how we'd manage without you.'

'Your dinner's in the oven.' She exited the room rapidly. The conversation was taking far too emotional a turn for her comfort level. There was only so much a body could deal with. Instead she went down to the kitchen and began making rather a lot of noise.

After Sheila had left to go back to her flat, P.J. continued to sit at the table, with Bones snoring peacefully by the Aga. He refilled his glass and went over the day's events, and eventually a lot more besides.

He thought of the early days, of him and Jilly so much in love.

He thought of Alex, the excitement he and Jilly had both felt, the incredible rush of love when he had been handed to him that first time, a tiny bundle to hold.

And he remembered then the unspoken promise he had made to him, there in the ward, with the team of nurses and his father's best friend – the watchful gynaecologist who had delivered him, now long dead – standing back, tired and happy, thankful for the safe arrival of another new baby. 'Well, P.J.,' he had said, smiling broadly, 'another new arrival! You have a son, young man – that means you have to step up to bat. No better man!' he added, winking as he left them to it.

Hello, my son, P.J. had said in his mind, gazing at the tiny bundle in his arms as he rocked him gently. *My precious, precious son. Welcome to this mad, bad, wonderful world. I'm your dad, and I promise, here and now, to do the best I can for you, now and always. I promise to teach you to throw a ball, to ride a bike, how to look like you're listening in class when you're not, and later I'll teach you about girls, at least the little I know, and hopefully one day you'll be as lucky as I was and you'll meet a girl as wonderful as your mum.*

Where had it all gone wrong? He had meant every word of it. Still did. But somewhere along the way, he had let Alex down, and badly.

Had he always suspected he wasn't really his son?

Had he loved Jilly so much that he was blinded to the needs of the young, insecure, uptight little boy who looked to him for support, guidance, approval?

The questions, once asked, kept on coming.

Sure, Alex had always had the best of everything, and P.J. had always tried to, if not *actually*, make the parents' meetings, the plays, the tennis matches and the swimming competitions. But whenever he showed up, it always seemed to make Alex more nervous. Even Jilly had acknowledged that. Eventually, he had stayed away – it seemed to produce better results. When P.J. was absent, Alex won tennis matches, broke swimming records and generally did well. If P.J. was there, things just seemed to, well, fall apart. Alex lost out and everyone else felt bad for him, and somehow P.J. seemed to feel it was all because of him. And so a chasm had formed, and try as he might to forge a bridge across it, P.J. knew his son was slipping further and further away from him. When he tried to discuss it with Jilly, she would dismiss it, make light of it. Now P.J. knew why.

What a mess, he thought miserably.

'Jilly?' he asked aloud. 'What should I do? If you can hear me, wherever you are, help me do the best for Alex. He needs our help now, and I could do with a bit myself,' he added, shaking his head. 'Now I know I'm drunk,' he said to the almost empty bottle in front of him. Then, as the full enormity of her loss and what it had done to him and the children threatened to overtake him again, he put his head in his hands.

He hardly heard his phone ringing.

'P.J.,' said Charlotte when he picked up, 'I'm so sorry for not calling like I said I would. I'm in the car on my way home. I've had the day from hell.' Her voice sounded shaky.

'You too?'

'You wouldn't believe it.'

'Try me.'

'I don't even want to discuss it over the phone. It's Candy, and it's pretty horrible, actually.'

P.J. thought he could hear her stifling a sob. 'If it's any help, I've had a horrible day myself.'

'I'm such a failure, P.J.,' her voice broke. 'I'm such a pathetic, lousy mother.'

'You couldn't be, even if you tried. I, on the other hand, am an egocentric, self-obsessed man and the worst father any son could be unfortunate enough to have.' He hiccupped slightly.

'Are you mad?' Charlotte was roused out of self-pity. 'You're the success story, the stoic widower with two perfect, well-adjusted and successful children, and by all accounts the only man in Dublin who ever had a happy, loving marriage.'

At his end of the phone, P.J. smiled wryly. 'Where are you?'

'I'm about to turn into Wellington Square.'

'Well pull up outside my house and come in for a drink. I could do with some company.'

There was the briefest of pauses. 'So could I,' she said. And for the first time that day, they both smiled like they meant it.

'You first,' said P.J., handing Charlotte a glass of red wine, which she accepted gratefully, sinking into the big sofa in the kitchen.

'Oh God, P.J. I really don't know where to start.'

'Try the beginning,' he prompted her, sitting down beside her and resting his arm around her shoulders.

So she told him. About how Candy had been behaving since she'd left home as such and went to stay with her father and Shalom, about the boob job, and then finally, the awful video clip and blackmail threat.

'It's so unspeakably awful. I can still hardly take it in. I feel like such a failure as a mother.' Her voice wavered.

'Of course you're not,' he said gently. 'Kids go off the rails all the time, Charlotte, no matter what. Marriage breakdown is tough on everyone, and we've all indulged our kids at times.'

'Yes, but Ossie ruined her and I let him. I have to take responsibility for that.'

'How's Candy about all this?'

'Not good, as you can imagine. I think she's shattered, actually.' Charlotte bit her lip, visions of women in porn movies creeping into her mind. She shuddered, thinking of the emotional damage it would do to Candy if the video got out. She just wanted Candy home, safe with her. 'She admits nobody forced her to do it. She was crazy about this guy. That says it all, really. I mean, how badly have Ossie and I screwed up to make her fall for a sleazeball like that?'

'It happens,' P.J. sighed. 'So where is she now?'

'Ossie has been keeping her under house arrest until he's decided how to approach this.'

'Which is . . .?'

'Well, he had his top security people on it immediately when Candy finally admitted she had been meeting some guy called Josh McIntyre, I think his name is. Clearly he's behind it. The thing is, she met him, or claims to have met him, at the Viper concert we brought her to. He's got something to do with the band, video directing or something.'

'Not for much longer, he won't. What a vile thing to do.' P.J. was outraged.

'But we have to be careful. This thing could end up on the Internet at any moment. For now, Ossie says it's best not to do anything, to make Candy sweat it out. He says it'll be a good lesson for her. Personally, I'm not so sure.' Charlotte put her face in her hands. 'I felt so sorry for her. I thought she was going to faint. And Ossie was so cold, so angry, although I can't say I blame him. He's shattered too – we all are. It's like living with a bomb ready to explode at any second.'

'So what happened today?'

'Well, Ossie and I were sitting in the study, and Candy was called down. When she came in, it was so awful. She looked sick, and petrified, as if she were being thrown to a bunch of lions. When she saw me there, I thought she was going to die of shame. I just wanted to run to her and take her away from it all.'

'If only we could protect our children from themselves,' P.J. murmured, shaking his head.

'Ossie made her stand there, just like that, in front of us, without saying a word. It was excruciating.' Charlotte felt sick remembering the scene. 'After that, I left,' she said miserably. 'I really don't know what's going to happen next.'

'It *is* a bit of a nightmare all right. If I can help in any way . . .'

'Thank you, P.J., I appreciate that, but right now I think we just have to do what Ossie says.'

'Don't forget that my mates in Viper will have something to say about all this.'

'Don't say anything, not just yet – there are so many legal implications and so on. Anyway,' she added, 'here I am wittering on about my day from hell. What happened with you?'

P.J. sighed deeply. 'It's my son, Alex. He – well, he's lost everything on this investment scheme he was involved in. The banks have closed in and he's been under terrible strain. He sort of fell apart a bit, I suppose, hit the bottle, told his wife she and the baby were better off without him.'

'Oh, P.J., how awful. How is he?'

'He's here, upstairs, asleep. I sedated him. I'll keep an eye on him for a few days. My guess is he'll be okay after a good rest, then we can sort the other mess out.'

'How bad is it?'

'Five million, at a rough estimate.'

Charlotte paled. 'Poor Alex and Catherine. What will happen? What will they do?'

'I think I might be able to help.'

'But P.J., five million? You'd have to sell your house, wouldn't you?'

'I don't think it'll come to that.'

'Well, all I can say is they're jolly lucky to have you to help them. You're a wonderful father.'

'That's the second time someone's said that to me today,' P.J. mused.

'Well there you are.'

'But I'm not. I don't think any of us are. We just do the best we can with what we have.'

'Do you think,' mused Charlotte, 'they have *any* idea, any idea at all, how much we love them? How we'd do anything? How we worry about them?'

'Nope,' grinned P.J. 'At least not until they have their own.'

'You're right, of course,' Charlotte yawned. 'I'd better go.' She hadn't slept at all, worrying about Candy, and although she hated the situation, she knew Ossie was right and that Candy had to face up to what she had done herself. Part of the problem was that Candy had the money of a grown-up but none of the responsibilities. Charlotte blamed herself for that too. She should have put her foot down more when Ossie gave in to Candy's demands, but she hadn't, so now Candy was learning the hard way that there were consequences. Much as it hurt Charlotte, that was what had to happen. She would be there for Candy as long as there was breath in her, but Candy had to grow up. Charlotte just hoped and prayed that Ossie was right and it was just a scam, that this guy didn't really mean business – but they had no way of knowing that yet.

'You won't stay?'

'I'd love to, but my mother will be chomping at the bit, waiting for an update. She's horrified to be left out of the drama. We didn't tell her, not the full story at any rate. I just told her Candy had been put in a very compromising situation and was in deep trouble. I'd better get back to her.'

'I wish you were staying.' P.J. took her in his arms as Charlotte got up to leave.

'So do I.'

'Nothing like kids to get in the way of a romantic evening, is there?'

'Or parents,' countered Charlotte as they walked arm in arm to the hall.

Then P.J. kissed her, and kissed her, and they stood there at the front door, reluctant to say goodnight, for quite a long time.

At first she thought she was imagining it.

She and Marco were sitting with her father. Marco had fallen asleep sitting in the chair, his chin resting on his chest, dark shadows under his eyes. Paulo and Bruno were both checking in with their families; both had wives and young children. Carla and Marco were on the afternoon shift, although Carla hadn't left her father's bedside since she'd arrived two days ago, except to grab a coffee or a bagel from the canteen. She was gazing out the window of the small room, looking out over the sprawling suburbs of New York, when she heard it.

'Carla.' It was a rasp, a whisper, then louder as she wheeled around. 'Carla.'

'Papa!' she cried, rousing Marco from his snooze and throwing herself on her knees beside her father's bed. She grabbed his hand and kissed it. 'You're awake! Marco, he's awake! Oh thank God.' She began to sob while Marco leapt from his chair and whooped, searching frantically for his phone to give his brothers the good news.

19

James looked at his watch and sighed. Ordinarily he got unpleasant tasks straight out of the way as soon as he could, but he'd been putting this one off all week. There was no way around it. He'd just have to bite the bullet. He should meet her, he reflected, he owed her that, but the thought of it made his heart sink. Suppose she began to cry? He would feel like such a heel. Then what would happen? No, much better to do it over the phone. Cowardly, perhaps, but safer. After all, things couldn't go on as they were. It simply wasn't fair to her.

After that, he had another task to complete, one he'd been putting the finishing touches to for quite some time now, ever since he'd heard about the ghastly incident in Rome from Sophia, when she'd been so upset. James had been incandescent with rage and vowed there and then to put a stop to this nonsense once and for all. It had required quite a lot of time and effort, not to mention considerable expense, but he could afford it. The result would be well worth it. Contracts had been signed last week and all the legalities had been taken care of. Now he just had to do his bit – make it personal, so to speak.

First, though, there was the other thing. James took a deep breath and dialled her number.

'James!' He could hear the delight in her voice, which made what he was about to do infinitely more difficult.

He cleared his throat. 'Sarah, I'm so sorry, but there's something I have to tell you . . .'

★　★　★

Cici didn't think her level of misery could plummet much further. She had reached a stage now where she was sort of bumping along the bottom, some days only slightly less awful than others. She was seeing Dom that evening. At least he was speaking to her. Sophia was still giving her the cold shoulder, although at Dom's request she had allowed her mother to explain her side of the story. At least after talking to her, Cici could tell that Sophia was thawing a little. She had listened to her, taken her phone call. That was a positive sign. It would take a lot of hard work, but Cici would make it up to her. She'd had such a great relationship with her daughter up until this and she couldn't bear to be cut off from her. It was like having her heart ripped out.

She checked the spaghetti and meatballs and gave them a stir, then put the finishing touches to the salad. As she opened a bottle of Chianti, the doorbell rang. Dom was as punctual as his father, she mused with a pang.

She could tell he was shocked at her appearance, though he tried to hide it well. Although they had talked regularly on the phone, it had been a few weeks since he had seen her. She knew she looked dreadful.

'Oh, Dommy, you shouldn't have. How thoughtful of you.' She took the flowers he pressed into her hands and tried very hard not to cry.

'I thought you might need a bit of cheering up,' he said jovially, although she could see the concern in his face.

'Have a glass of wine. You pour, and I'll dish up.' She found a vase for the flowers.

'It smells good, whatever it is.' Dom sniffed the air appreciatively.

'Your favourite, mine too,' she smiled.

'Spaghetti and meatballs,' he grinned. 'Excellent. Nothing like home cooking.' He sat down at the table.

Over dinner, they effortlessly slipped into Italian, as they always did, and chatted away, Cici deliberately staying away from her current domestic situation. She was afraid if she said anything, she might break down and cry.

But Dom brought it up before very long. 'What are you going to do, Mum?'

The forkful of food paused midway to her mouth, and she sighed and put it down. 'I don't know, Dommy. What can I do? It's all such a dreadful mess.'

'You can get a lawyer,' he said gently. 'You have to, Mum. You can't stick your head in the sand about this any more. You have to have legal representation. Dad is going ahead with this divorce whether you like it or not.'

She forced herself to reply. 'You're right. I've been looking into it, and I've been given the names of a few good people. I intend to ring them next week, make an appointment to see them.'

'Good,' Dom sounded relieved. 'The sooner all this is sorted out, the better. I know it's horrible, Mum, really I do. None of us ever thought – well, you know.'

'I know,' Cici filled the awkward pause miserably. 'And it's all my fault. If I could turn the clock back, I'd do anything. *Anything.*'

'I know you would, but you can't.' He was firm. 'And now we all have to move forward and get on with our lives.'

She changed the subject. 'Speaking of which, Dommy, what's going on with you? Here we are talking about awful depressing things, like me and Daddy. Let's talk about you and the restaurant. How is everything? It's so long since I've been to Dominic's.'

Dom sighed and decided to be truthful. 'Actually, Mum, things are pretty bad.'

'What?' Cici was astonished. 'How do you mean?'

Taking a sip of his wine, Dom launched into the whole story. He told his mother about being in the red, the deteriorating accounts that Tanya had kept from him that he should have spotted, and then about Carla, about how he had almost fallen in love with her, until the awful moment a couple of days ago when he had returned home and Astrid had thrust the awful newspaper article into his hands.

'I couldn't believe it,' he said despondently. 'I still can't. And now, well, you can imagine. Things are completely crazy. Rollo has left. His pride was fatally injured – understandably. The kitchen was on a skeleton staff anyway, Carla has conveniently run off back to New York and I'm barely managing to keep the doors open. Of course, the most ironic twist of all is that the story has piqued interest in the restaurant, so we're getting more bookings than ever. But the food is deteriorating by the minute. I've already put word out for a replacement chef, but I'll never get anyone of Rollo's calibre, and even if I could, I couldn't afford it. So things, since you ask, are looking pretty bleak.' He paused to draw breath.

'Oh, Dommy – I can't believe it!' Cici was appalled, listening to his account.

'Well, there you go – that's pretty much where I'm at.'

'But,' Cici was thinking aloud, 'you and Carla, why didn't you tell me? Although I did notice the way you looked at her in the restaurant.'

'You did?' He was astonished.

'Of course I did, what do you take me for?' She grinned impishly, a hint of the old Cici coming through.

'Nobody else did, I hope.' He looked sheepish, then scowled. 'Anyway, now I know that was just a ruse. How could I have been so stupid?'

Cici patted his hand sympathetically. 'Don't blame yourself, sweetheart. Look at your mother.'

Dom managed a weak smile.

'But still,' Cici looked puzzled. 'Something about this doesn't ring true.'

'What, exactly?' Dom tried not to sound sarcastic.

'I don't know. It just doesn't feel right. I saw Carla often in the restaurant, and apart from Harry,' she said ruefully,

'I'm not a bad judge of character. I can't believe she would be that conniving.'

'Yeah, well, that's the way it is – believe me.'

'Oh, I do, Dommy, I'm not suggesting for a moment that you're exaggerating or making it up – you couldn't,' she laughed. 'No one could. But that's just it – it sounds almost too ridiculous.'

'Nothing ridiculous about it from where I'm sitting.'

'There is just one thing,' Cici paused.

'What?'

'You said that you were *almost* falling in love with Carla.'

'So?'

'In my experience, there is no "almost" falling in love. You either do or you don't. *Are* you in love with her?'

'A girl who would set me up? Betray me? Put my restaurant, my reputation, at risk? Are you mad?'

'You haven't answered my question,' Cici pressed. 'And we don't actually know that Carla did *any* of those things. I for one always liked her tremendously. She's a great girl, and Italian. That's what feels wrong about all this.' She paused, nodding her head emphatically. 'Yes, that's it. I don't for one moment believe Carla would do that to anyone, let alone the man she loved. And believe me, she has loved you for a long time, Dommy, any woman could see that, let alone your mother. It used to drive poor Tanya mad – I'm pretty sure it still does. Does Tanya know you and Carla are together?'

'*Were* together,' Dom corrected her. 'I suppose she could have.'

'And have you talked to Carla about all this?'

'She left a message on my phone saying she had to go back to New York, something urgent had come up. Well obviously it had – her cover had been blown, for starters.'

'And you didn't call her back?'

'I got her voicemail – I left a message.'

'Not a very nice one, I'm guessing.'

'There's nothing to say.'

'Dommy, listen to me, and listen carefully.' Cici was serious. 'You're my son, and I know you. For what it's worth, I think that you *are* in love with Carla.' She held up her hand to stop Dom objecting. 'Just hear me out. I think that you are in love with her and I *know* she is in love with you – a mother can sense these things. You are in love with each other. Do you know how important that is? How precious? To find someone you can feel that way about? I think there has been some horrible misunderstanding, but even if there hasn't, even if it turns out that all this undercover stuff is true and her intentions were dishonourable, don't you think you owe it to yourself to talk it over face to face? Surely it's worth that much. If you have any Italian blood in you at all, if you have a shred of the passion I know you have, if you have even the smallest bit of your father's integrity, you will go now to Carla. Fly to New York, do whatever it takes to find out what has gone wrong. Otherwise – believe me – you will spend the rest of your life regretting it.' Cici drew a long breath. 'I know what I'm talking about here. I may have made a horrible mess of my life, but you don't have to. I have managed to lose the person I have loved most in all the world. Don't let foolish pride and misunderstandings stand in the way of finding out the truth – however difficult that truth may be to face.'

Dom was silent, wrestling with a myriad of conflicting emotions. Eventually he sighed and got up. 'It's late. I'd better go. Thanks for dinner, Mum.' He put on his coat.

'At least think about what I've said, will you?' Cici said, patting his face fondly. 'I know I'm not a very good example of relationship counselling right now, but I just have a feeling about this.'

Dom hugged her. 'Maybe,' was all he would say.

'Let me know what happens,' Cici said.

When he had gone, she poured another glass of red wine and sat down alone at the table. She had been right to say what she had. She was sure of it.

She liked Carla – almost as much as she had *disliked* Tanya. Carla would no more hurt Dom than his own family would. Cici would bet her life on it. Every motherly instinct she possessed was telling her so.

Carla was in her old bedroom, still maintained just as it always had been, in her family home. The old Victorian brownstone with steep steps up to the front door in Brooklyn was unchanged, except now her father lived there alone. When her family bought the house in the 1950s, it wouldn't have been considered a particularly good neighbourhood, just your regular big, blue-collar Italian families. Now, because of its proximity to the financial district just across the river and the stunning views of the Manhattan skyline, it was considered very trendy.

Now that he was recovering and off the critical list, she had, on Marco's insistence, gone home to shower, change and get some rest. She was just undressing, almost incoherent with tiredness and relief, when her phone rang. It was Astrid.

'Carla!' she said, sounding both exasperated and relieved. 'Finally, I get hold of you. What the hell is going on with you?'

'What do you think is going on with me?' Carla snapped. 'And thanks for asking, but my father came out of his coma just hours ago. He still has a long way to go, but he's out of danger – only just.'

'What are you talking about?' Astrid was bewildered.

'What do you mean, what am I talking about? My father had a heart attack. He almost died. I've spent the past two days by his bedside while he hovered between life and death, and neither the man I thought loved me or anyone else I work with even had the decency to ask how he or I were doing. I thought I had a good working relationship with everybody in Dominic's, never mind the one I clearly *don't* have with Dom.'

There was a pause at Astrid's end of the line. 'A lot's been happening since you've gone, Carla.'

'Well, clearly it's more important, whatever it is.'

'Carla,' Astrid said, 'why didn't you tell anyone who you really were?'

'Excuse me? What are you talking about?'

So Astrid told her everything – about the newspaper article, Dom's reaction and, of course, about Rollo leaving. 'We're up the creek without a paddle, you could say.'

By the time Carla had finished listening to Astrid's account, she was pacing around the room. 'I don't believe this,' she kept repeating. 'I don't believe it.'

'It's true. Take it from me.'

'And you, Astrid? Do you believe I would do such a thing?'

There was a pause. 'No, I don't. But it's a pity you never told anyone about your background, your career. You can see how it could be construed unfavourably.'

'Only one person could construe anything unfavourable out of this, and that's Tanya. Everything about this smacks of her. But still, I can't believe that Dom would believe I'd do such a thing – nothing could be further from the truth.'

'He said he tried to call you, but he just got voicemail. That confirmed his suspicions.'

'Oh for God's sake!' Carla cried. 'My father was dying! Phone calls and messages, unless they were a matter of life and death, were not at the top of my list of priorities.'

'Look, you've had a shock, Carla, and I'm truly sorry to hear about your father. None of us had any idea, really.'

'I told Dom – I left a message on his phone.'

'All these messages,' Astrid sounded exasperated. 'There's some sort of crossed wires or something going on. Call him – better still, come back and talk to him yourself. He's miserable without you and hell to be around. I thought Rollo could be difficult, but . . .'

'Dom can go to hell! I've done nothing wrong except ask

for a little privacy in my life. So what if I'm a chef? Who cares? I just wanted to get away from New York, away from my brothers, my father and away from cooking. I wanted to be invisible for a while, and now—' Her voice broke. 'I'm sorry, Astrid. It's not your fault. It was good of you to call me. I just can't cope with anything else right now.'

'Of course.' Astrid was sympathetic. 'Is there anything I can do?'

'No, thanks. Look, I'll call you in a couple of days.'

'Take care, Carla. I miss you – we all do.'

'Sure you do,' said Carla. If she hadn't been so tired, she'd have flung the phone out the window. She was stunned, stunned and hurt. How could they? How could he?

She had left a message on his phone, telling him her father was desperately ill, and he hadn't even called her back except to leave some accusatory message on *her* phone. And this was the man she loved, who said he loved *her*? She had thought she meant something to him – that they had something special. Clearly she had been wrong – again. He was judgemental, selfish and unappreciative, just like all the other men in her life.

Fully intending to have another good cry, Carla climbed wearily into bed and was asleep before her head hit the pillow.

Since Carla had gone, Dom had been working around the clock. It wasn't just a necessity, given his increasingly fraught kitchen arrangements – it was the only way he could keep his mind off what had happened between him and Carla. How could he have been so wrong about her? How could he have been so easily taken in by her charms? Tanya had never liked her either. Perhaps she'd been right, womanly intuition and all that. But then he thought about what his mother had said the night before and when he started thinking about that, he started thinking about other things, like how he'd always fancied Carla rotten but for some reason never admitted it to himself. He remembered how concerned she'd been when he was sick and she'd brought the soup up to him, and the look on her face, the look they'd both exchanged, full of meaning, before Tanya had all but physically turfed Carla out. Then he thought of that first night, and the many other nights and days that had followed when their bodies had spoken so eloquently of what neither one would say – which was that they were falling more and more deeply in love.

Why hadn't she told him?

Sitting at his computer, Dom googled her again. Scrolling through mentions of her culinary achievements, he had to admit they were right up there. No wonder Rollo had been upset! She outranked him any day.

And then he saw it. Under the same name, Berlusconi, *The New York Times* excerpt, dated only three days ago, reporting that Antonio Berlusconi, owner of the famous chain of Italian restaurants, had suffered a serious heart attack and was in a critical condition. His three sons were by his bedside and it was hoped that his only daughter would join the vigil, despite a family rift rumoured to have forced Carla, former executive chef of the M Hotel, to leave the country.

Dom's hands froze over the keyboard. He was reading it again, checking the date, when Astrid came in, looking uncomfortable.

'I'm really sorry to interfere, and I know it's none of my business, but I've just been talking to Carla and I think you need to talk to her. It's her father – he's really ill. That's why she had to go back to New York. She said she left a message on your phone, but . . .' She held her hands out helplessly. 'I told her about the article, and of course, well, you know the rest. She's really upset about it.'

Dom ran his hands through his hair and let out a long breath. 'What a bloody mess,' he said, shaking his head, then he stood up. 'I know it's an awful lot to ask of you, Astrid, but do you think you could hold the fort here for a day or two? Just tell everyone to do the best they can. I need to go to New York.' He grabbed his jacket and was already on his way.

'Of course,' Astrid smiled broadly. 'I was hoping you'd say that.'

What a difference a day made! Or in this case, four days. Carla swung through the doors of St Vincent's Hospital with a broad smile now the hospital was no longer a place that held fear and anguish for her. Walking along the by-now-familiar corridors and nursing stations, Carla smiled and greeted the medical staff who had taken such good care of her father and had been so supportive of her and her brothers during that awful night when he hovered between life and death. Now, pushing the door open to his room, Carla was overjoyed to see the change. Antonio Berlusconi was sitting up, declaring they weren't feeding him enough and flirting with the two nurses who were monitoring his chart and checking the apparatus. He was still hooked up to a few drips, but the man who greeted her was definitely the father she knew and loved, even though they were both so alike they drove each other crazy.

'Well, well, well, if it's not my hot-headed daughter,' he grinned at her, indicating that she should come and sit beside him.

'Papa,' she said, dropping a kiss on his forehead, 'you gave us such a scare.'

'You keep saying that,' he grinned at her. 'If that's what it took to get you to come home, I'd do it all over again.'

'Don't say that. Nothing matters any more except that you're going to get better again.' She settled down to eat the take-out lunch she had brought from the deli. 'You're going to have to take it easy from now on, Papa. No more stress, no more drama. You're going to have to learn to be calm, go with the flow.'

'Look who's talking!'

'I'm serious.'

'So am I. But I'd rest a lot easier if I knew my only daughter would stop running around and settle down, find a nice man, have some children,' he grumbled. 'Marco, Paulo, even Bruno, all married.' He looked at her. 'Now don't go getting angry with me – it's only natural for a father to want those things for his daughter.' He patted her hand. 'I didn't check out this time, but who knows when I will, and when I do, I'd like to think I was leaving knowing you were happy and loved by a good man. There must be someone out there who's right for you.'

'I thought so too,' Carla said, for once not challenging him. 'And I thought I had found him, in Dublin.'

'An Irishman? Well, I suppose . . .'

Carla smiled at his expression. 'He's half Irish, half Italian.'

'Good,' he nodded, encouraged. 'So what's wrong with him?'

'Oh God, Papa, you wouldn't believe it if I told you.' She rolled her eyes.

'Try me.'

'It would take too long.'

'Do I look like I'm going anywhere?'

So she told him everything, from her first day in Dublin, to getting the job in Dominic's as a waitress. At this, her father's eyes bulged. She told him about Dom and how she'd fallen for him, and then the awful call she'd received from Marco to come home immediately, and then, finally, the unbelievable newspaper article and the misunderstandings and accusations that had followed.

'Let me get this straight.' Antonio hoisted himself further up on his pillows, his eyebrows knitted together in a manner she knew all too well. 'You fight with your father. You run away to a strange city. You get a job in a restaurant, where you masquerade as a waitress, misleading your employer and the rest of the staff. You then fall in love with the owner of this restaurant, never at any time telling him that you are a world-class chef and by the time some wise guy gets hold of the fact and runs to the newspapers with the story, you have disappeared to New York.'

'You were dying!' Carla cried indignantly.

'Listen to me, Carla.' He was glowering at her now. 'I don't know anything about this Dominic guy. I don't know if he's worth it or not. I don't know if you love him or not – only you know that. But I can tell you that if you do, you had better do something about it. Your mother, God rest her soul, was, unlike her daughter, a patient, understanding, forgiving woman. I loved her more than my own life. She would tell you what I am going to tell you. If you find love, real love, then you don't run away from it! You don't let any misunderstandings or secrets destroy it.'

'It wasn't my fault!'

'Do you love him, Carla?'

'I don't know.' She made a face. 'Maybe.'

'Did you love him before you left for New York?'

'Yes, but—'

'No buts. Then this is what you must do. This is one piece of advice you must listen to – even if it is from your father. You must go back, Carla, immediately.' He held up his hand to stop her protest. 'You must go back and tell him everything. It is the only honourable thing to do.'

'I can't go back, they all hate me. The chef has even left because of me.'

'Then who is running the kitchen?'

'Astrid, the pastry chef.'

'A pastry chef in charge of a kitchen?' He was incredulous.

'They're on a skeleton staff already,' Carla mumbled, feeling the force of his disapproval.

'No daughter of Antonio Berlusconi shirks her responsibilities and leaves a kitchen in chaos, never mind in the hands of a pastry chef! You must go back to Dublin immediately and help them out. Otherwise I will have another heart attack.'

'Papa, that's not fair!'

'Who said anything about fair?' he shrugged, but there was a gleam in his eye. 'I'm fine now, they're sending me home at the end of the week. I'll have full-time nursing at home until I'm back on my feet. It will help my recovery to know you are doing the right thing. Now go!'

'I won't.'

'It's what your dear mother would want.'

'Papa, don't do this to me,' she begged.

'I don't want to see you again until this mess is sorted out.' And with that, Antonio lay back on his pillows and pretended to close his eyes.

When his considerably confused and subdued daughter had kissed him and left the room, Antonio took the photograph of his late wife from the bedside locker and held it to him. 'Maria,' he murmured. 'If you could only see her. She is so beautiful, so like you, and is so clearly in love.' He sighed, shaking his head. 'Wherever you are, watch over her. Don't let her screw it up!' Then he kissed the miraculous medal of hers that he'd worn around his neck since the day she had died.

20

It was a beautiful, clear, sunny day in Dublin, and the bright blue sky made Harry feel more cheerful than he had in weeks. He was particularly sensitive to the weather and convinced he suffered from seasonal affective disorder, although his therapist had challenged him about this. Not that he had seen her for months, ever since he'd waxed lyrical to her about his relationship with Cici and she'd been nonplussed. He could tell, without her having to say a word. She just got that look on her face, like she always did when he talked about his love life. What did she know anyway? All sympathetic and supportive when he was down, and then, when he was feeling positively euphoric about life, she would rain on his parade, telling him to take things slowly and did he think it was wise in light of his past experiences? Clearly she didn't approve, though unfortunately, she had been proved right. Women! They were all the same.

Since the Rome incident, he'd been lying low, confining himself to sending the odd derogatory text message to Cici, and a few times, when he'd sat up late having a couple of drinks (he didn't tell his therapist about *that* either), he had left voice messages telling Cici in no uncertain terms what he thought of her. He was still stung to think of what had happened, but at least he had wiped the smile off her face when he'd followed her and turned up at the restaurant that evening with her daughter. The look on her face had been worth it.

He got a good laugh too over that article about Dominic's

he had read in the paper. Made her son look like a right eejit! Harry knew the waitress to see – she was hard to miss, sexy too, if you liked that sort of thing. He had never liked Dominic anyway, arrogant sod. He had always treated Harry politely, but he could tell he was looking down his nose at him – that kind always did. Still, who cared about the Coleman-Cappabiancas anyway?

The other thing that was making Harry whistle as he strolled towards the offices of *Select* was that he had an appointment to see the new CEO of Marquess, the publishing company that owned *Select* and a variety of other top-class publications. The surprise takeover had increased the share price considerably, and since Harry had taken *Select* from being a rather fuddy-duddy women's monthly to one of the hottest new style bibles, he was pretty sure he was in for a promotion. Stephen Friar, the CEO, was a slick Brit and appreciated bright, young, driven talent. Harry had taken even more care than usual with his appearance. The new biscuit-coloured linen suit with pale blue lining had cost a fortune. At the time, he had thought of it as an investment. He'd bought it especially for the Rome trip, thinking, as he had then, that when he would be living with Cici he would need an extensive wardrobe for all the wonderful places they would visit and stay in. He scowled again, thinking of what he'd been deprived of. Still, at least he was looking the part today.

He strolled past reception and went to grab a coffee. He still had ten minutes to spare and was just about to head into his office when Lucy, one of the PAs, caught up with him.

'Harry,' she said rather breathlessly, 'you're wanted in the boardroom now. He's early,' she said. 'Just as well you are too.'

'Thanks, Lucy, I'm on my way. Ditch this for me, would you?' He handed her the coffee.

He walked down to the end of the corridor and opened the double doors into the huge room, where the long walnut table held pride of place, gleaming now in the sunlight that streamed through floor-to-ceiling glass windows.

'Mr Friar!' Harry moved forward eagerly, holding out his hand to greet the tall figure who stood looking out at the view from the end of the room, then stopped in his tracks as the man slowly turned around, keeping his hands casually in the pockets of his pinstriped trousers, making no effort to return the greeting.

This wasn't Stephen Friar, Harry registered slowly, but there was something definitely familiar about the elegant, handsome figure who regarded him with something that approached disinterest. The warning bells and recognition began to tug at his consciousness simultaneously, and Harry faltered halfway across the room. The man in front of him was none other than James Coleman.

'Sit down, Harry.' James indicated a seat. 'This will only take a few moments.'

'I don't understand.' Harry's throat was dry. 'Where's Stephen Friar?'

'I'll make it simple.' James's tone was pleasant, although he remained standing. 'Stephen had other business to attend to. As I now hold a controlling interest in Marquess, I said I'd be happy to stand in for him.'

A cold trickle of sweat began to run down Harry's spine.

'I'm afraid we no longer require your services, Harry.'

'You can't do this,' he began.

'Please don't interrupt.' He waved a hand dismissively. 'In view of your acknowledged contribution to *Select*, which we have taken into account, we have a position to offer you in our Manchester office.'

'This is a joke!' Harry blustered.

James continued, unperturbed by Harry's outburst. 'A smaller position, but similar. A challenge, if you like.'

'I won't be—'

'Be quiet.' The voice was like steel. 'The choice is yours,

Harry. You have half an hour to collect your belongings and vacate your office, or I will be forced to involve the police – and I have much to involve them with. I would have sooner, of course, but in light of your rather *unfortunate* history, and indeed proven records of emotional instability, I'm offering you a discreet way out.'

'I have a lawyer,' Harry spluttered.

'I'm sure you do, but the time for fantasy is over, Harry. And I mean *over*. You're playing with the big boys now, and you've already lost.'

Harry felt a strange roaring in his head. 'Cici's behind this. She made you do this.'

'My wife knows absolutely nothing about this.' James Coleman leaned on the table, his eyes boring into Harry's. 'And if you ever – *ever* – contact, much less approach, her or indeed any of my family again, I will have you locked up for a very long time. I'm prepared to offer you this position in Manchester because I'm a reasonable man, and I appreciate that you may not, as it would appear, always be able to control your behaviour. But if you think for one moment that I will stand by and watch my wife and daughter be taken advantage of, stalked and harassed by a delusional young man, however unfortunate the circumstances leading up to that behaviour have been, then you are sadly mistaken. If I were you, I would see Manchester as an infinitely preferable option to remaining here and facing what are bound to be unpleasant and distasteful consequences.'

'Are you threatening me?'

'No, I'm merely advising you. As I said, I'm a reasonable man, unless my patience, which is considerable, is taxed, at which point I become extremely unreasonable. I have not risen to the position I hold today without taking necessary action, however unpleasant that action may be – when required. I will not hesitate to do so where you are concerned.'

Harry sat there, immobilised.

'You may go now.'

Somehow he got up and made it back to his office, his breath coming in rasps. His throat felt tight, constricted. With shaking hands, he scrolled through the numbers in his phone for the one he so desperately needed. He wished now he hadn't stopped taking his medication. It had affected his sexual performance, so he'd ditched it. He would have to come clean and tell her everything, all over again. He didn't care how annoyed she would be with him. If she would only pick up the phone, he would never disregard his therapist's advice ever again.

Jennifer was feeling like a new woman. What with her new hip and two new front teeth implants, she was feeling twenty years younger. It was wonderful to be pain-free after all those years of limping.

She had already met up with most of her old friends for lunch or bridge to show off all the new technology. Now, though, she was bored, bored and a little lonely. Charlotte was always out and about with P.J., which she was happy about. Jennifer was immensely fond of P.J. She felt as if she had known him for ever; he was that sort of chap. But now she found herself on her own a lot of the time. She missed Candy about the place too and hadn't heard from her in weeks. According to Charlotte, her granddaughter had got herself into some sort of unspeakable trouble – so unspeakable that nobody would tell her anything about it. It was thoroughly frustrating. She had even tried phoning Candy once or twice on her mobile, but just got the recorded message.

Now, on her way back from the hairdresser's, in her ancient Mini Clubman, she was surprised when her phone rang.

'Gran?'

'Candice! I was just thinking of you.'

'I can't talk for long, Gran, the money's going to run out.' Candy was breathless.

'What? Where are you?'

'I'm in a phone-box thingy.'

'What on earth are you doing in a phone box?'

'They've taken my phone, Gran, and my computer – I'm under house arrest.'

'What on earth are you talking about?' Jennifer swerved, narrowly avoiding a parked car.

'You sound funny, Gran. Have you been drinking?'

'Don't be impertinent! Of course not. It's my new teeth, I haven't got used to them yet. Where are you?'

'I'm at Dad's house, or I'm supposed to be – they've locked me up. I only escaped now to the village. You've got to help me. Will you come and get me, please?'

'Oh, Candice, really! What's going on?'

'I'll tell you when I see you. Just come and get me, will you?' She sounded desperate.

'Who's there? Is that Shalom creature at home?'

'And her mother, that's all. Dad's out. Please, Gran, hurry.' The phone went dead.

Shalom and her mother! So Ossie was moving the family in, was he? Whatever her granddaughter had done, it couldn't possibly warrant being locked up with that sort of people – why, that was what had started all this trouble in the first place.

Jennifer pulled up abruptly and did a U-turn, blithely ignoring the rude oaf in the lorry who made some vulgar hand signal at her, and headed straight for the Stillorgan dual carriageway. When she reached it and got through the traffic lights at Donnybrook church, she put her foot down. She didn't care what Charlotte might say. Charlotte wasn't who Candy had rung for help, she had rung her grandmother – and quite rightly, by the sounds of things. Tearing along the motorway, Jennifer hadn't felt such an adrenaline rush since she had last ridden to hounds.

*　　*　　*

Carla pulled the cushion and patterned throw off the old trunk that served as a window seat in her old bedroom and knelt down in front of it. Opening it, she inhaled the familiar, slightly musty smell, a combination of old papers, yellowing photographs, old letters and, of course, her notebooks. Taking them out carefully, one by one, and flicking through them, she was immersed in culinary memories. Her first, childish, carefully printed recipes for baking, painstakingly copied in red pencil, hastily scribbled notes of inspired combinations of flavours jotted on the back of an envelope on a backpacking trip through Peru, famous recipes from Michelin-starred restaurants and, of course, her family recipes, tweaked and added to down through the years – wives, mothers, grandmothers all adding their own magic ingredients, their own words of wisdom. She found the ones she needed and put the rest back carefully. Then she placed them in her hand luggage (she would never have risked losing them in a suitcase) and gathered the rest of her belongings. Five minutes later she was on the street, hailing a cab. 'Kennedy,' she said to the Rastafarian driver as he pulled off into the stream of traffic. She was on her way back to Dublin to face the biggest test of her life so far – both in the kitchen and out of it.

Twenty minutes later, Jennifer pulled off the motorway, taking the exit for Annaderry. She knew the country house Ossie had bought and lavishly refurbished well, although in her day it had been a smaller and no doubt significantly more tasteful home than the one she now approached. All the same, she had to admit it was impressive. Driving slowly up the long, winding driveway, she pulled up outside the front entrance and parked her car, taking good care to keep her distance from the white Porsche (undoubtedly Shalom's) and the hideous mustard-coloured car beside it with lots of bits sticking out of it. Taking one final look in the mirror, she adjusted her headscarf, rubbed some lipstick off her teeth and got out. She rang the doorbell and waited, tapping her foot. A voice whispered through the intercom. 'Gran? Is that you?'

'Of course it's me, Candice. Stop this nonsense and let me in at once.'

The door opened and Candice let her in, looking over her shoulder nervously. 'Shh,' she said, holding her finger to her lips. 'I didn't think you'd be so quick. I just have to get my bag, it's in the kitchen.' She darted through a door and re-appeared with a holdall. They were just about to depart when a shrill voice beckoned. 'Candy? Just a minute, young lady, where do you think you're going? And who are you?' Bernie asked indignantly, emerging from the front living room.

Jennifer turned slowly, regarding the plump, blonde, overly made-up woman in the leopard-print top and tight white skirt from beneath arched brows.

'*I* am Jennifer Searson,' she said. 'And who might you be?'

'I'm Bernie. And she's under house arrest.' She pointed a blood-red nail at Candy. 'Ossie left strict instructions she was not to leave her room except to eat.'

'Is that so?' Jennifer was icily polite. 'Well, you may tell your employer, Bernie, that I have come to take my grand-daughter home.'

'Employer!' Bernie shrieked. 'I'll have you know my daughter is the lady of this house – I'm Shalom's mother.' She stood with her hands on her hips.

'That explains a lot,' Jennifer smiled.

'C'mon, Gran, let's go.' Candy tugged at her sleeve.

'What's that supposed to mean?' Bernie's eyes narrowed.

'Never mind. You may tell my son-in-law that Candice is coming with me.'

'Ossie's not your son-in-law, is he? Not any more!' she shot back. 'And he's not going to be happy about this.'

'You're quite right on both counts,' Jennifer said breezily. 'I never did think he was good enough for my daughter, and yes, I dare say he won't be happy about this. But you may tell him to ring me – he has my number on speed dial. Come along, Candice, let's go.'

'You'll be sorry,' Bernie leered at them. 'I bet he'll send the police after you when I ring him. She's got herself into a right heap of trouble, the little tart! Ossie's furious. We all are.'

'Please, Gran,' Candy beseeched her. 'We need to go now.'

'If Candice's behaviour has been in any way inappropriate, it is because her father has encouraged and enabled it, not least through his own example – or rather, lack of one. You may tell him I said that too. Good day to you.'

'What a frightful woman,' Jennifer said to Candy, starting the car and setting off. 'Is she anything like the daughter?'

'Peas in a pod,' Candy confirmed.

Jennifer shuddered. 'Now Candice, you'd better tell me what's going on.'

'I – I don't think I can. I'm too ashamed. Bernie was right, I *am* a stupid tart.' A tear rolled down her face and she brushed it away.

'Stop that snivelling right now. Whatever you've done, whatever trouble you've gotten into, I'm your best chance of getting you out of it, but I can't help you unless you tell me everything – and I mean everything. Now I want every detail, right from the beginning. How bad can it be?'

A little while later, Jennifer almost wished she hadn't asked, but to her credit she kept her eyes on the road, only spluttered once and tried not to look too horrified.

'So you see, Gran? You can't help me, nobody can,' Candy said miserably. 'Not unless Dad pays up.'

'I sincerely hope he does no such thing. On this occasion, your father is absolutely right.'

'Then there's nothing anyone can do.'

'I don't know about that – but I know a man who will.' Jennifer turned off the motorway and headed into town.

'Where are we going?'

'To visit a friend of mine. If anyone can help you, he can.'

Minutes later, Jennifer and Candice walked into the opulent offices of Whitaker, Willoughby and Turnbull, Solicitors.

'Mr Whitaker's office?' she enquired of the receptionist.

'Third floor, the lift is on your left.'

Exiting the lift, Jennifer approached an immaculately groomed girl tapping away on a computer. 'I'm looking for Mr Whitaker's secretary.'

'That would be me,' the girl smiled politely. 'Can I help you?'

'I certainly hope so. I need to see him immediately.'

'Do you have an appointment, Mrs . . .?'

'Searson. Jennifer Searson. No I don't, but just tell him I'm here and that it's a matter of great urgency. I'm quite sure he'll see me.'

'I'm terribly sorry, but Mr Whitaker is in a meeting. Without an appointment, I'm afraid there's absolutely no chance of him seeing you. He's a very busy man,' she explained.

'I'm sure he is, and he has me to thank in no small part for that. His late father used to shoe our horses. My late husband was responsible for putting the very busy Mr Whitaker through college and arranging his apprenticeship. Now if you won't let him know I'm here, I shall sit outside, right here, until he appears – but he will not be happy to know I have been treated in this manner.'

Candy studied the floor, wishing it would open up and swallow her. And they called *her* brazen!

The girl's expression hardened, but she seemed to waver. 'Take a seat, please. I'll interrupt his meeting to let him know you're here,' she said disapprovingly. The girl picked up the phone and murmured discreetly into it. Then, with a forced smile, she said, 'He'll be with you in just a few moments. Can I offer you some tea or coffee?'

Five minutes later, a tall, thin, austere-looking man appeared from around a corner. 'Jennifer!' he beamed. 'How lovely to see you. Do come into my office.'

'Forgive me for being so insistent, Nigel. It's terribly good of you to see us like this. I'm afraid my granddaughter here, Candice, has got herself into a most undesirable predicament. I'm hoping you can help her – and time is of the essence.'

'I'll certainly try. It would be a pleasure. Sit down, do.' He indicated two very expensive-looking antique leather tub chairs in front of his desk. Then he sat down behind it, rested his chin on his hands and, looking directly at Candice, said, 'Tell me the facts, right from the beginning.'

Candice looked at Jennifer, who nodded affirmatively, and for what seemed like the umpteenth time, launched into her nightmare account.

His face remained impassive throughout. He made a few notes and asked for confirmation of a couple of details. 'Did you sign anything?' he asked pointedly. 'This is very important. Think carefully.'

'No – no I didn't.'

'Are you quite sure?'

'Yes. Well, I almost signed something.' She looked worried.

'Almost?'

'Josh did ask me to sign some lease or something, to witness it for him.'

'And did you?' Jennifer held her breath.

'I was going to, but the pen wouldn't work – it had run out. So I couldn't.'

'That's good, Candice, that's very good,' said Nigel, smiling for the first time. 'Now how about some tea or coffee, and I'll tell you what I suggest we do?'

'You mean you can help us?' Jennifer asked eagerly.

'Jennifer, I'm not the foremost show-business lawyer in the country for nothing, you know. Legally speaking, I can't promise anything, but I'm pretty sure I can help. Now here's what I suggest . . .'

Cici had only gone to the hairdresser to get her roots done. She had no desire to leave the house if she could avoid it, but she was depressed looking at her disintegrating appearance. Things were bad enough. She didn't need to see a wreck looking back at her every time she passed a mirror. And besides, old habits died hard. She had found the buzzing atmosphere of the salon vaguely unsettling, she had been out of circulation for so long. Her colourist, Raymond, had been pleased to see her at least.

'Cici! It's been a long time – that's not like you,' he said, running his hands through her hair. 'Been burning the candle at both ends I suppose?'

More like my bridges, she thought, but stapled a bright smile to her face. 'Just work some magic, Ray, and make me look glamorous again.'

'You always look glamorous, Cici, although you've lost a lot of weight and you didn't need to.' He looked concerned. 'Have you been ill?'

'I'm fine, I just had a bad bout of flu, couldn't eat a thing,' she lied.

'Wish I could lose my appetite.' He pointed to a burgeoning paunch. 'Never mind, we'll soon have you looking perky. I think we should be a little adventurous. Let's put a mixture of copper and dark gold through it, it'll look fabulous with your dark base.'

She let him rattle on, relieved not to have to talk. She would have let him shave her head if he'd suggested it. Settling back into her chair, she picked up a few magazines, leaving aside and shuddering inwardly at the March copy of *Select*, which featured the spread on her. She cringed now when she thought of it.

When she was done, she had to admit the finished result

was worth it. Her hair had been freshly restyled in flattering layers around her face, and longer, just brushing her shoulders. The copper and bronze highlights gave her a much-needed lift without appearing drastic. Her hair seemed to shimmer now when she moved.

It was only when she got back to her car that she realised she had a message on her phone. She dialled her voicemail and chewed her lip as she listened to James's voice.

'Cici, it's me, James. I was wondering would you pop up to the house this evening if you're free? I'll rustle up something to eat. There are a couple of things I'd like to discuss if it suits. I'll expect you around seven. No need to ring me back unless you can't make it.'

Dinner with James, in the house – their home. Oh God, she wanted to, but under such awful circumstances, how could she?

And then she made a decision. Enough with the self-pity crap. This flaky, pathetic, crumbling creature she had turned into was not the woman he had married (or rather, thought he had married). She would go for dinner. She would make herself look fabulous – whatever it took. She would laugh and be cheerful and stoic. She had thrown away her marriage, her wonderful life, and put her family in jeopardy, and she would face the consequences. At least she could make sure they would have a civilised, friendly relationship from here on out. Whatever he threw at her, she would accept it with dignity and resignation. She would not object, she would not plead, she would not resort to tears. She would leave them with one last dinner they could perhaps remember fondly one day. She would look on the bright side. At least it was in the evening – the lighting would be flattering.

P.J. was feeling better about things. They had all come through a rough week. Alex, thank God, was considerably better, although he was still pretty shaken. He had been seen by a psychologist who had confirmed, as P.J. had suspected, an emotional breakdown rather than a nervous one – stress induced, not surprisingly. Alex had liked the man and had found talking to him helpful, and to everyone's relief had agreed to see him on a regular basis until he was feeling stronger and had come through this crisis. Catherine had been at his side the moment P.J. told her he was ready, which was after three days of complete rest. She and Charlie had come to stay – there was plenty of room – and their house was put on the market. The Ferrari, too, had been sent back to the shop. Everyone agreed that a fresh start and a more modest set-up was the best course of action.

Sheila was delighted with all the company and having young people in the house again, and Bones had taken to nightly preambles, sneaking up from the kitchen and checking on newly inhabited rooms, where he would settle happily for the night, nudging their surprised inhabitants awake with an insistent wet nose thrust in their face come the morning.

Behind the scenes, P.J. had been to see his own accountant, and together they had arranged a meeting with the investors in the various banks who had put up the cash for Alex to deduce exactly what the damage was. Then he and his accountant and investment people had gone away to formulate their plan.

'It's a big deal, P.J.,' Jim, the accountant, warned. 'Four point nine million's a lot of money.'

P.J. nodded. 'It is, but at least I have it. Might as well give it with a warm hand, as they say. Alex and Bella will get it one way or the other. It might as well be when they need it – which in Alex's case is now.'

'It's a big risk, this hotel resort business. Times are tough. How confident are you about it?'

'The music industry has been good to me, Jim, and financially speaking, the whole world is in disarray. Now I have it to give, but next year, who knows? As for the scheme, I don't know – but I do know I have confidence in my son. Alex is a hard worker; he was just unlucky with the timing. An awful lot of people are going to find themselves in the same boat.'

'And they won't have someone like you to bail them out.'

'I prefer to think of it as giving him another chance. I've had plenty of them in my time. I didn't invest in this scheme when Alex asked me to before. I'd like to now.'

'It'll take a few weeks to release the capital, but we can start with the initial tranche right away.'

He was looking forward to telling Alex and Catherine the news.

He smiled, thinking back to his student days. If anyone had told him that mucking about with a guitar and a penchant for writing lyrics would have proved so profitable, he'd have laughed. But that was before Viper made it big and before some of his lyrics had become big hits, before one had become a movie soundtrack and he'd been asked to write another, and especially before ringtones. It really was extraordinary how one thing led to another.

Sure, P.J. did well as a doctor, but it was his beloved hobby that made him worth an awful lot more than anyone had ever imagined.

Cici waited at the top of the steps outside the front door of what used to be her home, feeling terribly ill at ease, but she was determined not to back out now. This had to be done, had to be endured, however painful it might be. She had taken great care with her make-up (thank God she'd had her hair done) and had discovered a beautiful coral wraparound dress in Sophia's wardrobe that accentuated her new overly slender silhouette, rather than drawing attention to her drastic weight loss. She had even brought a bottle of champagne with her, but her heart was in her mouth as James answered the door.

'Cici,' he said, his eyes roving over her. 'You look wonderful. Come in. And champagne – how thoughtful.'

Following him down into the kitchen, Cici wanted to cry. How bizarre was this, to be invited into her own kitchen and have her soon-to-be-ex-husband cook dinner for her? Looking around her at all the familiar nooks and crannies, the memories flooded back of all the family dinners through the years, feeding the children as they fought to hold a spoon in chubby, uncoordinated little fingers, teaching them to sit at table, and later to cook. Shared confidences, comforting favourite foods in the bad times, celebratory dinners in the good times, but always, always family. How could she have been so stupid to throw all this away?

'The champagne was a great idea, Cici,' James was saying as he dished up. 'I think we ought to make this a fun occasion. There's been far too much doom and gloom recently. To new beginnings,' he said, handing her a glass and raising his own.

'Yes, of course, you're absolutely right. To new beginnings,' she said with forced brightness. *To new beginnings with you and Sarah de Burgh,* she thought as a savage twist of pain gripped her. No wonder James was looking so cheerful. He was getting rid of his stupid, selfish, self-obsessed wife (or non-wife) and making way for the new woman in his life, who by all accounts would appreciate and value him as he deserved to be. Cici took a quick gulp of her champagne to stop herself from sobbing.

'Now, there we are.' James set down a dish of spaghetti puttanesca. 'I doubt it's as good as yours, but I did steal the recipe. After all, it was our first meal together, remember?' he smiled. 'I thought it would be nice . . . for old time's sake.'

Cici felt sick. Was he trying to torture her? If so, he was succeeding. She smiled weakly. At least he hadn't mentioned how thin and gaunt she was looking . . .

'You've got awfully thin, Cici. You're not sick, are you?'

'No. At least, I don't think so.'

'Good. Well, tuck in.'

Desperate to change the subject, she brought up the restaurant and asked him if he had heard the news.

'Yes, I did. Dreadful business. Dom told me all about it. I must say I was taken aback. I don't know this Carla girl well, but I always found her very pleasant. But then, you never can tell, can you?' He shrugged. 'I rather liked Tanya, but I always was partial to good-looking, charming women,' he grinned.

'I just want him to be happy,' Cici said.

'He's rushed off to New York now, so he must be keen on her.'

'He went to New York?' Cici asked, surprised.

'Yes, called me from the airport. I have no idea what's going on, but I never was very good at playing games with all this romantic business. I always preferred to put my cards on the table.'

She nodded dumbly.

They chatted amiably about other, inconsequential things when all Cici wanted to do was break down and beg James for one more chance.

And then he asked the dreaded question.

'I don't like to keep harping on about it, Cici, but have you appointed a lawyer yet?'

Her throat constricted. 'Yes – no – that is, I'm going to. I've been given some names, I just . . . haven't got around to it yet.'

He looked at her across the table with no sign of emotion or regret. 'Because we really must wrap this up, make it legal.'

'Yes . . . I do know that. It just seemed . . . ' How could she say that it seemed impossible, unthinkable? Now she *was* going to break down. She put her hand to her mouth and stifled a sob.

'Come on, Cici,' he said, reaching over to take her hands. 'It's not so bad. There's no point in upsetting yourself about this. We've just got to take the next step. It's only sensible, in light of what's transpired.'

She could only nod helplessly as two big tears rolled down her face.

'Which is why,' he continued gently, 'I'm asking you to marry me. What do you say?'

'What?' she whispered.

'You heard me. Will you marry me? Properly, this time?'

'Is this your idea of a joke?'

'I have only ever asked someone to marry me once before in my life. I was dead serious then – and I'm serious now.'

'But how? Why?' She was unable to absorb what she was hearing.

'Quietly is the answer to your first question, and the answer to your second question is because I love you, I have always loved you and I always *will* love you. Life without you is a bit like this house, just an empty, meaningless shell.' He smiled at her, really smiled at her, for the first time in a long, long time.

'But after everything I've done . . . how could you forgive me?' She couldn't go on.

'What? Because you had an affair? Because you weren't always a perfect wife? Cici, listen to me. You have always had a certain penchant for . . . how shall I put it . . . drama. That was evident the minute I first set eyes on you. It was part of what I fell in love with. You were so very different from me. I always knew we could hit a rocky patch at any stage – and frankly, I'm surprised it wasn't sooner. You gave up so much for me. I know you want life to be like it is in the movies, with men rushing around waving swords and killing their rivals, but life isn't like that. Do you think my love was dependent on you always loving me back? Do you think I'd let you go so easily? What sort of man would that make me? A pretty weedy one, I think. I know things haven't always been easy for you, and maybe I did play too much golf and take you for granted, but we can work all that out. Let's just wipe the slate clean and start over.'

'Oh, James.' She put her hand to her mouth.

'Is that all you can say?' He arched an eyebrow. 'You still haven't answered my question.'

'Yes,' she sobbed, 'yes, a thousand times yes. You have no idea how miserable, how wretched I've been. I was so stupid, so selfish. I was afraid nobody needed me any more. You were so successful, and the kids were all sorted. I was afraid of growing old, becoming old and invisible, when all that really mattered was that *I* needed *you*. It didn't matter if nobody needed me.'

'You! Afraid of growing old!' James gave a shout of laughter. 'I don't believe it.'

'But it's true, James,' she protested. 'I *am* afraid of growing old, losing my looks. They're what I've always relied upon, traded on, and now . . .'

'But Cici, I adore you. You'll always be beautiful to me, whatever age you are. Nothing could change that.'

'Are you sure about this? Are you sure it's what you really want?'

'Absolutely sure – sure enough, and perhaps presumptuous enough, to have booked the registry office for the 7 November . . .'

'The 7 November,' Cici gasped. 'But that's—'

'Our wedding anniversary, yes. Rather a nice touch, don't you think? I haven't completely lost my sense of romance.'

'What will we say?' She began to laugh. 'What will we tell the children?'

'We won't say anything at all to anyone – least of all the children. It's none of their damned business!'

'I can't believe this is happening,' she said, shaking her head.

'Neither can I – although I'm very glad it is.'

'This is the most wonderful surprise I've ever had in my life. I love you so much, James, more than ever. And I'm going to prove it to you every day of my life for as long as I live.'

'Good. Then come upstairs with me now, Cici. We have only six months left to live in sin. It may all become quite dull after that.'

'And you say *I* have a sense of drama.' She shook her head in wonder.

Josh was in the studio editing Viper's latest promo video when he got the call.

'Mr McIntyre?'

'Yeah?'

'This is Mr Nigel Whitaker of Willoughby, Whitaker and Turnbull Solicitors.'

'Uh-huh.' Josh put down the mug of coffee in his hand as a slow smile spread across his face.

'My client, Miss Candice Keating, has instructed me to set up a meeting to discuss the, ah, proposed use of her video images.'

'Is that so? I think I can manage that. When did you have in mind, Mr Whitaker?'

'Would tomorrow at three o'clock be convenient?'

'It's short notice, but I guess I can make it.'

'It would be in your interest to make it, Mr McIntyre.'

'Is that what she told you?' Josh's eyes narrowed.

'That is what I am merely advising you of.'

'I would say it's pretty much in your client's interest too, Mr Whitaker.'

'We can discuss just such matters at the meeting, Mr McIntyre, if you would be so good as to confirm you'll attend.'

'Sure, I'll be there. I'll be counting the minutes,' he grinned.

'Very good. I'll inform my client and give you directions to my office.'

Josh put the phone down and sucked in a long breath. This would be fun, just as he had known it would be. Very lucrative fun, by the sounds of it.

* * *

'Please don't make me go, Gran,' Candy pleaded. 'I don't need to be there, the solicitor can do it on his own.'

'Don't be ridiculous, Candice, of course you need to be there.' This wasn't strictly true, but Jennifer had her reasons, one of which was making sure her granddaughter got to look this snake in the eye in the cold light of day and see him for what he was. Otherwise she would be forever cowed by the incident, and Jennifer wasn't having that. Quite apart from the fact that Jennifer wanted to get a look at him herself – not just out of curiosity, although there was an element of that; it was more a protective instinct on her part. She knew his type, and they never scrubbed up well. Nothing like a bit of harsh reality to do away with the veneer of dangerous glamour Candy had no doubt attributed to him. 'It's not as if you'll be on your own. I'll be there too.'

'You can't!' Candy shrieked in horror.

'Oh yes I can,' said Jennifer grimly, 'and so can you.'

The imposing offices of WWT Solicitors were easy to find on Clarion Quay. Josh had decided he'd better look like he meant business and had unearthed the only suit he possessed, a beige double-breasted number he had appropriated from a shoot he'd done with a boy band two years ago. He teamed it with a black shirt, a white tie and left his hair long and loose. The whole effect was *don't mess with me.*

Now, waiting in reception for what felt like an unnecessarily long time, he was becoming impatient, drumming his chewed fingernails on the arm of the couch. Just when he was about to complain, the lift doors opened and a very pretty, prim-looking girl addressed him. 'Mr McIntyre, if you would like to come with me, I'll show you up to Mr Whitaker's office.'

In the lift, he gave her the benefit of his practised once-over, narrowing his blue eyes speculatively as he took in her black pencil skirt and slim high-heeled pumps, but if she noticed, she gave no sign of either registering or responding to his interest.

Exiting the lift, Josh felt as if he lost at least two inches as his shoes sank into the deep pile carpet that lined the corridor, off which solid mahogany doors concealed their secrets.

'Here we are.' The girl knocked discreetly before opening the door. 'Mr Josh McIntyre,' she announced, showing him in before leaving the room discreetly, closing the door behind her.

What was this, the Three Stooges? Josh was momentarily taken aback. He had expected the lawyer guy, for sure, who stood up now to greet him and indicated that he take a seat at the long table, but he hadn't banked on seeing Candy – a very pale, un-made-up and surprisingly vulnerable-looking Candy. And who was the old broad with the stony expression and the weird hat? He had thought this would be a man-to-man thing.

'Do sit down, Mr McIntyre.' Nigel Whitaker resumed his seat opposite him and smiled pleasantly. 'I'll come straight to the point. There seems to be a fundamental problem with your, ah, proposal.'

'I wasn't aware I had made any proposal – yet.'

'Then now is as good a time as any to point out that you appear to have neglected to offer a consideration to my client, Miss Keating, for your proposed use of these video images.'

'Are you kidding? *She's* supposed to offer *me* a consideration for them.'

'My client, as far as I am aware,' he looked to Candy for confirmation, who nodded, then continued, still in the same mildly bewildered tone, 'has not signed any formal release for these images.'

'So what?'

'That leaves us with a predicament on our hands.'

'You said it.'

'I understand you work for another of my clients, the rock band Viper. Isn't that so? In the capacity of director of promotional videos – would that be correct?'

'Yeah, your point being?'

'I would imagine that accounts for a large part of your earned income?'

'What's that got to do with anything?'

'Well that depends, Mr McIntyre, on how much you value your association with Viper.'

'What're you getting at?'

'It has come to my attention, Mr McIntyre, that your company, Windvest, is involved in selling pornography on the Internet, isn't that so? Videos are made available to the procurers of such entertainment by downloading and so forth for a fee.'

'Nothing illegal about that.'

'Quite. But legal or not, I'm afraid my clients, Viper, would find it very unappealing to be associated with any such practices. It wouldn't, as they say, be good for the image. They would be forced to disassociate themselves from any such activity, and as their lawyer I would advise them quite strenuously to do so, never mind what the PR people would have to say. I imagine there would be quite a lot of noise made about it. Very undesirable noise.'

'What are you getting at?' Josh growled.

'We are willing to pay you a consideration for the time and effort spent in producing these images of my client.'

'So you do want to buy it, right?' he grinned.

'Indeed. My client is prepared to offer you the sum of one euro.'

'Funny.'

'There is nothing remotely amusing about the offer, Mr McIntyre. If you do not accept it and make any attempt to launch these images, we will sue for infringement of copyright – and it will be a very substantial sum we will sue for, make no mistake about that.'

Josh's face was working. He looked at the lawyer guy, who returned his gaze steadfastly, and then at the old broad, whose mouth was set in a thin line. Then he looked at Candy, who was squirming in her chair.

'Keep your money, Miss Rich,' he spat. 'I don't need it.'

'Oh, but I insist,' the lawyer continued. 'This has to be a legal transaction. Candy?' Nigel looked at her as she bit her lip and fished in her pocket for the amount they had decided on. She put the coin on the table and Nigel pushed it across to Josh. 'There you are.'

Josh stood up and swiped it off the table. 'Fuck you,' he said and walked out the door.

'Well,' said Jennifer, 'I must say I really can't see what you saw in him, Candice. Can you, Nigel?'

Nigel smiled.

'Neither can I,' murmured Candice. 'Thank you, Gran. Thank you, Mr Whitaker – I won't forget this.'

'And I hope you won't forget the promise you made me either.' Jennifer looked expectant. 'Quid pro quo.'

'I haven't forgotten, Gran. The hairdresser's appointment is booked for four-thirty.'

'Jolly good. Now I think it's time you called your father and told him you've sorted out this unfortunate incident.'

'Feel free to use my phone,' Nigel said, leaving the office discreetly.

Dom hadn't been in New York for a few years, and he certainly never expected to be there on a mission such as he was.

Arriving at 2:30 p.m. after the six-hour flight, he was tired, and viewing the vast queue of passengers from all over the globe, he thanked God he had been able to clear customs in Dublin. He jumped into a cab at Kennedy and told the driver to go straight to St Vincent's Hospital. As always, it was bumper to bumper on the Brooklyn-Queens Expressway and the stop–start motion of the cab and jet lag began to lull him into a mindless trance. They took the Queensborough Bridge at 59th Street and Dom looked out at the panoramic view of Midtown Manhattan, which never failed to impress him. Finally, after what seemed like an eternity, with the driver hunched over the wheel muttering under his breath about the delay, they reached the hospital. Dom paid him, grabbed his bag and headed for Reception.

He asked for Antonio Berlusconi's room number and went straight up. Outside the door, he took a deep breath, knocked and went in.

'Excuse me,' he said to the old man sitting up in bed who looked straight out of central casting for a *Godfather* movie. 'I'm terribly sorry to barge in like this, but I've come to find Carla – there's something important I need to explain to her.' He paused to catch his breath. 'My name's Dominic Coleman-Cappabianca,' he added as two younger men sitting by the bed, obviously Carla's brothers, regarded him quizzically.

The old man looked at him for a beat, then folded his arms and nodded slowly. 'So you're the Dominic guy, huh?' He turned to his son and said, 'Marco, get this boy a cup of coffee and let him sit down. I hate to tell ya, but your timing is crap.'

'I do realise you've been very unwell,' Dom began, feeling beyond awkward, 'and I'm terribly sorry to intrude, but this won't take long. If you could just tell me where I might find her . . .' The brothers were looking at him strangely.

'You won't find her here,' Antonio said, his eyebrows knitting alarmingly.

'Then where?'

The brothers were shaking their heads.

'What is it with you young people?' Antonio exclaimed, throwing up his hands. 'All this technology you have – cell phones, computers – and you still can't communicate with each other.'

'I just need to explain—'

'Then you've come to the wrong place,' he glowered at him.

Dominic's nerve was beginning to desert him, but then the old guy began to chuckle. 'You've come to the wrong place because Carla has gone back to Dublin to explain things to *you*.'

'I don't believe this.' Dom ran his hands through his hair.

'You better believe it,' said Antonio. 'But since you're here, sit down and tell us a bit about yourself.'

Marco handed him a coffee and Paulo slapped him on the back, laughing. Then they sat back and listened expectantly.

'Start from the beginning,' ordered Antonio. 'And don't leave anything out!'

21

'As we are making our final approach into Dublin, please ensure your seatbelts are fastened and your seatback is in the upright position.'

Carla rubbed her eyes and looked out at the emerald green map unfolding beneath her, bathed in early morning sunlight. It was six-thirty a.m., and all around her people were rousing themselves, chatting and laughing, glad that the flight was over and that they were almost home.

Inside the airport, she collected her bags, got a taxi and headed straight into town. There was no time to lose.

'Early start, love?' the taxi driver asked.

'You bet,' she said, 'and it's gonna be a long day.'

'What is it you work at?'

'I'm a chef,' she said.

'Get away!' He was clearly impressed. 'Would I know where you work?'

'Have you heard of a restaurant called Dominic's?'

'Dominic's,' he mulled it over. 'I *have* heard of that place, right enough. Haven't been in it though. I've heard the food's very good there,' he said.

'It's about to get even better,' she grinned.

It was seven-thirty when she arrived at Dominic's. She dropped her case in the staff room, which was empty, then quickly fished out her uniform, put it on, tied back her hair and fixed her white chef hat, taking one final look in the mirror before heading for the kitchen. She paused for a moment before pushing through the swing doors, took a deep breath and prepared to face the music.

Thirty seconds passed before anyone actually realised she was there, but it was more than enough time for Carla to see that the kitchen was in complete disarray. At first glance, her eagle eye took in wilted vegetables, drab prosciutto and, to her horror, some packets of bought, dried pasta.

'Carla!' Astrid's mouth dropped open. 'Thank God you're here.' She ran to give her a floury hug.

Pino turned from a blazing argument with the other sous chef, grinned and shook his head. 'If I had known . . .' He waved a knife at her.

'Jaysus!' said Paddy, the kitchen porter, looking up from the pile of potatoes he was peeling, 'Who'd have thought it!' He beamed as if his face would split in two.

'Look,' Carla said. 'I know you all have a lot of questions, and believe me, I want to answer them, but there's no time now. Where's Dom? I need to talk to him.' And then, 'What's so funny?'

'Dom's in New York,' Astrid explained, 'looking for you.'

'I don't believe this.' She put her hands to her face and shook her head.

After she'd fully taken in the deteriorating situation, she brought them all together. 'Here's the deal: we still have a restaurant to run. I'm in charge now. Anyone got any problems with that?'

They shook their heads in unison.

'Good, because this kitchen's a disgrace!'

'We're running out of supplies. We can't possibly deliver the menu tonight.' Pino was stressed. 'Nothing's been ordered. It'll be all we can do to get through lunch.'

'We'll get through it all right,' she said grimly. 'For now, Pino, get that dried pasta out of my sight. Those vegetables can go into a country minestrone, with garlic and pecorino cheese and anchovy croutons,' she instructed, making her way into the cold room. At least there were some decent steaks hanging, and a couple of large sole. Apparently a new fish supplier had dropped them in on appro earlier. It wasn't ideal, but it wasn't a disaster either. With a lot of work and even more luck, they could make it – dinner, though, depended on the suppliers. Since Dom always insisted on using the best fresh ingredients, they naturally varied from day to day and week to week – and nobody had ordered.

First, though, there was pasta to make. Within minutes, she had set up a mini pasta factory, covering every surface in paper-thin sheets of dough, remembering her mother teaching her that making pasta is an art as much as a science – and Carla was an artist.

'Let's go, people! If we put our backs into it we can still make lunch. Forget the dinner menu for now – I'll do a new one. Gary,' she instructed the other sous chef, 'those steaks can be braised. We'll do a Tuscan-style hearty casserole with borlotti beans, red peppers and red wine – make that our best Chianti. No skimping on quality.'

'Yes, Chef.'

'I'll make saffron angel-hair spaghetti for the sole. Pino, use the heads and bones for a fish stock to cook the pasta in. Waste not, want not.'

'Right away, Chef.'

Then it was time to get on to suppliers. Offering up a quick prayer to St Macarius, patron saint of chefs, she held her breath and hoped against hope.

First was the fish. She tried the new supplier who had dropped in the sole earlier that day. One of his boats had come back unexpectedly early with engine trouble, but they had a bumper catch of Dublin Bay prawns, monkfish and some magnificent turbot. She took five kilos of the monkfish and four of the prawns.

The meat supplier had just had an order cancelled for a lavish party, but yes, Carla was more than welcome to it –

finest aged Aberdeen Angus steaks, racks of lamb and sweet veal.

The organic vegetable supplier had a huge crush on her and was more than happy to accept a late order. He was still out in his fields and polytunnels selecting his finest crops and would do his best for her.

The strange herb lady, Tessa, was very fond of Carla, especially since she had given her a delicious recipe for vegetarian lasagne, and was eager to help. Just that morning she had picked a fine crop of exotic herbs, wild edible fungi and greens and Carla was welcome to them.

Astrid, of course, had already baked the breads and made the desserts, so those weren't a problem.

Finally, studying what was on order, Carla sat down, sipped an espresso and prayed for inspiration. In the end, it came easily, just like it always had, her instinct, talent and love of great food arising naturally. She wrote the evening menu confidently, and studied it with approval.

They got through lunch by the skin of their teeth. By the time the evening menu was being prepared, the kitchen had become a hive of activity, everyone working methodically and purposefully as instructed, intent on giving it their best shot. Carla presided over it all, offering advice, checking, scolding and stepping in to finesse when necessary.

By seven o'clock that evening, when the first bookings arrived, the elegantly dressed diners who sat sipping cocktails in the Chameleon Bar had no idea of how close they had come to not eating at all.

Exhausted but exhilarated, Carla and her team worked through the night, preparing and delivering the inspirational dishes that more than one table described as exceptional.

On the floor, there was no evidence that they were understaffed. The fewer waiters and waitresses just worked extra hard, quietly and efficiently, even though their faces hurt from smiling as much as their feet did from covering twice as much

ground. But it all worked. There were no disasters, no dropped
orders or dropped plates. Nothing at all out of the usual. The
crowd was as noisy and effusive as ever, so much so that no
one had time to notice the small, balding man sitting at the
corner table alone, glancing at his newspaper from time to
time. 'Can I get you anything else, sir?' asked Therese, the
small, relentlessly cheerful Lithuanian waitress.

'No thank you, just the bill,' he smiled. 'That was very
good.'

When the last dishes had gone out, the kitchen was bare –
they'd had just enough food to complete the service. Exhausted
and elated, Carla finished up with another family tradition.
Opening a bottle of grappa produced by her cousins in their
ancestral region of Italy, she poured a shot for everybody. 'Well
done, guys, I think we pulled it off. Here's to new beginnings.'

Charlotte and P.J. both agreed they had never had better food.
Back at P.J.'s house in Wellington Square, they had a nightcap,
enjoying the break from their respective family dramas.

Alex and Catherine had gone away for the weekend, leaving
little Charlie with Catherine's mother.

Ossie had taken Jennifer and Candy out to dinner in
Guilbaud's to celebrate the successful solution to the video
débâcle, as it was referred to now. Charlotte had been invited
too, but had declined, preferring to spend the evening with
P.J. Alone now for the first time in weeks, or so it felt, they
slipped up to bed like guilty teenagers.

'Do you think it's true what they say?' P.J. mused, propped
up on his elbow as he traced the outline of her mouth. 'You
know, about blood being thicker than water and all that?'

'I don't know.' Charlotte thought about it. 'I suppose so,
but I do know that when you love someone – *really* love
someone – there's no holding back.' She smiled up at him.

'Good,' he said, bending down to kiss her. 'I was hoping
you'd say that.'

Epilogue: One Year Later

It was Viper's last-ever concert – again.

Seventy thousand people had filled the new Lansdowne Road Stadium in Dublin for what promised to be the hottest gig of the decade. As it was for charity, several other big acts had come on board to join them and the atmosphere was electric.

Cici and James were there with Mimi, Sophia, Dom and Carla. Afterwards, there would be a special dinner at Dominic's, invitation only, for selected guests. Since winning their first Michelin star, and rumoured to be gunning for a second, neither Dom nor Carla had had a night off – not together, at any rate, except for the magical trip to the villa in Tuscany last New Year's Eve, which had been work-related, of course, and where he had proposed to her.

They had gone for an after-dinner stroll in the crisp December air. Behind them, the villa stood in the moonlight, its time-mellowed stone guarded by rows of picture-perfect cypresses, surrounded by vineyards and olive groves. Walking hand in hand in the moonlight, they stopped to admire an ancient moss-covered statue of Bacchus, the god of wine. Dom had turned around and got down on one knee. 'Will you marry me, Carla?'

'Oh Dom,' her eyes were shining, 'you know I will. Yes, yes, yes.' She laughed as he got up and swung her around.

Encased in their bubble of happiness, neither of them could ever have guessed that theirs would be the *second* wedding in the family of late. As Viper launched into one of their huge ballads, Cici and James held hands and exchanged a secret smile . . .

Ossie and Shalom were there, of course, and Bernie, who stood up regularly to gyrate to her favourite numbers, singing loudly and tunelessly. Becoming a grandmother hadn't slowed her down at all. Ossie watched Bernie in her gold leggings and wondered what Jennifer would have said looking at her. He missed the old girl. Shalom was leaning against him, tired. Kylie was almost a year old and Shalom was pregnant again, which had come as a surprise, seeing as she hardly ever let him near her, she was so sleep-deprived. Shalom's dad had nudged him and made jokes on hearing of the second impending arrival and Ossie had felt a bit sick. He was sleep-deprived himself these days. Three weeks ago, the third nanny had left, saying politely but firmly that she couldn't work with Ossie's mother-in-law (as she politely referred to Bernie) interfering all the time. Ossie could understand why. He sighed. He had seen Charlotte earlier on the way in and she looked fabulous. He thought about her quite a lot these days – and nights – more than he would have liked to.

Ossie's wasn't the only baby-in-waiting in the audience. Alex and Catherine were enjoying a night out on their own, for a change. Charlie was in the safe hands of a babysitter, and the young parents were singing along as loudly as everyone else. Catherine placed Alex's hand on her tummy and laughed. She was sure the baby was kicking along in time to the music.

Charlotte was there too, having a blast with Candy and her pals Emma and Katy. After her brush with disaster, Candy, along with Jennifer, had embarked on a small business venture running courses advising and coaching men and women about social etiquette and speaking skills. Jennifer did the coaching (she was superb) and Candy videoed the participants so they could review their performance as Jennifer critiqued it. They were doing remarkably well and had a constant waiting list of prospective clients. 'Hardly surprising, given today's appalling lack of manners,' Jennifer had pronounced. She had declined the invite to the concert, preferring to stay at home and watch *Gone with the Wind* – again.

Along with the other members of Viper's families and entourage, Candy and Charlotte had the best seats in the house – right up front. P.J., of course, was doing his stuff behind the scenes, playing doctor on stage.

As they wrapped up the last act of the night and Viper disappeared behind a screen of smoke and laser lights, the crowd bayed for more, stamping their feet and screaming, *Vi-per, Vi-per, Vi-per!*

After what seemed like an eternity, there was a sliver of movement, and Joey, the lead singer, scampered out on stage. The cheers were deafening as the crowd went wild again. He shouted into the mike for silence, '*Ciúnas! Ciúnas!*' and quiet descended. 'It's been a great night, Dublin, but we've got one more number for you. Our final act tonight – and I mean final – belongs to an old friend of ours. We owe him a lot – not least for keeping a bunch of old farts like us on our feet. He started out with us but left the band to pursue a more respectable career. Our loss was the medical profession's gain. We know him as Doc,' he continued, 'and not a lot of people know he's written some of our best lyrics. Tonight we've persuaded him to dust down his old guitar and play one last gig with us.'

As Charlotte's hands flew to her mouth, she gasped as a murmur of curiosity began among the crowd. And then, as the band ran back on stage, there he was, walking on with his guitar, grinning sheepishly but looking very sexy. As he settled himself on the stool, tuned up his guitar and nodded at Rory on keyboard, he picked out the first deliberately un-familiar chords of a haunting riff.

'Take it away, P.J.!' yelled Joey, slipping back to join Barry on base.

'This song is a very special one for me,' he began, keeping them guessing, 'and I know it is for all of you too.' He grinned as a roar of anticipation filled the stadium. 'I wrote it a long, long time ago, but tonight, I want to dedicate it to someone very special to me. I want to dedicate it to my wife.'

As the lights went down and a sea of hand-held lighters glowed and swayed in the darkness, he looked straight at her and said, 'Charlotte, this one's for you.'

When the band launched into the much-loved ballad and P.J.'s gravelly voice rang out into the night, a wild cheer went up as the fans recognised the famous track.

As he reached the chorus of 'Beautiful to Find Me', the great crowd sang as one.

Acknowledgements

Grateful thanks to Sue Fletcher of Hodder UK; Ciara Doorley and Breda Purdue of Hachette Books Ireland; Margaret Daly of Hachette; Louise Swanell, and my agent, Vivienne Schuster of Curtis Brown.

I am indebted also to Dr. Damien Rutledge for information on Von Willebrands disease and related medical implications.

And also to David Bergin of O'Connor & Bergin, for advice on family law.

If I have forgotten anyone, which is entirely possible; lunch is on me.

If You Like Happy Endings . . .

You have just come to the end of a book.

Before you put it aside, please take a moment to reflect on the 37 million people who are blind in the developing world.

90% of this blindness is TOTALLY PREVENTABLE.

In our world, blindness is a disability – in the developing world, it's a death sentence.

Every minute, one child goes blind – needlessly.

That's about the time it will take you to read this.

It's also about the time it will take you to log on to www.righttosight.com and help this wonderful organisation achieve its goal of totally eradicating preventable global blindness.

Now that would be a happy ending.

And it will only take a minute.

Fiona O'Brien supports RIGHT TO SIGHT and would love if you would too.